LALA PETTIBONE:

STANDING ROOM ONLY

Dear Anne,
This bears repeating:
Lala and I are
thrilled to know you!

Heidi Mastrogiovanni

Amberjack Publishing
New York | Idaho

AMBERJACK
PUBLISHING

Amberjack Publishing
1472 E. Iron Eagle Dr.
Eagle, ID 83646
amberjackpublishing.com

Publisher's Cataloging-in-Publication Data
Names: Mastrogiovanni, Heidi, 1957- author.
Title: Lala Pettibone : standing room only / Heidi Mastrogiovanni.
Description: New York : Amberjack Publishing, 2018.
Identifiers: LCCN 2017057661 (print) | LCCN 2018005271 (ebook)
| ISBN 9781944995744 (ebook) | ISBN 9781944995737 (pbk. : alk.
paper)
Subjects: LCSH: Women authors--Fiction. | Man-woman relationships-
-Fiction. | Choice (Psychology)--Fiction. | Los Angeles (Calif.)--
Fiction. | Paris (France)--Fiction.
Classification: LCC PS3613.A819943 (ebook) | LCC PS3613.A819943
L35 2018 (print) | DDC 813/.6--dc23
LC record available at https://lccn.loc.gov/2017057661

Cover Design: Mimi Bark

FOR TOM

ENCORE?

An especially unsettling energy was making an unlucky section of the second floor hallways in one of the main buildings of Sony Pictures Studios in Culver City, California vibrate.

Eliza in Accounting stood up in her cubicle and peered over the partition at Phillip, who wore headphones all day and hummed along to whatever he was listening to, which, if his aggressive "mmmm hmmmm mmmms" were any indication, was the entire songbook of a profoundly ill-tempered heavy metal band on a loop.

"What is that freaky . . . Oh, for heaven's sake, you can't hear it, can you?"

Eliza had taken an instant dislike to Phillip when his first words to her on his first day at work were, "What's cookin'? Numbers, huh? Am I right? Numbers?"

Just as she was about to sit down, Phillip caught sight of her out of the corner of his eye.

"DID YOU SAY SOMETHING, ELIZA?" Phillip bellowed, not taking off his headphones.

Eliza theatrically mouthed "NO!" and slammed herself back down into her chair.

Had the Accounting Department been any closer to the ladies' room, Eliza might have been able to hear blustering cries of distress, and she might have been able to make out identifiable sounds and individual words.

"Would someone PLEASE tell me what sin I committed on the Ides of March in a past life that made this BLEEPING day hold such a BLEEPING grudge against me?" Lala Pettibone demanded.

Lala's new colleague, Zoe Koehler, a fellow Wesleyan graduate more than a few years Lala's junior, paused in her frantic splashing of cold water all over Lala's eyes and face and head and shoulders.

"Why are you saying 'bleeping' instead of, well, what I assume should be 'fucking'?"

Lala grunted, imagining that her young friend hadn't quite yet learned the proper etiquette of doing business.

"I don't want to seem unprofessional, even in the bathroom, Zoe."

"We're in Hollywood," Zoe said.

She's right, Lala thought. "You're right. FUCK! FUCK FUCK FUCK FUCK FUCK!"

Lala's anguish had begun only a few minutes earlier when she had entered the ladies room after being ushered there by a genial young man who wore black pants so tight as to make them flirt with the realm of leggings, and who had welcomed them at the reception desk with a perky "Hello! And whom do I have the pleasure of greeting today?"

They were at the studio to discuss the possibility of Clive Ellis, acclaimed British actor and classic bad boy offscreen, starring in the film version of Lala's very popular comedic novel, *Dressed Like a Lady, Drinks Like a Pig*.

Zoe had met Lala at a Wesleyan alumni event in Beverly Hills and cornered her the moment she walked in.

"I loved your book," Zoe gushed.

"Okay, and whoever you are, I love you," Lala said.

Zoe thrust out her hand and grabbed Lala's.

"Zoe Koehler," she said. "Wesleyan class of—"

"Oh, no, no, no, that's okay," Lala said, shaking her head violently. "Let's go get a drink. I don't need to know how young you are."

Lala and Zoe didn't leave the bar area that night. They sat at a small high table by one of the floor-to-ceiling windows that offered a lovely view of the Beverly Hills Library and Civic Center.

Lala's feet did not reach the floor from the tall chairs that accompanied the high table unless she kind of sat/stood on the edge of the seat. When she was fully seated on the chair, Lala had to notice that she was not as tall as Zoe was standing.

Oy vey, Lala thought. *I look like a garden gnome next to her.*

Zoe told Lala all about growing up in New Hampshire and falling in love with movies when she first saw *Now, Voyager,* and as soon as she heard that, Lala suspected Zoe could quite possibly end up being one of her legion of adored adopted nieces and nephews.

"Is that a movie about second chances, or what?" Lala said, spearing a very large olive from her very dirty vodka martini and ramming it into her mouth. "I absolutely identify with Bette Davis in that movie. I did not find my stride until my . . . well, the actual number of the decade isn't important. What's important is, it's never too late. Trust me on this, my young friend, it is never, ever, ever, ever, ever too late. Thank goodness."

Lala told Zoe about being widowed at a far-too-young age and after that only dating men who lived in different cities, because she couldn't imagine a full-time life with anyone but her beloved Terrence, but that was all subconscious and Lala wasn't aware of it until her Auntie Geraldine had yelled it at her after losing patience with what Geraldine often described as "your ongoing crapfest."

"I'm so sorry you lost your husband," Zoe said, rubbing Lala's arm with care and affection. "Our glasses are empty. We shouldn't be talking about this with empty glasses."

She is entirely my kind of niece, Lala thought. *Done. I've adopted her.*

Lala told Zoe that her novel had originally been a screen-play that was eviscerated by a fellow Wesleyan graduate who was a literary agent, on the same day that Lala found out that the Frenchman who was her boss at the New York branch of a French publishing house, and on whom she had a wicked intense crush, "had a ridiculously fabulous girlfriend named Marie-Laure, can you believe anything so fabulous? And she's gorgeous and charming and she's around my age, so I can't even hate him for picking someone your age over someone my age."

"Wow," Zoe said. "I just want to keep rubbing your arm. Is that okay?"

"It's great," Lala said. "And on that same day—and who would even put this shit in a book or a movie or an alternately dark and hilarious series that you binge-watch on cable, because who could believe this shit, because life is way crazier than fiction . . . I lost my train of thought . . ."

"Something else awful happened on that same day?" Zoe prompted. "Wow, you can really drink fast. I'm getting you another one."

"Thank you, dear," Lala said. She watched Zoe scoot over to the bar and saw the handsome young bartender smile at her.

What a cutie pie she is, Lala thought.

Zoe came back balancing another very dirty vodka martini that had been filled to almost over the brim and a very large bowl of popcorn.

"Thank god," Lala yelped. "A base! A starchy base for the booze! Yay!"

"Yup," Zoe said. She grabbed a big fistful of popcorn and chomped it down. "I learned the importance of that at an all-night protest on Foss Hill senior year. Okay, so, that shitty day, part three."

"Yeah," Lala said. "So, then, get this: I go to the board meeting for my co-op building in the West Village, and I hear that we've all got to pay forty grand by the end of the week because the basement of the building is suddenly, like, some kind of contained post-apocalyptic nuclear wasteland. So I have to move across the country and live in a beautiful apartment in my adopted Auntie Geraldine's fourplex in Manhattan Beach, and, by the way, I am now your adopted auntie, okay?"

"That sounds great!" Zoe said. "Did you finish all the popcorn already?"

"I like to fantasize that the word 'savor' was invented to describe how much I enjoy food. At any rate, having to leave my beloved Island of Manhattan turns out to be a good thing—forgive me, Gotham, for even saying that—because I am taking in a bundle renting my co-op to visiting tourists, and I was able to start a charitable foundation and make a lot of donations to support my priorities, which include the environment and education and most of all animals—"

"I have seven rescued senior cats," Zoe said.

"WHAT?!" Lala gushed. The tight crowd of fellow Wesleyan graduates and their guests turned to look toward the direction of the outburst. Lala waved at them, bobbed her head, and grinned enthusiastically.

"I'm taking a car service home, so it's cool!" she declared. "Okay, so guess what? My specific passion is senior animals!"

"OMIGOD!" Lala and Zoe said in unison.

Lala told Zoe all about meeting Dr. David McLellan, a devastatingly handsome and entirely wonderful veterinarian whom she spent a delightful night "bonking like a lunatic. I mean, it's like I was back in freshman year and I was going nuts in my dorm room in Butterfield C," before he went on a months-long sailing trip with his sons, and all about David coming back to Manhattan Beach and moving in with her and her four rescued senior dogs, and about how life in Southern California was now absolutely lovely, and she felt a bit disloyal to her beloved Island of Manhattan, but she certainly intended to visit that unparalleled place at least once a year to spend quite a few tourist dollars of her own there.

Zoe and Lala ordered their car services at the same time and headed in opposite directions. Zoe told Lala that she had bought a small, adorable little bungalow in South Pasadena, having timed it just right when the housing market was being kind and having saved the down payment from her excruciating but very lucrative first job out of college as a personal assistant to a world-class actor who was also a world-class tool.

"Wow," Lala said as they eyed Santa Monica Boulevard for their grey Honda Civic and black Toyota Prius, respectively. "That is impressive. Owning a home at your age. Kudos, dear niece."

"So, can I take you out to lunch next week and talk some more about getting the movie version of your hilarious novel made?"

"We go out to lunch, I'm buying. That's what aunts do," Lala said. She waved frantically at two approaching cars. "Look! They're here at the same time! I'm taking that as a very good sign for our new partnership!"

Zoe had proved better than her pitch. She worked closely with Lala to encourage and elevate Lala's adaptation of her rejected screenplay into a bestselling novel, back into a screenplay that would not suffer the same fate as Lala's first attempt.

They alternated working at Zoe's house and at Lala's apartment, because each viewed the visit to the other's home as a superb opportunity to—in addition to getting work done—indulge an aching need to spend time with dogs and cats.

Lala's dogs—wonderful old souls who smelled quite ripe mere hours after their baths and who slept for the majority of any day and certainly right through each night—took to Zoe deeply and immediately. As did Zoe's cats take to Lala.

"Clever of you to name them after the Seven Dwarfs," Lala said on her first visit. She was sitting on Zoe's cute love seat in her clean but cluttered living room with all the cats walking over and around her and her laptop. The one named Grumpy wouldn't stop swatting Lala's shoulder and ear, something that Lala found quite charming. "What happens when you rescue another cat?"

"I start on another list of characters," Zoe responded. "I'm thinking the Seven Deadly Sins. Maybe I'll go with Sloth for the first one."

"God, that is a fabulous idea," Lala said. "Sloth. I love that. I may borrow your idea and name my next dog Gluttony. Do you have any more of these delicious stuffed olives? I can't stop eating them."

After they went through five drafts and got feedback for each version from writers Zoe had worked with and respected, Zoe sent the screenplay to a friend from high school who was an administrator at William Morris Endeavor and got it to Clive Ellis's representative at the agency.

Zoe had gotten an e-mail from her friend that the screenplay was in the hands of Clive's agent on a Friday. Lala and Zoe assumed that they would have to wait a long time for a response. The call from Clive's agent's assistant came on the following Monday. A meeting was set up for two weeks from that day.

"Clive will be in town and he'd like to get to know you both a bit so he can see if maybe working together would be a positive experience all around."

"You are SHITTING me!" Lala had screamed when Zoe called to tell her the good news. "We have got to celebrate! Let's go to that fancy-pants movie theater that I love in Old Town Pasadena. I don't care what's playing there!"

"The one where you sit in cozy Barcaloungers and you can order delicious food and drinks and stuff and the tickets are outrageously expensive but the popcorn is free? I LOVE that place!"

They went to a seven o'clock screening of a dopey college sex comedy that, after a non-stop series of mojitos because "I'm craving something minty fresh," Lala deemed "one of the funniest movies I have ever seen. I mean, EVER! What did he just tell his brother? That his brother's farts smell like Chinese food? That is comic GENIUS! God, I am SO happy about our MOVIE deal! I hope our movie turns out half as good as this one!"

And now it was potentially all about to go down the crapper

at Sony Pictures Studios because Lala had made the mistake of grabbing what she thought was a bottle of Visine from her purse and ended up drowning her eyes with the ear drops she picked up at the vet for her ancient beagle, Petunia, that morning.

"We need to get going," Zoe said. Lala straightened up and looked at herself in the mirror.

"I think I may be having a major cardiac crisis," Lala said. "Not really, though I do think I have a wicked case of heartburn brought on by sudden and excessive stress. And I look like shit," she sighed. "You, on the other hand, look fabulous."

Objective reality indicated that Lala did not look like shit. She looked a bit wilted and a bit damp and a bit red and rubbed, but other than that, she was a very attractive woman.

Objective reality also indicated that Zoe did indeed look fabulous. Lala suspected that Zoe was the kind of person who would look great at every stage of her hopefully long and happy life. She would remain accessibly beautiful because she had a warm, wide smile, porcelain skin with a cute smattering of freckles, and wavy, light auburn hair that was currently long and would probably look fabulous at whatever length and in whatever shade she would choose in the future. Zoe was a nice person, and Lala knew that would make all the difference, all the time.

"But we are strong, proud women. And we must never let it be about looks—"

"We're in Hollywood," Zoe said. "It is about looks. And also talent. And also about being easy to work with. We've got all of that, partner. So let's go show them how it's done."

"Holy shit!" Clive Ellis said. "Are you okay?"

He had opened the door to the small, sleek conference room and did a visible register of shock when he saw Lala's pulsating neon eyes.

Holy shit, Lala thought. *He is even cuter in person. Damn it! Why do I look like this? Now I can't flirt with him. Fine, fine, I'll leave that for Zoe. Fine. Whatever.*

"I am absolutely fine, Clive," Lala said, extending her hand. "What a pleasure to meet you."

"Jesus!" Clive fretted. "Sit down, please, sit. What happened to your eyes?"

"Oh, allergies. No big deal at all. It's not nearly as bad as it looks."

"Well, it couldn't be, could it? Are you sure you're okay?" Clive asked.

"Yup," Lala sighed.

"If you need us to call 911 . . ." Clive continued.

Sheesh, Lala thought. *I couldn't read the label? I couldn't check to see if I was dousing my eyes with hound dog ear wax dissolver?*

"I'll be sure to give a yell," Lala said.

"We don't need to call 911," a rather weaselly fellow sitting at the table grunted. "Let's keep this all in-house, Clive."

"I'm absolutely fine. Really," Lala said.

"Okay. Then let's get started. This is my manager, Garrett. And you must be Zoe. Sit, everybody, sit."

Lala and Zoe grabbed two plush chairs next to each other at the conference table opposite Clive's manager.

Garrett Olsen, a surly-looking beanpole who might have been Ichabod Crane's twin, had apparently never met a tanning booth he didn't like. He nodded at the two women and sneered a voiceless "Hello."

"He wants to do the movie," Garrett said.

Lala thought she might not have heard him correctly. Because nothing had been quite this easy for her since . . . well, certainly since she could remember.

Wait. Second grade was, in actual fact, fairly easy, Lala silently reflected. *I had no problem mastering any of the subjects, as I recall. I didn't much like dodgeball, that's true. That wasn't especially anxiety-free or effortless. But aside from that—*

"Yeah, I really wanna play Terry," Clive said. In a perfect mid-Western twang.

"Wow," Zoe said. "Nice accent. That's exactly how I hear Terry in my head."

Clive smiled at Zoe, and Lala noted that she was indeed being left out of any flirting that was going on in the room.

Unless Garrett's ceaseless frowning is his edgy way of courting me, Lala thought.

Just as Lala was about to return to savoring how bizarrely and unexpectedly smoothly this was all going, the door to the conference room opened and a deliveryman entered pulling a cart laden with multiple platters overflowing with all kinds of sandwiches and spreads and a wide selection of fancy beverages.

"Ohh, how nice of you," Lala said. "I didn't have an appetite all day because I was so nervous about meeting you, but now that you're being so enthusiastic about the project, I think I just realized I'm starving!"

"No!" Garrett suddenly screamed, lunging across the conference table and grabbing the closest platter away from Lala's orbit.

"Are there peanuts anywhere in there?" Clive yelled.

"Are there peanuts?" Garrett demanded.

"Or pineapple?" Clive bleated, keeping the frenzy going and reverting to his native Cockney.

Did he say poi-nah-pa? Lala thought. *What the fuck is poi-nah-pa? What the fuck are they yelling about?*

"Or super hot salsa? She's probably allergic to everything, damn it!" Garrett panted. "She dies here, and I have to go before the grand jury again? No WAY am I going before the grand jury again!"

"Holy shit!" Aunt Geraldine said. "What happened? Have you been crying? Didn't the meeting go well? Have you been crying because the meeting didn't go well? With your face in a bucket of red wine vinegar while you were crying because the meeting didn't go well?"

Lala spent the immediate hours after their brief and astonishingly successful (other than the brouhaha over her freakish eyes and the fact that she had to watch everyone else eat the delicious catered food while she was only allowed water because "that's probably safe for her") meeting at Sony sitting with Zoe at a charming oceanside café near her home in Manhattan Beach. They drank a sublimely refreshing bottle of Prosecco on an empty stomach, and then Lala placed her dear producing partner and adopted niece in a car service to head home to the east side.

Lala walked the short distance to her lovely apartment in the fourplex owned by her treasured adopted Auntie Geraldine so she could, as she explained to Zoe before the car drove off, "clear my head and maybe start making some sense again, if that cute bartender's quizzical look at my repeated attempts at flirtation were any indication of the state of my actual degree of intoxication, which I was apparently too hammered to be aware of." For some reason, Lala felt she had to repeat that monologue aloud in a loud tone of wonder and awe as she walked home, to the confusion of the adorable dogs she passed on her trip and the tentative amusement of their owners.

Lala's Aunt Geraldine was sitting in the lush courtyard of her fourplex—a classic Southern California, mission-style, two-floor real estate marvel—waiting for her adopted niece, the child of her best friends who had passed away a few years earlier at a comfortably old age, to get back from her meeting at the movie studio. Lala walked in, stumbling far less than she expected to— perhaps thanks to the sea air—and saw Geraldine surrounded by Lala's four dogs and by the other residents of the fourplex.

With Geraldine were Stephanie and Chuck, a married couple who met in veterinary school and who were, as described by Lala, often and with great affection, "the most earnest youngsters I have ever met. Seriously, they have no concept of irony, and I love that about them."

Chuck was cradling their brand new baby, named Trixie because they thought—without a trace of irony—that it sounded empowering.

Lala and Geraldine had been in the hospital waiting room while Stephanie gave birth and Lala had, upon Chuck's entrance to announce that it was a girl and after hugging Chuck, informed him that he should make sure his daughter knows as soon as she can comprehend that she is Lala's adopted grandniece and that she will be "taking care of me in my dotage."

Thomas, who lived in the last of the fourplex apartments, was also eagerly awaiting news of the meeting.

Thomas bore a shocking resemblance to Salman Rushdie, but was not in fact Salman Rushdie—a fact that Geraldine could not, even in the face of all the convincing her husband and friends and family had tried to do over several years, and in the face of actual government-issued documentation to the contrary, accept or acknowledge.

"He's in hiding," Geraldine would always whisper. "He has to say he's not who he actually is. Because of that nasty *fatwā* on his precious keppie."

"The *fatwā* has been lifted," Lala would sigh. "The real Salman Rushdie appears on television."

"That's a body double," Geraldine would crow. "And a face double, obviously. And that proves my point!"

Geraldine's second husband Monty was away, having gone on a motorcycle ride up the coast with Lala's boyfriend David, who lived with her at her gorgeous apartment in the fourplex. Geraldine and Lala had been invited on the trip, but then the meeting at Sony came up, and the ladies decided to let their men make it a Boys' Journey.

"I didn't really want to ride for miles on the back of a motorcycle," Geraldine had said as they smiled and stood by the road, waving their men off.

"God, neither did I," Lala agreed, smiling and waving in a wide arc, and speaking through clenched teeth so David couldn't turn around and lip-read her betrayal. "It sounds like Hell on God's Earth. They're going to be camping. Outdoors. I, for one, need a clean and spacious bathroom nearby if I'm going to be enjoying any kind of travel adventure."

As soon as Lala entered the courtyard after her meeting, Geraldine rushed over to her and wrapped her in a hug.

"My god, darling, you look like hell. Thank goodness David isn't here to see you like this. I'm so sorry your meeting didn't go well."

"I don't need a consoling hug, Auntie Geraldine," Lala said, "but I appreciate the impulse."

Lala noticed that Stephanie and Chuck were giving her what appeared to be the visual assessment of medical professionals, albeit medical professionals whose area of expertise encompassed life forms with fur, fins, and feathers.

"Did you, in a moment of understandable confusion, given how important this meeting was, put those drops we prescribed for Petunia in your eyes?" Stephanie asked.

"Yes, you dear young veterinarian!" Lala said. "That's why I look like hell! The meeting was great! We're moving forward with the project! There is NO business like SHOW business! I have got exclamation points jumping around in my head like so many Tasmanian Devils!"

Geraldine led the mood of the group as it moved from concern over a dream dashed and a mild horror at Lala's eyes, to exuberance and starting to plan what to wear to the Academy Awards ceremony, by executing a sudden and quite odd sliding motion back and forth on the polished stones of the courtyard while fluttering her hands together in an odd rhythm, which seemed to be trying, quite unsuccessfully, to approximate clapping, that made Lala, for a terrifying moment, fear that her beloved aunt was having a stroke. She was greatly relieved when Geraldine articulated her joy in crisp and clear words.

"Ohhh, we've got to celebrate! I'm thinking road trip! Road trip to Paradise! With nice bathrooms!"

Heaven

David and Monty wanted to get started on their celebratory drive up the spectacular California coast early in the morning. Very early. Ridiculously early.

"I don't wanna get up at five o'clock!" Lala whined.

The four of them were relaxing in Geraldine and Monty's apartment after having enjoyed a simple but elegant impromptu meal that Geraldine had whipped up from a box of risotto, a jar of capers, and a can of Kalamata olives that were just this side of their sell-by date.

Before the announcement of their departure time that sent Lala into a siren-like snit, Lala had cheerfully dubbed the dinner "so sinfully sodium-laden, I think I can hear my blood pressure rising."

"Seeing the waves crashing as the sky brightens is going to be worth it," David said, ignoring Lala's protests by not looking away from the documentary about scaling the north face of the Grand Teton that he was watching with Monty.

"What is wrong with you boys?" Geraldine huffed. "When did you both become so rugged? I did not sign up for rugged, Monty."

"Gerry," Monty chuckled affectionately, also not taking his eyes off the television, "nothing rugged about early morning waves when you're watching them from a Lexus."

Lala and Geraldine slept soundly through the magnificent sight of dawn on the Pacific as Monty's Lexus, driven by David, cruised up Highway 1.

Stephanie and Chuck and Trixie—who were so much like family that the distinction between *de facto* and *de jure* had been rendered irrelevant—were of course invited to join them on their trip, as was Thomas, also a member of the extended family. But Stephanie and Chuck had to stay home to host a visit from Stephanie's parents, who lived in Michigan and found an excuse to visit their beloved first grandchild on an almost bi-weekly basis, and Thomas was going away to New Orleans for the week with his new girlfriend.

"Mazel Tov!" Geraldine said when Thomas shared his travel plans. "When do we meet her?"

"So happy for you!" Lala added. "When do we meet her?"

Lala's dogs would be staying with Stephanie and Chuck because Trixie loved them, and Stephanie and Chuck, of course, knew exactly how to care for geriatric pets. Stephanie's parents were volunteers for the Humane Society of Huron Valley in Ann Arbor and were, according to Stephanie, "maybe more excited about spending time with your dogs than they are about seeing Trixie for the second time this month. I'm being ironic, of course."

"I don't think that's irony," Lala said. "And I just love you, you earnest and adorable young gal."

And then she hugged Stephanie and added, "You know, half the time I'm not really sure what constitutes irony anyway. Which, given how self-righteous I am about words and syntax and grammar and punctuation 'n' stuff, might be ironic. Or not. I'm not entirely sure."

By the time the Lexus got to Santa Barbara, and they stopped for lunch at a cute little bistro right on the beach, Lala was awake and crowing about charitable giving as she shoved big bites of a delicious veggie burger in her mouth.

"Why are you taking a picture of my profile while I'm eating?" she demanded of David.

"Because you look like a chipmunk storing up veggie burger for the winter," David said from behind the safety of his iPhone.

"If you weren't so adorable, I'd smack you right now," Lala giggled. "I'm kidding, of course. This may be the best veggie burger I've ever had. OMIGOD, look at that Doge de Bordeaux!"

Lala jumped up and assaulted a young couple who were walking a dog, which could have functioned as a pony for toddlers, on the path skirting the beach. Monty poured Geraldine and David another glass of iced tea from a large carafe as they watched Lala bob her head and chat animatedly with the dog and his owners. Apparently her question of "Is he/she friendly?"—which was always Lala's first query when she met a new dog to adore—had been answered in the affirmative, because they saw Lala fall down to her knees and proceed to rub her face in the cheerful beast's endless jowls.

"I am COVERED in drool!" Lala cheerfully announced when she bounded back to the table. "Is this California coast HEAVEN, or what? Okay, okay, on to business."

She pulled out her cell phone and started pounding on it with her index finger.

"Wait. Wait. I just need to find that notepad thingie. Got it. Okay, so we'll donate as much as we're spending on this luxurious celebratory weekend, yes?"

"Yup," David said.

"Mmm hmm," Geraldine echoed.

"Sure, of course," Monty concluded.

"Charities?" Lala demanded. "I'll go first. Compassion Without Borders for me. They help animals everywhere, and I love them."

"Excellent," David said. "This time around, I'm going with a foundation that helps the Chicago public schools."

"I love you," Lala drawled as she jabbed at her phone. "Auntie Geraldine?"

"The Nature Conservancy."

"Lovely. Monty?"

"My favorite. Habitat for Humanity."

Lala stood and waved her cell phone at the large crowd of tourists and smiled as she yelled.

"A village! It takes a village, people!"

They arrived at the Post Ranch Inn in Big Sur just as the sun was starting to set. Geraldine was awake for the impressive sight. Lala was also conscious and somewhat out of her mind.

"It's so NIIIIIIICE!" she trilled, leaning out the window as the entrance to the insanely lush and environmentally conscious hotel loomed before them. Geraldine and Monty had loved the place when they honeymooned there, and this would be Lala and David's first visit.

"Welcome, Mr. and Mrs. Briller!" Lars, the dashing manager of the Post Ranch said as he opened the passenger side door to the Lexus. "We're so happy to see you again."

Monty's last name had been Miller for all of his life until he married Geraldine after losing his first wife several years earlier. Geraldine, also widowed, had taken her first husband's surname when she married. She had been born into a family named Kaplan and had become Geraldine Bronson. When they married, Geraldine and Monty decided to "mash our names together and create a new beginning, because that's very sexy and bold, isn't it?" as Geraldine explained to Lala. "I considered melding my first last name with Monty's only last name, but then we would end up with Maplan or Killer, neither of which sounded very charming. I like Briller because it sounds like someone from Ireland is pronouncing Brillo. And I think that's adorable, don't you?"

Lars escorted his special guests to the Pacific Suite, a two-story edifice with a private suite on each floor that looked out on the ocean and was—as Lala would later describe to her many actual and adopted nieces and nephews who were caring for her in her rambunctious dotage during many a "Day-Long Happy Hour, because why should the party ever stop, huh, kids, huh?"—"a prime example of the reason the masses rise up to overthrow the aristocracy."

Lars showed them the details of the suites and left them with a promise to bring his signature macadamia nut bread pudding to their table for dessert.

On the drive up, Lala had been enumerating all the things she planned to do in and around beautiful Big Sur, including going shopping in nearby Carmel, walking down the literary legend that is Cannery Row in Monterey, hiking at Julia Pfeiffer Burns State Park, and ogling the real estate along 17-Mile Drive.

When the door closed behind wonderfully gracious Lars, Lala turned to her boyfriend and her adopted aunt and uncle.

"I am not leaving here. I shall never leave the Post Ranch Inn. My nieces and nephews, all of them, shall have to journey here to care for me, for I shall grow old here, and I shall die here."

Not two days would pass before Lala came to deeply regret that last choice of verb.

"Okay, so here's the deal," Geraldine said. She slipped her arm under her dear husband's and clutched him close to her. "We're gonna go off to our magnificent, thankfully soundproofed suite and fuck. Fuck all over the many luxurious variations of all nine-hundred-and-seventy gorgeous square feet, until the last second we can, leaving just enough time to get cleaned up and make it to the incomparable Sierra Mar restaurant for our reservation. We'll see you at dinner."

Lala smiled at her aunt. She reflected on what a fun quartet they were. There was Geraldine with her entirely timeless elegance. Geraldine was lithe and striking, and she could easily put her chin on the top of her pixie adopted niece's head and would, in fact, probably have to stoop a bit to get it there. And there was Monty, a strapping, adorable man with all the grace of a diplomat. And her David. So handsome. When Lala met him, he was sporting a modernized mullet, and still, she couldn't resist him. Thankfully, the mullet had been replaced, at Lala's very unsubtle urging ("No, seriously. That thing has got to go. I mean, like, now."), by a short cut that was quite flattering.

And here I am, Lala thought. *Still no grey hair. And still the most short-waisted woman on the planet. What can you do? Genetics. They'll work for you, they'll work against you. Look at us. The Fab Four. Living proof that sexy just gets better in your forties. And seventies. Yay!*

And then, still smiling, she huffed at her aunt as Geraldine and Monty were walking out the door.

"Damn it, Auntie Geraldine, I was just going to say exactly that same fetching and saucy thing about fucking all over the place, and you beat me to it! You always get the jump on being a sexy, edgy woman in her prime. Next time I want a head start."

The California wines at dinner were quite possibly the best Lala had ever tasted, and the bread pudding Lars had promised was indeed incredible.

"This delicious dessert might soak up some of this wonderful wine," Lala mused as she hoisted yet another overflowing forkful. "I could end the evening on a relatively coherent note."

"Dream on, cookie. That'll never happen," Geraldine chuckled. She grabbed what was left of Monty's dessert and shoveled it into her mouth. "Monty, hurry up and finish, we need to have some boozy sex before we fall asleep."

Despite her aunt's pessimistic prediction, Lala felt remarkably lucid when she got back to her suite with David. They made out in their plush king-size bed until Lala said she was starting to lose feeling in her jaw, and David said maybe they should catch a few hours of sleep and then wake up and screw.

"I like the way you think, sexy animal doctor," Lala purred.

They turned on their left sides and spooned, and it didn't take more than a minute or two for Lala to hear the steady, rhythmic breathing and feel the delicate exhales that indicated her adorable live-in boyfriend had fallen asleep.

Jesus, Lala thought. *That monsoon he is unleashing on my ear is going to drive me crazy.*

Lala spent the next fifteen minutes turning onto her back, moving imperceptible degrees at a snail's pace so that she wouldn't risk waking dear David. And, once she was on her back, she spent an at least equal amount of time sliding herself upward so that she could ultimately be sort of sitting up against the headboard.

She looked down at David, who was still asleep. And whose breath was hitting her naked waist.

My skin is weirdly hypersensitive tonight, Lala thought. *Seriously, I may have to sleep on the couch.*

She stretched her neck and looked toward the sofa in the living area.

It does look very comfortable, Lala thought. *And spacious. And inviting.*

But Lala wasn't quite ready to give up. She slowly inched the blanket up until it was between her skin and David's lips.

I'm exhausted, Lala thought. *What time is it? I think I can sleep semi sitting up.*

Lala counted backward from three hundred with "Mississippi" between the numbers because that would approximate five minutes. And then she counted from one to three hundred in French with "Mont-Saint-Michel" between the numbers, having determined right after *deux-cent-quatre-vingt-dix-sept* that counting backward in French was just way too challenging after so much wonderful wine.

Well, Lala thought, *whatever time it might actually be, and however exhausted I am, I don't seem to be able to fall asleep. What to do, what to do. I know! Time for some deliciously diverting TV!*

Lala scanned the room. The remote was on the nightstand next to David's side of the bed.

Damn it, Lala thought. She paused. *Smooth. Smooth and swift and subtle and seamless. God, I do love alliteration.*

Before she could lose her resolve, she spun around, taking David with her in a move that turned them both toward their right and ended up with David on the opposite side of the bed to the one he had started out on, putting her on top of him, still spooning and within reaching distance of the remote. She froze. After another moment, she once again heard the soothing sound of David's slumbering breath. Soothing now that it wasn't falling on her.

Yay! Lala thought. She moved quietly and gently back to the other side of the bed and positioned herself against the headboard. She clicked on the television and then immediately clicked on Mute and Closed Captioning so she could read the screen rather than listen to it.

After a delightfully brief scroll through the channels that once again served to sustain Lala's belief and hope that the universe was an ultimately merciful place, Lala found exactly what she was looking for. *Say Yes to the Dress.* Also known as Heaven on Lala's Earth.

Uh oh, Lala thought. *Hush.*

She had quite suddenly noticed that the snack basket in the living area was yelling her name.

Be quiet, she thought. *You'll wake him!*

Lala looked at David. He was entirely undisturbed by what had grown to be a cacophony from the bounty of treats.

Fine, Lala thought. *You can sleep through that, you can sleep through anything.*

Lala bounced off the bed and sprinted out of the sleeping area.

"Whre doon?" David mumbled, turning over on his back.

"Nothing!" Lala yelled. "Go back to sleep!"

She ran to the counter in the wet bar, scanned the large basket in a moment, and grabbed a can of Pringle's potato chips, which she popped open on the way back to the bed. Lala slid back under the covers and commenced crunching.

"Whr makn smuch noise?" David grumbled, not opening his eyes.

"Go back to sleep!" Lala said as she scooted under the covers.

Lala tried, fairly unsuccessfully, to eat the delicious chips more quietly and focused once again on the screen.

Wow, Lala thought. *Heaven.*

The brides at Kleinfeld in Manhattan and the wedding dress consultants who were helping to make their matrimonial dreams come true did not, as they never, ever would or could, disappoint. This, Lala felt sure, was storytelling at its best. Relationships. Conflict. Reconciliation. Transformation. It was all there. In lace and satin and tulle, mermaid, ball gown, and sheath styles. All of it real and meaningful and entirely over-the-top.

Would you listen to that gal? Lala thought. *Who refers to herself in the third person? "Desiree is the star of her wedding! Desiree will be the center of attention, because that is who Desiree is!" She's talking about herself, for god's sake! This third person stuff? It drives Lala crazy!*

Lala read the dialogue between the next bride and the consultant. The consultant asked the bride to tell her about her fiancé. The bride gushed and said they had met in college and he was her best friend and she had the best fiancé in the world and she knew he would be the best husband in the world.

Nuh uh, Lala thought. *Your fiancé may be quite spectacular. And he may end up being a superb husband. But he won't be the best. I had the best.*

Lala remembered her late husband Terrence proposing to her in Central Park in her beloved Island of Manhattan. She remembered shopping for the dress for her wedding to Terrence.

She remembered losing him far too soon.

"Whre cryin'?" David muttered. He turned on his other side and wrapped his arm around Lala.

"I'm not," Lala gulped. She grabbed her pillow and dabbed at her wet face with it. "Everything's fine. Go back to sleep."

Lala settled back on her damp pillow and shut her eyes. The television remained on.

I've got to get some sleep, Lala thought. *Don't think about Terrence. Don't think about how precious and fragile life is. Don't think about David breathing on me like he's running a fucking marathon.*

I may need to unbutton my pants, Lala thought.

"This complimentary gourmet breakfast buffet thing?" Lala said. She seized a mini almond cherry scone from the breadbasket and bit it in half. "It's yet another reason why I never want to leave this place."

Geraldine and Lala were alone at their table while Monty and David stood in a short line at the omelet station. The men were wearing their tennis whites, having gotten up for an early game after a quick room service breakfast of egg whites and steamed spinach. Geraldine and Lala had woken a bit later and had gone to a hot yoga class, with Lala complaining that she was "schvitzing like I'm literally standing under a shower, and I think that's the correct use of literally in this context, no?" and Geraldine urgently hissing at her in a whisper to "shut up because we're in YOGA class, for god's sake!"

Lala and Geraldine had not eaten anything before their yoga class, as per the directions in the brochure in their suite, and Lala was now on a tear.

"Okay, I'm done with this current sweet cycle, so on to the savory. I think I'll have another round of risotto. Doesn't David look cute in his tennis whites? I think he looks like his name should be Sven. I think I'll start calling him Sven."

After brunch, they all retired to their suite to nap before enjoying a guided nature walk together on the seemingly endless grounds of the Post Ranch. Their guide was a strapping Swede named Sven, and Lala took that as a sign that she should never leave this place. They were joined on the walk by a young couple from Chicago. The husband was a journalist and the wife was an attorney. The man, Lala would later recall to one of her nieces and nephews who were taking care of her in her golden years, "had a voice that conjured what I imagine to be the sound those really big dinosaurs—I can't remember what they're called— make. And I mean that as a compliment."

And after that, it was back to their suite for room service lunch and afternoon sex and yet another nap before they met at the heated lap pool that overlooked the ocean so that Lala and Geraldine could do their own version of an Olympic swim meet while David and Monty sunbathed, and then the four of them would soak in the heated Meditation Spa, also overlooking the ocean, before they would go back to their suite to get dressed for dinner.

"And it was in the Meditation Spa," Lala would later recount to one of her nieces and nephews who were taking care of her, "that it all went to shit that day."

And when, decades later, she would reflect on that god-aw- ful day that had started with so much comfort and luxury and so many trips to the Happy Endings dessert bar at the compli- mentary gourmet breakfast buffet, Lala would have a hard time deciding which part was the worst.

"I vacillate," she would admit to one of her nieces and neph- ews, at this point a different one because this particular story in their Auntie Lala's repertoire was an especially winding one, and so they'd schedule shifts to listen to it.

The niece or nephew would try very hard to focus and to not let her or his eyes flutter anywhere near shut, because a betrayal like that would cause Auntie Lala to snap, "WHAT? I'm BORING you?"

"Not at all, Auntie Lala," her niece or nephew would assure

the grumpy-but-good-hearted-old-grande-dame. "You were saying?"

And at that point Lala would grandly swoop up her martini glass and loudly slurp up the remaining drops of vodka and olive juice. And if her nieces and nephews had scheduled it so that two of them were there at the same time for a visit on that particular Sunday "because, y'know, it's easier to listen to those same stories that were perhaps interesting the first few times but are now bordering on psychological torture when you've at least got a fellow prisoner to roll your eyes at," one would turn to the other while their aunt was gulping and whisper something amusing, and the other would silently giggle, and their aunt would grandly slam her martini glass on the table.

"I can HEAR you! And quit rolling your eyes! Okay, as I was saying, I'm not sure if the worst part was sitting in that fabulous Meditation Spa and suddenly noticing—it seemed the three of us noticed it at the same time—that Monty's eyes had closed, and it wasn't because he was luxuriating but because something was terribly wrong, and suddenly the three of us were lunging across the pool to get Monty out of the water before he went under. Or maybe the worst part was that interminable ride to the hospital through all those fucking endless roads in 'glorious and majestic' . . ."

And at this point, Lala would lift her ancient but still very shapely arms and grandly make air quotation marks around the compliments, having never in all those decades forgiven that particular section of her beloved California coast for causing so much terror that particular day.

". . . Big Sur. Or the way my Auntie Geraldine looked when she saw her husband faint. Or sitting in that emergency room waiting for forever until a doctor who looked like Methuselah's grandmother and ended up being quite possibly the kindest and most brilliant person I ever met, so listen to me being such a putz thinking about old people in that kind of negative way back then, when that doctor back then looked like a spring chicken compared to the way your beloved Auntie Lala looks now, WHY AREN'T YOU PICKING UP YOUR CUE FASTER?!"

And her niece or nephew would jerk her or his head back because she or he had understandably been finding it nearly impossible to stay awake, and would yell to compensate for the lack of enthusiasm implied by the transgression of almost falling asleep, and also because they had been so startled by Lala's yelling at them while they were almost asleep, even though the same scenario with the trying not to sleep and the almost sleeping and the yelling and the missing cues had played itself out multiple times before.

"YOU LOOK GREAT, AUNTIE LALA! You look much younger than you are!"

"Yeah, yeah," Lala would chortle. "Anyway, as I was saying, there I am, silently being snotty about how old this wonderful doctor looked, and then she comes in and says that awful word. P.S. Sweetheart, I'm not a scientist, but I don't think that martooni pitcher is gonna fill itself."

David was at the cafeteria getting them all coffee when Dr. Celentano came back to the waiting room to find them. She sat down next to Geraldine and consulted the file she held.

"The good news is that he hasn't had a stroke, and he hasn't had a heart attack. The other news is that there's something on his thyroid that I don't like, so I rush ordered a biopsy."

God, do I hate that fucking word, Lala thought.

"I know that's a terrifying word," Dr. Celentano said.

That's what Terrence's doctors said, Lala thought.

"Let's try to think of it as a diagnostic tool and not as a conclusion in itself."

Yup, that's more-or-less what they said.

"And even if the results are not what we want to hear,

thyroid cancer is among the most curable."

Okay, that one we never heard. Because fucking stomach cancer. Decidedly not among the most curable of fucking cancers.

They rented a room at a Super 8 motel less than a mile away from the Community Hospital of the Monterey Peninsula so that they could shower and so that, as Monty insisted, Geraldine could leave his side for a couple of hours and get a little sleep in an actual bed. Lars from the Post Ranch brought over his special bread pudding.

And then on the second day they heard the word that Lala and Terrence hadn't heard.

It was late in the afternoon and they were all sitting around Monty's bed. Dr. Celentano came in and, when she saw the four of them there, she smiled.

"Good. You're all here. It's benign. You can go home tomorrow. Is that Lars's signature macadamia nut bread pudding? That stuff is incredible! Gimme a bite!"

The next morning, as she was signing the release forms, Dr. Celentano gave strict instructions for the drive back home to be leisurely.

"Seize the moment. Seize the day. Don't drive like a crazy person. Stop and smell the sea air. None of us know how much time we've got on this planet, right, Montgomery? So all of you pretend you're Italian like I am and add lots of *mangia*, *vino*, and *amore*. That's all the Italian I know. Oh, wait, one more. *La Dolce Vita*. Yeah. You know, I did the typical immigrant child thing. My parents come from Sicily, they settle in New York, my mother doesn't even speak English. My mother was illiterate, isn't that a tragedy. She died when she was fifty-six. She looked older then than I do now, and I'll be ninety-four on my next birthday."

Wow, Lala thought. *I would have guessed older, but I'm such a pill.*

Dr. Celentano had plopped herself down on a chair while they waited for an orderly to come up with a wheelchair to get Monty out of the room and back to their car. "So my parents spoke to all of us in Sicilian, and we all answered in English because we wanted to be Americans. Such a shame, losing the language of my people. Oh, look, you've got Keith, he's my favorite orderly. Hi, Keith. Okay, so I'll call Montgomery's regular doctor and fill him in, and, Geraldine and Lala and David, I'll count on you all to get this nice young man in to see his physician right after you get home. Not urgent, but don't dawdle. Lovely to meet you all. *Arrivederci, Roma.*"

And it was indeed, as ordered, a leisurely and very relaxing trip back to Los Angeles. Dr. Celentano had put no restrictions on Monty's activities, so they stopped at a lovely winery at the southernmost edge of Big Sur, then stayed overnight at an adorable BnB right on the beach in Cambria. After that, they went to another charming winery just outside Santa Barbara in the adorable Danish village of Solvang, where they stayed overnight at the cozy Svendsgaard's Danish Lodge, which made Lala momentarily fear that the name "Sven," in a myriad of terrifying variations, would haunt her for the rest of her life.

Throughout the trip home, Lala did a wonderful job of being her usual chatty self. Her usual very chatty self. Her usual incredibly chatty self. She basically didn't shut up for two days and two nights.

"Wow! Look at those waves! Monty, can you see those waves? Wow! Nice, huh? I love the ocean. Isn't this nice? All of us together. Riding along the beautiful coast. Together. Alive. Nice. So. Waves. Fun."

"What's with the staccato delivery?" Geraldine demanded. "Are you okay?"

Uh oh, Lala thought. *Subconscious cries for help escaping. Damn.*

"I am GREAT!" Lala yelled.

"Good," Geraldine said. "Let's modulate our enthusiasm, shall we?"

And so whenever she saw that Monty was dozing off, as he should have and did while they were driving between scenic stops, Lala didn't stop talking, she just lowered her voice to an indecipherable whisper.

"I do love the idea of all of us dressing up as the Beatles for Halloween this year, don't you? If it's okay with everyone else, I'd like to put dibs on Ringo. Is that okay with you both? Auntie Geraldine, don't feel you have to answer for Monty. I can wait until he wakes up. Though I am eager to find out, so maybe you could give me your okay and then promise to persuade him if he's not keen on the idea?"

And then Lala would wait for an answer, and when none was forthcoming from David, who was driving, and from Geraldine, who was in the backseat with Monty stretched out with his head on her lap, she spun around to stare inquiringly at her aunt.

"I couldn't understand a word, dear," Geraldine said. "David, did you get any of that?"

"I wasn't listening," David said.

And still Lala didn't stop chatting. She couldn't figure out any other way to maintain the perky energy that might prevent them from knowing that she couldn't stop replaying the last months of Terrence's life in her head. She didn't want them to know that the images of IV drips and syringes and vomiting and wonderful hospice nurses, whose non-stop kindness only made it more difficult for her not to be constantly sobbing in front of Terrence as they upped the doses of his morphine to help keep him out of pain, were flooding her mind in a way that they hadn't since the awful years immediately after Terrence died.

When they got back to Manhattan Beach, it was just before dinnertime. Lala asked David to please wait just a minute and she would come right back to help him with the bags.

"I'm not an invalid," Monty insisted. "I'll help him with the bags."

"NO!" the three of them yelled.

Lala ran from the parking spots behind the fourplex and through the courtyard to Stephanie and Chuck's place.

Got to see my puppies, she thought. *Got to see them now. Must hug puppies. Now.*

"Hi, Mr. and Mrs. Stephanie!" she crowed when Stephanie's mom and dad opened the door.

I can't remember their names, Lala thought. *Damn it. I am such a putz.*

Stephanie's mom, Linda, was holding her granddaughter and was also balancing Yootza, Lala's dachshund, in her arms. Yootza, who was normally a complete grouch, a quality that Lala found ceaselessly endearing, was snuggled up against Linda and Trixie. Lala thought she could hear him purring.

"Look, Yootzie," Linda cooed. "Mama's home!"

She gently handed the grey-faced little hound to Lala, and the moment that Trixie realized that her best buddy was being taken from her, she began to wail with wrenching, full-body sobs.

"Ohh," Stephanie's dad Leland said. He patted his granddaughter on the top of her head, which only seemed to add to Trixie's distress.

Linda nodded at Lala and Yootza and smiled.

"Babies," Linda sighed. "When they're sad, they cry with their whole little souls."

Yeah, Lala thought. *I know how they feel.*

You Know What You Can't Do?

As she had done from her earliest memories, Lala retreated to find solace with her animals. Her regular work routine of sitting on the couch with her dogs and working on her laptop while her television show addictions played at a low volume in the background brought Lala a lot of comfort as she relived memories of her life with Terrence with a vividness that hadn't really been with her since shortly after he died.

It took a week of popping half an Ambien so that she could fall into blissful oblivion fifteen minutes after swallowing the little bisected pill for Lala to start to feel somewhat righted again. And throughout this unexpected period of upheaval and adjustment, Lala worked very hard to make sure that everyone, especially David, couldn't tell that she was in a fresh phase of non-stop, low-grade widow's agony.

I'm David's girlfriend, she silently mused while *Say Yes to the Dress* once again played in the background. *And I guess I really do still think of myself as Terrence's widow. Maybe I can combine the two words for all of us who have to move on after we lose our mates. Gidow. Wirlfriend. I love words. Oh, honey, do not buy that dress. Don't listen to your stepmother. You do not want to look like that on your wedding day.*

Most of the time, Lala was successful in being her usual self so no one would worry that something was amiss. But then there were those moments when forming complete sentences in conversation was just beyond her abilities.

"I feel like making a chopped salad for dinner," David said one evening after he had gotten back from speaking at a day-long conference at UCLA for undergraduates interested in going to veterinary school.

"Yum. Delish. Greens. Yes. Thanks."

"Are you okay?" David asked.

Oops, Lala thought. *Gotta up the vigilance.*

"I am great!" Lala said. "I feel so great, I think I'll make the chopped salad while you relax and play with the pups."

David peered at Lala with increased concern.

Oops, Lala thought. *Overcompensating again.*

"You never cook," David whispered, sounding somewhat terrified.

"Kidding!" Lala brayed. "I'm kidding, you silly goose! You make the damn salad! Everyone knows I never cook!"

Thankfully, high-powered distraction arrived shortly after their return from Big Sur in the form of another meeting at Sony Pictures Studios. Zoe drove to Manhattan Beach on the day of the meeting to get ready with Lala and to travel to the studio together.

Getting ready involved Zoe talking Lala off the ledge she had gotten herself onto.

"Check again! Are you sure? Check again, please, Zoe!"

"Lala," Zoe said with an exaggerated level of calm that she desperately hoped might make her producing partner less crazy. "There are no drops of any kind in your bag. I promise you. I've checked four times now. All is as it should be. Your notes are in there. Several pens and a highlighter are in there. Your phone, your not-tested-on-animals blush, and your not-tested-on-animals pressed powder compact is in there."

"Good," Lala gasped, her voice still trembling. "Let's hope I don't poke any of the stuff in my bag in my eyes before we get to the conference room."

Clive and his manager Garrett were already in the conference room when an assistant brought Lala and Zoe in to join them.

Clive stood when they walked in and extended his hand, first to Lala and then to Zoe.

Garrett remained seated.

I'm thinkin' Garrett's a dickhead, Lala thought, smiling broadly at Clive and pumping his hand.

"Lala, you look great!" Clive said, sounding astonished.

"Ohhh, thanks," Lala said unenthusiastically, Clive's note of surprise having been entirely impossible to miss.

"I'm sorry," Clive added. "It's not because I'm shocked that you could look great, Lala, it's just that your eyes were in so much distress last time we saw you."

Okay, I have to admit that that's a rather endearing save, Lala thought.

"Yeah, okay, Clive, can we get this meeting started?" Garrett growled.

"Garrett, don't be a total dickhead," Clive chuckled.

Clive, you are growing on me at a rapid rate, Lala thought as she sat in the chair that Clive had pulled out from the table for her.

The meeting was light and gregarious and fun, all of it coming from Clive's end because Garrett didn't do a whole lot more than sit there and scowl. Lala and Zoe and Clive talked about possible casting choices, about songs that had come to Clive's mind while he was reading the script that might work on the soundtrack, and about location ideas, including actually filming the Parisian scenes in the novel in Paris, which made Lala's *couer* skip a beat.

Garrett ate all the deviled eggs that were on the once again bountiful cart of savory and sweet snacks and legions of varied beverages.

Damn, Lala thought, *I love deviled eggs. Greedy schmuck.*

"Give 'em the DVD," Garret growled through a mouth full of yolk.

"Excellent idea. Thank you, Garrett," Clive said with what Lala immediately recognized was genuine and completely inexplicable affection.

Wow, Lala thought. *You are a far better person than I, Clive.*

Clive grabbed a DVD case from the seat next to him and handed it to Zoe.

"We'd like you to please consider Matthew Finch as the director for *Dressed Like a Lady*. Take a view of his latest film, and let us know what you think."

Zoe looked at the cover and smiled.

"We saw this!" she said. "Lala, it's that comedy we just saw!"

"It is? That's the director you want? We loved that film!"

"Excellent!" Clive said.

"Good," Garrett huffed. He slid over to the cart, grabbed a Perrier, and ostentatiously wrenched the top off. "Meeting's over."

While Lala and Zoe were standing and smiling at the sinks and mirrors in the bathroom that had once been the location of so much random trauma and was now transformed to a place of optimism and exuberance, Eliza from Accounting ran in. Her eyes were bright red and wet and she was panting.

"Omigosh, dear," Lala said. She grabbed a paper towel and held it under the faucet. "Here, wipe your poor eyes."

"Thanks," Eliza gasped. Lala patted her back while she gently dabbed her eyes over the sink.

"Did you put drops that were intended to dissolve wax in your beagle's ears in there?" Lala asked sympathetically.

Eliza lifted her head and peered with her anguished eyes at

the possibly misleadingly stable-seeming woman.

"Did I what?" Eliza said.

"Did you—"

"Lala," Zoe interrupted, "that's not a thing."

"Oh. It's not a thing. Right."

Eliza started crying anew.

"Oh, dear," Lala said. "I didn't mean to add to your distress."

"You're not," Eliza sobbed. "I don't know what just happened. This stupid guy in the cubicle next to mine always wears headphones, and usually I can steer clear of him, but today he started singing along. It was quiet at first so I could kind of ignore it, and then it got louder. I thought I should probably just go out and get my own headphones so I wouldn't hear him, but then I just lost it. I stood up and I started screaming at him, and my supervisor came over and I quit my job! I did it without thinking. I just got so fed up with everything. What am I going to do?"

"Which department are you in, dear?" Lala asked.

"Accounting," Eliza sniffled.

Lala and Zoe looked at each other. There was an immediate understanding between the partners.

"I think we could use a good accountant for our production, don't you?"

"I sure do," Zoe said.

"Are you a good accountant?" Lala asked.

"I am," Eliza said. "I work very hard."

"Excellent," Lala said.

The three women walked out of the building together. On the way, they established that Eliza lived in Santa Monica in a small apartment she shared with two roommates.

"Well, I don't live far away from you at all. I'm in Manhattan Beach," Lala said. "Do you have plans for tonight?"

Eliza said that she didn't, and so they agreed to meet at the Whole Foods in Venice, where they shopped for sandwiches and side dishes and wine and dessert.

When they got to Lala's place, her dogs were waiting at the door. David was doing an overnight shift at a 24-hour veterinary hospital in West LA.

"Look at your pups!" Eliza crowed when she walked in. She got down on the floor with the dogs and started rolling around with them, much to the immediate and complete delight of Chester, Petunia, Yootza, and Eunice. Lala and Zoe gave each other a look that clearly indicated they were quite pleased with this confirmation that they had made a good choice in hiring this fellow fan of animals to work with them.

The women and the dogs got themselves comfortable in various locations in the living room. Wine was poured and deemed superb, sandwiches were devoured and deemed sumptuous, and potato salad German-style, as well as potato salad with mayonnaise dressing and macaroni salad with capers, were sampled and were deemed "Omigod, SO tasty!"

The women chatted while they ate and exchanged pieces of biographical information. Eliza had also gone to school in Connecticut, at Trinity College in Hartford.

"Loved it. Hated the winters," she said.

"I know, right?" Zoe said.

"Right, I know," Lala agreed.

They settled back on the sofas and in the cushioned chairs with their vegan blueberry scones, vegan carrot cake, and English Breakfast tea that had ample shots of brandy in it.

It had been decided early on that this would be a slumber party so that there would be license to, as Lala explained to the young women, "not worry about if it's getting late while we brainstorm regarding the project and also get completely hammered." And they would watch the DVD of the film helmed by the director they would most likely be working with.

Lala switched on the TV and the previews leading up to the film began playing.

"*Tooters*," Lala said, reading the DVD case. "Is that the same movie that we saw? I didn't remember it being called that."

"It's the same one," Zoe assured her. "Look at the cast and the character names."

"Oh, yeah. Gosh, you'd think I would have remembered a title like that. Well, there were a lot of mojitos involved."

"I love mojitos," Eliza said. She had Yootza on her lap and was holding him like a baby. Lala watched as her grumpy dachshund gazed at Eliza with serene adoration.

"I do not know how you managed that, Eliza," Lala said. "Yootza is such a grouch. You're like canine Valium."

The previews were over, and *Tooters* began. Lala sat back, looking forward to being delighted and diverted as she had been at the first viewing in the movie theater. It took about fifteen minutes for confusion to begin. She tried not to start worrying and decided to give the film another half hour to transform back into the quality entertainment she fondly remembered. Five minutes into that pledge, Lala had seen enough.

"I'm sorry, did he just say his brother's farts smell like Chinese food? Who writes crap like that?"

Lala grabbed the DVD cover and read the credits.

"He wrote and directed this! That guy they want to direct our movie wrote and directed this piece of crap."

"It's not that bad," Zoe began, and when Lala and Eliza immediately looked at her as though she'd had an instant lobotomy, she had to agree that it was not good.

Clive wants him, Lala thought. *We are fucked*.

"We are fucked," Zoe said. "Clive wants him."

The room went quiet, but for the sounds of Petunia snoring and a character in the movie named Bart telling a character named Brody that they should go to town and "Get dick-deep in the radical, man."

I doubt they're talking about protesting in favor of single-payer healthcare, Lala thought.

She picked up her teacup. It was nearly empty. Eschewing the pot of tea on the coffee table, she grabbed the brandy bottle and filled the cup with that. Lala sipped steadily as she continued to watch the screen and reflected on the dream of a quality creative future that was crumbling in front of her. And that reminded her of another time when her plans for the future were suddenly lost. And that made her quickly get over herself *vis-à-vis* her career.

"You know what?" Lala said. "It's not life and death. If Clive wants this guy and having this guy gets our movie made, we'll make it work. Let's look on the bright side."

She drained the last drops out of the brandy bottle into her cup. Zoe and Eliza watched her in hopeful anticipation of hearing what the pluses to this silver screen slop festival might be.

"We're out of brandy," Lala said. "But I've got a full bottle of Bailey's Irish Cream in the cupboard. See? Things are already looking up!"

Life, Lala observed, continued as it always did unless the Grim Reaper had other plans, and she did her best to push any thoughts of loss out of her mind. Thankfully, life was newly quite busy and helped distract her. The filming of *Dressed Like a Lady, Drinks Like a Pig* was fast-tracked when Clive's production company came aboard, and Clive kept Lala and Zoe, and now Eliza, busy with all aspects of the production. He made his admiration for the women clear, and Lala appreciated the extra activity in her life. Until they moved into their own office space, Clive gave them complete access to two of the five offices that Sony had given him on their lot for the project, and Lala spent many hours, often seven days a week, at the studio, doing anything that would help get the job done.

"I really think we should film the Paris scenes on location," Clive said one day.

"*Mais bien sûr!*" Lala cooed.

"*Tu parles français?*" Clive asked.

"*Tu n'as pas idée, mon cher.*"

I'm not entirely sure what I'm trying to indicate with that, Lala thought. *But it sounds knowing. And rather insouciantly French, I think.* J'espère.

Lala's conscious attempts to banish the painful memories of losing Terrence started to work, and her conscious efforts to behave as though she were feeling confident and optimistic about life also started to work, so that acting—something Lala had to admit to herself she had never been especially good at, even during all those years in college and when she was auditioning in New York ("How in god's name I didn't realize I absolutely sucked in just about every role I ever had is entirely beyond me . . .")—like she was okay was proving surprisingly effective. Whenever she thought about someone she loved—specifically David—dying, she just imagined a big stop sign and silently yelled "STOP!" to herself. And doing that really started to help. It really did.

But there were those stray moments when the interior voice slipped into the exterior.

At dinner . . .

"Honey, do you want more ice—"

"STOP! I'm sorry . . . You were saying?"

While hiking up to the Hollywood sign . . .

"Lala, look at that cute puppy over—"

"STOP! I'm sorry . . . Puppy! Cute!"

During sex . . .

"STOP! No, I'm sorry, David . . . don't stop . . ."

On her personal horizon, there was a lovely event coming up that would also serve to help Lala feel distracted. Monty was turning seventy-five, and Geraldine decided that a big birthday weekend celebration, especially given his recent health scare, was a must.

Monty's daughter Helene, who was spending a year as writer-in-residence at the Iowa Writers' Program, was to visit from Iowa City, where she was living for the year with her boyfriend Clark, whom she had met when he was the chauffeur for

Geraldine's bachelorette party in Las Vegas.

Also at the festivities would be Lala's best friend from high school, Brenda, and Brenda's husband Frank, who would be visiting from New York City. Brenda, having been like family to Lala and her late parents, and subsequently to Geraldine and her late husband, and then to Monty and Helene and David, was always included in every celebration, and of course that feeling of family extended to Frank as well.

Helene and Clark were staying in Geraldine and Monty's second bedroom. Brenda and Frank would be staying with Lala and David. The festivities were going to begin on Friday evening, with an outdoor movie screening at Will Rogers State Historic Park in the Pacific Palisades. *It's A Wonderful Life* was showing.

"*It's A Wonderful Life?*" Lala said.

"I know it's not even close to Christmas, but I love that movie," Monty said, and everyone agreed that the seasonal imbalance was irrelevant if the birthday boy was happy.

Food trucks of every variety would be at the screening in abundance. They all got there early to scope out a great location with a clear view of the screen, and to spread out their cushiony blankets and low-slung beach chairs. Chuck and Stephanie came and brought Trixie, who slept like a little angel in her papoose throughout the entire show. Because it was outdoors, dogs were allowed, and Lala brought all four of hers. Yootza insisted on staying in his papoose, and Chuck offered to keep the little dachshund slung to his chest while Trixie slept on her mom's, so that the two best buddies could be next to each other. Thomas, a.k.a. Salman Rushdie, brought his new girlfriend, Marina, who was warm and gracious, and everyone instantly loved her. As soon as Thomas and Marina left the group to wander over to the bathrooms, Lala and Brenda and Helene got into a furtive huddle.

"Okay, is it just me?" Lala asked.

"Are we thinking the same thing?" Brenda wondered.

"I'm not going crazy, am I?" Helene demanded.

"I know Thomas isn't really Salman Rushdie," Brenda said. "No matter what Geraldine says."

"Right," Helene agreed.

"But," Lala said, "is it just me, or does Marina look exactly like someone put a curly blonde wig on Aung San Suu Kyi, winner of the Nobel Peace Prize who was kept under house arrest for years by the military junta in Burma, now Myanmar?"

"I was thinking exactly the same thing!" Brenda said.

"Thank god I'm not going crazy," Helene said.

"What are you three whispering about?" Geraldine yelled over from the far side of several blankets, where she and Monty were stretched out and had been mashing on each other since they all got there.

"NOTHING!" Lala and Brenda and Helene yelled back.

The next afternoon included bowling, one of Monty's favorite leisure activities, after brunch at Monty's favorite restaurant in Pasadena, one that of course served bottomless mimosas, which Lala deemed a necessary part of any celebration in a civilized and forgiving world.

Lala was not a good bowler even when sober.

"Honey," David said, watching Lala's intense concentration as she stood at the head of the lane clutching the bowling ball to her chin and shifting from the toes to the heels of her feet and back again in an offbeat rhythm, "are you—"

"Not now, David," Lala hissed. "I'm bowling."

"I'm sorry, sweetie, I don't think I can manage to get the sarcasm out of my voice, but I really am genuinely curious. Are you trying to pitch them all in the gutter?

The plans for Saturday night were for everyone to relax at Geraldine and Monty's place with Chinese food, champagne, and charades.

Lala was not good at charades even when sober.

"Cheek? Gouge? Cheek Gouge? Gouge Cheek?" Lala guessed.

"*Scarface*," Frank sighed. "It's the movie *Scarface*, Lala. If *Cheek Gouge* is in fact a movie, it's not one I've seen."

On Sunday, the actual day of Monty's birth, Geraldine and Monty spent a long afternoon being pampered at a spa, the gift that Lala and David had gotten *L'anniversaire Garçon*, as Lala insisted on calling him. They got home, their muscles kneaded and their fingers pruney from spending so many hours soaking in the spa's hot tub, just in time to change into elegant evening-gwear for a visit to the Magic Castle in Hollywood, as guests of one of Helene's friends who was a member there.

The last time Lala had been to the Magic Castle was when she and Brenda were in high school in Santa Monica and they went there with their then-boyfriends because Brenda's boy-friend's stepfather was a character actor who also did magic as a hobby. Lala eschewed all the shows and the rest of the delights of the place to spend the entire evening making out with Patrick Eliasoph, the star of the theatre department at Santa Monica High who had played Stanley to her, as Lala freely and cheer-fully admitted in hindsight and after switching her career ambi-tions from acting to writing, unbelievably awful rendition of Blanche DuBois.

Though Patrick was, as Lala boasted at the time, "a superb kisser, world class, really, in my admittedly limited experience, and I'll get back to you if my assessment changes with a wid-ening of my reference pool," Lala regretted missing seeing the much-heralded mysteries of the Magic Castle, and she was thrilled that she would be partaking that night.

Because they had all known that Monty's special birthday weekend would include a visit to the Magic Castle, and because the dress code at the Magic Castle required elegant attire, and because Lala really, really, really, really hated shopping and really, really, really, really wasn't especially good at picking out clothes, she fretted about what to wear. Lala didn't share her concerns with Geraldine, because she didn't want to drag her beloved aunt into "my ceaseless mishegoss," despite the fact that

Geraldine had always cheerfully offered to go shopping with Lala and had always been an excellent source of advice on what to try on.

"I can't bring myself to take advantage of her kindness yet again," Lala confessed to her dogs as they were all spread out on the couch while Lala worked on her laptop. "At some point, I am going to have to stand on my own two, boringly-clad in uninspired footwear, feet in terms of getting myself dressed like a big girl."

So Lala snuck off to every department store and every chain clothing store at the classic American mall that is the Beverly Center in Los Angeles. She scoured the racks of fancy dresses at Macy's and Bloomingdale's and Banana Republic and Anthropologie, and when all the warm and helpful salespeople asked her if they could help her with anything, Lala answered as though she were channeling Eeyore.

"I'm okayyyyy. Thanks."

If there was one constant in all this grief, Lala noted in each and every store, it was the cruel and mocking lighting in the dressing rooms.

Nothing worked. Absolutely nothing. Sheaths, off-the-shoulder, patterned, tea-length, a slew of little black dresses . . . Lala stood staring at herself in the legion of three-way mirrors and felt that she would have to pretend to have caught a sudden stomach virus on the day of the Magic Castle excursion. She came home from an entire day spent at the mall exhausted and devoid of any shred of hope.

David opened the door when he heard Lala's key turning in the lock and grabbed her for a big hug. When he let go, he saw her face more clearly in the light of the entranceway.

"Are you . . . Is something . . . You look . . . What happen—"

"I'm okayyyyy. Thanks," Lala sighed miserably. "I think I'll take a bath. Do we have any vodka in the freezer? I mean, the good stuff, not one of those freakishly-large bottles from Trader Joe's. Though I'll certainly drink that if that's all we've got."

Lala knew several people at her gym to smile at whenever they saw each other and to chat pleasantly with about whatever struck their fancies on any given workout day. It was to one of these people, a retired high school English teacher named Clarissa, that Lala blurted her dilemma when Clarissa came over to say hello while Lala was on the stair climber.

"Clarissa, apropos of nothing at all germane to us happily bumping into each other today, I need a fancy dress and can't find anything, and so I'm working out my wardrobe angst by upping my climbing speed to a nine setting from my usual five. God, am I schvitzing."

"Pin Up Girl," Clarissa said. "It's in the Valley, on Magnolia. Just go there. Trust me."

The next day Lala, after having checked the store's website and having been surprised to find herself feeling an odd and unfamiliar sense of optimism when she saw the pages and pages of vintage-inspired dresses and tops and skirts and pants that would have fit in perfectly on any sitcom of the 1950s and that—if the way they looked on the models in the photographs was any approximation of reality—were shockingly flattering, drove to Burbank. This would have been a long trip even on Southern California's web of freeways, but Lala never drove on those freeways, and always and only took surface streets to get wherever she was going.

"Have you *seen* how people drive on the freeways here?" Lala would ask with incredulity whenever anyone stared at her with incredulity when they found out that she never drove on freeways. "They tailgate on the freakin' freeways! They're constantly an inch away from your butt going eighty miles an hour, and I need stress like that in my life?"

Lala found a parking spot very close to the store, right outside the legendary and insanely popular bakery Porto's, where she went in to stand on line for almost half an hour to buy a large iced tea and a muffin that must have had a stick of butter all to itself baked in to fortify her for the merchandising task that was looming large.

Lala squeezed herself into a little corner table and sipped and ate while she read the unabridged, 1,500-page version of *The Count of Monte Cristo* for the "umpteenth time," a designation which Lala often employed and which she maintained did in fact reflect an actual number, "and the fact that I don't actually know exactly what that actual number is doesn't make it any less valid as a description of quantity."

"Well, Edmond Dantès," Lala sighed when the muffin was consumed and the refill of iced tea had been savored, "you may have it rough as a prisoner in the Chateau D'If, but at least you don't have to worry about what you'll be wearing."

The first thing Lala saw when she got to the store was a large sales rack filled with a rainbow of colors and styles in the center of the small courtyard entrance.

Lala studied dresses with patterns, dresses with sleeves, sleeveless dresses, short dresses and longer dresses, eschewing skirts and tops and pants because she wanted to wear a dress. She figured it would just be easier, because it was one thing rather than two and that had to be twice as uncomplicated. And just as Lala's eye rested on something in a gorgeous shade of green and she picked a dress out of the rack, the door to the store opened and a tall, pretty young lady wearing a superb Pin Up Girl outfit consisting of red capri pants and a cropped white top, along with black pumps that looked to Lala like a modified version of stilts, exited.

Would you look at how fabulous she looks, and can you even imagine how awful that fabulous outfit would look on me with my short waist and my gnome-like stature? Lala silently asked herself, smiling at the young lady with genuine admiration. *Plus, I would fall and break my ankle on those shoes in a New York Minute.*

"You've got the Erin!" the young lady said.

"The clothes have names?" Lala said.

"I know, that's fun, isn't it? They all have names!"

"Wow," Lala said. "That is fun! There wouldn't be a dress

named Lala, would there?"

"Hmm," the young lady said. "I don't think we have a Lala."

"Okay. No problem."

"But the Erin, that is going to look absolutely amazing on you!"

The young lady, who introduced herself as Kelly, took the dress from Lala and held the door to the store open for her.

"Come on, let's go see."

The lighting in the Pin Up Girl boutique, Lala was grateful to see, was calm and cozy. The other salespeople were also wearing the store's styles, and they all looked sexy and beautiful.

The bar here, Lala thought, *is set very high.*

Kelly escorted Lala to one of the dressing rooms. Lala pulled the curtain shut and got herself out of her clothes and into the dress. She looked at herself in the mirror before she emerged. The green dress fell just below her knees. The skirt was full and had pockets. The top was tight, and the belt cinched her waist. Her cleavage was showing, and it was looking very sexy.

Wow, Lala thought.

Lala smiled and reflected that the last time she felt this good in a dress, other than in her wedding dress when she married Terrence, was probably back at Wesleyan when she played the sassy friend of the ingénue in *She Stoops to Conquer.*

"A role," Lala whispered to herself in the dressing room, "that was mercifully simple and straightforward, with some darn funny lines, so my subpar acting abilities couldn't make me screw it up too badly."

The costume department had created an opulent Eighteenth-Century aristocrat's dress in deep rust and yellow—two colors that Lala would have thought would look awful on her and ended up looking wonderful.

Lala dated the senior who was playing her love interest in the play throughout the production.

"Let's be frank," Lala whispered, tightening the belt on her Erin dress one notch, "plays are wonderful literature. Theatre is an art for the ages. And a lot of us majored in drama because it's a great way to steep yourself in make-out sessions under the guise of rehearsing."

"Wow!" Kelly said when Lala exited the dressing room. "You look even more amazing than I thought you would!"

Gosh, Lala thought. *I guess I really do look good.*

And then she very suddenly thought about how much Terrence would have loved to see her in this great dress. She didn't know Terrence in college, so he didn't see her in her *She Stoops to Conquer* costume. Other than her wonderful, simple wedding dress, Terrence hadn't really seen her in another exceptional outfit. Shopping and clothes were never her thing. Terrence had loved her in jeans and tee shirts, most of them emblazoned with aggressively liberal political messages or quotations that paid homage to centuries of writers. He didn't need much more than that to think she looked gorgeous. But he really would have loved this dress.

"Sorry," Lala said. "I guess finding the perfect dress makes me all verklempt."

"Happy tears, right?" Kelly said, handing her a tissue.

"Yup," Lala said.

And also really, really, really sad ones, she thought.

"Wow," David said. "You look absolutely amazing!"

Lala had gotten dressed in her new Erin while David, already looking quite handsome in his Hugo Boss suit, sat in the living room with the dogs and worked on an article on feral cat colonies for the *Journal of the American Veterinary Medical Association*.

David stood and swept Lala into a twirl that ended in a bent backward kiss. When they stood and Lala looked at him and started laughing, he looked down at himself and started laughing because his black suit was covered with dog hair. They rushed to find the masking tape roller that so miraculously removed all manner of stuff from clothes. Lala ran it over him again and again like she was a member of the TSA at airport security, until David was gleaming like hairless new.

When they left the apartment, everyone else was already downstairs in the courtyard having a cocktail before the car service van would come to pick them up. They all heard the door to Lala and David's apartment close, and they looked up toward the stairs as Lala and David were descending from the second floor.

"Wow! Lala! You look absolutely wonderful!" Geraldine said. "When did you buy that exquisite dress? And where? And without me? I am very impressed! Come, darlings, I've made a signature cocktail in honor of my beloved, and it's got tequila and ginger and cayenne pepper, and I'm calling it The Full Monty, and we have to finish both pitchers before the car gets here!"

Geraldine handed each of them a large goblet filled to the top. Lala and David raised their glasses and blew a kiss to Monty. Lala took a big sip.

"Wow!" she said, gasping for air. "That is wicked, Auntie Geraldine! So tasty! And I think my sinuses just cleared up."

There was a festive limousine ride over to the Magic Castle, and Helene's friend Kirwan met them at the entrance wearing a tuxedo and a sweeping black cape. Kirwan had the debonair air of the Clark Gable era of Hollywood, complete with a pencil-thin black moustache.

"Welcome to the World's Finest Emporium of Prestidigitation!" he said. He made a low bow, and then he hugged Helene, kissed the other women's hands, and shook the hands of all the men. "First to the library, my dear guests, then to the bar!"

The happy party and their gracious host entered the richly-paneled lobby of the Castle. After driver's licenses were shown at the front desk, they made their way through the door that blended within a wall of books to the large area that was surrounded by staircases leading up and down to the many fascinating levels of the building. The place was packed with people in elegant eveningwear and the atmosphere was thrilling.

Kirwan lead them through a lounge to the Castle library. A gorgeous Tiffany window was the first thing that they all saw. The next charming sight was a huge jug of treats on the main table.

A stately woman, whom Lala suspected might have been a descendant of exiled European royalty, approached the door to the library, essentially blocking the group from entering.

"Kirwan," the woman said with a lovely and tranquil voice, "I welcome you and your guests."

She smiled at them all and added, "To a point."

"Thank you, Lisa," Kirwan said, bowing again. "My friends, this is one of the Castle's librarians, my good friend Lisa."

Kirwan smiled at the party and yelled.

"You can only go as far as that big desk over there! THAT'S SIX FEET FROM THE DOOR! AND WE'RE ONLY ABLE TO DO THAT BECAUSE LISA IS MY FRIEND AND SHE IS WELCOMING US IN! OKAY?"

"Yikes," Lala whispered.

Kirwan handed everyone little paper cups.

"Eat! Eat!" Kirwan said. "I'm sorry I yelled. I take this all very seriously."

Lisa gave Kirwan's face an affectionate little smack.

"You are adorable," she said. "Yes, please enjoy. Members bring in snacks, sometimes it's pretzels, sometimes, like tonight, it's a sumptuous *mélange* of Chex mix and what looks like an addition of some serious amounts of salted peanuts."

"Yum," Kirwan said. "The cups are so we don't just shove our fists into the jug because that would be, like, yuck. So scoop and eat and enjoy!"

"Yes," Lala chimed in without thinking that she might be speaking out of turn and perhaps unintentionally taking the thunder away from their charming host and the equally charming librarian. "Because we will—well, I certainly will—be doing a lot more drinking and—"

"Yes," Kirwan said, "and if one is, it's good to—"

". . . have a base," Lala and Kirwan said in unison.

Great minds, Lala thought.

"Great minds," Kirwan said.

"Uh huh!" Lala said. "What's that room over there?"

"Ohhh," Lisa whispered. "It's locked. That's where the historic books are kept. Some date back a couple of hundred years. There are also several books in the locked room that belonged to Houdini. They're not books that he wrote, but books he owned and annotated, quite humorously, in the margins. I believe one of the books is one of Conan Doyle's spiritualism books, and Houdini's notes are hysterically dismissive and rather smug and nasty."

"And you certainly can't go in there," Kirwan added. "Sorry. Not for civilians."

"Cool!" Lala said.

"Indeed!" Kirwan said. "Okay, we must be on our way. Thank you so much, Lisa. Time for drinks. Because we can't linger here, as ninety percent of the books are about methodology and we are not taking *any* chances with our secrets."

"Indeed," Lisa said. "They're grouped on the shelves by subject. Cards, coins, large illusions, which are books that contain construction plans for, say, sawing a person in half, tarot, mysticism, mentalism, and just about any other magic effect there is. That's what they're called. Effects. Not tricks. Effects."

"Very cool!" Lala said.

Everyone thanked Lisa, and Lisa wished them a lovely evening, which she said she was sure they would have.

Kirwan led them back through the crowded main room and up a flight of stairs to a small bar that was essentially the entirety of a half floor between the first and second levels. A very pretty young woman with a full head of gorgeous curly black hair piled on top of her head, secured with a circle of small silver skulls and crossbones, yipped when she saw Kirwan enter and motioned toward a row of empty barstools with the cocktail shaker she was wielding like a handle-free, cylindrical maraca.

"Hi, punkin'! I saved your seats!" she announced.

"I love you, Janeen!" Kirwan trilled. "Okay, you're all having Janeen's signature cocktail. It's called a Magic Bullet and it will wax your bikini line!"

Lala loved the cocktail, she loved the many appetizers that Kirwan ordered for them all to share, and she thought that Janeen was absolutely delightful.

"Janeen," Lala said, "what's in this cocktail? It is heavenly."

Janeen told her. Lala wrote it down. She made the cocktail several times in the ensuing years, to great acclaim at her parties and of course always giving Janeen full credit. And then the slip of paper was lost. Whenever Lala would, in her extreme and delightfully vibrant old age, try to remember the ingredients, after a few sputtered insistences that "Simple syrup is involved in some capacity, I'm quite sure . . . I think . . ." Lala would then smile and tell her great-niece or great-nephew, "Fuck it. Let's just throw some vodka into some lemonade and call it a party, shall we?"

Janeen entranced them all with a history of the bar.

"It was built in the 1880s by Brunswick Bowling, one of three bars they built. Sometimes, after hours, we set up nine empty bottles at one end and roll oranges down the bar. Don't tell anyone. The bar was shipped by boat around Cape Horn before arriving in Crescent City, where it survived a tidal wave. However, it was water-logged. A friend of the Castle's founder, Milt Larsen, called him about the bar, and Milt had NBC pick it up. The bar was restored and was on a TV show that I don't remember, but then it was used on Dean Martin's Gold Diggers show before it was installed at the Castle. And the backdrop was the original nighttime backdrop for *The Tonight Show* with Johnny Carson, a long-time member of the Castle. Who's ready for a refill?"

"I am! I am!" Lala chirped.

"Let's ask Archimedes some questions," Kirwan said.

"Archimedes?" Lala said.

"The owl," Kirwan said.

"Owl?" Lala echoed.

"Over the bar," Brenda said.

"That huge owl," Geraldine said. "Right there. Over the bar."

"Ohhh," Lala said. "See, this is why I could never be a detective. I am essentially oblivious to all the details surrounding me. Just about all of the time. Did not see that owl. Would have bet good money there was not an owl anywhere near here."

"It has to be a yes or no question," Kirwan said. "And I can't tell you how he answers, so don't even ask me."

A question leapt into Lala's mind, and it startled her to hear it in her unspoken voice.

Will I die of sadness?

"Questions! Questions, people!" Kirwan said.

"Will we all be delightfully hungover tomorrow?" the Birthday Boy asked.

All eyes looked to the imposing owl. Very slowly, Archimedes nodded his head.

"I knew it!" Monty said. "Clever bird!"

Die of sadness? Lala thought. *Where the fuck did that come from?*

"Will we get up before noon tomorrow?" Geraldine asked.

After a pause, the owl solemnly shook his head "No."

Everyone nodded and applauded the bird's wisdom.

"Am I going to," Lala began.

Lala paused and took a big gulp of her Magic Bullet.

NO! she silently yelled at herself. *That is not an appropriate question for a birthday celebration! I can't think of any celebration for which that would be an appropriate question, for god's sake!*

". . . frantically search for my glasses tonight when they are, all the while, right there on top of my head?"

Archimedes did not hesitate to nod quite confidently. Everyone giggled. Lala took another big gulp of her Magic

Bullet and smiled.

Saved by the booze and the glib banter, she thought.

After more appetizers and more drinks, everyone said good-bye to wonderful Janeen with Lala declaring that Magic Bullets were "THE best things EVER!"

Kirwan led them to a small theatre, one of many at the Castle. The chairs were covered in red velvet, and the etched black and red paper on the walls was reminiscent of what Lala imagined a New Orleans house of very ill repute might have. Kirwan was going to do his magic act there, and he warned Monty that he would be called on to be a volunteer for the show.

Shortly after they settled in their seats, the room filled to capacity and the lights were dimmed. Kirwan swept onto the stage to applause. He was carrying a classic briefcase with hard sides, about four inches in thickness.

Kirwan put the briefcase on a table that had a round surface and a completely visible pole supporting it. Nothing was hidden from sight. Kirwan opened the briefcase and pulled out a bowling ball. Lala smacked her cheeks with her palms in a universal gesture of amazement.

"How is that even possible?" she gasped.

Lala leaned toward Brenda and whispered in her ear.

"Yeah, he had me at takes a bowling ball out of a briefcase. This show could end right now, and I'd be in eternal awe."

"Thank you, thank you all so much," Kirwan said to the applause and hoots. "I'll need a volunteer and there's no point in raising your hands, because my dear friend's father has a birthday today, so please welcome Monty to the stage."

Monty ran up the side stairs to the stage and Kirwan gave him a big hug. Kirwan then took two decks of cards, in their unopened boxes, out of his briefcase.

"How is there room for them in there?" Lala asked quite loudly and with a tone that bordered on mild hysteria. "There was a bowling ball in there, for god's sake!"

"Monty, would you please select one of these decks."

Monty tapped the deck in Kirwan's left hand.

Kirwan put the other deck on the table and pulled out the cards from the deck that Monty had chosen. Kirwan shuffled the deck, and then held the cards in a fan behind his shoulder.

"Now, Monty, unless I have eyes in the back of my head, I can't see the cards, can I?"

"No, you can't," Monty agreed.

"Excellent. Would you please pick a card, not from the deck, but in your mind? Just think of a card. Okay?"

"Yes," Monty said.

"You've got it?"

"I've got it," Monty said.

"Excellent. Please take the deck from me."

Monty did.

"Excellent. Please spell out the name of the card you selected, silently, as you count out a card from the deck to correspond with each letter, placing the cards face down in my palm. When you get to the last letter and thus the last card, please turn that card face up in my palm."

Monty slowly counted out nine cards, placing them face down in Kirwan's hand. He placed the tenth card face up.

"Are you done?" Kirwan asked.

"Yes, I am," Monty said, smiling as he looked at the card that was face up in Kirwan's palm. Kirwan held that card up toward the audience.

"Is the card you were thinking of the Ace of Clubs?"

"Yes," Monty said, "it is."

"How is that even POSSIBLE?" Lala exclaimed, applauding wildly along with the audience.

"Thank you so much," Kirwan said. "Monty, would you please open the second deck of cards."

Monty did.

"Excellent. Would you please shuffle the deck?"

Monty did.

"Thank you. Now, would you please once again count out the number of cards corresponding with the card you picked."

Monty counted out nine cards and placed the tenth one face up. Kirwan held up for the audience to see. It was the Ace of Clubs.

"NO!" Lala shrieked. "How is that possible! The second deck, too? What! I can't BELIEVE IT!"

"Lala," Geraldine said, "maybe you switch to club soda after this?"

Kirwan smiled and bowed. He then pulled a large manila envelope out of the briefcase.

"Okay, SERIOUSLY," Lala yelled. "How much stuff can he fit in that freakin' briefcase?"

Kirwan asked Monty to open the envelope, take out the piece of paper inside, and show it to the audience, all of which Monty cheerfully did.

Written on the paper, in thick black letters, were the words "ACE OF CLUBS."

It seemed at that moment to everyone in the theatre that this wonderful piece of mentalism was the straw that broke the camel's back of Lala's vulnerable grip on composure.

"I CAN'T BELIEVE IT!" Lala yelled. "How? SWEET MOTHER OF GOD, how could he know that! He wrote that before the show started? HOW DID HE KNOW THAT WAS THE CARD BEFORE MONTY PICKED IT?!"

After the show, everyone went to the large bar on the main floor to share a lovely bottle of brandy that the manager on duty that evening had offered to Kirwan as a special gift for the birthday guest.

Lala sat on a bar stool between Kirwan and David and imagined that she was Vivien Leigh sitting between Laurence Olivier and Marlon Brando.

This is so sublime, she thought. *Here we are in this entirely magical place, dressed to the nines, sipping impossibly smooth brandy. I don't think I've ever felt quite so elegant before.*

"Kirwan, how *the fuck* did you know which card Monty was going to pick?"

Kirwan graciously declined to illuminate, and Lala repeated the question two additional times, each time putting the emphasis on a different combination of words.

"*Kirwan, how* the fuck did you know which card Monty was going to pick?"

"Kirwan, how the fuck did you know *which card* Monty was going to pick?"

When it became clear to Lala that she would not be able to wear down Kirwan's resolve, she was seized with a sudden, overwhelming desire in a completely different direction.

"Guys," she said, "can you excuse us for a bit? I've just now gotten a desperate urge to recapture my youth."

Lala grabbed David's hand and lead him down an arbitrary staircase to the right of the lobby.

Okay, this is looking a little spooky down here, Lala thought. *I hope we don't disappear forever into the vapor of magic. Or something like that.*

"Let's find a nook and make out," Lala whispered to David. "And pretend we're in high school."

"Let's," he said.

They stopped on their way down a long and narrow hallway to admire a wall of indented glass cases that held an array of artifacts from the history of the castle, along with fetching details and explanations in intricate calligraphy.

Terrence would have loved this, Lala thought. *It would have really appealed to his sense of drama.*

Without letting herself think about that for one moment longer, Lala pulled David down the hall at a run and grabbed the handle of the first door she saw.

Please let it be unlocked. And please let it not be an unearthly portal to the vapor—whatever the fuck I mean by that.

The door was unlocked. It led to a very small, very dimly lit, empty theatre. Lala pushed David down onto the first chair in the first row and glided onto his lap.

David is definitely a way better kisser than my high school boy-friend Patrick. He's really as wonderful a kisser as Terrence. Terrence never got to see the Magic Castle. We talked about moving to Los Angeles, but we always kept putting it off because I thought I hated LA and because we thought we had all the time in the world.

Lala managed to resist the impulse to start slapping herself in the face so she could get her mind to focus on something, anything else.

I can't believe these ideas that are popping into my head. This definitely never happened after Terrence died when I was only dating men who lived thousands of miles away and whom I only saw on a stray weekend or two, every other year. Which is clearly why I never dated anyone in my same zip code until I met David. Like I would need a Ph.D. in psychology to have figured that out.

David continued to kiss Lala as he lifted her to stand. Then he stopped kissing her and held her at arms' length for a full view.

"That dress is amazing. You look so beautiful. I'm so lucky I found you."

"Ohh," Lala whispered. She had been able to not cry until that moment, but at that moment it wasn't going to be possible.

David looked surprised to see her eyes overflowing with tears. He ran his index fingers over her cheeks to help wipe them away.

"Happy tears," Lala whispered.

That's not strictly a lie, Lala thought. *I am happy. And I'm also so sad, I think I might die.*

CHANGE THE PAST

What was most painful for Lala to remember was the suddenness of it. And when she remembered it, she would chastise herself for not noticing that something was wrong, for not seeing the signs that were painfully clear in hindsight.

On that morning, it seemed to Lala, everything really did change in a blink. Yootza looked normal to her that morning. He ate his breakfast—as he always did—with gusto, standing next to his three siblings in the kitchen of Lala and David's apartment. But it seemed that she only looked away for a moment, and suddenly Yootza's belly looked horribly swollen.

"Honey!" she screamed out the front door at David, who was sitting in the courtyard working on his laptop. "Something's wrong with Yootza! His tummy! Something's wrong with his tummy!"

David ran up the stairs. He picked up Yootza and cooed to him.

"It's okay, Little Man. Let Papa have a look."

I love you, Lala thought. *I love you for being a veterinarian. For being such a kind and good veterinarian. Omigod, my sweet little boy.*

Lala was too upset and frightened to notice in that moment that Yootza wasn't growling and snapping, as he normally would have when being picked up was anyone else's idea other than his own. The dachshund let David put him on the couch and let David rub and poke his tummy without any protest at all. Lala tried to be as calm as possible while she waited for David to say something.

"Let's take him to the hospital."

Lala tried to be as calm as possible while she walked Eunice, Chester, and Petunia downstairs to Geraldine and Monty's apartment so they could stay with them in case Lala and David and Yootza would be gone for a long time that day. She tried to be calm when she got in the car and saw that David was sitting in the driver's seat and little Yootza was on his lap looking very tired and worn out. She tried to be calm while David spoke into the speaker on his phone and let the nearby 24-hour veterinary hospital where he was a part-time surgical fellow know that he was coming in right away.

Beatrice, the sweet woman who might have been on the north side of eighty had been working at the hospital for decades as a vet tech. Lala had met her many times because Beatrice was a volunteer at Dogs of Love, the rescue group whose board of directors Lala served on and for whom Lala was one of the main benefactors.

When they walked in with an urgency that Lala was trying to keep on a less-than-hysterical level in her mind, with Lala cradling Yootza like a baby and David holding all the doors open for them, Beatrice jumped up from behind the reception desk where she had been waiting for them.

"X-rays and blood?" she asked rhetorically as she gently took Yootza from Lala.

"Yes, please," David said. "We'll wait here until you can get him into an exam room."

Everyone on the staff stopped by to share hugs and care while Lala and David sat in the lobby. The tests were rushed, and David was able to look at the x-rays shortly after Yootza was brought into a room for them to sit with him. Lala peered at the photographs of her little fellow's insides while she held him on her lap and bent in half to give him almost constant kisses on his precious little head. David studied the x-rays with one of his colleagues, a young vet from England who was interning in the States. Lala waited for the two men to decide something.

"We'll try draining it," Dr. Elias Scollan said. David nodded.

Dr. Scollan smiled at Lala. "Is it okay if I take him with me for a little bit?"

"Of course," Lala said. She kissed Yootza again many times, and then handed him to the kind young man.

"I'm going to go with Elias, okay?" David said. "And then I'll come right back and we'll talk, okay?"

"Of course," Lala said. "Thank you so much, Elias."

Lala took out her Kindle and tried to read the novel about a love that lasted decades after beginning in a tiny seaside village in Italy and ending with the old man and old woman finally brought together again. She had been enjoying the story via this device that she had resisted for as long as she could—because she loved the feeling of actual books so much—but finally decided she liked because it was light and thus a fine adjunct to actual books when she was leaving the house for long or short trips.

She always bought a lot of actual books, and she also bought the Kindle version of every book she was reading, and she found that she was now reading more than she ever had before, which had always been a lot anyway because there were few things Lala loved as much as reading, and really nothing she loved more.

She couldn't make out anything on the screen of the Kindle. Whatever the words were, they didn't seem to be actual English. She tried to sound them out phonetically, but that got her nowhere. So she closed the Kindle and took out her phone to look at all the photographs. She found the folder that had images of her dogs, and she looked at all the images she had snapped of actual old photographs she had taken of Yootza when she first got him, so that she could have electronic images of those photographs with her all the time via her fancy and modern phone. The old photographs showed a senior dog, but one that wasn't quite old enough yet to have his face entirely covered by grey fur, as Yootza's was now. And then the door opened and David came back in with Yootza.

David placed the little dog back on Lala's lap. Yootza looked very sleepy, and his entire tummy had been shaved.

"Sweetie, here's what we're dealing with," David said. He sat down next to her and put his arm around Lala's shoulder. "Yootza has a lot of fluid around his heart and in his lungs. That means his heart isn't working the way it should. My fear is that he has cancer, and I'm afraid the blood tests seem to support that. So we've drained the fluid and we need to see how long it takes for the fluid to come back. If it doesn't come back today, I think that means we can take him home for a few days and keep him comfortable so we can all say good-bye. I'm so sorry, Lala."

Lala put her head on David's shoulder.

"I should have known. He's been different. He hasn't been adorably grumpy like he always is. I should have known something was wrong."

"No, Sweetie, if anyone should have known, I should have."

"Nuh uh, you're the best, David. We're all so lucky to have you."

He really is, Lala thought. *We really are.*

"I'm afraid I'm going to start keening," Lala said. "And that will scare my little Yootza, so I can't do that, but I don't want to leave him, so can I babble? So I won't start crying?"

"Sure, sweetie," David said. "Do whatever you want. Whatever you need."

"While you were gone, I was looking at photos of Yootza and I kept thinking about how quickly things can change.

Sometimes for good, other times for ill, of course. Like I happen to meet James Lancaster and he's a publisher, and suddenly I'm a published author and they're making a movie of my book."

"A very successful published author," David said. He kissed the top of Lala's head. Lala suddenly started giggling.

"Oh, god, honey, it's going to be one of those things where I'm laughing and the next thing I know, I'm crying in a very loud and unattractive way, and I really don't want to scare little Yootza. I suddenly had this image of Terrence on the phone in New York in our minuscule apartment where we were so happy. He had gotten some kind of notice from our health insurance carrier and it was signed by Alvinia S. Baxter, so he called the number on the notice and he asked for Alvinia S. Baxter, and when I hear this I can't stop laughing because he felt compelled to say her middle initial because, who knows, maybe they also had an Alvinia F. Baxter working there."

Lala could barely get the words to this memory out to share it with David because she was laughing so hard and she was trying so hard not to cry, so she'd get stuck on one word and keep repeating it until she somehow managed to move to the next one. As a result, a story that should have taken a minute or two was now well into its seventh sixty-second segment.

"And I'm remembering that, and I'm also—all the time that I'm remembering, I'm simultaneously thinking about my poor little Yootza and how ephemeral life is. It's like you look in the mirror, you look away and immediately look back, and I'm sorry, was that massive GASH of a wrinkle there on my forehead five seconds ago? Everything can change in one instant. For good or for ill. Like with Terrence. He seems fine. It's just that his stomach is bothering him, and I'm sure it's an ulcer at worst, and then I hear the words 'Your husband has a growth on his stomach' from his doctor and it's all over. My life as I knew it then was effectively over."

Lala had gotten herself so worked up in the disjointed telling of these vaguely overlapping tales, she hadn't noticed that

David had gently put his hand on Yootza's chest and had been running it over the dog's stomach and back to his chest again, carefully feeling the long undercarriage of the dachshund. At the same moment when Lala finally saw that he was doing this, she heard Yootza's labored breathing.

David picked Yootza up and walked to the door of the exam room.

"I'll be right back."

Everything happened so quickly, Lala didn't have time to panic even more than she already was. She sat in her chair, not moving, just staring at the closed door until David came back. She wasn't sure how long he'd been gone. He didn't have Yootza with him. David sat down next to Lala.

"He's got more fluid around his heart and in his lungs, sweetie. And if we drain it again, it'll come right back. He's having a hard time breathing. If we take out the fluid, it'll come right back again. I'm so sorry. We have to decide what to do."

"Geraldine and Monty love him," Lala said. "So do Stephanie and Chuck. And Thomas. I don't think Thomas's new girlfriend has had a chance to form an opinion yet. We have to let them come here to say good-bye."

David called Geraldine. She came right over with Monty and Stephanie and Chuck and Thomas. Yootza had been brought back to the exam room and Lala was sitting on the floor next to the large, soft bed that David had placed there for Yootza to rest on.

Geraldine got down on the floor next to them and hugged her adopted niece and her niece's little dachshund. She stayed there next to Lala and Yootza while Monty and Stephanie and Chuck and Thomas bent down to hug Lala and give Yootza a gentle little rub on his dear little head. And then they all left the room to wait in the lobby of the hospital while Lala and David said their final good-byes.

Lala lay flat on the floor and put her head next to Yootza's. David had two syringes ready. Though Yootza was already dozing much of the time, the first injection would let him drift off completely to sleep. And then, as Lala knew from having helped so many precious animals pass from their far-too-short lives, lives far too short even if they were passing in their old age, the second injection would, as she always told herself, set her precious boy/girl free.

"I love you so much, my sweet little Yootza," Lala said over and over.

When it was done, David got down on the floor next to Lala and Yootza. Lala put her head against David's chest and buried her nose into his shirt. She realized for the first time since Yootza's crisis had begun that this was the first beloved pet she had lost since Terrence died.

She turned her head so David could hear her.

"I don't think I could get through this without you, David. I don't know what I would do without you. I can't bear to even imagine it."

Lala and David slept, or tried to sleep, on the couch that night, with the television on and with Petunia, Chester, and Eunice crowded into the space on the cushions with them. Lala was on her left side, draped over David's torso and legs. Their beagle, Petunia, was squished with not a fraction of an inch to spare in the triangular space behind Lala's bent knees. Chester, their very large former racing greyhound, was on the other side of David, wedged between David and the back of the sofa. Eunice, the wrinkled borzoi/Shar Pei mix, was draped over Lala's head like a large, furry shawl.

It had been a long time since the space surrounding Lala felt so empty.

Lala and David could tell that the dogs missed their brother. Everyone was uncharacteristically quiet. They would all fall asleep for a bit, then wake up in staggered shifts. Someone would try to change his or her position and quickly realize that the effort alone, nevermind the completion of the actual action, would be highly disruptive of the extremely tentative equilibrium they had achieved on that couch.

Darn, Lala thought, *I really have to pee. Oh well, maybe later . . .*

She dozed off and woke up a half hour later to the sound of David and the dogs snoring and the low-volume narration of a wedding gown alteration crisis on *Say Yes to the Dress*.

I've seen this episode, Lala thought. *They'll be able to fix the neckline in time. She'll look gorgeous at her wedding. It will all work out in the end. Please, god, let that dress be a metaphor for life. Mine, specifically. Darn, I'm really hungry. Maybe I can move my legs really slowly . . . Nah, maybe later . . .*

When Lala woke up the next time, David was sitting propped up by many of the couch cushions. The dogs were all awake and were staring very intently at the large bowl of potato chips that David was enjoying.

"How did you all move around so much without me noticing it?" Lala asked. "Do we have any white wine? Of course we have white wine. You want a glass? Not you, Petunia. I'm talking to Daddy."

Lala shuffled to the kitchen and brought back a bottle of Pinot Grigio swathed in a flexible ice wrap, and two glasses. She filled both the glasses and balanced hers as she cuddled with David on the couch. They sipped and crunched and watched a syndicated episode of *Law and Order*.

Lala kissed David's shoulder because it was the closest thing to her head and because she loved him.

"I miss his platypus feet. I miss the way they used to wap, wap, wap against the hardwood floors when he walked."

"Man, those paws of his," David said. "Mitts. Like hams, they were. Such a wonderful boy. Such a grumpy, wonderful boy."

"Don't die before I do," Lala said before she let herself

consider the comment. "Promise?"

Lala got the clear sense that David was trying very hard not to make a big deal out of what she had just blurted.

"I promise," he calmly said.

Liar, Lala thought. *I love you for lying to me.*

"Look!" Lala said. "I love when this show does an outdoor shoot in our beloved New York City. Central Park! Let's go to Central Park together soon, okay?"

"Okay," David said.

Lala grabbed a handful of chips and shoved them all in her mouth at once.

"Eating my feelings," she sputtered through the crunching.

"Watch out, honey," David said. "You don't want to make yourself choke from voicing subtext that pretty much didn't need to be spoken. We all get it. Petunia really gets it. She eats her feelings all the time."

I love you, Lala thought.

Lala and David eventually got up off the couch and moved into the kitchen, where David made a big bowl of pasta. Lala went to feed the dogs and gasped when she pulled four food bowls out of the cupboard. David quickly took Yootza's bowl away from her and put it in a bottom drawer before she could fully freak out.

They took the pasta back to the living room after the dogs inhaled their dinner, and the dogs joined them in repose on the sofa. A classic episode of *Saturday Night Live* was playing on the television.

Wow, Lala thought, *a reference to Nixon is always funny. And tragic. What a metaphor for life. I think. I may never have fully understood what the word "metaphor" actually means.*

"Honey?" Lala said.

"Yes?" David said.

"Maybe tomorrow we'll go to Dogs of Love and see which animal we're going to adopt next?"

"Sure," David said. "If that's what you want, we'll go tomorrow."

Lala had said that because that was what she always did, right away, when one of her beloved pets passed. She always opened her heart to another animal that needed a home. Because there were so many animals that needed homes, and she felt sure that the dog that had passed wanted her to share with another dog the family that he had been such a treasured part of. And so Lala opened herself to having her heart broken again and again; sometimes sooner, when she adopted a really old animal, and sometimes later, if she adopted a slightly less old animal.

And she reflected on that fact of her life as she thought of the prospect of adopting another animal now that Yootza had died, now that her first dog had died since she lost Terrence.

Not this time, Lala thought. *I can't.*

"You know what, Honey?" Lala said. "On second thought, it might be too soon for me. I think I might have to wait."

That was the first time in Lala's adult life of rescuing animals that she had ever said those words.

Eventually they all got into bed that night, and Lala managed to get in a few fitful hours of sleep. She was surprised to find the next morning that she didn't feel as tired as she expected to.

I'm going to take that as a sign from the universe, Lala thought. *I'm not sure of what. Maybe a sign that I should take all this sadness and be energized by it? Maybe. I better give it a try and see.*

David had woken up earlier and left her a note saying that he had taken the dogs out for a morning walk and had fed them their breakfast before heading out to meet a colleague with whom he would be teaching a seminar at the UC Davis School of Veterinary Medicine, his alma mater.

"How did I sleep through all of that?" Lala asked Petunia and Chester and Eunice. Lala was especially amazed that she hadn't been woken by her beagle's baying, a foundation-shaking aural onslaught that occurred whenever Petunia thought that there was something—anything—going on anywhere near her that involved food of any kind.

Petunia's definition of "food" included, as Lala had come to discover over the years, any grotesque thing on the sidewalk or in the grass that wasn't a rock.

"I slept through all of that," Lala continued. "Maybe I slept really, really, really deeply and intensely. For a short amount of time, but in a freakishly restorative way. Maybe me feeling peppy right now isn't a sign from the universe."

Lala looked over at her three beloved dogs, who were sleeping on their beds in the living room. Her three dogs, who had very recently been a four-pack.

"Well, sign from universe or no," she said, "I'm going to bring more joy into the world, starting right now. In honor of Yootza."

Lala picked up her cell phone and hit the number for the veterinary hospital. Beatrice answered.

"It's Lala."

"Ohh, sweetie. How are you?"

"Sad."

"We're all so sorry."

"Thanks. You are the best. All of you. Listen, I want to pay for people who come to the hospital and might not be able to get their pets the care they need because they can't afford it. Can we figure out how to do that together? Can I take you out to dinner so we can figure that out?"

Lala heard the catch in Beatrice's voice when she answered. She knew they were both trying not to cry.

"I'd be honored," Beatrice said.

"Thanks. How's tomorrow night for you?"

"Perfect."

Lala's next call was to her aunt.

"Is Monty home?" Lala said.

"He's playing handball and then going for a schvitz at his club."

"That man is so vibrant," Lala said. "So that means we can

have a Gals' Day, yes? I know you know I'm not asking because I think we need permission from our partners, right? Partners sounds like such a stupid word in this context. I didn't know how to mash your husband and my boyfriend into one collective noun off the top of my head. David's busy all day, and I just didn't want Monty to feel left out if I needed my beloved auntie to myself for a few hours. Spa?"

"Spa," Geraldine said.

"One deep breath," Sasha said.

Oh, merde, *here it comes again*, Lala thought.

Lala inhaled and exhaled, and Sasha dug her elbow into a stubborn knot in the muscle of Lala's right shoulder blade.

"OY, SASHA," Lala yelped. "That is FABULOUS!"

Another hour of exquisitely painful kneading later, and Lala just barely managed to get herself off the massage table, get her robe on again, and shuffle herself down a long hall to the outdoor patio of the spa. Geraldine was already there, lounging on a wicker recliner and reading a copy of the *New York Times Book Review*.

"You look relaxed," Geraldine said. She poured a glass of lemon water from a large pitcher on the table next to her recliner and handed it to Lala, who had gotten herself down onto a recliner next to Geraldine's with many contented grunts and huffs as she descended.

"I am. Sasha is a beast. That tiny little woman is amazing. It's what I imagine getting a massage from the Incredible Hulk would be like."

"I think our grumpy little Yootza is happy that his mama is okay."

"Oh, Auntie Geraldine, I miss him."

"Yup," Geraldine said. "His absence is profound."

"He was such a dear little grump. I'm thinking I'm going

to up the ante on trying to put more joy in the world. In his grumpy little bastard honor."

"Atta girl," Geraldine said. She dabbed at her eyes with the end of her robe's sash. "You know, I get the feeling he's watching from Grumpy Little Bastard Heaven, and I think he's really happy, Lala."

They nodded and sipped their drinks. They paused, letting themselves enjoy the warm California sunshine, each savoring a special memory of Yootza.

Lala was reliving the first moment she saw Yootza at the shelter in New York City and his pronounced, crooked underbite immediately stole her heart.

Geraldine was recalling that funny, adorable, terrifying time Yootza mistook her left index finger for a Snausage.

After a few minutes, Lala spoke.

"Are you wishing this lemon water stuff had vodka in it as much as I am?"

"God, yes," Geraldine said. "More."

"What are you and Monty doing tonight?" Lala asked.

"Bonking."

"GOD, you are my inspiration, Auntie Geraldine," Lala said.

"What are you and David doing?"

"Well, in keeping with my renewed commitment to joy, I've decided I'm going to take my sweetheart out for dinner and a movie."

"Lovely," Geraldine sighed.

"And then I'm going to take him home and bonk him within an inch of his life."

"Atta girl," Geraldine said.

Lala and David drove to Redondo Beach. Lala had discovered that there was yet another movie theater that featured recliners and seat-side full bar service and food menus. This

particular movie chain was housed in a massive and quite sumptuous shopping mall.

"Look at the architecture!" Lala exulted. "It's just so pretty
here! And more and more movie theaters have Barcaloungers
now, and in more and more places I can order several lovely
flutes of sparkling rosé, and we're going to see a comedy that
wasn't directed by the guy directing my movie, so it actually
might be good!"

David took Lala's hand and kissed it and they continued
walking through the crowds.

"David," she said. "I'm so happy I found you. If I ruled the
world, I would . . . I guess I'd need a magic wand. If I were in
charge of the world and I had a magic wand, every person and
animal would be as happy as I am. Ingrid?"

Lala stopped at the same moment a woman walking in the
opposite direction stopped. The woman was tall and sporty and
maybe a few years younger than Lala. She had long black hair
pulled into a ponytail and her face was shiny and make-up free.

"Lala?"

The two women grabbed each other and hugged. Then they
held each other at arm's length and did a mutual assessment.

"Seriously, is there a portrait of you in an attic somewhere
that looks like a dissipated old slattern? Because you have not
aged one iota!"

"Shut up," Ingrid said. "You're the one who hasn't aged!"

Ingrid's voice was deep and had a subtle accent that defied
identification beyond "pan-European."

"Ingrid, this is my boyfriend, David McLellan," Lala said.
"David, this is Ingrid Garlin; we used to take acting class
together in New York. And then, after class, we would go out
and get hammered. We were birds of a feather. Except Ingrid
has actual talent."

"Shut up, you do, too," Ingrid said.

"Oh, okay, so you're not as good an actress as I thought. Not
that Streep herself could have made that sentence convincing.

How long have you been in LA?"

"I just got here. I've got a small part on a new sitcom."

"WHAT!" Lala said. "See, David, I told you she has talent! I am thrilled for you! Where are you going right now?"

"Home," Ingrid said. "I tried to find a new dress at Macy's for a party, but everything looks awful on me."

"I've got just the store for you," Lala said. "It's in the Valley."

"Lala," David said, "if Ingrid's not busy, I think maybe we skip the movie tonight and go out for a drink together?"

Lala grabbed David's face, which involved her standing on her tiptoes, and kissed him.

"This is one of the many reasons I love him. Are you busy, Ingrid?"

"Not too busy to catch up."

They found a restaurant in the mall with a bar that wasn't entirely overflowing with people. David grabbed them a small table in the corner and took their orders. Lala would have her flute of sparkling rosé, and when Ingrid heard that she said she thought that sounded lovely, which made David decide that they needed a bottle of sparkling rosé, which he then went to the bar to order. Lala kissed him again and watched him walk away.

"I'm so glad you're happy again," Ingrid said.

Ingrid had met Terrence several times in New York. She had attended Terrence's funeral, as had so many people—family, close friends, casual friends, acquaintances. Terrence was much loved, and it didn't take having spent a long time with him or having seen him often or knowing him well for people to want to honor his life and mourn his passing.

"Thank you, Ingrid," Lala said. "I didn't think it could happen twice in my life."

"I'm jealous," Ingrid said. "I haven't met anyone nice since I got here."

"I am on it. I am in full matchmaker mode. I'm doing a mental inventory even as we speak."

Ingrid giggled and shook her head.

"I wish I could be as lucky in love as you are. David is so handsome. And your ex-husband was such a great—"

My what? Lala thought.

And that was the last thinking Lala did before she spoke. Before she interrupted Ingrid and started speaking quickly and fairly loudly, and got quicker and louder as she went on.

"Oh, no. No, no, no, no, no. No, Terrence was my *late* husband. He was not my *ex*-husband. We weren't divorced. I was widowed. Late husband. Not ex-husband. Big difference. Very, very, very big difference. We weren't divorced. We would never have divorced each other. We loved each other."

And in the midst of that, Lala, at some point that she wasn't aware of, did start thinking enough to realize that David was standing next to her holding an ice bucket with a bottle in it.

"Hi, Honey!" she said.

Merde, she thought.

If David had heard her and if he was in any way upset about what she had said, he was in fact a very accomplished actor, because nothing in his voice or demeanor indicated anything but comfort and contentment. He put the bucket on the table and gave Lala a quick kiss.

"Three flutes, in a flash."

And he was off again. And Lala felt awful.

"Ingrid, I am so sorry I lost my mind."

"No, not at all," Ingrid said. "It's my English. I got confused. I'm so sorry. I meant late husband. I just misspoke."

"No, no, no, it's all my fault, and I'm so nuts and I'm so sorry."

"David's coming back," Ingrid said.

And David was back, smiling and placing three champagne glasses on the table. He took the bottle out of the bucket and popped the cork.

"Such a happy sound!" he said.

They drank the sparkling rosé, and it was delicious. David

insisted that he stop drinking after having only half a glass because he was the designated driver, and he would be driving Ingrid home too, since she lived in Venice and that wasn't far at all, so Ingrid and Lala drank almost the entire bottle by themselves. They ordered appetizers to share, and the conversation never lagged as they talked about movies and Lala's book and Ingrid's role on the sitcom and David's uncanny ability to calm terrified feral cats. And then it was time to go home. They took Ingrid to the cute little guest house in Venice that she was renting from an adorable elderly couple named Bess and Marjorie. Bess and Marjorie were in the front yard when David's car pulled into the driveway, and they toddled over to the passenger window and cooed at them that they had to come in for cake and tea.

With the first bite, Lala realized that the cake had a lot of rum in it.

"Bess? Marjorie?" she said.

"Yes, dear," the two precious women cheeped in unison.

"Please sign me up as your niece. Please count on me to take care of you, should you ever need it. Because I love you."

"That's nice, dear," Bess said. "Thank you."

"We'll certainly keep you in mind, dear," Marjorie said. "Thank you."

Bess and Marjorie had twelve cats. They were all sitting on David's lap, or trying to shove off their siblings who were sitting on David's lap so they could sit on David's lap, or winding their way around and through David's ankles in a rhythmic dance that might have gotten the choreographer a Tony award.

"Cats know," Marjorie said. "They know good people."

"They do," Bess said.

They sure do, Lala thought.

Everyone hugged good-bye at the back door to Bess and Marjorie's cozy house. Lala and David walked Ingrid across the small yard to her door. When they were in the car and headed home, Lala realized that she really was relaxed and she really felt confident that she should be relaxed, because maybe David hadn't even heard her lose her mind at the bar and if he had, it clearly hadn't hurt his feelings, which was the last thing she ever wanted to do.

Ohh, thank goodness, Lala thought. *Everything's okay. Everything's great, actually.*

"What a lovely evening," she said. "Such a wonderful unplanned adventure."

"Yup," David said. "Listen, I need to . . . I'd really like to talk."

Merde, Lala thought. *And there goes the likelihood of us bonking tonight right down the drain, too.*

David paced. He looked over at the dogs, who were huddled together on one of their doggy beds sitting bolt upright and whose eyebrows, as much as the area above their eyes could be described as such, were knitted in distress.

"Daddy's not angry," David said, not letting up his pacing for one moment to reassure Eunice and Petunia and Chester.

Lala and David had driven home from Ingrid's place in relative silence, and once home they had both changed into comfy sweatpants and flannel shirts because no one was feeling very sexy at that point, and now they were in the living room, and David was walking a trench into the hardwood floor.

"I think they're upset because their papa is choosing such a clichéd physical manifestation of distress," Lala said.

David stopped pacing.

"You're trying to be funny?"

Oops, Lala thought. *Too soon?*

"I am," she admitted. "Sorry."

"No, no, don't apologize. I'm laughing. On the inside."

Ohh, David, Lala thought. *I don't deserve someone as nice as you.*

"You are so sweet. If the roles were reversed, I'd be screaming right now about how you're being glib in the face of my entirely understandable angst about our relationship."

"You would?" David said.

Oops, Lala thought.

"Yup," Lala said. "Did I just overplay my hand? You don't want to hitch your wagon to a hypocrite?"

"I'm not really worried about that. I love you."

"I love you," Lala said.

I do, Lala thought. *You're wonderful and I love you.*

"And you love Terrence."

"Of course I do. And if . . . god, I can't even stand to think about this . . . If you died, I'd still love you. I will love you forever, too. Unless you do something really shitty. I'm not a saint."

David came over to the sofa where Lala had been trying unsuccessfully to sit comfortably since they had gotten home and sat down next to her. He took her hand and kissed it.

"Okay, in the context of this evening, a little glib."

"Oops. Sorry."

"I get that you'll always love Terrence. I just need to make sure we're on the same page about our future. When I heard you say 'late husband, not ex-husband,' I understood it. I really did. It just made me have to face the fact that if Terrence were still alive, you'd still be married to him."

Of course I would, Lala thought.

"Well, yes, if things continued to be as wonderful as they were between Terrence and me. But . . . I mean, what about you? Would you still be with your ex-wife if you could? Because it's actually possible that you could, because she's still alive. She's more of a threat to me than Terrence is to you."

David leaned his head on the back of the sofa and pressed his palms onto his closed eyes. He was silent for several long moments.

"No, see, that's kind of exactly the point," he finally said. "I didn't want her to leave me, but once she did, I ended up not wanting her to come back. Not now. Not ever. Because what I would really like is for us to get married. When you're ready. So this is my proposal that we move on the path toward getting married, okay? Wait. Don't answer yet."

David ran into the kitchen and ran back carrying a bottle of champagne and two glasses. He popped the cork, poured, and handed a glass to Lala.

"I promise the actual proposal will be much more involved and premeditated," David said. "But right now I'm wooing you with champagne so you'll say that we're going to go in the direction of getting married. If that's what you want us to be doing."

I . . . I do, Lala thought.

"Yes," Lala said. "In that direction. Walking, running, driving, flying. Being instantly sent there by that transporter thing on *Star Trek*. I really want to. I would love to."

I really would, Lala thought. *As long as you don't die before I do.*

David smiled and chugged his glass of champagne and Lala copied him. They grabbed each other and kissed, and the dogs finally exhaled and flopped down in the bed and fell asleep.

This is wonderful, Lala thought. *David is happy. I'm happy. Puppies are relieved that the* mishegoss *around here has abated. Win, win, and win.*

She was surprised to suddenly find herself feeling wide awake, even after the long night. Lala shimmied her shoulders in a kind of involuntary, but nonetheless quite delicious tic of joy and swung her hips over onto David, pinning him to the couch with her legs. She kissed him and ripped his flannel shirt open, sending buttons leaping into the air.

"How's that for a clichéd physical manifestation?" she purred. "Sorry about your shirt."

"Like I care about my stupid shirt," David whispered.

I will just have to choose not to be terrified that David will die before I do, Lala thought. *I think I can definitely not be terrified. I will focus on joy and faith and love and hope. And I will focus on the fact that bonking is definitely back on the agenda for tonight.*

OR MAYBE EVEN THE PRESENT?

I am terrified, Lala thought. *I am utterly and entirely and unreasonably and irrationally and completely understandably and just about constantly terrified.*

She was sitting in her new production office with Zoe and Eliza. The night before had ended with Lala and David having utterly delightful sex.

"Wow," Lala said. They were on the couch wrapped in a blanket. "Our first sex as an engaged-to-be-engaged couple. Very excellent sex, I might and just did add."

They put their sweatpants back on, and Lala put her flannel shirt back on, and David got a sweatshirt to put on because his flannel shirt had been torn open, and they went downstairs and knocked on Geraldine and Monty's door. They had clearly interrupted Geraldine and Monty while the older couple was not asleep in bed, and Geraldine and Monty invited them in. Lala told them she and David were "engaged-to-be engaged," and Geraldine said, "What the hell does that mean? Don't tell me, I don't want to know."

And now Lala was in her production office and it was taking every bit of strength she could muster not to hyperventilate as she sat at a small table with Zoe and Eliza, and they all ate the sandwiches they had gotten at the best sandwich place ever, which Lala had been introduced to by Monty's daughter Helene shortly after she moved to Southern California, and which was right next door to the office and was a major factor in Lala deciding on the office space she chose.

"Sometimes it's just easier to not think about certain things," Lala said. "Sometimes, and I know this sounds counter-intuitive, but sometimes it's less lonely to have a boyfriend who lives thousands of miles away. Because you can't really miss them and obsess about them dying, because they're kind of not really there anyway."

The subject of the lunchtime discussion, up until a moment before Lala's pronouncement, had been selecting locations for the film.

"Are you okay?" Zoe asked.

"Seriously, is this the best tomato, brie—because I substituted brie for mozzarella—and olive tapenade on a baguette in the universe, or what? I'm great! Why?"

"Because that was like your twelfth non sequitur today," Eliza said. "And, no offense, but you look kinda weird. Not unattractive at all. Just weird."

"Oh, okay," Lala said. "Hey, you know what happened to me yesterday? I was at the Beverly Center, and I wanted to check out a book at the Beverly Hills Library—which is ridiculously gorgeous, isn't it—and so I walked there on Burton Way because I love the architecture on Burton Way, and it's such a lovely, wide boulevard, it feels like you're in Europe. And this guy driving a Bentley pulls up next to me as I'm walking and rolls down his window and says, 'How much?' And I look at him in utter and entirely understandable confusion and say, 'Pardon?' and he says, 'How much? Nothing kinky, just straight missionary position.' And I think I must be losing my mind and I say, with visible astonishment, 'I'm not a *hooker*. I'm a pedestrian!' The nerve of that guy, huh?"

Zoe and Eliza were staring at Lala with what she was happy to recognize as sympathy and understanding. Lala smiled at their reaction, because she always loved it when people shared her outrage.

"I don't get it," Eliza said. "Why were you walking?"

"Why . . .? What do you mean why was I walking?"

"You walked from the Beverly Center to the Beverly Hills Public Library?" Zoe said. "Why would you do that?"

"Why are you both asking me why I walked?" Lala demanded. "It was a beautiful day. It's a beautiful boulevard. Why wouldn't I walk?"

Zoe and Eliza looked at each other and shook their heads.

"I can see why the guy was confused," Eliza said.

"Yeah," Zoe agreed.

"Are you kidding me?" Lala asked. "Didn't you two walk when you were in college? Like, a *lot*. Across campus and everywhere else 'n' stuff?"

"Sure," Zoe said.

"Sure," Eliza echoed. "But that was in Connecticut."

"Yeah," Zoe said. "This is LA"

"Oh, for heaven's sake," Lala huffed. "Never mind. Forget I said anything. Let's get back to work."

Lala did her best to focus on the tasks at hand in the office for the rest of the day. She went to the gym after work, and when she got home Geraldine was tending to her lovely, drought-resistant garden that took up large swaths of the court-yard of the fourplex.

"Are you okay?" she asked when Lala opened the front gate and entered.

"I'm great!" Lala said. "Why?"

"You look weird. Should I be worried about you?"

"No, no, not at all."

Yes, Lala thought. *You should.*

She gave her adopted auntie a big, reassuring hug and went upstairs to walk her dogs and then shower. David wasn't home yet, and when he got home a few hours later, Lala was on the couch with the dogs working on a new idea she had for a novel that centered on a miserable old Siberian nun who is granted a dying wish by her Guardian Angel and ends up in Manhattan as a beautiful young model, but it's not until the nun reforms the bitterness inside her so that her soul is as wonderful as her body that she finds love in the afterlife with the sexy angel.

Love after death, Lala thought, just before she heard David's key in the lock. *I'm guessing I'm not going to be able to write about much of anything else for the foreseeable future. Well, I can only hope that I'll be able to make it funny and charming.*

David walked into the living room, pushed their snoring beagle aside so he could sit next to Lala, and gave Lala a kiss. Then he took a second, more studied, look at her.

"Are you okay?" David asked.

"I'm great!" Lala said. "Why?"

"You look a little weird. Not bad weird. Just not like yourself."

In the weeks that followed her demi-engagement, Lala did her best to distract herself and move forward in her future and not dwell in the past that she still missed so much. And, other than being asked by many people who knew her well or casually if she was okay and other than the adjective "weird" being applied to the way she looked a lot more than she would have liked, Lala was successful in staying focused and staying very busy. She put in extra hours and devoted extra energy to working on the film and to working on her new novel. The new novel involved lots of discarded drafts and lots of heavy-handed editing to remove "bathos, miles and miles of bathos," but she kept at it, and she also put in her usual time at the gym, and she stuck to her willing determination to spend fun time with David, all of which had the happy side effect that when she got into bed every night she, after having wonderful sex with David which was just getting more and more delightful, fell sound asleep because she was too exhausted to be terrified.

Lala could tell that Zoe and Eliza were continuing to be sensitive to her weirdness, and that her two lovely young colleagues were treating her with extra tenderness. And that touched her heart profoundly. She brought treats to the office every day, and got them little gifts, and bought them lunch every day and dinner too if they worked late, which they often did. And so as each week passed, Lala got used to her new state of generalized anxiety that had been the result of the prospect of being married again, to a wonderful man she loved.

I should be on Say Yes to the Dress, Lala thought one morning at the office. *Not just to pick out my dress, which would be way too much fun, but because they get widows on that show. They understand how difficult it is to move on. The ambivalence. The fear. They get it. Granted, I haven't seen any widows quite as whacked out as I am on the show. But I feel sure they can deal with me. I'll have to look into getting on that show. I'll probably have an epic meltdown while they're filming my episode. Which will make for great television.*

"Lala?" Zoe said.

"Mmm?"

Before Zoe could respond, the phone rang. Lala watched Eliza grab the receiver.

"Were you doing another inner monologue just now?" Zoe asked.

"Lala!" Eliza whispered fiercely. She had her hand over the mouthpiece of the receiver and a look of aroused terror in her eyes. "Clive Ellis is on the phone! For you!"

"Why are we whispering?" Lala whispered.

"He's so cute!"

"That's why we're whispering?" Lala said. "Because cute boys have super hearing?"

She took the phone and patted Eliza's hand with maternal affection.

"Hi, Clive. 'Sup?"

I sound like an idiot, Lala thought. *'Sup. Who says that anymore? I guess maybe I'm being a doofus because Eliza is right, because he really is quite cute.*

"Hey, Lala. I've been wanting to film the Paris scenes in Paris, right? Well, the director and I really want you to be there while we're filming, right?"

"Why am I getting the feeling that this is not a good idea?" Geraldine fretted.

Lala had gotten home from the production office to find Geraldine sitting in the courtyard of the fourplex. Geraldine told Lala when she walked through the gate that Monty and David had gone to their favorite Chinese restaurant to get take-out so they could all enjoy dinner al fresco. Before Lala got home, Geraldine had brought Petunia and Eunice and Chester out to lounge in the sunshine with her. And now the two women and the three dogs were sitting together waiting for dinner, and Lala had just told Geraldine her incredibly exciting news.

"I can't imagine why," Lala responded, sincerely and obliviously perplexed. She studied the goblet of sangria Geraldine had poured for her from a large pitcher Geraldine had whipped up following "a treasured family recipe, because my Bubbe Rachel lived in Mexico at the end of the Nineteenth Century and she knew how to make sangria." Lala tried very hard to think of a reason why being on the set of her film in the City of Lights would be anything but delightful. "I love Paris. Terrence and I went to Paris on our honeymoon."

"Right! And you're thinking of going there now and your new fiancé-to-be-your-fiancé—which is the most ridiculous thing I've ever heard, and it makes you sound like a sorority girl during the era of the Cold War—can't go with you because he's scheduled to teach a class at UC Davis! There's something off about that."

"Don't be silly," Lala said uncertainly. Her aunt's frenzy was starting to have an effect on her enthusiasm, and she was not happy about that. "Damn, this sangria is insane. Your Bubbe Rachel must have been fierce. I wish I could have met her."

"Half your darn book takes place in Paris," Geraldine grumbled.

"More like two-thirds."

"Right!" Geraldine spat, aggressively grabbing the pitcher and refilling her niece's glass. "You'll be there forever! When will you and David start planning your wedding? My GOD, when are you getting officially engaged? What exactly is going ON here? Should I be worried about you?"

Yes, Lala thought. *Absolutely.*

"Of course not," Lala said. "I'm great!"

"Then when are you getting married?!" Geraldine wailed.

"What's the rush?" Lala said. She took a big gulp of sangria and giggled. "It's not like we have to hurry to have kids before my biological clock tolls a death knell that would make Big Ben's chiming sound like a whisper. He's got grown kids and I don't want to have kids. I want to follow in your gorgeous footsteps of being the best childless aunt in the world. We've got all the time in the world. Look who's here! Two of the handsomest, kindest, smartest, sexiest men in the world! And they come bearing Chinese food! *La vie est trop belle!*"

Lala ran over and kissed David and grabbed the take-out bags Monty was carrying. Lala and David brought the bags over to the table, and Monty sat on Geraldine's lap and kissed her.

"Oof," Geraldine grunted when Monty landed on her.

"We got two jewels here, David," Monty said. "Our lovely ladies are our beautiful pearls."

"They sure are," David agreed.

"Monty," Geraldine grunted. "My legs are falling asleep."

The dogs woke up while Geraldine was distributing the chopped tofu and mushroom and ginger mixture into four lettuce boats on four plates. The greyhound put his head on Lala's thigh and looked at her with pleading eyes. The borzoi/Shar Pei mix walked around the table, stopped momentarily at each occupied chair, and sighed loudly and constantly as he traveled.

Petunia watched all of this activity by her canine siblings unfold for a couple of minutes. And then she let out a resounding beagle bay, which conveyed outrage a dowager empress would have labeled excessively self-righteous.

"Sweet Mother of GOD!" Lala yelled. Her sangria goblet jumped in her hand and she scrambled to hold onto it. "Monty, are you okay? Has the shock affected you adversely? Do we need to do CPR?"

"I'm fine," Monty said, looking quite composed. "Dogs make noise. That's life."

"Don't be so flappable, Lala," Geraldine said. "Be unflappable, like Monty."

Okay, Lala thought. *She has a point. I have been way too skittish lately. I need to get my balance back on track.*

"You are right, my dear auntie," Lala said. "Look at us. Lovely food. Lovely sangria. The best men in the world. And precious dogs who think I don't know that their great-auntie fed them dinner half an hour ago. Nothing to worry about. Everything to savor."

The dogs seemed to sense, in unison, that their scam, which they attempted to perpetuate on an at-least-daily basis ("Did she tell you she fed us? Because she didn't. She must have misunderstood your question, because we haven't had dinner yet. Nope. We sure haven't."), had once again been busted, and they reluctantly returned to their outdoor beds and went back to sleep.

A leisurely and convivial dinner hour among the humans began. When everyone was done eating, there were no leftovers, even though David and Monty had ordered more food than four people with very hearty appetites could normally be expected to eat, because Lala went kind of nuts over how exceptionally delicious the dry sautéed string beans were that night. When half the carton was remaining and David and Geraldine and Monty were leaning back in their chairs, clearly beyond any level of sated that would register below glutinous, Lala kept pointing to the carton and kept asking "Anyone want more? Because if you don't, I'm gonna finish it, okay? Anyone want more string beans? Because if not, I'm—" and Geraldine told her to eat the rest of the darn string beans already, for goodness' sake.

They had grapes and sliced watermelon for dessert, and then Lala told Geraldine and Monty to go back to their apartment and relax while she and David and the pups cleaned up outside.

"And when I say that the pups will be helping with the clean up, I am, of course, kidding, because they don't do much of anything except sleep and eat and be wonderful and precious and loving and very loud on occasion and, like Yootza and so many before him, leave an eternal memory in your heart. Which is more than we have any right to expect or indeed deserve."

After they finished cleaning, David and Lala went back to their apartment and Lala made some chamomile tea. As the evening went on, she had been feeling more and more nervous about telling David that she would be going to Paris for at least a month or two, especially because she knew he wouldn't be able to join her.

I don't want him to think I'm being glib about this, Lala thought. *I don't want him to think I'm skipping town and that marrying him isn't a priority for me. I have to be really calm and reassuring about this.*

"DAVID!" Lala suddenly yelled. David's mug clattered to the floor and chamomile splattered around the kitchen. "I NEED TO GO TO PARIS FOR THE MOVIE AND I KNOW YOU CAN'T COME BECAUSE OF YOUR CLASS AND I AM *REALLY* GOING TO MISS YOU!"

Lala was euphorically amazed when things didn't go deep south after her outburst. Though David's pants were caught in the flying tea and were quite wet, he seemed to be wonderfully enthusiastic about Lala's travel plans.

"That's great! Ow! Delayed OW! I think that tea was hotter than I realized."

Lala grabbed David's arm and led him to the bathroom. She sat him on the edge of the bathtub, undid his belt, and slid his pants off. She got a washcloth out of the linen closet and ran it under the faucet to soak it with cold water, then she wrung it out and handed it to David.

"Hold that on your thigh," she said. She got another washcloth, ran it under the cold water, and handed it to David. "And this one on your other thigh."

Lala ran to the kitchen and got a bottle of water from the refrigerator. She brought it to David. She opened the medicine cabinet and got out a bottle of Tylenol. She handed two pills to him.

"Take these," she said. "I'll hold the washcloths."

Lala knelt on the floor and held the compresses while David swallowed the pills and finished the bottle of water. They were silent for several moments.

"Better?" Lala asked.

"Better," David said.

"Good?" Lala asked.

"Good," David said.

That night began an epic sex-a-thon that put a veil of joy on the two weeks leading up to Lala's flight to Paris that was almost too much for Lala to endure. Sex with David had always been great, and this elevated phase left Lala unbearably happy, because beneath all of it was the scar left by Terrence's death, the scar that put the fear that it might all disappear never far from her thoughts.

The drive to LAX on the afternoon of Lala's overnight flight to Charles De Gaulle Airport was much more cheerful than Lala expected. Maybe it was because of the just-about-always reliable California sunshine. Maybe it was because David had not deviated from being calm and encouraging from the moment he heard about Lala's travel plans. Maybe it was because Lala was consciously refusing to do anything other than pretend everything was going to be just dandy.

Petunia and Chester and Eunice were cozily dozing in the backseat of David's car, and Lala was chatting at them.

"Okay, so, Papa will be going to teach in Davis, and I'll be going to work in Paris, but we'll be back soon and you'll be staying with Great-Auntie Geraldine and Great-Uncle Monty, and you know how much they love you. You will have so much fun together! And of course Papa and I will miss you very much, and before you know it, we'll all be together again."

Before I know it, Lala thought. *It's all going to be okay. Nothing to be worried about.*

"It's all going to be okay," Lala told her dogs. "Nothing to be worried about."

Petunia snorted, turned over on her back with her legs in the air, and in short order began snoring again. Chester suddenly yipped, presumably because of a very exciting dream. Eunice passed gas, quite loudly. The sound did not wake her up.

"Do you think they're listening?" Lala asked David. "I mean, as a veterinarian, what is your expert opinion?"

"I do think they hear you, sweetheart," David assured her. "In their subconscious."

"You're humoring me, aren't you?" Lala asked, rhetorically and with great affection.

"Maybe to some extent," David admitted. "I do think you should feel assured that they did in fact hear you when you told them all that this morning at breakfast, when they were actually awake. And on their walk, when they were actually awake. And at the beginning of this ride, before they fell asleep."

David took the car off the freeway and guided it through the always massively congested traffic at LAX to the curb outside the Air France gates of the Tom Bradley International Terminal.

The dogs slept through Lala's anguished exit from the vehicle.

"Mama! Loves! You!" she gasped in loud staccato outbursts that might have been better suited to grand opera than to an adult going on a fairly brief journey. "Mama and Papa love you and we will all be together again we promise so please . . . Are you seriously going to not wake up to say good-bye to Mama?"

Yootza would have woken up to say good-bye to Mama, Lala thought sadly. *That's actually not true at all. The grumpy little bastard would have been on my lap and he would have growled in his sleep when I moved to get out of the car. I miss him so much.*

David had taken Lala's suitcases out of the trunk and was showing Lala's boarding pass and driver's license to a curbside employee of Air France. When her bags were on the way and she was set to enter the terminal, she started to find it hard to breathe.

"I'm going to miss you so much," Lala said. She put her arms around much-taller David's chest and crushed her face against it, like a toddler not wanting to go in for her first day of school.

"We'll Skype tomorrow," David said. He had to stoop forward to kiss the top of Lala's head. "We'll write long and passionate e-mails all the time. We'll be back together before you know it."

Lala looked back at David and waved with each step toward the doors of the terminal. A series of people walking behind her smacked right into her because she was disrupting the smooth flow of traffic on a second-by-second basis.

"I love . . . oops, sorry . . . you . . . sorry, my mistake . . . so much . . . Did I crush your toe, I'm so sorry . . . David."

Once inside, Lala searched for the nearest empty bench and collapsed onto it. She cradled her carry-on bag that contained her laptop, her Kindle, and a large bottle of Ambien. There was a thought weighing on her, and it was an echo of a thought that had haunted her ever since Terrence died. The frequency and the intensity of the thought diminished with time, but it never fully disappeared.

There's nowhere I can walk to or drive to or fly to, there's no number I can call. I can't ever find Terrence again. He's gone forever. I can't ever see or speak to him again. If I hear or see or read something that would make him laugh, I can't share it with him. Not ever again.

"Ma'am, are you okay?"

Lala looked up to see the worried, kindly face of an Air France representative looking at her.

"I'm great!" Lala said.

The woman handed Lala a tissue. Lala studied it, then looked back at the woman with a confused expression. The woman hesitated for a moment, then dabbed at her cheeks with her fingertips. Lala couldn't think of anything else to do in response to the woman's gesture except imitate it. So she did, and found that her cheeks were completely wet.

"Omigoodness," Lala said. "Allergies. Sudden allergy attack. Thank you so much."

"Of course," the woman said. "Can I do anything to help?"

"Yes, please, can you point me in the direction of the nearest lounge I can get into with my Amex Platinum Business Card, registered trademark—I don't know why I always have to add that—and my first class ticket?"

"That would be the Korean Air Lounge, ma'am. Please, let me escort you. I'd feel better knowing you got there okay."

The woman, whose name, Lala discovered on their walk to the lounge—after Lala assured her that she didn't need to find a cart to transport them because Lala could probably walk and wasn't, god willing and the creek don't rise, going to have a full-on mental and physical collapse anytime soon—was Peggy, brought Lala to the lounge and insisted on finding one of her colleagues, a lovely young man named Sean, so she could ask him to please take extra special care of Ms. Lala.

Lala hugged Peggy and realized she might start crying again, so she distracted herself with positive action. She grabbed her phone and started to pound on the screen.

"Peggy, would you please give me your e-mail address, and would you please pick a charity I can donate to in your honor, and would you please give me your boss's contact information so I can tell her or him how sanity-savingly kind you are?"

"Dachshund Rescue of Southern California," Peggy said without hesitation. Lala gasped.

"You have got to be kidding. Were you concerned that I didn't adore you enough already? Done. I'm staying in touch with you, my new friend. And, yes, that is way more of a threat than a promise."

Sean escorted Lala inside the lounge. He pointed toward the bar area.

"Yes?"

"Oh, yes, dear Sean," Lala said. "And you go right ahead and start thinking about your charity-of-choice."

Sean settled Lala into a very comfortable chair in a corner of the area surrounding the bar. He helped her adjust her seat so that her feet were elevated, and he very quickly got her in possession of a very large glass of premium white wine from Sonoma and a lovely cheese plate.

"Sean, your place in heaven is assured, and I'm adopting you as one of my slew of nephews. That means you'll be taking care of me when I'm old and, I hope, agreeably dotty."

"Great!" Sean said. He gave Lala a sweet little nod and left her to relax.

Poor dear boy, Lala thought as she watched Sean walk away. *He has no idea how demanding I intend to be in my dotage.*

Lala surveyed the spacious lounge. The colors were soothing. There weren't many people there. It was a calming, cozy atmosphere, and Lala was very grateful for that. She propped a pillow under her head and leaned back with her Kindle screen on the most recent page of *The Count of Monte Cristo*. After maybe a few more readings, Lala felt happily sure, she would probably have all 1,500 pages memorized.

Maybe this wasn't such a scary plan after all, Lala thought.

She looked around the lounge again. *When I went to Paris the last time, with Terrence, we left from JFK. And we certainly didn't fly first class. And we stayed in a cheap, wonderfully small hotel, and now I'll be in a charming apartment. So the memories might not be able to flatten me.*

Lala took a big sip of wine and visited with the Count as he formulated his escape from the Chateau D'If. After a half hour of wonderful transport to a completely different place and time, Lala shut her Kindle cover for a moment.

I'm okay, she thought. *I think I may even have bested the Dread Memory Demons for now. Yup. Going to Paris is actually a very good plan, and I don't feel a bit frightened. God, this bleu cheese is fabulous. What a harbinger of bonnes choses to come!*

This was a very terrible plan, and I should not have done this!

That upsetting thought had actually been kept at bay for far longer than Lala had any right to expect. She had done very well during the long overnight flight, other than a momentary blip while she was getting comfortable in her big first-class slumber pod. The Air France jet had not yet left the gate to head to the runway when Lala suddenly blurted.

"Sweet Mother of God, what am I thinking going to Paris alone?"

Lala just as suddenly clapped her hand over her mouth and tentatively half-stood to see if her outburst had been loud enough to be heard by anyone. First class was fairly empty, and the air hosts were gathered at the galley in front of the plane, so it seemed possible that she had not branded herself a whack job from the beginning of the flight.

Lala had settled back in her seat. Champagne service began almost immediately, and Lala didn't have an empty glass through the delicious vegetarian dinner and the viewing of movies that was interrupted only by trips to the bathroom and reading breaks to visit with her forever-loved Edmond Dantès, until she fell asleep without even needing to pop an Ambien.

She woke just before landing. A smiling young man holding up a sign with her name on it was waiting for her when she exited customs.

"*Bonjour*, Madame Pettibone," he said.

He pronounced her last name "Puh-teee-boh," and Lala had to try not to swoon.

My god, he is adorable, Lala thought. *Frenchmen. My god.*

The car the production had hired to take her to her apartment was very comfortable, and, after chatting with the driver, Fabrice, in French and English, Lala fell into a bit of a nap in the backseat. When she lifted her head, the Eiffel Tower loomed in the distance against a clear blue sky. And that's when the Memory Demons recaptured their hegemony.

This was a very terrible plan, and I should not have done this! Lala thought.

"I'm sorry," she gasped. "Could you please pull over?"

"Of course, Madame," Fabrice said. He found a spot around the corner from the main road they were on and parked. He turned toward the backseat. "What can I do for you?"

Lala couldn't answer right away. She tried not to hyperventilate.

It has been a long time since I felt so alone, Lala thought. *Maybe not since the months right after Terrence died. Oh, and that summer during college when I worked on that midnight-to-seven shift at that phone sex line in Tarzana because the pay was so good.*

"Madame," Fabrice said. "Are you ill?"

"I'm great!" Lala forced herself to say. "Sudden and thankfully momentary attack of jet lag, I guess. *Merci mille fois pour votre gentillesse.*"

They got back on the road and arrived at the gate leading to the courtyard of Lala's new home without any additional mishaps. Fabrice had phoned ahead to alert the concierge that they would be arriving. A stooped old man was standing at the entrance when the car pulled up. He slowly opened each side of the wide iron gate, and the car pulled in to the cobblestone courtyard. Lala looked up at the charming old three-story building that wrapped around the center.

Oy vey, she thought. *SO gorgeous. I'm kvelling. Alone. Oy.*

The concierge leaned into the open window on the driver's side and spoke to Fabrice in rapid-fire French. Lala couldn't catch many of the words. She did manage to make out "*la femme*" and "*bien sûr que non*" before she saw the concierge hand Fabrice a huge, elaborate key. The old man then shuffled away from the car and disappeared into a nearby door. Fabrice leapt out of the car and ran over to Lala's door to open it.

"Madame, let me show you up to the apartment so you can relax while I bring the bags upstairs."

"God, no," Lala said. "Pop the trunk and let's schlepp them to my place together so you can be on your way, you sweet young man. And your big tip is assured, *mon ami.*"

Fabrice protested that he didn't want her to have to carry anything, and Lala wouldn't hear of it, so they hauled Lala's suitcases up one flight of stairs together. Fabrice used the fancy key to open the door to a small, utterly charming one-bedroom, all the windows of which faced the courtyard. The sun made every corner of the apartment bright. The furnishings were clean and crisp and cozy. Lala wanted to cry.

"Wow," she said. "Listen, Fabrice, you are wonderful. Thank you so much. I think I'm going to have a shower and a nap. Don't be a stranger. Come visit the set sometime, yes?"

Fabrice promised Lala he would, and he gave her a cheerful wave on the way out the door. Lala had a long, hot shower. She wrapped one of many big, fluffy towels around herself like a sarong and unpacked. There was a gorgeous armoire in the bedroom, and it was just the right size for all her clothes and then some. The bed was big and had an ornate headboard carved in a wood Lala couldn't identify because she had no idea about anything having to do with interior design other than what was comfortable and comforting for her. And this apartment was profoundly that. It felt like a sanctuary. It felt like just what Lala needed at that point.

My fear of losing David to his untimely death that would occur anytime before I kick it, and my resulting urge to run and hide from our relationship aside, I may need to fly him over here so we can bonk on that bed, Lala thought.

She set up her laptop on the small desk in the bedroom. One of the first e-mails she saw was from Clive, inviting her to dinner that night. She wrote a quick response to ask for a rain check. Having to maintain a sustained conversation with anyone at any point during at least the next twelve hours didn't really seem that appealing to her. Clive responded immediately that they would definitely reschedule and that, if it was okay with Lala, he would pick her up to take her to the set the next afternoon.

Lala sent a quick e-mail to David to tell him that she had landed safely, and that she loved him and couldn't wait to Skype with him, and could they please do that tomorrow as she was exhausted from jet lag and desperate to get to bed.

Part of the e-mail was a lie; Lala felt wired and not a bit tired, and she knew she wouldn't be able to sleep anytime soon.

David wrote back immediately to say that he loved her and missed her, and they would definitely Skype tomorrow. Lala sent another e-mail that consisted of rows and rows of 'X's and 'O's.

Her next e-mail was to Geraldine, to tell her that the trip was wonderful and she was safely in her adorable apartment, and she would write more tomorrow because right now she was exhausted from jet lag and desperate to get to bed.

Geraldine wrote back immediately to say that she suspected that was a load of crap and that Lala would be too agitated to sleep, but she loved her anyway, even though she was a bald-faced liar.

Lala chose to completely ignore Geraldine's P.S., which stated that Geraldine "better not find out you are trying to peddle the same bullshit to dear David, tonight or any other night, or there will be hell to pay."

Lala decided a long constitutional was an absolute must. She put on a comfortable pair of jeans, a cozy cotton sweater, and her walking sneakers. They were certainly not her workout sneakers, which had been left behind in Los Angeles, as they were fairly pungent and she hadn't planned to visit a gym while she was in France. Lala wanted to get her exercise like a real Parisian, by traveling on foot everywhere. She stuck her credit cards and her international driver's license in her back pocket so she could travel light. She grabbed her sunglasses and her key and was out the door, skipping down the stairs.

Act like you're feeling safe and confident, she thought. *And you'll end up feeling safe and confident. God, I hope that's true.*

Lala's apartment was in the Fifth Arrondissement, on a charming little side street not a hundred steps from the Seine and in a direct line to one of the many bridges across the river, this one leading to the Île Saint-Louis. The end of the street also boasted a stunning view of the back of Notre Dame. Lala marched toward the water and smiled.

Ice cream, she thought.

Her first stop was at Berthillon, a wonderful ice cream shop she had visited with Terrence on their honeymoon. The line leading to the store stretched around the block. Lala cheerfully took her place behind the last person in line, a cute and tiny woman who looked like a sweet grandma-for-hire. The older woman smiled at Lala and nodded.

"*Bonjour*," she said.

"*Bonjour, Madame*," Lala said, nodding and smiling a bit to excess. "*Comme il fait beau aujourd'hui!*"

The woman's smile instantly became broader.

"Oh, you are American," she said.

Yikes, Lala thought. *It's that obvious? Well, I never was a good actress.*

"Yup," Lala said.

"Where are you from?"

"Los Angeles by way of New York," Lala said.

"*J'adore* New York," the woman trilled. "I live there for many years right after the war, with my parents. In the Greenwich Village!"

"*J'adore* Greenwich Village!" Lala crowed.

By the time they got to the front of the line, Lala had to tell the woman, whose name was Mimi, that she would love to meet her grandson if she were single, but she was in fact engaged-to-be-engaged to a lovely man, and Mimi responded that that sounded "adorable, but is my English perhaps not of high enough quality for me to understand why that is not entirely fucking ridiculous *en même temps*," and Lala couldn't stop laughing. She bought them both a double scoop of lavender and vanilla, and they made a date to have dinner together over the weekend. Lala told Mimi she had to promise to come visit the set of the film.

After hugging Mimi good-bye, Lala walked along the bank of the Seine and made her way over to Notre Dame. She walked around the cathedral and remembered dancing with Terrence to a violinist who had been playing in the long square in front of the cathedral years ago.

Lala sat on a bench and listened to a guitarist play and sing to *Et Maintenant*. It was one of the songs she memorized to help her learn French, and so she sang along in French, while also astonishing herself by simultaneously translating in her mind.

Now that you're gone . . .

A young man had been standing next to the bench on the other side to listen to the song, and when he heard Lala singing in French, he turned and spoke to her.

"You're American?" he asked.

Sheesh. My accent sucks when I sing, too? she thought. *Well, I never was much of a singer. Like, not much of one at all.*

"Yup," she told the young man, smiling. "How are ya?"

They chatted for a few minutes and Lala complimented him on his excellent English. Then Lala walked back to the Left Bank and continued walking for several miles, past bookstalls and all kinds of other vendors. She made it all the way to the Musée d'Orsay, also a much-loved memory from her honeymoon. It was closed at that point during the early evening, and she resolved that she would visit the museum as soon as possible.

By the time she got back to her street, Lala was ravenous. She noticed a small Italian restaurant right across from the entrance to the courtyard of her building, and she felt a welcome and familiar craving for carbs.

The little bistro was full, and Lala was surprised to see that the concierge of her building was also the host of the restaurant. He shuffled over to her and made what might have been an attempt at a smile, or possibly just a facial indication of a sudden and quite dreadful attack of gout.

"*Bonsoir, Madame,*" he said in an utterly uninflected tone.

"*Bonsoir, Monsieur. Avez-vous des plats végétariens?*"

The concierge/host responded with an extensive, muttered monologue, none of which Lala could understand, but he was speaking as he was shuffling toward the only empty table in a far corner, so Lala decided to assume that somewhere in all those rushed words there was a "*Oui.*" She followed him and beamed when he handed her the menu.

"*Merci mille fois!*" she said with extra gratitude.

Lala instinctively—really, since she was a toddler—had never been able to abide it when people were grumpy around her. She either removed herself from cranky people, or she mounted a sustained attack.

I swear, I will win over this crotchety old chap, she silently declared.

She cheerfully regarded the menu and decided almost immediately on a small green salad and penne with pink sauce.

Lala scanned the room. It looked like a nice group of

people; a few families with children, couples on a date, one other single person . . . a young man in hiking shorts and a turtle-neck. What looked to be the only waiter in the restaurant, also a young man, was having a spirited debate in French with the solo diner. Lala listened attentively to the discussion and was quite pleased with herself when she managed to understand a complete sentence.

"Tu es complètement fou ou quoi?"

Okay, unless I'm way off on this, he just said the other guy is totally nuts. Delish! Lala thought. She watched the two men high-five each other and watched as the waiter walked over to her table. He was maybe in his late 20s and he had the muscular grace of a ballet star. His head was shaved and there was a small red heart tattooed on each earlobe.

"Bonsoir, Madame," the waiter said. *"Vous désirez?"*

"Bonsoir, Monsieur," Lala said. *"S'il vous plaît, je souhaiterais—"*

"Oh, hi. You're an American. Cool. Welcome," the young man said in a native Brooklyn accent so thick, Lala imagined it could function quite nicely as a doorstopper to one of the massive portals leading into Notre Dame itself.

"Wow," Lala said. "You're not French. You're from New York?"

"Sure am," the young man said. He held out his hand and shook hers. "Kenny."

"Lala."

"Ahh, you're our new guest in the building! Pleasure to meet you.

"Ditto. How . . . your French accent. Is it me, or is it superb?"

Kenny nodded toward the concierge, who was sitting behind the small bar and was reading *Le Monde*.

"That's my grandpa. We visited him every year. I learned French when I was two years old."

"Sheesh. Do you ever have an ear for accents. Wow. And I

think you got my share of that talent because rumor has it that I was born totally without any."

"That's not true," Kenny said. "Your French accent is—"

"You are so sweet," Lala chuckled. "My French accent is appalling. Who knew? Okay, no more lying, however kindly intended. Which red wine do you recommend, truthfully?"

Kenny brought her a lovely glass of Bordeaux, and when she finished that, he brought over a bottle and another glass. Between serving the other customers, Kenny sat with Lala and they shared the bottle while Lala ate. At the end of the evening, when the restaurant was empty, Kenny's grandfather, Maurice, still scowling, came over with three apple tarts.

Now's my chance, Lala thought. *Get ready to smile, mon cher Monsieur. Of course, there is that language barrier. I'll just have to flirt with my eyes and enchant him that way.*

"Are you okay?" Kenny asked.

"I'm great!" Lala said, winking spastically at his grandfather and then at him.

Maurice rather quickly proved to be surprisingly chatty. He started telling a story that involved different voices and many elaborate gestures and facial expressions.

Lala was able to follow the first sentence of the speech. "*Chère Madame, écoutez, je vous prie.*"

Ohhh, boy, Lala thought. *I . . . Wait . . . What did that teacher tell me? Just nod and say, "You find?"*

Lala smiled and nodded at Maurice.

"*Vous trouvez?*" she asked.

Maurice stopped his narration and stared at Lala. He abruptly stood and went into the kitchen.

Uh oh, Lala thought.

"Did I just misremember and say something unforgivably rude?" Lala asked Kenny. "Like, 'Shut your pie-hole, Napoleon'? I think I'm really drunk."

"Did you have a French teacher who told you how to get through a conversation and not sound like an idiot, even if you had no idea what was going on?" Kenny asked.

"Yes," Lala said. "Yes, I did."

"*Vous trouvez*. You find? You got it right."

"Thank goodness," Lala said.

Maurice marched back carrying a bottle of champagne and three flutes. He popped the cork and giggled. And then he started on a fresh monologue. Lala looked at Kenny helplessly. Kenny gave her a thumbs-up and whispered, "He says the young lady speaks excellent French. And that deserves a special toast."

Lala scrunched her shoulders up in delight. The old man handed her a glass of champagne.

"*Vous êtes très jolie*," Maurice said.

Okay, that I understand, Lala thought.

She patted Maurice's hand and smiled.

"*Vous trouvez?*"

Kenny escorted Lala upstairs to her apartment.

"My grandpa is actually quite a fluff ball when you get to know him," Kenny said at the door to the apartment.

"Fluff ball," Lala repeated. "That's a comforting image. I think maybe next time someone is making me nervous, I'll imagine that they're a large ball of fluff with a nose and eyes and a big smile and little spindly legs. Thank you, Kenny."

"Glad to be of help," Kenny said. He kissed Lala on both cheeks and told her he looked forward to seeing her at the restaurant again soon.

Lala had another long shower and wrapped herself in her thick robe. She was surprised that she wasn't a bit tired. She turned on the small television in the bedroom and was ecstatic to find, after flipping through only a few channels, that there was a dubbed version of *The Young and the Restless* playing. In French, the title was *Les Feux de l'Amour*.

The Fires of Love, Lala thought. She propped herself up

against the headboard of the bed with all the available pillows against her back, and balanced her computer on her lap.

Lala watched the episode and realized it was one she had seen many months earlier. She was very happy to also realize that the script sounded even more overwrought in the language of the Gauls.

Mon Dieu. C'est superbe, ça. *God, my accent really is for shit, even in my internal voice.*

Lala opened her laptop and checked her e-mails. There were a bunch from David. He had arrived in Davis and was happy with his studio apartment just off campus. He missed her already and he wanted to Skype with her as soon as possible.

Lala tried to subtract nine from the time on the digital clock on the nightstand next to the bed.

2 a.m.. Okay, so, it's . . . 5 p.m. in California. Merde. *He'll be awake.*

Lala slammed her laptop shut, as though it were somehow communicating to David that Lala was awake and could Skype with him at that moment, but she was choosing not to.

I just can't. Maybe I'm realizing that I have to get used to being without him? Because life is so fragile, and there are absolutely no guarantees, and we're all going to die, and it's just a question of how and when? Maybe that's what I'm doing? Maybe I'm protecting myself? Or maybe I'm just out of my fucking mind?

Lala tried to distract herself by watching the impassioned shenanigans on *Les Feux de l'Amour.*

Catherine would agree with me, she thought. *Jeez, she's buried how many husbands already? Not to mention all those divorces, which I'm sure are in the double-digits by now.*

Lala fell asleep with the television on and the computer still on her lap. She woke up the next morning because someone was knocking on her front door.

Is that the Grim Reaper, she thought. *God, I have got to get off this death thing. Having been a young widow can only excuse so much obsession.*

Lala shuffled over to the door, assuming it was Kenny or Maurice. She opened it to find Clive standing there.

"*Merde*. What time is it?"

"It's not too late. I made allowances for jet lag," Clive said. He handed her a coffee and a small paper bag. Lala opened the bag and inhaled the incredible scent of a fresh croissant. A fresh, warm croissant. A fresh, warm croissant in Paris.

"Ohhh," Lala sighed.

"You've got time to shower," Clive assured her. "I drive really fast."

Or Maybe You Can?

"My god, do you drive fast."

Lala had been trying to send David a message during the 80-kilometer trip from Paris on one of those international-doesn't-cost-a-cent thingies on her phone, but she couldn't type coherently because Clive was driving so fast. Plus, the countryside was far too beautiful to ignore. They were headed to Villers-Cotterêts to film on a farm just outside the small town where *Alexandre Dumas, père*, the author of Lala's favorite classic novel, had been born and was buried. Lala had reserved a room in a charming small hotel that had once been a monastery so she could spend the next morning touring the town.

She put her phone in her bag and concentrated on the lovely fields and scattered towns that were warming under a strong sun. And she concentrated on not freaking out over Clive's driving.

"The studio lets you drive this fast?"

"I'm not going much above the speed limit."

"Is it like it is on the Autobahn here?"

"Not quite."

Okay, I sound like a grandma, Lala thought. *Enough.*

When they got to the farmhouse, Lala grabbed a minute

before she got out of the car to send David a quick text saying that she had overslept (darn that darn jet lag!), and she was going to be on-set all day (darn that darn movie making magic!), and she couldn't wait to Skype with him as soon as they could coordinate a time when they would both be awake (darn that darn nine-hour time difference!).

Clive popped his head back in the open driver's side window.

"Oh, I should mention one thing before you meet the director. He brought his brother here to work with you on adding a new scene. We think it would be a good idea for Terry to have more of an edge."

What the FUCK? Lala thought.

"Cool!" she said. "Anything for the project!"

Okay, I do actually mean that, because I will do whatever it takes to get this movie made, but fuck you, Clive, you cute, sneaky British bastard.

Lala had a smile plastered on her face as she and Clive walked past the extras and the crew, who were taking a break around the outdoor craft services table. She had to use all her restraint not to trip Clive and send him flying into what she hoped was a mound of natural fertilizer.

I guess it's not cow poop, she thought. *It doesn't smell like cow poop. In the movie version of our madcap behind-the-scenes adventures, it will be cow poop. And in the movie, I will trip him. And he will land in cow poop.*

"Helllloooo, my friends!" Clive trilled. The crowd of actors and tech people applauded. "No! Stop that! Look who I've got with me. It's Lala Pettibone! The screenwriter! She's the one who deserves your applause!"

The crowd started clapping again, and Lala halted her internal revenge scenario to quite suddenly and quite genuinely feel very touched by their warm welcome.

"Omigosh, thank you so much. Thank you all for being here. I'm so thrilled. Thank you."

A very compact young man wearing what looked to Lala like a unitard made of camouflage material came striding out of the tall open doors that took up an entire side of the barn next to the craft services area. A slew of assistants followed him, one looking more nervous than the next.

The young man grabbed Clive in a bear hug and they kind of danced around together in a circle of ostentatiously heterosexual embrace. The young man just as abruptly broke it off and barreled toward Lala. She had to stop herself from lunging out of the way in fear of being flattened by him, because she didn't want to come across as a big baby in front of everyone.

"Hi!" Lala said. "You must be Matthew!"

"Get over here!" Matthew Finch, the director, yelled. He grabbed her hand and pumped it vigorously. "Lala! Lala! LALA! MAY I HUG YOU?"

"Sure!" Lala said.

Why has everything suddenly gotten so loud? she thought.

Matthew wrapped his arms around Lala's waist and swung her around so that her feet were flying off the ground.

"Lala PETTIBONE!" Matthew yelled. "I love your name, and I love your work!"

Matthew put her back down and kissed her on both cheeks.

"I'm getting to be really French here!" he announced at a reasonable decibel level.

Oh, thank goodness, Lala thought. *We've stopped shouting.*

"I love your work, too," Lala said. "*Tooters* was so much fun."

Another young man exited the barn and made his way over to Lala and Clive and Matthew. His genetic connection to Matthew was unmistakable in terms of his looks, but he moved with all the exuberance of a tree sloth who was looking to conserve his energy.

"ATTICUS, GET OVER HERE AND MEET LALA!" Matthew shrieked.

Is Matthew having difficulty with his ears? Lala thought. *Can he not hear his sound levels? Wait a minute, what name did he just say . . .*

"Hi," Matthew's brother said. He gave Lala a sweet, lazy smile.

"Hello . . . Atticus. Is your last name also . . . Finch?"

"My parents have a really twisted sense of humor," Matthew

said.

Okay, now we're suddenly back to normal decibels, Lala thought. *What the classic fuck?*

"Do you have any idea what it's like for me to try to order a pizza?" Atticus asked glumly. "Let alone subscribe to Hustler?"

"BERNADETTE!" Matthew screamed. A nervous young woman came rushing over. "PLEASE GET MY HEADSET CHECKED! I CAN'T HEAR MYSELF THINK!"

Matthew ripped his headset off and handed it to the young woman, who ran to a tent on the other end of the small field that had technicians and tables of equipment at the ready.

Matthew shook his head and then stuck an index finger in each ear, for some reason choosing to use the finger of the hand opposite each ear and ending up with his arms awkwardly crossed around his neck. He vibrated his fingers in his ears and hummed. For quite some time. Lala stared at the ground, not knowing where to look. Finally, Matthew stopped.

"Okay, that's better," he said. "Lala, I have to tell you that my brother is your biggest fan. He loves your script. Would you consider maybe taking him under your wing? I can say with all objectivity that he is an excellent screenwriter, and I'd love to see what you two could come up with for a new scene? Something for right when Terry gets to Paris. To give him a little more of an edge? Maybe?"

Fuck this noise, Lala thought. *Though Matthew is considerably more diplomatic than Clive. Whose name is mud right now in my book. Mud mixed with cow poop.*

"Clive already told me about the new scene," Lala said.

"Cool!" Matthew said. "Thanks, Clive! So, Lala, whaddya think, huh?"

"Absolutely!" Lala said. "Anything for the project!"

Lala was given a chair next to Matthew's when they began shooting again. She was thrilled to be watching the scenes in her script unfold before her, and she loved the actors' work. Even Clive, whose name continued to be mud in her book, was superb as Terry. She smiled at him and gave him a joyous nod whenever he caught her eye, while, in her mind, slapping him around for springing that shit about the new scene and her new writing partner on her. Lala didn't move from her seat until the assistant director announced that it was a wrap for the day, because she was too happy to go anywhere.

The next day's shooting would take place in the same location, starting in the afternoon. Clive bounded over to where Lala was standing at the craft services table eating fistfuls of peanuts because she was so excited about the project. Other than that part where she had to add a new scene and up the conflict. Her Terry character didn't like conflict. Neither did she.

"You were great!" Lala trilled. Clive grabbed her and hugged her.

"Yeah?"

"Yeah!"

Dickhead, she thought.

"Let's celebrate! I want to take you to my favorite restaurant, right by the Hôtel de Ville. We better hurry. Traffic might be a bit of a bitch."

"I'm staying overnight here," Lala said.

"You are?"

"*Dumas, père* was born here. He's buried here. No way I'm not spending all of tomorrow morning reveling in his brilliance."

Lala said "*Dumas, père*" with an exaggerated French accent that would have made Maurice Chevalier sound like a hillbilly.

Clive nodded sagely.

"Until the day when god shall deign to reveal the future to man, all human wisdom is summed up in these two words, 'Wait and hope'."

Awww, man, Lala thought. *Now I have to like you again.* Merde.

"Yup," Lala said. "I like to add, 'and take action.' You know, while you're waiting and hoping."

"Good point." Clive agreed. "I don't have any reason why I have to go back to Paris tonight."

"You don't?" Lala said.

"Where are you staying?"

Shoot, Lala thought. *He is way too cute. And I am way too only human.*

"I'm really sorry," Clive said. "I'm not good with conflict. In life, I mean. I'm great with it on screen."

"You are," Lala admitted. "In *Partisans*? You were painfully good with conflict. I couldn't sit still when I was watching that movie. I was so tense during that damn movie, I thought I would lose my mind."

"Thanks," Clive said. They were sitting in the small, charming restaurant of the Hôtel de l'Abbaye de Longpont, sharing mushroom crepes and an abundant selection of local cheeses and olives, along with a loaf of crusty bread that Lala had deemed obscene in its gorgeousness. Clive had ordered the entire meal in flawless French. His accent was equally flawless. The hotel's owner was clearly smitten with the movie star and so was the nervous young waitress, who couldn't stop giggling at everything Clive said.

"Maybe don't thank me," Lala said. "I'm going to have to say that I could never sit through that film again. It made me way too nervous. I much prefer a comedy with a happy and hopeful ending. No offense."

"None taken," Clive said. "I'm already thinking about what we should have for dessert."

"Yes," Lala said. She smiled at Clive, and then she snuck in another glare at him, one she assumed went unnoticed as had all the others, she assumed, in her passive-aggressive wallowing during that entire dinner.

"I'm really sorry I sprung that new scene stuff on you," Clive said. "I don't blame you for glaring at me. All night. All the time."

"Okay, that's not strictly true. I have also smiled at you. Damn, I didn't think you noticed the glaring."

"I'd have to be wearing an industrial-strength sleep mask not to notice."

"Shoot," Lala said. "I was never a very good actress."

"It's just that I knew that Matthew was going to talk to you about the scene, because we really do think it would add so much to the film if we up Terry's edge and enhance the conflict."

Terry doesn't like conflict, Lala thought. *He's sensitive and wonderful and perfect.*

The character of Terry in *Dressed Like a Lady, Drinks Like a Pig* was based on Lala's late husband, Terrence. Who was sensitive and wonderful and perfect in Lala's mind, and always would be.

"I wanted to say something as soon as I picked you up, you know, to give you some warning so Matthew wasn't springing it on you as a surprise."

"Instead you sprung it on me."

"I'm really sorry about that."

"It's okay," Lala said. "I think I forgive you."

"Thanks for being so gracious during the shoot today."

"I was thinking really aggressive thoughts in my mind," Lala admitted.

As opposed to thinking them in my ass, Lala thought. *I hate when my dialogue is sloppy.*

"Where else would you be thinking them?" Clive said. "In your ass?"

There was a moment's worth of a pause while Lala glared at Clive, and Clive looked worried that he had unintentionally been rude by referencing Lala's bum in this relatively early stage of their artistic collaboration, until Lala started guffawing and after a half beat Clive joined her in guffawing, and the hotel proprietor stared guffawing from this place behind the bar, and the sweet little waitress came over and brought them the dessert menu and giggled.

On the owner's suggestion, they shared two desserts, *crème caramel* and *mousse au chocolat*.

"Sweet Rockin' Kazoo," Lala mumbled through the mouthful of beige heaven she had just ladled into her mouth. "If I die tonight, I will die happy."

Where did I get "Sweet Rockin' Kazoo" from? Lala thought. *And why am I talking about dying tonight?*

"Amen," Clive said. "Not to you dying. To you being happy. Oh, and I like that 'Sweet Rockin' Kazoo' bit. Did you just come up with that?"

They ended up in the hotel bar, where the owner brought out a special bottle of Cognac for them.

And it was at the adorable bar that Clive made what was a big mistake . . . unless he really, really, really desperately wanted to hear a very late-night, very effusive monologue.

"So. Who's Lala Pettibone? Details, please."

The bottle of Cognac was half-empty by the time Lala paused for a breath.

"My GOD, this is good Cognac. Where was I? Oh, yeah. So, Clive, the thing is, when my parents died, it wasn't the same. I miss them, but my day-to-day life didn't really change. With Terrence, nothing was the same. In everything I did, I felt his absence. Maybe that's why I haven't spent every day with anyone until I met David. I thought I was ready. Now, I'm not so sure."

"England is my primary residence," Clive said. "And I travel a lot for filming. So we wouldn't be in the same town most of the time. If that's an incentive for you to maybe consider . . .? I have to say, I love women of a certain age—"

"Please put air quotation marks around that phrase," Lala said, even as she was annoyed with herself for blushing and for being delighted that Clive was flirting with her. "And I'm sorry, but David and I are in fact engaged-to-be-engaged."

Clive didn't say anything right away. Lala watched him as he lifted his brandy snifter and twirled the liquid inside it before he took a deep and soulful draught.

Poor sweet man, Lala thought. *I've hurt him. I hope he can deal with the disappointment. I hope this doesn't interfere with the movie.*

At last, Clive spoke.

"What are you, seventeen?" Clive said. "What are you, seventeen and it's the 1950s and you're a character in a black-and-white film where you've gotten a scholarship to college, but you've got this boyfriend who's a laborer so you're eventually going to throw it all away and get married?"

Lala took a long look at Clive. She curled her upper lip and wrinkled her nose in an affectionate sneer and winked at him.

"Yeah, yeah, very clever, Mr. Smart Ass Movie Star. You are one blunt British bastard, and I hate to admit that I find that rather adorable."

Lala stood, a bit woozily for a moment, but she got her sea legs back in a blink. She stepped out from her side of the table and did a full, dramatic curtsy. She then stood erect and gave Clive a full military salute.

"Lala out," she said. "You stay here and finish the bottle with our charming host. Do NOT follow me upstairs! If you do, and if any"—and at this point she made sweeping air quotation marks that began with her arms stretched overhead as high as she could reach and that ended with her arms spastically pumping out rapid-fire quotation marks around her ankles—"'funny business' is attempted, there will be"—air quotation marks again with, if anything, even more intensity—"'hell to pay.'"

Clive nodded and blew her a kiss as she exited.

"*Dors bien, ma chère amie*," he said.

Lala skipped up the stairs off the lobby to the second floor and opened the door to her small, cozy room. She took a quick shower and, after just dabbing her skin with a large, fluffy towel, slathered moisturizer all over every easily-accessible part of her body.

"My sincere and heartfelt apologies to you, oh little area at the middle of my back which I cannot reach coming from the top over my shoulders and not coming from the bottom by wrenching my hands around my waist either, you poor, last-kid-picked-for-the-team-every-time-in-elementary-school of my personal body politic."

While she was walking around the room naked, waiting for the lotion to dry into her skin, Lala realized that she felt optimistic enough to chat with David, and she seized that momentary pause in her seemingly bottomless fear of death and loss to open her laptop and smack the keys until her Skype operator was trying to contact David's Skype operator.

How does it work? Lala thought. *How? France talking to and seeing Southern California. Effortlessly. Such fascinating and bold times we live in. And yet we cannot conquer death, can we? Sheesh, I'm starting to sound like an overly caffeinated publicist for the Grim Reaper.*

She saw a message pop up on her computer, one telling her that Dr. David was not available to Skype.

Merde, Lala thought. And she just as quickly felt an unbidden sense of relief.

Lala wrote a quick e-mail to David to tell him that she had tried to call him and she missed him and she loved him and she was going to sleep now, *bisous, bisous, bisous.* She slammed her laptop shut, fretted once again that she might, in her exuberance, have broken it, and jumped into the large, soft, billowing bed. She propped the pillows against the headboard, always one of her favorite things to do, and she scooted under the thick comforter.

That should have been her segue into a blissful night of sleep, but an unsettling idea barged in before she could nod off.

I know what I'm doing, she thought. *I'm forcing myself to get used to not being with David. Just like I had to get used to being without Terrence. Because David might die before I do. Just like Terrence did. Well, this lovely little moment of self-awareness has shot any chance of sleeping all to crap.*

She seized the remote control for the small television that was comfortably encased in an antique bookshelf opposite the foot of the bed.

I swear, there better be *Les Feux d'Artifice* on some channel in this precious little burg.

Lala flipped channels and frowned.

That's not what it's called, she thought. *Feux d'Artifice means fireworks. Literally, it's "fake fire," and how cool is that? What is it called, The Young and the Restless? Oh, yeah, The Fires of Love, whatever that is in French. I can't remember right now. I swear, it better be on.*

There weren't many channels to check on the cable service in the small hotel that was once a monastery in the small town where Alexandre Dumas, *père*, was buried, so it didn't take long for Lala to realize that she wouldn't be watching her favorite soap that night. The last channel she checked before she was about to return full circle back to the first channel she had checked was a movie channel. It was playing Matthew Finch's blockbuster hit, *Tooters*, dubbed into French. Lala sighed heavily.

Fine, fine. I'll watch this stupid movie again. Any voices will have to do, so long I don't have to listen to the voices in my head.

Lala had slept fitfully, if much at all, that night, and she woke up determined to remind herself that the Count of Monte Cristo had way more to worry about on a good day than she had ever had in her remarkably lucky life, early widowhood notwithstanding. So she showered and got dressed quickly and ran downstairs to convey to the lovely proprietor of their hotel in carefully considered French that Monsieur Clive would be having breakfast in his room, and could she please bring a tray with *pain au chocolat* and coffee for two upstairs with her. Balancing the bountiful and lovingly-provided tray, Lala carefully walked up the small staircase and banged on Clive's door with her foot.

"Up and at 'em, *mon cher ami*," she yelled. "We have got some Dumasing to do!"

They started out at the Fifteenth Century church of St. Nicholas, where Dumas was baptized. Their next stop was the Alexandre Dumas Museum, where Lala proceeded to have a shimmying meltdown on her happy tippy toes over "all this stuff from his actual life that he actually read and used and looked at 'n' stuff!" They visited the house where Dumas was born, and after that they stood in front of the bronze statue of Dumas. Clive read from his tattered copy of *The Count of Monte Cristo*, which he took with him whenever he traveled anywhere.

"Clive, you would be perfect but for the fact that you take the abridged version with you," Lala said. She had been savoring his reading of the section of the novel in which Edmond Dantès meets the man who will help him escape his imprisonment on the Château d'If and will lead him to the fortune which will transform him into the Count of Monte Cristo, so that he can enact his terrible revenge against those who have betrayed him.

"Calm it down, buttercup," Clive said rather adorably. "I have my unabridged version at home. God, you can be so damn smug sometimes, Ms. Thing."

"I would like to go on record," Lala said as they had walked to the cemetery where Dumas had been buried until his ashes were reinterred in the Pantheon in Paris for the bicentennial of his birth in 2002, "as saying that I love flirting in general. I am not flirting with you specifically, Mr. Adorable Movie Star. And I guess my penchant . . ." Lala pronounced the word with an exaggerated French accent—*pohshoh*—that made her giggle and made Clive wince, ". . . for flirting in general is something that my fiancé-to-be-my-fiancé—"

"Which remains an entirely ridiculous concept," Clive said.

"Kindly do not interrupt. It is something to which he will have to get used. My dear late husband wasn't happy that I am quite such a flirt, but he ultimately accepted it as being an integral part of that which makes me who I am. Or something like that."

They walked around the cemetery and saw the resting places

of Dumas' parents and several other members of his family.

"We are steeped in Alexandre Dumas, *père*, on this fine day in the lovely town of Villers-Cotterêts" Lala said. "And I am loving that."

"*Moi aussi*," Clive agreed.

They returned to the hotel and checked out. A short drive to the set, and they were there in plenty of time for Clive to get into make-up.

Lala said hello to Matthew and looked around for his brother.

Where is the little pisher? Lala thought.

"Where's Atticus?"

"He stayed in Paris. He said he wanted to get ready for your first writing session together. Lala, I am so excited about this, and I'm really appreciative of your enthusiasm and flexibility."

Is the blank stare on my face conveying enthusiasm and flexibility? Lala silently asked herself. *Because that is definitely not my intention.*

"You bet!" Lala said. "Anything to elevate the project!"

Which is actually true, Lala thought. *Oy. Ambivalence! Oy vey*!

"I'll e-mail Atticus as soon as I get back to Paris tonight so we can set up a time to start working."

It was a short shoot for that afternoon, and they wrapped in time for Lala to insist to Clive that she would catch a fast train back to Paris rather than ride back with him because she needed "to be alone with my obsessive thoughts."

Kenny was washing the outside of the windows of the apartment building when Lala entered the courtyard.

"*Salut, mon ami!*" Lala called out to him.

"Hey! Welcome back! How was the shoot?"

"Really something else. Details over a bottle of wine as soon as possible. You need help?"

"No, *mon Dieu*, no, my grandfather would kill me if I let you help me with the windows. Or anything. You coming to the restaurant for dinner?"

"I'd love to, *mon trésor*, but I am exhausted. I think I might go out and get a little something and then curl up with a book."

"How about I bring you a brie sandwich on our signature crusty French bread and a salad with my own special mustard dressing?"

"How about I faint from joy and gratitude?"

By the time Lala had changed into her comfortable flannel pajamas, Kenny was at the door to her apartment with a box filled with food and wine.

"Sweet Sassy McGillicudy," Lala said. "This is paradise in a box, Kenny. I don't know where I'm getting these exclamations from. The other day I said 'Sweet Rockin' Kazoo,' if you can believe that."

She was going through the treasures and finding, in addition to a gorgeous cheese and bread creation and a huge salad, a *Tarte Tatin* that definitely did not look like an individual serving, and a box of madeleines and a jar of homemade strawberry jam for breakfast tomorrow.

"Kenny, you and your grandfather are now officially family to me, and I should warn you that that probably entails more obligation than it does advantage."

Lala sat at the small dining table in her living room and ate the entire sandwich and all the salad.

Merde, she thought. *This is the best food I have ever had. I'm going to convince Kenny to go into business with me to sell this mustard dressing. Seriously.*

While she was eating, she was audibly expressing her utter delight in increasingly louder outbursts of ecstasy, none of them actual words and all of them accompanied with the impassioned slapping of palms against her chest or the raising of her open hands to the heavens in a universal gesture of "How the fuck is something so delicious even possible?"

The lovely food gave Lala a fresh wave of energy and inspiration, so she spent the next two hours on her brand new novel, which she had given the working title, *A Woman of a Certain Age.*

It was almost eleven o'clock when she signed off on the manuscript efforts for that day, and she did a quick calculation to determine that it was afternoon in California.

"You free?" she texted David.

Her phone dinged to announce a response in a heartbeat.

"Yes, but I'm not cheap."

What followed was a Skype sex session between Lala and her intended-to-be-her-intended that, as Lala subsequently described to Geraldine in an e-mail she composed right after logging off with David, was basically a walking letter to *Penthouse*.

"Well, thank goodness you've surfaced again," Auntie Geraldine wrote back. "David and I were wondering what the heck was going on with you and your sudden radio silence. He called me, and I assured him that I hadn't heard from you either."

Yikes, Lala thought. *My "head-in-the-sand" approach to the rest of my life is becoming noticeable. Yikes.*

Despite her concern about that, Lala somehow managed to focus on the matters at hand long enough to get an e-mail off to Atticus that suggested they meet at either her place or his place to work, whichever location suited him best, and would tomorrow, late morning-ish, be a good time for him? Atticus joined the ranks of the distressingly prompt men in her life whose seeming self-assurance acted as a stinging rebuke to how vermischt she was currently feeling when he wrote back immediately to say that that would be "swell, and why not meet at your place since I think that might be more convenient for you, plus, I'm kind of an instant pack rat wherever I go, so there's not much open space here in my hotel room."

And despite her concern that people, specifically David and Geraldine, were noticing that she was, subconsciously or not, trying to fade away from any kind of life that had the possibility of the death of loved ones in it, Lala slept surprisingly well that night. She had the Madeleines and the jam Kenny brought her for breakfast, and they surpassed her high bar of expectation.

It was early enough that she thought she might have plenty of time for a long and invigorating walk along the Seine before she got together with Atticus. She put on a pair of yoga pants and a sweatshirt, and as she was zipping up the front, she looked at herself in the mirror and froze.

No, she thought. *Please. No.*

Kenny was in the restaurant stocking the shelves in the kitchen when Lala found him. She tried to be nonchalant as she asked him if he had a doctor he knew and trusted that preferably was female, and if his doctor wasn't female, could he maybe get a referral from one of his friends for a female doctor? Like, right away? Like, now? She had already sent Atticus an e-mail to ask if they could please postpone their writing session to sometime in the afternoon because something urgent had come up.

Kenny's family doctor was a woman. He called her office, and her nurse said he should bring Lala over right away.

"*Mon cher ami*, you don't have to come with me. Just give me the address. I'll be fine by myself," Lala told Kenny without any conviction whatsoever.

"Yeah, no," Kenny said. He was walking down the street with her to the nearest Metro stop. "If anyone else saw your face right now, I mean, like, in the movie version of the Lala Pettibone saga, and then in the next scene they find out that I let you go to the doctor alone, they'd be, like, what a *dickhead* that guy is."

It was a short subway ride to Dr. Sandrine Barraya's office. The receptionist got up from behind the desk and kissed Kenny on both cheeks. She extended her hand to Lala and smiled.

"We will take good care of you," the young woman said. "Doctor will be with you in just moments."

Lala and Kenny sat in the very comfortable chairs in the

small waiting area. Lala put her head on Kenny's shoulder.

"Does everyone in Paris speak English? Dr. Barraya speaks English, yes?"

"Better than I do," Kenny said. "Better than you and I do, put together."

In just a few minutes, the nurse opened the door and motioned for Lala to come inside. She was led to a small exam room and was given a gown to change into. There were a few magazines on the counter next to the exam table, and Lala did her best to distract herself by trying to read an article in *Paris Match*. As best she could figure out, there was a lesser royal in Belgium who had eaten an entire wheel of premium cheddar at a country fair in Wisconsin while representing his country's trade delegation there.

That can't possibly be right, Lala thought. *I think I'm translating that verb wrong. And that noun. And just about all of those adjectives.*

The door to the exam room opened, and a woman who looked like she couldn't have been more than a month out of medical school came in. Lala put the magazine back on the counter and started sobbing.

"My . . . I . . . my . . . my husband . . ."

There was only a momentary pause in Dr. Barraya's reaction, perhaps long enough for her to wonder if Lala's first language also wasn't English. Dr. Barraya walked the two steps toward Lala and held both Lala's hands in her own.

"Let's just breathe. Let's just focus. You're safe here. I'm here to help."

Wow, Lala thought, even as she was trying to concentrate on not hyperventilating, *her English probably is better than mine.*

"Tell me what's wrong," Dr. Barraya said. "Long, deep breaths, okay? Let's figure out what's going on."

Lala inhaled and exhaled and got her heart to stop racing to some reasonable extent, and when she finally found herself able to put sentences together, she couldn't stop.

"My husband had stomach cancer. He died in less than six months. I don't want to enter the world of cancer again. If I have to die, I just want to be up and then I want to be down. I want an aneurysm or something. I don't want to know that I'm sick. And I don't want my boyfriend to die before I do. I can't go through that again. And I feel like an idiot wanting all these things. Like any positive force in the universe, whatever that might be, is going to listen to me? Little kids in Syria are dying, but I want a better exit from the world than cancer? Their pleas go unheard, but mine should be acknowledged for some reason? I'm sorry, I think I'm going to barf."

Dr. Barraya had let go of Lala's hands only long enough to pass her a box of tissues. As Lala was speaking, the doctor nodded and focused all her attention on what Lala was saying.

"Why don't you lie back," Dr. Barraya said. She helped Lala swing her feet up and she propped a pillow under Lala's head. She then put a pillow under Lala's knees. "How's that?"

"Better," Lala whispered.

"Can you tell me why you wanted to see a doctor today?"

"I think I have breast cancer," Lala said.

"Okay," Dr. Barraya said. She patted Lala's shoulder. "Can you tell me why you think that?"

Lala had to take many deep breaths again before she could speak.

"I was getting dressed, and I saw a red lump. Red's not good, is it? It must mean it's really advanced. I don't know how I didn't notice it before. I have to admit that I don't do monthly breast exams. I figure I'll just make myself crazy thinking I have cancer all the time. But I do get a mammogram whenever my gynecologist says I should."

"May I take a look?" Dr. Barraya asked.

"Of course," Lala said.

Lala opened the top right side of her robe and looked down to find the exact location of the horrible sight she remembered with so much terror so she could show it to Dr. Barraya. Lala pointed at the noticeable spot on her breast.

God, it's even bigger than I thought it was, Lala silently gasped.

Dr. Barraya leaned in to take a closer look. She paused for several long moments as she studied the spot. She turned to the cabinet next to her, took a pair of latex gloves out of a dispenser, and put them on.

"I'm going to touch it," Dr. Barraya said. "Let me know if this hurts."

Oh, god, Lala thought. *Please, just let me die now.*

Dr. Barraya gently ran her index finger on the lump. She picked something up off of Lala's skin and rubbed it between her index finger and her thumb.

"I think that's jam," she finally said. "I would say, strawberry."

"Jam?" Kenny said. "Seriously?"

"Yeah, the delicious stuff you gave me last night, so thanks fer nuthin', pal."

"Seriously? Jam?"

"Okay, in my defense, I found out in one hellish week that my husband had stage four stomach cancer that had spread to his bones and lungs. I'm a little skittish vis-à-vis that particular disease."

They were walking back along the Seine to the apartment building because it was a beautiful day and, as Lala kept repeating, "I'm alive! You're alive! We're alive! *Marchons!*"

And then she began singing *La Marseillaise*, all the lyrics of which she had memorized once upon a time, in her less-than-stellar French accent and less-than-stellar singing voice. But what Lala lacked in authentic Gallic enunciation and pleasing tonal delivery, she more than made up for in pure *joie de vivre*.

"*Allons, enfants de la patrie, le jour de gloire est arrivé!* Come on, bubbeleh, sing it with me! You know the words, right?"

"Of course I do," Kenny grunted, nodding at the staring

passersby with an apologetic expression.

"*Contre nous, de la tyrannie!* Can you sing? You have to sing with me! Apparently I do something that's called 'singing in perfect thirds.' I have no idea what that means. I think I'm singing the right notes. Apparently I'm harmonizing. Who knew? Which, I've been told, doesn't sound all that great on its own."

"It really doesn't." Kenny pulled her into their courtyard. "Come on, let's get you upstairs. Don't you have a meeting to write or something? A meeting that doesn't involve singing?"

Lala kissed Kenny on both cheeks and skipped across the courtyard. She took the stairs by twos and made a tempting platter of cheeses and breads for the new writing partner who had been imposed on her. Which, at the moment, wasn't bothering her at all.

Lala had her front door open before Atticus could deliver a second knock.

"Hi, there, *mon cher* colleague! Come on in! We are writing together because we're both *alive*! YES! Let's do this, huh!"

Lala smiled warmly at Atticus. Her voice was like ice. The really deep kind in Antarctica.

"Terry wouldn't do that." *You smug little pisher*, she silently added.

If Atticus noticed that Lala was hoping her words might magically form into tiny little daggers that would keep flying and swooping to torment Atticus like villains in a twisted Disney movie, his convivial enthusiasm was working as a very effective diversion.

"Okay. Sure. I understand that. But, you know, just for the heck of it, what if he did? Because he and Frances get back together, right?"

"Yes, of course they do," Lala huffed. "They're in love. They'll always be in love."

"Right, which is so wonderful. I love that. What I'm thinking is maybe we try a scene in the beginning, right when Terry gets to Paris, after he's broken up with Frances? And she's desperately trying to get in touch with him, and he's ignoring her. And we see how hurt she is. Wow, this brie is really good."

"This film is a comedy, Atticus," Lala said, trying very hard not to sneer quite as much as she wanted to.

"Right, and I love that. It's hilarious in such a smart way."

Oh, jeez, Lala thought. *Don't even try to make me like you, because I swear I will get really pissed if it starts working.*

"I mean, I don't even miss having any fart jokes. I love it, and it's great, and I'm kinda just wondering if maybe Terry were kind of a shithead in the beginning—"

Terry would never be a shithead, Lala thought.

"Terry would never be a shithead," Lala said. "Never."

"Okay, but if he maybe were, maybe there could be a great payoff because maybe that could set us up to love him even more at the end, when he does get back together with Frances. I know we'd have to adjust part of Act Three, because he'd have a lot to make up to Frances, but maybe it could be really sweet?"

I do like really sweet . . . Wait a minute!

"No bathos!" Lala yelled. "Maybe a little pathos! But absolutely no bathos!"

"Right! No, I agree! Bathos! Yuck! Where did you get this crusty French bread? This is especially wonderful crusty French bread."

Man, is this kid playing me, or what? Lala thought. *And is it working? Should I give this little pisher's idea a try?*

"What's next? You tell me that, in addition to being very talented and smart, I'm also very attractive and I look much younger than I am?"

Atticus peered at Lala, looking confused.

"I kinda figured that wouldn't work with you. You seem way too smart for that. Sincerely, you do. And I also figured you'd clean my clock if I went for superficial instead of substantial."

Oh. Okay. Good point.

"Would that have worked? Because you really are very pretty and—"

Lala, before she could stop herself, guffawed.

"Oh, knock it off, you little pisher! And I am so annoyed at myself for laughing at the ridiculously charming way you delivered that comment. Fine, fine, fine! Let's give it a try. But I am not, *je répète*, I am NOT committing Terry to anything. Got it?"

Barf, Lala thought. *Damn it, this scene is looking really good.* Merde.

She had been standing behind Matthew for most of the day while he directed Clive and Rebecca, the superb New York-based actress who was playing Frances, a character that was a very thinly-disguised version of Lala's younger self. They were in an apartment that the production had rented to serve as the place where Terry crashes with an old college friend when he first gets to Paris.

And jeez, can that woman act. Her talent is a justified slap in the face to my own lack of thespianic ability. That's not a word. Thespianic. It's not, but it should be.

Rebecca went in to give Clive's character a desperate kiss, and Clive put his outstretched arm up to stop her from coming any closer. Matthew slapped his hand on his thigh.

"Cut!" he said. "Excellent work, you two! Okay, let's take a break."

The crew applauded with spontaneous enthusiasm.

Okay, okay, Lala thought. *No particular need to rub my nose in it. I generally have a fairly acute sense of when I'm entirely wrong.*

Rebecca and Clive hugged each other, and then turned to Lala and Matthew, and Atticus, who was standing behind them at the craft services table shoving one granola bar after another into his mouth virtually whole, and blew them all a kiss.

Matthew turned around to look at Lala with the nervous questioning of a beagle who had eaten her usual breakfast and lunch and who feared, as the sun set, that perhaps this might be the day that her devoted mama decided to not provide her with her usual dinner.

"Is it okay?" he asked her.

"Oy vey. It's great, and you know it."

Matthew jumped out of his director's chair and grabbed Lala and danced her around in a hug that grew into a trio when Atticus ran over, spewing bits of unchewed oat and nut as he moved, and tried to circle Matthew and Lala with his arms.

"I just really love working with you two," Atticus said through far too many organic snack items.

It came out as, "Rm mss lff wrrrr" followed by a series of unnerving coughs that made Lala wonder if she still knew how to properly execute a Heimlich.

"I can't take credit for this," Lala said. "It was Atticus's idea."

"So?" Atticus sputtered. He seemed to have cleared his mouth of food, if the copious crumbs that covered his jacket were reliable evidence. Lala and Matthew watched with a lingering bit of concern as Atticus swallowed loudly and dramatically several times. "You wrote just about all the dialogue." He frantically swept his hands on his jacket to get the chomping debris off. "I eat when I'm nervous."

"Right there with ya, pumpkin," Lala said. "And, P.S., dialogue is bupkes without a great idea. Ideas? Not always my strongest suit. I appreciate you, Atticus. I really do."

They finished shooting just a little more than an hour after they took that last break, and it was early enough in the day for Lala to be able to call David in California, no matter how much she stalled.

"*Merde*," she said, glancing at her watch. She was sitting on a bench with Clive facing the Seine and the back of Notre Dame at the end of the street from her apartment. They had walked from the day's location. Clive had invited Lala to dinner, but she asked for a rain check so she could get some work done tonight. Her new novel was turning out to be a lot of fun, and she looked forward to spending a few hours on it before she went to sleep. As a compromise, because they both had to eat, Lala had taken Clive to a little sandwich shop she had found on one of her walks, and they had gotten brie sandwiches and Diet Cokes, because, as Lala announced, "sometimes you just need a fizzy low-cal drink, y'know?"

"Too late to call David?" Clive asked.

"No, plenty of time," Lala admitted. "Okay, let's change the subject."

"I had no idea I loved Diet Coke so much," Clive said.

"You know, there's something I've been meaning to ask you. Your manager?"

"Yup," Clive said. He nodded vigorously, smiled, and took a big bite of his sandwich.

"Was he in prison?"

"No," Clive said. "Why do you ask?"

"He made a reference to a grand jury at our first meeting."

"Oh, no. He's a bit melodramatic. He had to go to traffic school once when we were in LA"

"Oh. Okay. Well, I was also wondering . . . Is he just grumpy round me?"

"Oh, goodness, no. He's that way with everyone," Clive assured her.

"Well, what is he, in the Witness Relocation Program? Or he's a spy or something? And that grumpy persona is just a character he's using to be undercover?"

"No," Clive said. He chuckled and took a big swig of Diet Coke.

"I . . . Well, maybe you can guess what my next question is?"

"Why do I keep such an unpleasant person around?"

"Umm," Lala began. She paused. "In a nutshell, yeah."

Clive took apart what was left of his sandwich and studied it as though the bread and cheese and lettuce and tomatoes and

Dijon mustard offered the key to all the riddles of the ages. He spoke to Lala without looking at her.

"I don't want to tell you about my manager."

"Why not?" Lala asked.

"I'm afraid it's going to hit way too close to home."

Oy, Lala thought. *And I had to ask.*

There was a pause in their conversation, and then Clive looked at Lala again. Lala studied his expression.

"Are you looking at me like you're the Ghost of Christmas Future and I'm Ebenezer Scrooge?"

"Yes, that's actually exactly what I'm doing."

"Damn it. You're literate. And you're a movie star. Damn. And you're adorable. Damn, damn, damn."

"And I love women of a certain age." Clive leaned over and gave Lala a relatively chaste peck on the cheek.

"That's the title of my next novel," Lala told him. "And the character based on you is being skewered in the manuscript, trust me."

"Ohh, I love being skewered. Can I play him in the movie version?"

Lala laughed. "What am I gonna say? No?" She put her head on his shoulder for a moment, and just as quickly lifted it again. "Fuck it. I can't let it go. Tell me about your manager."

Clive sighed.

"If you insist. Garrett is my aunt's widower. She died just a few years after they were married. He never got over it. That was decades ago. He completely changed. He was a sweet guy before he lost her. I let him think he's my manager. I don't really need a manager at this point, but I take him most everywhere with me when I'm conducting business. It gives him something to do. He's so alone."

Lala put her sandwich down on her lap and put her head in her hands.

Don't cry, she thought. *Your face gets so red and puffy when you cry. Really, much more than might be considered normal.*

"God, you are a sweet man," she said through her fingers. She lowered her hands. "But . . . but . . . doesn't his . . . well, you know . . . his remarkably unpleasant attitude cost you work?"

Now it was Clive's turn to guffaw.

"Oh, you darling, naïve woman-of-a-certain-age. Of course it doesn't. I'm a fucking movie star."

They both chuckled and smiled and didn't feel the need to say much else as they sat for a few more minutes to finish their sandwiches. Lala insisted that Clive leave her at the end of her street and not walk her all the way to her door.

"I can't flirt with you anymore today, Clive. I just can't. I feel like I'm back in college. And I'm liking that feeling. I have to call time-out on this. At least for today. Okay?"

Lala kissed him on both cheeks, lingering a moment too long on each, and sauntered up her street, turning once to see if he was watching her walk away, seeing that he was, and waving and smiling with an insouciant wink.

He probably can't see my fetching little wink anyway, Lala thought by way of an excuse for continuing to flirt with the sexy movie star.

She pivoted back toward her building and managed to resist a churning urge to turn around yet another time.

Okay, so, when I get home, I'll . . . I wonder if Clive's still watching me . . . Stop that! Okay, let's change the subject. David. Mon cher David, David, David. I have got to think of something more creative than "Busy on set, bisous, bisous, bisous." I'm suddenly inspired by my new novel? That's actually true. File that for future use. I'm walking around Paris every moment I'm not on set or not writing or not sleeping and I wish you were here to enjoy this beautiful city with me? Also true on all counts. Filed. I've hit my head and lost my memory, who are you and why do you want to Skype with me?

While Lala was still musing, she walked into the courtyard and saw Kenny being berated by a young woman. As she got closer, she saw that he had a small bowl clutched in his left hand, which was bent behind his back to hide what he was holding. The young woman was dressed immaculately if in a somewhat clichéd fashion in a suit that was most probably an actual vintage Chanel. Her jet-black hair was closely cropped and her pale, pinched face was surrounded by tight curls. But for the huffing tirade that was spewing from her bright red lips, she might have been very attractive. She was yelling in rapid French, and Lala couldn't make out many of the individual words.

Did she just say . . . yeah, no, other than the ones that are also words in English that she's just saying in French with her prissy little French accent, I'm getting nothing here, Lala thought.

She didn't pause to debate her options. Largely because she couldn't think of more than one. She quickly crossed the courtyard and got right in front of Kenny, positioning herself between him and his tormentor. She stuck out her hand.

"Lala Pettibone. *Nous sommes nous rencontrés?*"

Okay, not the most innovative dialogue, but I'm working on the fly here. And I'm working on the fly in French. So I think I deserve to be cut rather a large swath of slack.

The young woman visibly softened in response to Lala's words. Which meant she had gone from looking like a prison warden dealing with a jailbreak to a prison librarian dealing with a severely overdue book.

"Ohhh," the young woman oozed. "Madame Pettibone! Our American. How lovely to meet you."

And we immediately switch to English because my French accent is obviously so entirely for shit. And how is it that she's hitting every consonant in my name with quite so much aggression? That's not what the French do. It's Puh-teee-boh, babe.

Lala turned and opened the circle to include Kenny. She immediately saw that he had both his hands back in front of him, and she was relieved that he had grabbed the opportunity of her intended distraction to stash a bowl that was, for some reason, strictly forbidden.

"I am Celestine Barrault. My father and I are honored to be

your hosts."

"Then you are exactly the person I wanted to speak with," Lala said with forced conviviality. "Please convey to your father, as well, that I couldn't be happier with my accommodations. And Kenny and his grandfather have been absolutely wonderful to me. I appreciate them tremendously."

Celestine wrinkled her nose and pursed her lips. She gave Kenny a curt little nod, and then, while still wrinkling her nose in a royally disdainful fashion, spoke to Lala with unctuousness that could rival Uriah Heep's.

"How nice. Well, Madame . . ."

And here she paused.

". . . Pettt-eeeettttt-BOWWWNNN. I won't keep you."

Celestine turned on her white and black patent leather kitten heels and clip-clapped out over the cobblestones. Lala and Kenny were silent as they diligently listened to the sound of her footsteps continue down the sidewalk and disappear into the ether. And then they burst out laughing.

"What the fuck was that, Kenny? And where's the bowl? In your butt crack?"

"Yeah, more or less," Kenny wheezed through short, rapid bursts of cackles.

Lala stopped chortling. She saw a quick, sudden movement in the doorway leading to the small garden directly behind the building.

"Is that cat feral?" she whispered.

Kenny was immediately silent and unmoving. His response was barely audible.

"She was. She's been letting me pet her."

"I need to think. Let's go to my apartment."

As calmly and quietly as possible, they made their way out of the courtyard to the staircase leading to Lala's apartment. Once inside, Lala turned to Kenny and spoke with urgency.

"Have you seen other cats in that garden?"

"Yup," Kenny said. "I leave food out for them. Madame

Defarge suspects something, I'm sure."

"We need humane traps. And we need to see if any are tame and if they are, we need to find homes for them. And we need to get them all spayed and neutered. And we need to get the feral ones into a safe situation so we can maintain a managed colony for them."

And I think I just found another supremely sympathetic reason why I'll be much too busy to Skype with David very often.

At Minimum, You Should At Least Try, N'est-Ce Pas?

Kenny went downstairs to the restaurant to make sure his grandfather and the chefs and servers had it all under control. He came back with an enormous Caesar salad.

They put the large bowl in the middle of Lala's small dining table and ate directly from it.

Lala told Kenny all about her life as an animal rescuer.

"The cats are lucky I found you," he said.

"Well," she responded, "let's hope we can do something to help them together. Without Fifi de ForFuckSake catching on. Did you make this dressing, too?" It was a light ranch concoction that Lala already adored.

Kenny nodded, his mouth too full to respond verbally. Lala's mouth was also full, but that wasn't going to stop her from gabbing.

"Damn. We are manufacturing and marketing all your stuff, I swear to god. Okay, okay, okay, I really want to go out and just grab that semi-feral kitten and just bring her in here because I've seen her and now it's personal, and I don't want her to spend another night outside, cold and afraid, but, *MERDE,* that's not a good idea because if we don't succeed in catching her, she'll be spooked and she'll never come near us again, and it's too late to get humane traps tonight, so we should—"

"Lala, I think it's either got to be eat or pontificate, or it may get dangerous in terms of the possibility of you choking."

"Yeah, you're probably right."

They finished the salad, and Kenny rushed downstairs to get some homemade lime sorbet for them to share. During the few minutes he was gone, Lala fretted about the cats and about what the time it was in California because she was having trouble subtracting nine hours. When Kenny ran back in, she jumped out of her seat.

The sorbet was delicious.

"Don't tell me you made this. We are going to have a food empire, *mon cher*."

They made a plan to find humane traps the next day so they could start trapping the following night, and to figure out where to take the cats for spaying and neutering. Wonderful David, Lala felt sure, would be a big help with this.

"Good humane rescue work, Kenny," Lala said at her door as she bid him goodnight. "You're a natural at this. You saw the cats, you stepped in to help. Apparently you were concerned that I wouldn't adore you enough for your expert cooking and your humbling grasp of the beautiful French language and your excellent accent and all the warmth and kindness you've shown me. *Dors bien, mon cher*. Hey, do you like men or women? I'm a natural yenta, and if you're not seeing anyone, I'm going to make it my mission, along with saving the cats, to find the perfect match for you."

"Men," Kenny said. "And I'm currently single."

"Not for long," Lala said, and she winked at him.

Lala changed into a pair of sweats and a cotton sweater. She put on the television for the background soundtrack of her life, and she got comfortable on the sofa with her laptop.

I miss David, Lala thought. Merde, merde, merde, *I miss him so much.*

She focused on the TV screen, where a panelist on a talk show was, as far as Lala could tell, either furious about the bottled water that was being provided in the green room or about election tampering in Monaco.

Fuck it, Lala thought. *Sometimes you just have to make yourself vulnerable to the uncertainties of love. Plus, I'm feeling exceptionally horny.*

She flipped open her laptop and then clicked on her e-mail, intending to write to David to see if this was a good time to Skype. There was an e-mail from her Auntie Geraldine waiting for her, with a lot of shouting in the subject line.

EMERGENCY! SKYPE WITH ME IMMEDIATELY!

Oh, no, Lala thought. *No. Please. Don't let anyone be dead. Don't let anyone be sick.*

Lala's hand shook as she tried to get the mouse to bring up the Skype connection. It was probably no slower than usual, but it felt like eons to her. At last, she was able to smack the cursor on the number to connect with Geraldine.

Please pick up. What time did she send that e-mail? Please, please, please be there.

The screen of the laptop flickered as Geraldine answered on her computer. She was sitting at her desk with a large mug of coffee and a bagel. Petunia was squished onto her lap and was whimpering for a taste of breakfast.

"Hush, sweetheart," Geraldine said. She kissed the old dog on the forehead. "There you are," she then said in an accusing tone to Lala.

"Omigod!" Lala yelped. "What's wrong? Is anyone sick? What's wrong!"

"No one's sick," Geraldine said, looking at the screen as though her cyber conversation partner had completely lost her mind. "What makes you think anyone's sick?"

"YOU WROTE 'EMERGENCY'!" Lala yelled. Geraldine frowned, and Petunia tilted her head in the universal hound symbol of confusion.

"It *is* an emergency," Geraldine huffed. "You have been in touch with David with less and less frequency, and he is very concerned about that. Do not tell him I told you that. He asked me not to tell you."

"THAT'S NOT AN EMERGENCY! ILLNESS AND DEATH ARE AN EMERGENCY!"

"STOP SHOUTING!" Geraldine shouted.

Petunia grabbed the opportunity provided by the loud ker-fuffle to snatch the bagel out of Geraldine's grasp.

"Petunia!" Geraldine said. "Bad girl!"

Good girl, Lala thought. *One for our side.*

Geraldine turned her attention back to being annoyed with her adopted niece.

"I am not here to debate the definition of emergency with you. Power outages are emergencies. Running out of gas is an emergency. Eating too much delicious ice cream last night after seeing a movie with your wonderful husband and waking up feeling bloated but still eating, well, in this case, half a bagel for breakfast can be considered, on some level, an emergency of sorts. If I had had any idea you were going to be so excitable, I would have used a different word. Why aren't you talking to David every day? When are you coming home? We should be planning your wedding! WHAT IS GOING ON?"

"I am very busy, Auntie Geraldine," Lala spat through clenched teeth. "Filming is very exhausting. I had to write a new scene."

It was clear to Lala from Geraldine's facial reaction that her aunt thought she was kidding. Unsure what else to say in her inadequate defense, Lala waited for Geraldine's verbal reaction to her barrage of bullshit.

"*One* scene?" Geraldine finally said.

"It was a complicated scene," Lala sniffed.

I guess I don't need to add that I had a writing partner who worked on it with me . . .

"I was just about to see if David is available to Skype when I was shanghaied by your exaggerated and misleading subject line."

"Good!" Geraldine said. "You call him right now!"

"I will," Lala said. "I'll do it 'cause I wanna do it. Not because you told me too."

Geraldine gave the screen an *okay, now you have just got to be kidding* look.

Yeeeaaahhh, that was pretty ridiculous of me, Lala thought.

Geraldine hoisted up Petunia, who had fallen asleep, by her armpits and wagged the beagle, who did not wake up, at the screen. "Tell mama we are watching her. Tell her that we will no longer put up with her crap. Tell her we will call her on her crap, non-stop. Right, my sweet little Petunia?"

"Yeah, yeah," Lala grumbled. "Hug them all for me, okay? And you and Monty hug each other from me, 'kay?"

"Will do!" Geraldine said with smug confidence and exaggerated cheerfulness and assurance that she had won the argument she instigated. "Love you!"

"Yeah, yeah," Lala said.

She clicked off the connection and sunk back on the couch.

Merde, she thought. *I really miss David. And I also really need to expand my vocabulary of French swear words.*

Lala violently shook her head in an attempt to stop herself from thinking too much before she acted.

Great, she thought. *Now I just feel like I'm going to barf.*

She typed a short e-mail to David and hit "Send" before she had a chance to second-guess herself. Then she reread it in her Sent folder and cringed because there were two typos. Before she had much time to silently berate herself for not proofreading, a dinging sound loudly requested her presence in the Skype interchange.

When Lala saw David sitting at the desk in his apartment at UC Davis, she burst into tears. He was wearing the sport coat she had bought him when they took a short vacation to Ventura.

"What's wrong?" David asked. "Lala, darling, why are you crying?"

"I love you so much and I miss you so much and I'm really busy with the film, and I can't really do math when time is involved because it's not a ten-based system, and I keep getting confused about the difference between California and France, and I've also been on set just about every day, and when I'm not on set I've been walking all around Paris because it's so beautiful, and I wish you were here to see it all with me . . ."

And you're going to die one day, she thought. *And I just don't think I could bear that . . .*

". . . and there are feral cats in the garden behind the building where I'm living and I have to make them a managed colony and at least one of them is probably tame—"

"You and the cat looked at each other, didn't you?" David asked.

"Yup," Lala said. "Gimme a minute, okay?"

She buried her face in the blanket next to her on the couch and gasped and groaned and finally forced herself to stop crying. She popped her head back up and smiled weakly at David.

"That took longer than I expected," she said. "David, it's still afternoon there, yes? Can you maybe check if any of your colleagues there know any rescuers in Paris? I need humane traps, and I need to get all the cats fixed."

"Absolutely," David said. "I'll get the information, sweetheart. Please try not to be so sad, okay? I'm sure someone here has a contact in Paris. I know you'll get that tame cat inside and I know you'll find her a wonderful home. Everything's going to be okay."

Lala looked at David sitting there with that sweet, guileless face of his. She remembered how happy he was when she ducked into that small store because she had seen that gorgeous jacket in the window. She remembered walking back to the hotel in Ventura with David and their then four dogs, because her precious Yootza was still alive. She remembered—vividly, as though she had been transported back in time and to another continent—ripping each other's clothes off and having spectacular sex right after they had waited with ever growing impatience for the dogs to settle down in their beds and fall asleep because Lala had a "hard time really letting loose in the *eros* department when the beasts are conscious in the same room and are often given to staring at us. Unblinkingly staring at us, which is especially creepy."

Apparently she had been sitting there in a reverie for several minutes.

"Lala? Honey? Shoot, I think the screen froze . . ."

"No, no, I'm sorry, David. I was just having sex with you in my mind. In Ventura, specifically."

"Could you please write up an extensive list of colorful, emphatic, and intellectually-admirable French swear words and phrases for me?"

"Just use '*merde.*' Trust me, it's the easiest way."

Lala and Kenny were on their way to meet with a French veterinarian who had studied at Tufts Veterinary School with one of David's fellow visiting professors at UC Davis. The French veterinarian had recently added a small animal rescue foundation to her medical practice.

"It's like she's the French me. I mean, the French me if she's also short and slightly out of her mind, and minus the ability to actually understand science and math," Lala had said when David had Skyped with her that morning to give her Dr. Veronique Dermond's contact information. It was the first time since she had arrived in Paris that they had seen and spoken to each other more than once in a 24-hour period. It had broken Lala's heart to be reminded twice in such a relatively short time how much she loved David and how constantly terrified she was that he would die and leave her as her first husband had died and left her.

Dr. Dermond's clinic was in the Eighth Arrondissement. Lala and Kenny were walking along the Champs-Élysées toward the Arc de Triomphe. Lala saw that Ladurée, the classic, world-famous emporium, was coming up on their left.

"Is it me," she said, "or are *macarons* . . ."

Being the self-proclaimed worshipper and guardian of words that she was, Lala pronounced the name of the dessert as a French person would . . . if that French person had a French accent that was for shit.

". . . just as boring as a treat can be? I do not get the fascination. They're dry. And kind of tasteless. Or is it just me? I have never craved *mah-cah-roh*—"

"Lala," Kenny said, "please just call them 'macaroons,' okay? Please. Your accent is driving me nuts. And I do agree that they are highly overrated."

Lala whacked Kenny on the back of his head with great affection and giggled. They turned left just before getting to the overwhelming flow of merging streets and traffic leading into and around the Arc de Triomphe.

"Man," Lala said, "every sentient being in Paris should be grateful that I have not gotten behind the wheel of a car here. Look at that. How do they manage not to smack into each other?"

Just as Lala noticed it, Kenny also saw a little girl walking up ahead leading an Irish Wolfhound by the leash who dwarfed her. The two of them skipped through an archway just a few buildings ahead of where Lala and Kenny were marching.

"Ohhhh," they both said in joyous appreciation.

"I have a good feeling that we're in the right place," Lala said.

"Yup," Kenny said.

They followed where the little girl had gone through the archway and checked the first door they saw. A small plaque outside read: "Dr. Veronique Dermond, *Clinique Vétérinaire*."

Kenny grabbed the door and they rushed in together. The waiting room was beautifully jammed.

"Ohhhh," they both said. Lala sought out and found and smiled at the little girl and the Irish Wolfhound, who were sitting together in a corner. The little girl was perched on a chair and had her feet sticking straight out, resting on her dog's head. The large beast was stretched out on the floor next to his girl. A long-haired Chihuahua was valiantly humping the big dog's leg, a gesture which no one, including the Wolfhound, noticed or commented on. Lala, smiling like someone who might be dangerously happy, approached the little girl.

"*Votre chien est absolument adorable!*"

Everyone in the room, including, Lala thought for a moment, the animals, chuckled.

"You're from the United States!" the little girl said.

Oh, for god's sake, Lala thought. *My accent is really that bad? I swear, I don't hear it . . .*

"Yeah," Lala said.

"I love New York!" the little girl continued. "And Washington, DC and Seattle and San Francisco!"

"Wow, you're English is really good," Lala said. "And I shouldn't have used the formal form of 'you' with a young person like you, should I?"

"No!" the little girl said with surpassing sweetness and enthusiasm. "You should use '*tu*' with someone my age! That's why we were all laughing!"

"Okey-doke," Lala said. "Anyway, your dog is adorable. And I really like that English has only one form of 'you'."

"I do as well!" the little girl said.

Her Wolfhound had not moved during their conversation, and the Chihuahua was still madly humping away. A sturdy young woman wearing a lab coat opened the door that lead from the waiting room to the inner part of the clinic. She stood in the doorway and scanned the room. She waved to Lala.

"*Madame Puh-tee-boh?*"

"*Oui*," Lala began, "*je suis . . .*"

Fuck it, Lala thought.

"Uh huh. That's me."

The young woman walked a few quick steps to Lala and held out her hand.

"Veronique Dermond. A pleasure. My American colleague told me all about you. I'm afraid I've gotten quite a bit busier than I expected today. Please accept my apologies."

"No, no, *pas du* . . . not at all," Lala said.

"Can I ask you to perhaps go next door to the bistro? Please tell Vincent that I sent you. My wife and I will join you as soon as we see the patients."

"That sounds great! I love a nice bistro."

"Excellent," Veronique said. She pointed to Kenny. "You are Kenny? So nice to meet you. We will see you soon, yes?"

She smiled at them both and then motioned for an elderly woman, who was carrying an equally elderly looking cat wrapped up in a blanket like a baby, to follow her into the clinic.

"Ohhhh," Lala and Kenny said.

"She is so nice!" Lala gushed.

"Nice!" Kenny echoed.

"Your name means 'little good'!" the Irish Wolfhound's young guardian said.

What? Lala thought.

"I . . . it . . . it does?"

It does, Lala thought. *How have I not thought of that before? Little good. Always better than no good at all, I guess.*

"Okay, Kenny, in my defense, it's not like I spent my life walking around pronouncing my name as if I were a Parisian, okay? *Peh-tee-bown* doesn't bring to mind the French words for little and good, okay? Though I have to confess, now that I've heard it, I can't fathom how it never occurred to me before."

They were sitting at a table for four at the window of *Les Petits Fromages* next to the veterinary clinic. Their host, Vincent, had spoken to them in the French of a sailor in Marseille who had decided to imitate Professor Henry Higgins's lesson for Eliza Doolittle that involved talking with a mouthful of marbles. Lala couldn't catch anything after Vincent said, "*Bienvenue!*" so Kenny had to simultaneously translate in their own mini-version of the United Nations.

"He went to high school with Veronique's father in Provence. He says she's like a daughter to him. He wants us to try a special bottle of Sancerre."

And now they were loving that special bottle of white wine, which Vincent had just brought to the table and opened, and for which Lala thanked him profusely. In French.

"*Merci mille fois, Monsieur. Vous êtes trop gentil!*"

Vincent smiled and winked at her and had a blank look in his eyes that clearly indicated that everything she had just said had been Greek to him. Lala scrunched her face up as she watched Vincent toddle back to the kitchen.

"Kenny, I would just like to point out that my current boyfriend, who is fluent in French and a bunch of other languages, complimented my accent when he met me, and I sang *Hier Encore* with him at a karaoke night, and also when I spoke French with him after we—"

"Oh, well, okay, Lala, obviously he was trying to fuck you. And I say that with all due affection. Wait . . . He heard you sing and he still wanted to fuck you?"

Lala snorted a laugh and kicked Kenny under the table, just as Veronique and a very petite blonde woman, who was probably shorter than Lala, came in. Vincent rushed over to them and embraced them both. There was much kissing on both cheeks and many smiles. Lala beamed at the women as they approached the table. They were very quickly followed by Vincent, bearing another bottle of Sancerre.

"You all are so nice!" Lala crowed. "And I haven't even

officially met your wife yet, and I already like her! And I would say that all in French, but you'd probably all have to try to not laugh, and dear Vincent wouldn't understand me! How do you say 'exclamation points' in French?"

Veronique introduced her wife, Camille, while Vincent ran off and came back in what seemed like no time with four plates covered with omelets and salad and round little *pommes frites*.

"Omigod, this food is delicious!" Lala said. "Kenny, can you translate for me so Vincent knows that I think he's amazing? You're both veterinarians? That is SO cool! WOW! I have to tell you, I made a very brief visit to the Island of Lesbos. In college. During a generously populated make-out session at an off-campus house that was the closest I've ever come to participating in an actual orgy. After making out with Willis Daniels, my then-boyfriend, I spent the rest of the party mashing on Diane Delehanty. She was a senior, and I was a sophomore, and she was the star of the theatre department. My lips were numb for the better part of the next day. No one had any tops on, but that's about as far as it went, nudity-wise. I guess that makes me sound quite puritanical."

"No, not really," Veronique said.

"Not really even by French standards," Camille agreed.

Vincent made a huge chocolate soufflé for the table, and a big pot of very strong tea. Veronique had explained to him that Lala and Kenny would be helping *les chats*, and it was going to be a long night.

"I've got seven traps in our car," Camille told Lala and Kenny. "We'll drive you home. You have a place to keep the cats until tomorrow morning?" Lala nodded.

"They'll stay in my apartment." And just as she spoke, Lala was surprised that she suddenly gasped and started crying. "At least one of the cats is tame. Or she could be."

Camille took a tissue out of her purse and passed it to Lala. "You'll know what to do with her, I feel certain."

Lala dabbed at her eyes. "Thanks. She could be a boy. I swear, I can never tell with cats. I just don't get where the penises are supposed to be."

Veronique nodded and smiled. "I still have trouble with that."

Lala had her nearly empty wine glass in one hand and a full cup of tea in the other. She slugged back the rest of the wine and followed it with a caffeinated chaser.

"This wine is really tasty. And this tea is very strong. Which is clearly a very good thing."

"I am both hammered and wide-awake, which is an uneasy combination and one that, alas, I am not unfamiliar with," Lala whispered to Kenny. They were sitting squished behind a corner door where they had a view of the three humane traps they had set up in the garden. "I remember being at Downey House drinking beer my senior year and suddenly remembering that I had forgotten I had a linguistics exam the next morning. So it was nothing but Diet Coke and cramming until I dragged myself to the test the next morning, bleary-eyed and functionally incoherent. P.S., I aced it. I really have to pee."

"Go, go, go," Kenny whispered. "I'll keep watch."

The evening which had started out so enthusiastically and supportively with the loaning of the humane traps and the delicious food and wine, had hit a major snag on the way to the actual rescuing of the feral cats when, at an hour that was entirely too late for anyone to be out and about on a Monday, regardless of how pinched and bloodless they might seem and regardless of how many comparisons to actual vampires they might inspire, Celestine Barrault, the building owner's dreaded daughter, had appeared at the building in a lather which had been inspired by an Amazon France order that was intended as a toadying gift from Celestine for a wealthy tenant on the top floor being accidentally delivered to Celestine's home . . . a mistake which was based entirely on her own flawed entry of the details of the desired transaction online, but one that she was determined to blame on Kenny, despite his total lack of any association whatsoever with the ordering or delivery.

Luckily, Lala and Kenny had gotten the traps secured in their hidden locations just before Celestine's abnormally high boots came clacking across the cobblestones. The volume of her voice was not modified in any consideration of the late hour.

"Kenny!" she brayed. "*Où es-tu?*"

Lala gasped and pulled Kenny off to an opposite side of the building where Celestine couldn't see them.

"You two *tutoyer* each other? You use the familiar form of 'you' with that harpy?"

"She calls me '*tu.*' I, of course, have to call her '*vous,*'" Kenny explained.

"That bitch," Lala hissed. "That aristocratic hypocritical *bitch*. Okay, no time for righteous indignation. I'm going to get her out of here. You man the barricades. Let's pretend we're in the French Revolution."

Lala stomped out into the courtyard and, without consciously deciding to do so, affected what she imagined was the tone of a stern aunt, a way of speaking which she, as a demanding but also incredibly indulgent aunt to her actual and informally-adopted nieces and nephews, had never in fact used in real life.

I'll just pretend I'm Geraldine, and Celestine is me, and I'm really pissed off at her, Lala thought. *Thankfully, there will be no actual acting involved in this scene.*

"Mademoiselle Celestine! People are trying to sleep!"

Celestine wobbled on her heels and narrowed her eyes at Lala.

She's drunk, too, Lala thought. *Okay, good. Even playing field here.*

"Pardon me, Madame," Celestine said. "Would you possibly know where Kenny is?"

"I imagine he's *asleep*, as is the rest of the civilized world. Come on, you're buying me a drink."

They ended up at the bar in a small hotel two streets over. The atmosphere was dark and romantic. Lala found herself wishing she could be there with David. Or Terrence. She quickly dismissed the thought and ordered them very dirty vodka martinis, all of the communication with the attractive young bartender being done wordlessly. Lala pointed dramatically at the nearest vodka bottle, and then mimed tossing large green olive after large green olive in the two martini glasses she had seized from behind the bar.

"*Elle veut dire*—," Celestine began to say to the bemused bartender.

"Zip it, Celestine!" Lala snapped. "We've got a universal language goin' on here! Back off!"

They drank a round of delicious martinis while Lala listened to Celestine blather on and on about how difficult it was to find the right kind of people to work for you. Lala did her best to keep her eyes open and to suppress a desperate impulse to smack the obnoxious young woman.

"Look, I'm going to have to jump in here and state, unequivocally, that Kenny and his grandfather are wonderful and heavenly, and if you don't start appreciating how lucky you are to have them, I'm going to hire them away from you and bring them to Los Angeles with me."

Celestine, who was at that point ever drunker than Lala, cackled. Her voice in amusement, Lala reflected, recalled to mind the overwhelming enthusiasm of feeding time at the zoo.

"We will be agreeing to disagree, shall we, Madame Pettt-eeeettttt-BOWWWNNN?"

"Oh, for god's sake," Lala snapped. She raised two fingers to the bartender and nodded frantically. "Call me Lala. Unless you're able to make my first name, which even I know is in fact a doubled-up actual musical note, sound clipped and curt and cutting."

Lala was a bit chapped to see that Celestine was too drunk to appreciate how much Lala was hoping to convey her contempt by way of a small degree of subtlety. As in, Celestine would know that Lala couldn't stand her, but quoting Lala's actual words wouldn't be sufficient evidence that Lala had actually said that she couldn't stand her. Instead, the vodka seemed to be resulting in Celestine thinking she and Lala were new best friends. There was now some burping and some giggling coming from Celestine, all of which sounded even more blood-chilling than the recent loud cackling.

"*Si tu veux,*" Celestine cooed.

"Whoa!" Lala snapped. "Whoa whoa whoa whoa whoa. I'm the senior in the hierarchy here, young missy. I decide when we *tutoyer*. Which *we* do not. I do. You don't. *Tu comprends?* I am *vous* to you, got it?"

Though Lala would have readily admitted she didn't have an actual plan when she hauled Celestine away from the courtyard, the plan that had appeared worked quite well. Celestine seemed to have forgotten that she was even looking for Kenny when Lala escorted her into a cab to go home.

"*Lala, à bientôt! C'était très sympa de boire un verre avec vous!*"

"Yeah, yeah," Lala grumbled. "Not if I see you first."

When Lala got back to the courtyard, Kenny reported that there had been some suspicious sniffing of the traps by a few of the cats, but none of them had taken the smelly tuna bait. So they sat together and waited. And Lala complained. And drank from a large bottle of warm Diet Coke that she had found in the pantry of the restaurant when she interrupted Kenny's grandfather's cigarette-and-demitasse fueled late night reflection on the state of the world via his reading of Machiavelli's *The Prince* at a table near the window of the restaurant, upon which Lala had tapped, startling the old man and causing him to spill his demitasse, and, once she had gotten his attention, where she did a dramatic mimed rendition of someone dying of thirst.

"She said it was your fault the package wasn't delivered correctly," Lala told Kenny.

"And of course I knew nothing about the package. *Rien.* I

have no idea what she's talking about."

"And of course that's what I assumed. I swear, it drives me nuts when people don't take responsibility for their actions. Nuts. I see red. I contemplate assault and battery. You need to pee?"

"Nope. I'm good."

By the time Lala returned from the bathroom in her apartment, there had been activity. Kenny was silently jumping up and down with delight. He raised three fingers.

Three? Lala silently mouthed, and Kenny nodded like a bobble-head.

"In two traps," he whispered. "Let's go."

He had already covered the front of the traps that had been tripped with the flap of the large towel that had a slit cut in it so that the handle of the trap was easily accessible. Kenny grabbed the trap that had two cats in it, and Lala picked up the other one. They made their way up the stairs and into Lala's apartment. Because they were in a covered space inside the traps, the cats were silent, their fear eased by the darkness. They would stay in their traps until the next morning, when Lala and Kenny took them to Veronique and Camille's clinic to be spayed or neutered, vaccinated, and treated for fleas, and to have one of the tips of their ears docked so that fellow rescuers could identify them as already having been trapped and fixed.

Lala and Kenny placed the traps in a corner of the living room where the hardwood floor was covered with newspapers. They sat on the couch at the other end of the room and each had a big glass of milk.

"There's no chance I'm going to fall asleep," Lala said. "This milk won't help me sleep," Lala said.

"I think it's making me feel more awake," Kenny said.

"Are you thinking what I'm thinking?"

"You're wondering if our tame cat is in the trap?"

"Bingo," Lala said. "We can't look. The light will upset them. We could shut off all the lamps and then look so they don't get upset. But then we couldn't see if she's in there."

They were both silent for a few minutes.

"Thoughts like these are going to keep me awake all night," Lala said. "All night of which there's maybe, what? Four hours left? Tops?"

They did not in fact sleep for anything more than a random moment here and there when they nodded off while watching *Les Feux de l'Amour*, which Kenny had never seen in English or French and which he dubbed "over-the-top to an almost delicious degree, 'almost' being the operative word." Kenny's grandfather drove them to the veterinary clinic the next morning before he opened the restaurant because, as he said in French and Kenny translated for Lala without her asking him to do so, "You both look like shit." To which Lala responded, "Kenny, I caught the *merde* part and I presumed the rest. Give me some credit."

While the cats were sedated, Lala and Kenny slept on the couches in Veronique and Camille's office.

The little tame cat had not been among the three they caught.

"If I had even slept half an hour last night, I wouldn't be able to sleep now because I'd be so upset about her not being safe. The only reason I can sleep now is because I'm crazed with exhaustion," Lala said just before she shut her eyes and lost consciousness.

"We'll get her tonight," Kenny said before he did the same.

Veronique woke them up when the cats were safely out of surgery. Camille drove Lala and Kenny home with the cats still asleep in their three separate carriers, which Veronique and Camille had lent to Lala and Kenny. The cats would rest, covered with towels to keep them peacefully in the dark, in Lala's apartment until nighttime. Then Lala and Kenny would release them back to the garden by the building. They were all deemed by the vets to be at least five years old. They would stay feral and would be best served by being in the garden they were already calling home.

The garden had high walls and was relatively safe for them,

Lala silently reflected as Camille drove them back.

"We need to build a shelter for them in the garden," Lala said aloud, though she had intended it to be just for herself.

She was sitting in the front passenger seat. Kenny was in the backseat wedged next to one of the carriers. The other two carriers were in the trunk of the hatchback. He leaned forward and put his chin on Lala's shoulder.

"Cruella de Vil won't let us do that," Kenny said.

"You're right," Lala said. "And we have to do something about that."

After they settled the cats in Lala's apartment, Kenny went to the restaurant to take over managing so his grandfather could catch an afternoon nap.

"He won't actually nap," Kenny told Lala. "He'll be in our apartment on my laptop, posting quotations from his favorite films on the Facebook group page he created, *Les Enfants du Paradis, et les Autres*."

"God, your granddad is adorable," Lala said. "Give him a big hug from me, 'kay?"

After Kenny left, Lala started to feel antsy almost immediately. She tried to do some writing, but determined that everything she was going to come up with that day was probably going to be, as she described it to the still slumbering kitties, "what I can only dub hyper-crappity crap, and I think I'm being charitable."

Lala went out and began a brisk walk by the Seine. After just a few energetic strides along the banks of the river, she missed a step and fell flat on her face.

Several people rushed over. There was much concern and many gracious offers of help, to which Lala responded that she was fine, if a bit entirely embarrassed.

Lala carefully shuffled herself over to a bench and sat down. She fished her phone out of her purse and called Clive.

"I need some distraction," she told him. "I'm suffering from *weltschmerz* and *ennui*. Plus, I just did an utterly ungainly pedestrian wipeout right by Notre Dame. Are you on set today?"

"As it happens, I just got back from an early morning shoot and I have the rest of the day off," Clive said.

"Want to go to the Pantheon with me?" Lala asked.

"I do want to go to the Pantheon with you. But tell me one thing."

"Of course."

"Are you flirting with me, Madame Scribe?"

"No, I am definitely not, Sir Movie Star. Okay, yeah, maybe a little. But don't get any ideas."

"Dumas. What can I say? This man doesn't know it . . . I mean, he does know it if there's an afterlife, which I certainly hope there is because then maybe Alexandre and Terrence are enjoying a lovely sparkling *bev-raj*—if I may be so bold as to pronounce the word 'beverage' in my dreadful French accent with the only goal of amusing myself and without you making a face as though you've just caught a powerful whiff of old gym socks, thank you very much, Clive—together right now and are watching me effusing here . . . Anyway, he may or may not know that he saved my life during one utterly miserable summer in New York before I met Terrence. I lived in a fifth-floor walk-up with the bathtub in the kitchen and no air conditioning, and it was as humid as the tropics that August. I finally managed to get an unabridged version of *The Count of Monte Cristo* via inter-library loan from a branch in Queens, and I walked from my apartment on 64th and First to the main branch of the New York City Public Library on 42nd and Fifth, and you know I was covered in schvitz by the time I got there."

Clive, who had been signing autographs and posing for photos with an adorable foursome of elderly ladies from Phil-adelphia, did his best to indicate that he was staying engaged with Lala's heaving monologue by nodding and glancing toward her on occasion while he was multi-tasking by simultaneously charming the Pennsylvania women.

"Betty, you're lucky you're married, because if you weren't, well . . ."

"Ohhh, Clive," Betty cooed. "We just love your work so much."

"We just love *you* so much," Abigail added.

"I had just been very unceremoniously dumped by my boyfriend of two years," Lala continued. "I didn't know what I was doing with my life, and I was just on the cusp of realizing that I had no business trying to be an actress. And all fifteen hundred pages of the Count's travails immediately absorbed me and made me forget entirely about feeling sorry for myself. Man, did that guy survive a total *merde* storm, or what?"

"Yes, Lala, he sure did. Ladies, if you are ever in Los Angeles or London, I've listed my management company's phone number on your maps of the Paris metro system, right underneath my autograph, so you be sure to contact me so I can take you all out to lunch."

"Ohhh, *Clive!*" the women trilled as they scurried away, sounding rather charmingly like a female barbershop quartet at an assisted living facility.

Lala smiled at the women and waved to them.

"Bye, Ladies! Enjoy the crypts!"

She linked her arm in Clive's and they stared at the three resting places that shared a hallowed space in the Pantheon. Clive was contemplative and absorbing. Lala was beside herself. Her entire body remained on a low but clearly discernible level of jubilant, highly-strung vibration. Lala shook her head in awe and whispered an homage to those she revered.

"Is this a triumvirate, or what? Dumas. And Victor Hugo. It's Victor Hugo. I just . . . I . . . Victor Hugo. Right here. Dead. Victor Hugo. Wow. I mean . . . What can you say, except . . . Victor Hugo. *Les Misérables.* He *wrote* that. Wow. I . . . I . . . Wow."

"Lala, do you need some water or something?"

"And like Dumas and Hugo aren't enough? Zola? Émile Zola. He wrote *J'accuse*."

"Yes, he did," Clive said.

"His words helped get Alfred Dreyfus freed," Lala said.

Clive did his best to look at her without turning his head, feeling somehow, instinctively, that any excessive movement could send her over the edge right now. And if the twitching she was engaging in was any indication, he was right.

"Lala, I'm thinking maybe we should find a bench and sit down for just a few—"

"After the poor man had been falsely convicted and sentenced to life imprisonment on Devil's Island. 'The truth is on the march, and nothing shall stop it,' Zola wrote. This sepulcher is, like, mecca for devotion and words and justice, and I am profoundly moved and humbled, and I think I might be about to have an aneurysm. And if I do, this would not be the worst way to go."

"Okay," Clive said. "I'm giving you five more minutes here, and then I'm taking you outside to get some air."

Clive held the door open for Lala as they exited the Pantheon. They blinked in the bright sunshine after having been in the darkened interior of the building for so long.

"Shall we go to *Père Lachaise*?" Clive asked.

"Oh, god, yes. Today has somehow become all about death and mourning and memory and devotion, and that is somehow a-okay with me. Terrence and I went to *Père Lachaise* when we were here on our honeymoon. It was very romantic. Abelard and Héloïse are buried there. Together. Talk about undying love. Sheesh."

They walked to the nearest metro station and took the underground to the 20th Arrondissement. When they got out at the station for the cemetery, Clive grabbed Lala's hand and led her on a run up the stairs to the outside. They found the nearest gate leading into *Père Lachaise* and then followed the signs for the Conservation Center, where they picked up two maps of the graves. Clive scanned his copy and made an announcement.

"I know which one I want to see first."

He grabbed Lala's hand again and started them on a quick walk through the paths around the graves.

"Running would be disrespectful," Clive said. "But I am hearing a running soundtrack in my mind."

"I did suspect you were starting to think that we're in an Audrey Hepburn movie," Lala said. "That's not a complaint."

"Here it is," Clive said.

Lala looked at a bust of a man on top of a tall white marble base. There was a short, ornate wrought iron fence around it.

"Honoré de Balzac," Lala said. "*The Red and the Black*. My college colors. And one of the best novels ever written. In my forever-less-than humble opinion."

"I giggle every time I hear his name." Clive confessed, not sounding a bit guilty.

"Because it sounds like 'ball sack,' of course. You are such a boy." Lala consulted the map. "Where's Édith Piaf's grave?"

They found the great chanteuse's tombstone and stood close to each other in silence, both of them swaying a bit in an unsung rhythm of her signature song. Unsung until the humming started. And especially unsung when the singing began.

"*Non!*" Lala sang, "*rien de rien, non, je ne regrette rien!*"

"What in the hell!" Clive barked.

"I've been told I sing in perfect thirds, which doesn't—"

"Let's just be on our way, shall we?" Clive said. He took Lala's hand and led her away. "No need to disturb poor Edith's eternal repose."

They stopped at Sarah Bernhardt's grave and Marcel Proust's, and then they looked at each other, nodded in an agreement that required no words, and raced over to Oscar Wilde's mammoth tomb, where they stood in reverend awe of the great writer and whispered favorite quotations.

"I never travel without my diary. One should always have something sensational to read in the train."

"If I am occasionally a little over-dressed, I make up for it by being always immensely over-educated."

"I can resist anything except temptation."

"The only way to get rid of temptation is to yield to it."

"Fucking fabulous," Lala concluded.

"Fabulous as fuck," Clive agreed.

Lala opened her bag, pulled out her lipstick and ladled it heavily on her mouth. She leaned forward and planted a big kiss on an upper corner of Wilde's tomb, next to the hundreds of other lip prints already there.

They lingered over the graves of other inspiring and interesting individuals, including Molière, where Lala informed Clive that Molière was his stage name and his actual name was Jean-Baptiste Poquelin, and Clive told her he knew that because he had, after all, gone to the Royal Academy of Dramatic Art.

After leaving *Père Lachaise*, they took the metro back in the direction of Lala's apartment and, en route, decided to get off at a stop near the Luxembourg Gardens. Clive took Lala to a tiny sandwich shop where the owner/chef, an adorable, grandmotherly old woman, came bounding from behind the counter to give "*mon cher* Clive," a big hug and to then kiss Lala on both cheeks and bid her a warm welcome, and where they got, per Clive's enthusiastic recommendation, scrambled egg and onion sandwiches on baguettes that Madame Pinson had baked there and just taken out of the oven a half hour earlier.

Their first stop inside the park was at seats near the entrance to the Luxembourg Palace to eat their lunch, where Lala bent Clive's ear about Celestine and the cats.

"Right off the bat, I disliked her. She's got very negative energy. You can tell she's not kind. Something has to be done. Yeah, we could relocate the cats to someplace safe. But then other cats will show up. That's how it works with ferals. I need to do something. We need a stable feral colony in that garden. I need to make it happen. I'm sorry, I think I might be boring you?"

"Actually, you're not. And if I can do anything to help save the cats, let me know."

"Seriously?" Lala said.

"Yup."

"Okay, at some point you may be sorry you said that." Lala grabbed their napkins and empty wrappers and tossed them in a garbage can. "Man, you are lucky I'm engaged-to-be-engaged, because I would be such a crazed fan of yours if I weren't. I'd be that nut job who thinks you're her boyfriend when you've never actually met. You'd need a restraining order, trust me on this." She seized Clive's hand and yanked him up out of his chair. "Come on, I want to walk all fifty-plus acres of this fabulous garden right now."

After they covered maybe ten of those acres, they left the garden and Clive dropped Lala off at the entrance to her courtyard.

"Oh, Clive, while I'm thinking of it, do you know if Matthew's brother likes men or women?"

"Men," Clive said.

"Cool! Is he single?"

"Dunno," Clive said.

"Can you please find out for me? I have some notions of matchmaking ping-ponging around in my head."

Lala raced up the stairs, newly hopeful because she might have found a blind date for Kenny and because of Clive's offer to help her help the cats.

What time is it in California? Cool! They should be in the office.

Lala grabbed a bottle of sparkling water from the fridge and sat at her desk. She opened her laptop and sent an e-mail to Zoe and Eliza asking when they could Skype and could that when please be now.

Come on come on come on come on, Lala silently chanted. Her computer pinged and she happily clicked on to the call. The screen filled up with the smiling faces of Zoe and Eliza in the production offices in Los Angeles. They were both holding their morning coffee cups in one hand and waving cheerfully to Lala with the other hand.

"Hiiii!" Lala trilled.

"Are you dating Clive?" Eliza asked.

"Are you sleeping with Clive?" Zoe demanded.

"Is he amazing in bed? I bet he's amazing in bed!"

"Ladies!" Lala wagged her scolding index finger at the screen. "Of course not! You know I'm engaged-to-be-engaged!"

Zoe and Eliza looked at each other and shrugged their shoulders. They looked back at the screen and shrugged their shoulders at Lala.

"I really have tried to not think that sounds stupid," Zoe said.

"I reread *Pride and Prejudice*," Eliza said, "and I still think 'engaged-to-be-engaged' just sounds ridiculous."

"Okay, Ladies?" Lala said. "This is, as I'm sure you can imagine, not the topic I had in mind for this meeting."

"Sorry," Zoe said.

"Sorry," Eliza echoed.

"I see you both trying not to giggle. Don't think I don't, because I do. Okay, here's the thing. I think I need to buy the building where I'm staying in Paris. And I would really like your help in figuring out how to do that. Eliza, I'm feeling very confident that your exceptional accounting abilities . . . hang on a sec . . ."

Lala switched her attention to her cell phone, which had just beeped to indicate that a text message had come in. It was from David.

"Are you on Skype? Let's talk! Love you!"

Merde, Lala thought. *I love him.* Merde. *And I am so freakin' horny.*

"Ladies, I'm so sorry, give me just a minute. Talk amongst yourselves. *Not* about my engagement status."

Lala started typing on her phone.

Though I do have to give myself credit for maintaining my sassy libido while I'm terrified of death and dying and loss. I am one sexually sassy woman of a certain age.

She hit "Send" and her message to David was on its way. The message she had typed told him that she was on Skype with her office, and she was working on a way to help the feral cats, and she loved him and she missed him, and she would Skype with him as soon as she possibly could, and she was covering him with hugs and kisses, every day, every moment.

"Okay, my dear ones," Lala said. She put her phone back down and refocused on her laptop. "Here's what I'm thinking. We send ideas to each other and we figure out how to do this, yes? Eliza, I can put my New York City condo up as collateral.

"On it," Eliza said.

"And I'll start brainstorming," Zoe said.

"I just adore you both," Lala said. "I'm thinking I need a face-to-face with the owner of the building. I've only met his daughter so far. She's a nightmare. I plan to tell him I will do whatever needs to be done to make the sale work. Short of offering to let him take it out in trade, of course."

"Of course," Zoe said.

"Talk to you soon," Eliza said.

The screen went blank. Lala sat for a few moments staring at the screen and drinking her sparkling water. Then she reread her text to David while she sipped.

Well, Lala thought, *everything I wrote is true. The only problem is that I'm misleading him when I say that I'll call him as soon as I possibly can. "Soon" sounds . . . like I mean soon. And I'm not sure how soon I can handle seeing David's sweet and kind and sexy and not-immortal face again . . . My epic lust for him notwithstanding. Damn you, mortality. Damn you for raining on my passion parade.*

IF IT'S NOT ONE THING . . .

Lala had stopped by the restaurant to check in with Kenny and his grandfather before she went to charm Clément Barrault. Their meeting had been arranged by Eliza after countless e-mails and phone calls between Lala and her wonderful production staff, her new veterinarian friends, and Lala's bank in Los Angeles.

"Is there a French equivalent for 'getting my ducks in a row'?" Lala asked Kenny. "Veronique and Camille are in enthusiastic agreement. They can move their clinic to that large apartment on the ground floor and they can live in the apartment just behind it. My condo will be collateral for the loan. First order of business after the sale, build a structure in the garden for the feral cats to find shelter."

Maurice poured the three of them large shots of tequila. They clinked glasses and downed the contents.

"Ohh, yeeeah," Lala said. "That is some kinda smooth stuff. I'm feelin' good. 'Feelin',' No 'g.' So you know I've got my game on. And 'kinda.' Not 'kind of.' Mama ain't comin' to play, Monsieur Barrault. 'Ain't.' Not 'isn't.' 'Comin'.' No—"

"Right. We get the idea, Lala. *Bonne chance, chère amie.*

Knock him dead."

"Right. Of course, I would have said, 'Knock 'im dead,' you know, just to use the folksy quality to indicate my level of grass-roots commitment to—"

"Absolutely," Kenny said. He and his grandfather linked their arms on either side with Lala's and marched her to the restaurant door. "On your way, *chère amie*. You don't want to be late."

Lala crossed the Seine to the First Arrondissement. Monsieur Barrault's office was on a small street near the Louvre. When she rang the bell, the imposing, ornate wood door was quickly opened by a tall, grey-haired man, possibly in his late sixties or so, in a perfectly-tailored navy blue suit. Lala's first thought at seeing him was that, in a lovely pan-European fusion, he looked like a Gallic version of Marcello Mastroianni. Her second thought was that, if she were not engaged-to-be-engaged, she might at that moment be hoping for a rather different conclusion to the day's negotiations.

"Madame Pettibone," he said. He took her hand and shook it. "*Bienvenue.*"

His pronunciation of Lala's last name was as lyrical and appreciative as his daughter's pronunciation had been hard-edged and aggressive.

Clément Barrault led Lala down a small hallway to the inner door to his office. The room was tidy and well-organized, and almost overwhelmed with books. Every wall had shelves and every shelf was filled.

Monsieur Barrault motioned for Lala to sit in the chair across from his desk. He brought over a tray with a large coffee pot, cups, and a platter of assorted small pastries.

"*Puis-je vous offrir un café?*"

"*Oui, merci,*" Lala said. "*Noir, s'il vous plait.*"

"Shall we continue our chat in English?" Monsieur Barrault asked.

"Oh, I guess that's probably a good idea, isn't it?" Lala said.

Monsieur Barrault sat behind his desk and picked up the platter of treats to offer them to Lala.

"You must try these. They are from my favorite *patisserie*."

"If I must," Lala said. She scanned the platter and chose a small strawberry tart.

"Ah, you picked my favorite of my favorites," he said. "How charming of you to have such excellent taste."

Are we flirting? Lala thought. *Because this is fun, so I think we're flirting.*

"Yum," Lala said.

"My daughter tells me she greatly enjoyed meeting you. It seems you had a lovely evening getting to know each other. I'm so glad."

"Mmm," Lala said. She looked out the window and managed to smile. Weakly. Out of the corner of her eye, she saw Monsieur Barrault nod.

"My daughter has been overindulged by her doting mother and grandmother and aunts. I have had a very difficult time combating her . . . how shall I say . . . rather brittle attitude. Perhaps you can help me with that today?" He opened a file on his desk. "The numbers your very capable Mademoiselle Eliza sent me are a very tempting beginning to our discussion."

"Oh, I'm very glad," Lala said.

"Eliza tells me you are here in Paris working on a movie?"

"Well, 'working' might be giving too generous a description."

"You know, I was thinking . . . As I looked at these numbers . . . I was thinking of something that might make this transaction rather more appealing for me. Perhaps you and I could discuss the possibility of—"

Whoa, Lala thought. *He's gonna hit on me! Cool!* Bien sur, *I'll say,* "Désolé, mais non, *but I have to confess*—"

The door flew open, and Celestine ran in.

"Pa-PA!" she barked.

Oh, merde, *Celestine! Sucky timing!*

"Celestine!" her father scolded. "Do you not understand the

concept of knocking?"

Celestine ignored him. She ran over to Lala and leaned over Lala's chair to embrace her.

"Ohhh, Madame Pettt-eeeettttt-BOWWWNNN!"

Lala saw Celestine's father wince at his daughter's attack on her family name.

"How lovely to see you again!" Celestine said. "We must make a plan for another fun evening together *bientôt, oui?*"

Celestine didn't wait for an answer from Lala. She stood and squared off against her father, standing at the side of his desk with her hands on her hips.

"*Je suis très en colère contre nos employés au bâtiment de Madame Pettt-eeeettttt-BOWWWNNN! Ce n'est pas acceptable et j'insiste—*"

"Celestine!" her father said, his voice rising. "It is extremely rude to speak French in front of our guest when she can't—"

"I did catch a few of the words," Lala said. "I think I may have gotten the gist—"

"Fine, fine, pardon, Madame," Celestine whined. "Pa-PA, I am simply not willing to tolerate—"

While she had been listening to Celestine gas on and on in her princess voice, Lala had been debating making the comments she was forming from a seated position, but she quickly decided that standing and imitating would provide a much more deliciously mocking presentation. She stood, turned a bit to face the snarling young woman, and put her hands on her hips.

"Celestine, could you excuse us? We're havin' a kinda important conversation here. Kinda. Not 'kind of.' And 'havin'.' No 'g.' So you know I'm not screwin' around here, Celestine. 'Kay?"

Lala had stayed up all night working. Before she got started on completing her urgent task, she had called Clive and

Matthew and Atticus and asked if she could take them out for breakfast. She got to the restaurant that Kenny and his grand-father managed just under the wire, not having showered and still in her sweatpants and her "WESCREW" tee shirt, the cute cotton top that the crew team issued at Wesleyan that could be read as a running together of "we screw" and that she had found endlessly hilarious in her undergraduate years and every year since.

Lala walked into the restaurant. The three men were already seated. When she saw all of their eyes widen at the sight of her upper garment, she remembered what she was wearing. It had slipped her mind that she had put the tee shirt on the night before when she started writing.

Oh, dear, Lala thought. *I think I'm sending the wrong message to my colleagues.*

Kenny came over to take their drink orders. When she saw him, Lala remembered that Clive had, just the other day, confirmed that Atticus was in fact not seeing anyone at the moment. This would have been foremost on her matchmaker's mind, but it had been bumped off first place by the more imme-diate urgency of helping the cats.

"Hi," Kenny said. "Okay, you're all here. Great tee shirt, Lala!"

"Hi, Kenny!" Lala said. "I've been wanting you to meet my friends-slash-colleagues, Clive and Matthew and . . ."

And here she stopped for a nearly unnoticeable, but none-theless reasonably portentous, moment or two to add an air of passionate gravitas as a boost to what she hoped would be a love match to rival Abelard and Héloïse's, but without all the taboos.

". . . Atticus."

And just as she said the name, she saw Kenny and Atticus smile at each other.

Ohh, look at that, Lala thought. *I didn't need to add the dra-matic pause at all. Some things might just be meant to be.*

"Kenny, I'm kind of chilly. Do you by any chance have a

jacket I could borrow?"

"Sure thing," Kenny said. "And what can I get everyone to drink?"

They ordered coffees and teas and Kenny recommended his grandfather's Omelet du Jour, which he explained was a new creation of Maurice's, inspired by just having seen *A Passage to India* again and one that involved a lot of curry and chickpeas.

Kenny brought Lala a comfortable sweater that Lala buttoned up to cover the collegiate advertisement regarding sex. The food was delicious, and everyone chatted easily about this and that. Kenny's and Atticus's mutual interest was palpable, and Lala was starting to lose her mind from nervousness about how important this all was for the future of those poor cats, so she did what she always did when she got agitated.

"Okay, enough cordial banter!"

Merde! Lala thought. *Now I'm fully committed to blurting.*

"Here's the thing. Clive knows about this colony of feral cats in the garden of the place where I'm living. Now I need to buy the whole building because the daughter of the owner is not a nice person and . . . Kenny! Get over here and help me with this, please?"

Kenny came over brandishing a fresh pot of coffee. He started pouring and gave Lala a quick hug with his free arm.

"Okay, yeah, I heard you dive in. Because everyone in the restaurant heard you dive in. I'm here, backing you up. Go on. You were saying?"

"So the daughter's not nice, and she would probably have the cats killed if she found out about them, and that is not me being melodramatic because I'm hyperventilating and I feel pretty dizzy right now. So I met with her dad, and I don't think he much likes his daughter. He didn't actually say that, but I really get the feeling that he's looking forward to rubbing her spoiled nose in it by selling the building to me so I can banish her from having any influence over the building and its inhabitants and this restaurant, which is also part of the deal, and, last but certainly not least, those poor cats. He's giving me a really good price. There's just one thing he wants, and I'm a little insulted to say that it wasn't sexual favors from me. I'm kidding, of course. Kinda. What he wants is to be in the film."

She paused to catch her halting breath, and Matthew jumped in. As she listened to him, Lala suspected that he was being cooperative to a great extent as a means of getting her to shut her jabbering pie-hole for a few precious moments.

"Okay, well, Lala, I would have to say that that shouldn't be a problem. He can be an extra when we film at the—"

"He wants lines," Lala said. "I've taken the liberty of writing a short scene for him."

Lala grabbed her large bag and pulled out three copies of four-printed pages that were stapled together. She handed one to Clive, one to Matthew, and one to Atticus. Kenny turned away from the table and called over his shoulder as he walked off to the kitchen.

"Let me get you all a special assortment of breakfast desserts! Back in a jiff!"

"Take your time, gentlemen. I don't need an answer until this afternoon. Matthew, I kept thinking back to what you had said about the character of Terry needing more of an edge. It was such an inspiring insight. Clive, I can only hope this draft showcases your fabulous acting in a way that it so richly deserves."

God, I am cascading this over these poor guys with a bucket . . .

"Atticus, I know that the scene absolutely needs your talent to elevate it. I would be so grateful if you would help me with the next draft?"

Lala noticed that Matthew had been nodding during the last words of her monologue. She turned to him with a hopeful, desperate smile. Matthew stopped nodding. He didn't say anything.

Come on, Matty, my man! Don't leave me hanging! You've got to realize I don't do well under pressure.

"Are you playing on our epically fragile male egos?" Matthew finally asked. "Egos that are clichéd to an extent that they can be easily manipulated in just about every case?"

I am if it's working, Lala thought.

"Is it working?" she asked.

"Yup," Matthew said.

"Definitely," Clive agreed.

"And count me in as a big, fat 'Yes' on that," Atticus said. "Especially if Kenny is single."

"Great! Because I've also been promising some of the lovely people I've met around the city, like the driver who picked me up at the airport and this very adorable little old lady I met on the line at Berthillon, that they could visit the set, so I've taken the liberty of writing them into the scene since they'll be there anyway . . ."

The number of participants in the midnight vigil had grown by fifty percent. The vigil had also changed in tone thanks to the threat of Celestine's interference being delightfully eliminated by the verbal agreement, soon to be finalized on paper via appropriate documentation and whatever Lala imagined was the French equivalent of a notary public, that Lala was the new owner of the building. As a result, Lala and Kenny and Atticus were hidden in a corner huddled together with their eyes focused on the humane traps that had once again been set up in the garden. They were silently passing between them and drinking directly from a bottle of very good port that Kenny's grandfather had supplied. Atticus, as it was discovered after breakfast when he stayed in the restaurant to flirt with Kenny under the guise of working on the new scene with Lala, was, in addition to being smart and cute and talented, a person who had always done whatever he could to help animals.

"There she is," Lala whispered. "I think."

"I think so," Kenny whispered. "Shoot, she's not going near the opening."

Please, please, please, Lala silently begged. *I know it's scary, but I promise you'll be okay.*

The cat sniffed at the side of the trap. Lala watched her as she turned and scampered away, and she got a better view of the cat as she ran beneath a brightly-lit window on the second floor.

"Damn it," Lala whispered. "That's definitely our girl. Come on back, sweetheart, please. We want to help you. Quit hogging the booze, Atticus."

And it was almost as though the cat heard her. In the moment that Lala unceremoniously grabbed the bottle from Atticus as he was in mid-sip, causing a small shower of port to splatter on Atticus's chin and neck, the little cat turned around yet again and made a mad dash immediately into the opening of the trap. Lala and Kenny and Atticus heard the cat loudly chomping on the pungent tuna cat food that was in the trap as bait, and in the next moment they heard the trap loudly snap closed.

The cat started howling. Lala and Kenny and Atticus jumped up from their hiding place. Kenny folded the towel over the front of the trap so that the cat would be in complete darkness. The terrified little girl was immediately silent. Atticus picked up the trap and calmly walked up the stairs to Lala's apartment with Lala while Kenny stayed behind to monitor the two other traps that remained and were still empty.

"It's okay, little girl," Atticus intoned in a soothing voice as they quietly made their way to Lala's front door. Lala held the door open and Atticus gently put the cage down on the thick rug on a spot next to the couch.

"Okay," he said. He gave Lala a quick hug. "I'll head back down to help Kenny monitor the other traps."

"And make out," Lala said.

"Definitely," Atticus said as he closed the door behind him.

Lala stood at the door and quietly drummed her fingers

on the wood as she debated what to do with herself so that she wouldn't run to the trap and grab the poor terrified cat right out of it so she could shower the little creature with hugs and kisses.

I know, Lala thought. *The comforting quality of carbs.*

Lala took off her shoes so she could keep the apartment as peaceful and quiet as possible so the cat could get a chance to relax. She opened the cabinet and the refrigerator with a stealth that would match an attempt to surprise an entirely unsuspecting James Bond with her superior spy skills before he engaged in edgy, contentious, incredibly hot flirtation with her that ended with the two of them in a huge canopy bed in a luxury hotel in Monte Carlo.

Lala came back into the living room with a large bowl of cold spaghetti. She had chopped the spaghetti, with silent energy and enthusiasm, into very, very small pieces using one of those salad choppers that looked a bit like a guillotine blade with a handle on it. Lala sat on the couch and turned on the television at a very low volume.

I should name this little girl, Lala thought. *Assuming she's a girl. It's just so hard to tell with cats. I think we need a pan-gender name. Robin. Let's go with Robin.*

"Robin?" Lala said in a gentle and low voice. "Have you ever watched *The Young and the Restless* in French? Assuming you understand French, *mon petit ange?*"

Lala sat back and scooped the bitty pieces of pasta with a large spoon.

"This is the only way to eat pasta, in my forever-less-than-humble opinion, Robin. I know some people swear by the spear and twirl with a fork and spoon method, but I don't seem to have the manual dexterity to pull that off. Oh, okay, I remember this episode. They're about a year behind here with the show. This is a whole months-long shit storm where Nick and Sharon are getting back together and Adam is being a total tool. Sit back and listen and learn, my little Robin."

Lala watched dubbed soap opera episodes and did an

ongoing patter to Robin for the next two hours. She hoped that the cat would be starting to get used to her voice and to being inside. And then she got twitchy and crazy and she, against her better instincts regarding what to do with a terrified cat who might very well be entirely feral, picked the trap up off the floor and put it on the sofa next to her and lifted the towel off the front so that she could see the cat and the cat could see her. The cat was sitting near the opening of the wire trap. She looked at Lala when the towel was lifted and she let out a tiny hiss, but she didn't move away toward the back of the trap.

"Okay," Lala said. "So far, so good, huh, Robin?"

Lala turned back to the television and calmly continued to talk to the cat.

"So, Robin. You should keep a close eye on Victor. He is not to be trusted. Personally, I have always been Team Jack. Victor never takes responsibility for his mistakes. That is something I find quite insufferable in a person."

Lala and Robin stayed on the couch dozing in front of the television until it started to get lighter outside. Kenny and Atticus had texted Lala several hours earlier to report that they had trapped two more cats and would be keeping them in Kenny's apartment until they could be taken to the veterinary clinic in the morning.

Lala had the sense that Robin was getting used to being around her, so she took another risk and moved closer to the trap. When that didn't make the cat move away, Lala was thrilled. She put her feet up on the small coffee table and leaned against the back of the sofa, her right arm draped over the top of the trap.

"Let's get some rest, little pumpkin pie."

When Lala woke up, a not entirely soft-core porn film was playing on TV.

"Robin, avert your eyes!" she gasped. She looked at the trap and was relieved to see that the cat was curled up against the mesh and had not moved from being quite close to her, nor had it been disturbed by the continental coupling on the screen.

Ohh, I've got a kind of crazy idea, Lala thought. *What time is it?*

Lala stayed on the couch until she determined the best sequence of events.

I'll need a cushion for the floor, she thought.

Once again moving very slowly and quietly, Lala took a cushion from the couch to the bathroom and put it on the floor against the bathtub. On her next trip, she took her laptop in and put it on the closed toilet seat. She came back out into the living room. Robin was awake and was staring at her.

"Okay, young missy," Lala said. "Let's get a little crazy. I would not be doing this if I weren't so exhausted and if I weren't feeling so unmoored in my life."

Lala lifted the trap off the couch and carried it into the bathroom. She put the trap on the floor next to the cushion and closed the door of the bathroom so she would be safely in a small space with the cat so the cat would feel secure and wouldn't be able to wedge herself behind the stove or something else crazy that would necessitate calling a repairman. And then she let out a deep sigh and opened the door to the trap. For a moment, no one moved or breathed. And then Robin slowly came out of the trap and sniffed Lala's knee, and Lala felt like she was having a joy heart attack as the cat calmly walked over her legs. Without standing and while moving to the minimum extent, Lala grabbed a thick bath towel off the rack and bunched it up on the floor and Robin curled up on it and feel asleep, purring loudly.

Yeah, she thought, *and that is what rescue is all about, people.*

"David needs to meet you," Lala told the cat.

She inched over to get the laptop, moving at a pace that would have made a snail's travels look like it was winning the Indy 500, all in the service of not startling or upsetting Robin. Her return to the cushion on the floor with the computer proceeded at an equally somnambulistic speed. At last she was sitting next to the still-sleeping cat. She sent an e-mail to David, asking if he was available to Skype. He responded in just a few minutes to say that he was just about to go out to dinner with a few of his colleagues from school and could they Skype later today? Lala wrote back that they could and that she was looking forward to introducing him to the tame cat they had finally managed to get safely inside, to which David responded with, "Excellent! Love you!"

Lala shut her laptop and, without thinking, put her hand on the cat to pet it.

Ohhh, merde, she thought, but before she could pull her hand away in fear of getting it slashed by a possibly and understandably still nervous cat, Robin just snuggled against her hand and purred more loudly.

"That is what rescue is all about, people," Lala whispered.

As they sat together in their new and comfortable friendship, Lala thought about the cat Terrence had had when she met him. Mr. Joe was a devastatingly handsome grey tiger with a perfect white triangle on his nose. He was full grown when Terrence adopted him from the ASPCA in Manhattan four years before he met Lala. Mr. Joe had clearly been miffed when Lala moved in with them, but she won him over by taking charge of the task of putting his tasty wet food in a dish three times a day and putting it on the kitchen floor for him to lap up. Once Mr. Joe started associating Lala with food, he was besotted with his new mama, and Lala was equally madly in love with him. She was always carrying him around the apartment, wrapped up in her arms in a big hug, or she was reading or working with him on her lap. He started sleeping on her side of the bed, which made Terrence happy because of the harmony in their home and jealous because Mr. Joe had chosen to stop sleeping next to him.

After eleven wonderful years, Mr. Joe developed kidney failure and had a stroke. Their vet came to their apartment to put him to sleep. Lala and Terrence were stretched out on the floor next to their beloved cat and whispered to him about how much

LALA PETTIBONE: STANDING ROOM ONLY • 173

they loved him as he passed away.

"You and Mr. Joe would have loved each other," she told Robin. "And you and Terrence, too."

But you'll never meet them, Lala thought. *I can tell David about you. I can't tell Terrence about you. I can't tell Terrence about anything ever again. Oy vey, this is getting way too intense for so early in the day.*

"Robin, when Terrence got sick, we were surrounded by our wonderful friends and family. And when he died, they all continued to surround me with love and care. Our friend Gary? He's a hoot. Sometimes I kind of want to smack him because he likes to argue a point just for the sake of arguing. About two years after Terrence died, people were starting to think about maybe finding someone for me to date. I was thinking about it, too, truth be told. So Gary asks me if I would consider dating someone who wasn't mean to animals, but didn't love them the way I do. You know, someone who was basically indifferent to animals. I'm, like, ewwwww, Gary, no."

The cat woke up and stirred beneath Lala's hand. Then she stood up, did a downward facing cat stretch on the towel, and then head-butted Lala's laptop. Lala quickly moved the laptop to the floor and Robin quickly took over the space on Lala's lap, where she turned around twice, kneaded Lala's thighs, and then curled up and fell back asleep. Lala wrapped her arms around the cat and gently rocked her.

"It's scary," she said, "but we promise we'll be okay, right, sweet girl?"

The day's filming was going to involve scenes with Clive's co-star, Rebecca, sobbing at a small jazz club on the Île Saint-Louis after Clive's character cruelly rejects her attempts to win him back. As a result, Clive had a day off. He called Lala early that morning to invite her to a "sojourn of stimulation."

"Clive," Lala had said during their phone call, "I really enjoy spending time with you. You are delightful. So when I say 'yes' to your invitation, I just want to make it clear that you shouldn't have any expectations. I am, as you will remember, and please don't snicker because I will have to smack you if you do, engaged-to-be-engaged."

"My only expectation," Clive had responded, "is to have an intellectually and culturally stimulating day with a very smart woman."

"Okay, well, in my defense, I feel quite sure you intended for your invitation to be misleading when you said 'stimulation' without adding any qualifiers," Lala had huffed.

They started the day with a walking breakfast. They stopped at Clive's favorite *patisserie*, which by delightful coincidence was located not far from Lala's apartment. Clive asked how many *pain au chocolat* Lala wanted, and she responded, "We better get four. For me. How many are you having? Wait, if we also get croissants, which look delicious so why would we not, I can probably make do with three of each. For me. How many are you having?"

They each clutched their white paper bags filled with treats and their small paper cups of espresso. They had decided, on quite a whim, to walk back and forth across the gorgeous bridges of the Seine until they crisscrossed their way to the Musée d'Orsay. On each bridge, they paused in the middle and gazed out over the river and the buildings along the banks. After stopping on the *Pont des Arts*, Clive started to walk toward the other side of the river, and Lala reached out to touch his arm to halt his retreat.

"This is my favorite view," she said. "Let's stay here a bit longer?"

They stood together and looked at the *Île de la Cité* in the distance and the medieval-looking *Pont-Neuf*, which they had crossed a few minutes earlier.

"You are so nice," Lala said. "I'm thinking of women I can

fix you up with." Clive gave her shoulder a quick squeeze and chuckled.

"Lala, I'm a movie star. I do pretty well on my own. But I really appreciate the thought."

"You've never been married, have you?"

"Not yet. I was engaged once."

"Right," Lala said. "I remember reading about that. You were both very young. You went to the Royal Academy together, right?"

"Yup. She's with the Royal Shakespeare Company now. Which is why I can never set foot in Stratford-upon-Avon because my heart would break."

Lala wrapped her arm around Clive's waist and hugged him.

"While there is life, there is always a chance," Lala whispered.

"I don't know," Clive said. "I was awful to her. I have spent years regretting it. If I were Tara, I wouldn't ever forgive me. Never ever."

"You know what the Count of Monte Cristo would tell you. Wait and—"

". . . hope," Clive said.

They leaned their heads together and looked out over one of the most romantic views of one of the most romantic cities, the city where Lala and her late husband had spent their romantic honeymoon.

Ohh, Terrence, Lala thought. *I could wait forever and still be without any hope of ever seeing you again.*

"Terrence?" Lala gasped.

She had just walked through the main entrance of the Musée d'Orsay with Clive and had just finished announcing that the first thing she wanted them to do was make a beeline for *Whistler's Mother,* when she saw a man walking not far up ahead of them who really seemed to be her late husband.

Lala stopped walking. It took Clive a few steps to realize that she was no longer advancing with him. He turned around.

"What's wrong?" Clive asked. Lala ignored him and ran in the direction of the beloved ghost.

She lost sight of him in the crowd, but then there he was again. As she got closer, she saw that he had, while he was out of her view, taken the arm of a thin, elegantly-dressed woman with gorgeous silver hair.

Terrence? Lala thought. *You're . . . you're cheating on me?*

Clive caught up with her and kept pace as she moved forward.

"What are you doing?"

"I'm trying very hard not to jump to conclusions about my late husband's fidelity. This could all be completely innocent. OMIGOD, GÉRARD?"

Lala had to keep reminding herself not to stare. She had to silently check in with the small part of her brain that wasn't stunned to see if her mouth was agape, which it usually was, and she then had to snap it shut. She was able to converse, but only at the most elementary levels. Thankfully, Clive was holding court.

"I think the best time I ever had, though, was when I was in school and I played Sweeney Todd. Such soaring lyrics. Absolute poetry."

"Ohh, I can just imagine you in that role! And you must have had fun on the set of *Pulling Rank, non?*" Marie-Laure flirted. "Such a treat to meet you and to talk about your bodyyyyyy of work with you, Clive."

And judging by the beguiled smile on Gérard's face, he was equally smitten with the handsome movie star and his tales of stardom.

"That's one of my favorite movies," Gérard gushed.

"That shoot was delightful," Clive boomed joyfully. The man was in his element. "And if any of the pleasure we took in our work translated to the screen for you, well, then I'm glad."

Lala was sitting at a small table in a bistro near the Musée d'Orsay. The day's planned visit to see the beautiful art for all four of the people sitting at the table had been cut quite short when Lala caught the attention of her former boss and heart-throbbing crush by braying his name across the first floor of the museum.

Gérard had turned around, had seen his former employee, and had marched over to give a warm embrace to the woman he hadn't seen since she had a raging breakdown at the New York offices of the French publishing house of which he was a partner.

I've got a doozie of a story to tell Clive when I get him alone, Lala thought as she smiled in the bistro and took nearly non-stop sips from the delicious glass of champagne that had been poured from the delicious bottle of champagne Gérard had ordered.

At the museum, Lala hadn't been able to say much more than that she used to work with Gérard when she lived in New York by way of an explanation to Clive of why this man had so profoundly caught her attention. Gérard had introduced them to the woman with him, Marie-Laure, his girlfriend, and Lala had assured them that she remembered meeting Marie-Laure in New York on the day Marie-Laure arrived to begin working at *Atelier Du Monde*, also known as the First Ides of March That Busted Lala's Balls To An Epic Extent.

And now they were all sharing a lovely assortment of breads and cheeses and olives, and Lala had only been marginally successful in getting the roaring sound of crashing waves that started pounding through her ears the moment she saw the man who resembled her late husband to an extent that was too sur-real to abate.

Yeah, I could also tell Clive that Gérard could be Terrence's twin.

Identical. Eerie identical. Creepy identical. And I could share the fact that I didn't even notice the resemblance until I went batshit crazy on that March fifteenth and my best friend Brenda pointed out the utterly uncanny similarity.

The four of them spent hours together that day. Lala learned that Gérard and Marie-Laure had recently left the New York branch of the publishing company and returned to work at the Paris offices. They lived together in an apartment near the Eiffel Tower, and they often spent weekends at Gérard's grandmother's estate in Reims, where they insisted that Lala and Clive must join them for the weekend sometime very soon.

They walked along the Seine together for a few blocks and exchanged contact information when they parted company. They made a plan to make a date to get together again the following week.

"They are great fun!" Clive enthused on the way back to Lala's place. "I am so glad we bumped into them. I had a blast!"

"Yeah, yeah," Lala grumbled. "Listen, you are coming up to my apartment. And do NOT get any ideas."

Lala and Clive were lying on the sofa in Lala's living room. Charles Aznavour was playing. The lights were low. Wine had been poured. Robin the Now-Much-Loved-Cat was sleeping next to Lala and was purring almost loudly enough to distract from the *chansons*. Lala and Clive had the tops of their heads pressed together, so that they were stretched out on their backs facing in opposite directions. Clive was expounding. Vividly.

He's acting it all out, Lala thought. *The sofa is bouncing from his theatrical gesticulations. What a freakin' ham.*

"I mean, seriously," Clive said. "I knew you were formidable, but I had no idea how strong you are."

Oh, for god's sake, Lala thought.

"You went right up to the guy at the museum. You let him see you. And you let her see you. After experiencing what really is one of the most poignant stories of humiliation that I have ever heard, you marched right up to the guy and you stood proud. Lala Pettibone, I admire you!"

"Clive, you have got to quit so emphatically lifting your head and smacking it back down on the sofa, or I may get seasick and, worse still, spill some of my wine."

Clive lifted himself on his elbow and turned to look at Lala, who had her eyes closed and was managing quite beautifully to choreograph the dance that delivered her wine glass to her lips over and over again without losing a drop, despite her concerns regarding Clive's acrobatics.

"Lala, I grant you that I haven't heard much of anything about the manuscript for your new novel, what's the title . . ."

"*A Woman of a Certain Age.*"

"Of course! That was my idea!"

"No, it was what you called me. I had the idea of writing a book about it. In which your character gets taken down a few pegs, I might remind you," Lala said. She switched the wine glass to her left hand and used her right hand to once again pet Robin. "What a good girl. Who's a good kitty?"

"I like that! I like to play heroes who suffer."

"Who says you've got the part? Who says the part based on you is a hero? Are you getting me more wine? That might go some way toward at least getting you an audition for the part."

Clive leapt off the couch with enviable energy and ran to the kitchen. He modulated the volume of his voice on his travels so that he could continue his lecture and be heard.

"Anyway, I want to very, very, very strongly suggest that you include this entire story in your new novel. The whole thing about you and Gérard and Marie-Laure."

He bounced back onto the couch. Lala lifted herself onto her elbows so Clive could refill her wine glass. Then they both plopped onto their backs again.

"It's just such a *story*," Clive continued.

I know, Lala thought. *I was there. Remember?*

Lala noticed something going on outside the window.

"Clive, I think the sun is starting to come up . . ."

"There you are, in love with your boss and thinking he's in love with you, though how you could believe that when he hadn't made a move on you in a year is just so delightfully . . . well, I was going to say naïve, but I think ludicrous is a better word . . . and then his girlfriend shows up at work and she's moving to New York and you have a full-on bat-shit-crazy meltdown at work! And then you see him at a museum in Paris, and you don't run screaming in shame and humiliation!"

Okayyyy, I think we've had just about . . .

"Clive, it's getting late, so maybe—"

Without any warning, and certainly without wine having been called for again so soon after it had just been fetched, Clive—in one incredible leap that involved bending his back and going entirely up on his shoulders and then thrusting himself into the air in a high arc and securing his landing like a gold-medal gymnast—got himself off the couch.

"Whoa," Lala said. "All those stage movement classes at the Royal Academy of Dramatic Art clearly paid off."

Clive seized Lala's wine glass and put it on the table next to the sofa.

"Whoa! Let's not get crazy here," Lala yelped.

Clive grabbed her hands and lifted her off the sofa so that she was standing and was facing him.

"Lala," he said, "you're my hero."

Ohhh, man, Lala thought. And she let herself give Clive a tight little smile. Because she was genuinely pleased that Clive had paid her that oddly charming compliment, despite having had to relive her epic, overwrought non-history with Gérard via Clive's one-man-show to get to the point where she ended up being the victor of the tale. In a manner of speaking.

"Fine, fine, I'm very impressive. Listen, grab that bottle of wine, and you can come impress me by helping me put fresh food and water out for my feral cats."

It's Another

Lala's computer had been grinding her last gear all morning. Not because of any failure or shortcoming on the part of the machine's technology or service, but because it was the unhappy and blamed messenger of way too much mishegoss for Lala to have to put up with on a good day. Which this one was decidedly not turning out to be.

By the time she and Clive had cared for the feral cats and Clive had headed home to get some "magical beauty sleep, luv," Lala had tried to take a nap but was forced to admit after less than fifteen minutes of spinning and twirling underneath the covers of her bed that she was wide awake and that that wasn't going to be changing anytime soon. So she opened her laptop and got to work. Her plan was to deal with any urgent correspondence, then check in with her aunt and avoid checking in with David, and then work on her new manuscript.

The positive forward momentum of that trajectory was immediately halted by an e-mail from her colleagues, Zoe and Eliza. Lala opened the e-mail, instantly got herself agitated before she even finished reading the first sentence, and, with stiffened self-righteousness, hailed the young women via Skype.

"Hiiiii!" Zoe trilled cheerfully into the screen.

"Hiiii!" Eliza said.

"Yes, hello," Lala said with clipped disappointment. Ample use of air quotation marks punctuated the words that followed. "I got your 'e-hyphen-mail' about the 'e-one-word-no-hyphen-mail' from our film supplier. I'll deal with that right away. What I wanted to discuss with you is that we in our production company *always* hyphenate the word 'e-mail.' I thought that went without saying."

"Umm . . ." Zoe began. Lala cut her off.

"We do that because *The New Yorker* does that."

"Umm," Eliza said, "it's just that when you look at most of the world, I mean the English-writing world, they don't hyphenate—"

"My dears," Lala interrupted, "you must realize that I don't give a royal shit that the rest of the world has chosen to cease using the hyphen, because if a hyphen is good enough for *The New Yorker*, it's good enough for me. And, as a result, for our production company."

Lala's foster cat had jumped on her lap while she was fussing and sputtering at Zoe and Eliza. Lala picked her up and cradled her like a baby. The cat immediately fell asleep and purred loudly. The sound and the vibration against her arms had a much-needed soothing effect on Lala.

"I'm sorry," Lala said. "I'm just not myself lately. Nevertheless, we are still going to use the hyphen."

"Are you okay?" Zoe asked.

"I'm fine," Lala lied.

"Are you upset because you're sleeping with a very, very sexy famous movie star while still being engaged-to-be-engaged to a very, very sexy veterinarian?" Eliza asked.

"I am *not* sleeping with Clive!" Lala yelled at the screen. "And I saw you two smirking about that 'engaged-to-be-engaged' part, don't think I didn't. Okay, I love you both. Get back to work."

Lala clicked off on their Skype connection. She cuddled the sleeping cat with even more aggressive urgency and kissed her precious little head.

Robin the Cat had been renamed Minou by Kenny, her official new papa, because her status as a female had been confirmed at the veterinary clinic. When Lala returned to the United States, Minou would have a wonderful forever home with Kenny. But for the present, Minou spent a lot of her time and most of her nights sleeping in Lala's apartment because Lala was aching from missing her precious dogs so much, and so she especially needed to have an animal's comforting presence and energy with her.

Lala was especially aching and missing her dogs because her aunt was being a real pill whenever Lala spoke to her. And as a result, Lala wasn't contacting her as much as she would have if all were well with their relationship. And so she wasn't seeing as much of her pups. And that was breaking her heart.

With equal measures of anticipation and dread, Lala called her aunt.

"Hi," Geraldine said on the Skype screen. She was in her loungewear and Lala could see just the top of Petunia's grey head peeking over the side of the desk in Geraldine's study.

"Hello, my dear ones!" Lala said with an attempt to convey the comfort and security of nothing being wrong between them. Lala felt as though she could almost hear her aunt thinking, "The envelope, please . . . And the award for Least Believable Performance by a Profoundly Disappointing Niece goes to . . ."

Other than Geraldine's blank face and Petunia's snoring, Lala's greeting elicited no response.

Oy vey, Lala thought.

"So, how's everyone over there?"

"Fine," Geraldine said. Her voice was Switzerland in its dedicated neutrality.

"That's great!" Lala cheered. "I'm fostering a kitty!"

Lala smiled broadly and imagined that her smile looked

incredibly forced. She held Minou up to her chin to show her off. Her aunt's face allowed only a tight little smile to transform it from the blank slate it had been since the Skype call began.

Words, once again, were not going to be forthcoming.

Okay, so she only responds to direct questions, Lala thought. *Fine.*

"So, anything new going on over there?"

"No."

"Do you think you'll ever respond to me in more than one syllable ever again for the rest of our lives?"

Geraldine shrugged. Lala sighed and decided to put the issue to rest for the present.

"Could you maybe hold up my little Petunia so I can see more of her?"

Geraldine silently complied.

"Look at mommy's baby!" Lala cooed. "Mama loves her Petunia sooooo much!"

The sight of her precious old girl banished, for the moment, any concern about her aunt's coldness. And any thought of why her aunt was angry with her. Geraldine had been surprisingly reticent on the subject of David for the past few weeks. And her silence had spoken volumes.

Petunia and Minou slept through all of the audible and inaudible tension of the call. Lala felt a tear leave her eye and start to roll down her cheek. She quickly wiped it away, and as she did, she saw her aunt's facial expression soften for just a moment, before Geraldine caught herself and put on her disdainful mask again. It looked to Lala as though her aunt wanted to convey that she almost couldn't be bothered to make the effort to hold Lala in as much contempt as she did.

Lala had to quickly numb her soul so she wouldn't start crying.

I know how much I'm disappointing you. And I won't give you the satisfaction of seeing that I know, she thought.

"Okey doke! Well, thanks a lot, Auntie Geraldine! Talk to

you soon!"

With a prim click of her mouse and her head held high, Lala ended the Skype call. Without much debate, she made a rapid series of decisions.

"Must have Ambien," she told Minou. "Want to *dors comme cher chat*, without a care in the world or much of a thought in the *keppie*, either. No disrespect intended, Minou. Will rest on the couch with the TV on in the background. Not sure why suddenly allergic to the use of pronouns. Probably delirious from exhaustion and stress."

Just before Lala fell asleep with Minou curled up right next to her head, she had a passing thought that she was just so damn grateful to be falling asleep. When Lala woke up hours later, it was almost a good time to go out for an early dinner. She decided to check her laptop in case anything urgent needed to be handled, and that was when the wonders of modern computer technology brought an initially unwelcome conversation.

Despite all of Clive's commentary about how fun Gérard and Marie-Laure were and how he and Lala just had to do something fun with them again soon, Lala was determined to avoid spending more time with her late husband's doppelganger and his lovely girlfriend. So when she saw an e-mail from Gérard with the subject line, "*Encore une fois?*" she shuddered.

"*Merde*," she whispered to Minou, who had turned over onto her back when Lala sat up on the couch and still wasn't conscious. Lala remembered how cats sleep eighty percent of the day and once again envied them. She opened the e-mail and immediately noted that it had been sent to her and to Clive.

"*Merde*," she repeated. "Now I can't just pretend that this communication never happened. Because Gregarious Movie Star has seen it as well. Double *merde*."

Lala began reading the text aloud, clearly of the opinion that Minou needed to hear a version of the correspondence with editorial comments appended.

"*Salut, nos chers amis!* We had such a great time at dinner with you both! How about another adventure *par quatre*!—okay, Gérard, I'm thinking we're overdoing the exclamation points, and that's quite an observation, coming from generally-quite-excitable me—Marie-Laure and I have two high flying adventures in mind for us, if you're game?"

Lala wrinkled her forehead downward in a frown and tapped Minou's little tummy.

"Is he suggesting we all join the Mile High Club together? Twice?"

Lala continued reading to Minou.

"Give a call and we'll discuss. And, P.S., Lala, we got your novel on our Kindle, and we binge-read it to each other, and we both absolutely LOVED it! Brava and congratulations! Can't wait to see the movie!"

Lala paused. Her lips slowly melted into a thin, wide, reluctant smile.

"Oh, okay, well . . . who doesn't love kudos?"

Her phone rang. She looked at the caller ID and snorted.

"Let me guess," she said.

"I just got off the phone with Gérard!" Clive gushed. "We're meeting them at 3:00 p.m. tomorrow afternoon, okay?"

"Why? Where? To do what?"

"IIIIII'm not gonna tell you, because it's a surprise!" Clive crowed.

"Okay, fine, but I just want to make it understood right off the bat that I am not having sex with any of you in an airplane, 'kay?"

Getting dressed for almost anything was almost never a fun or energizing or even vaguely tolerable event for Lala. And this day was especially daunting, because Lala's wardrobe for her trip to Paris had not benefited from her chic aunt's guidance. Geraldine had made it clear that she was annoyed that Lala was choosing to put a continent and an ocean between herself and her "What? Fiancé? Boyfriend? What should I call him at this point, Lala?" and as a result the most help she would be giving Lala as she got ready to leave would be to remind her that carry-on liquids had to be in small bottles, which Lala had testily reminded her was something she and the rest of the world knew, *merci mille fois, ma chère tante.* So Lala had enlisted her new friends Zoe and Eliza to go shopping with her, warning them that her saturation point at stores was usually reached after about fifteen minutes in a dressing room. The young women had hatched a plan together to keep Lala comfortably distracted from the task at hand by locating their spree at the Third Street Promenade in Santa Monica, with the idea that walking from retailer to retailer in the fresh ocean air and sunshine, and taking in the sounds and sights of their fellow pedestrians and the cute dogs and the street musicians, would refresh Lala on each passage so that the fifteen-minute limit could be extended to maybe half an hour in each store and result in a substantial and successful day of shopping.

Their hopes had been dashed at Banana Republic, their first stop. They had gotten Lala into the dressing room with three shirts and with a pair of sleek black pants.

Lala hated the way the shirts looked on her. She loved the pants.

"Okay," she announced as the salesperson was ringing her up at checkout. "Let's go to lunch and then maybe we'll catch a movie. I'm buying."

"But, but . . ." Zoe sputtered.

"We . . . we've got to . . ." Eliza began.

"We've got more shopping to do!" Zoe declared.

"Nuh uh," Lala said. "I'm done."

And so now she was trying to figure out how to dress for her second double-date. She had been told by Clive, when she whimpered, "Where are we going? What should I weeeaaaare?" that she should put on comfortable shoes and bring a sweater in case the wind got very strong.

Lala decided to put on the cute new black pants and her sneakers. That part was relatively easy.

"Which top, which top, which top," she muttered to Minou, who was asleep on her bed. "Like you're any help. DAMN IT!"

Clive had suddenly knocked on her front door loudly enough to startle Lala, but not to wake up Minou.

"Let's go, Lala! We're going to be late!"

In an entirely unnecessary panic, Lala grabbed the first shirt she saw, pulled it on, and picked up a black sweater on her way through the living room. She opened the door and Clive smiled when he saw her.

"Ahh, the lovely lady's got my favorite top on! We screw!"

"Oh, for god's sake, Clive," Lala huffed. She took his arm and yanked him down the stairs. "I told you, it's for the crew team. The Wesleyan crew team. Get your mind out of the gutter."

It was a gorgeous, sunny day. Lala put her sunglasses on when she got to street level.

"You lead the way, Keeper of Secrets," she ordered.

"I've allowed time for us to walk where we're going, unless you'd prefer to take the metro?"

"To whom are you speaking, young pup?" Lala demanded. "I LOVE to walk! I am a walker in every city I visit. Point me in the right direction and try to keep up, sonny boy."

Clive wrapped Lala's hand in his and led her down the short street to the Seine. At the bank of the river, they headed in a direction that offered Lala no clues as to their destination. They could have been going to meet Gérard and Marie-Laure at the Tuileries Gardens, or the Place de la Concorde, or the Champs-Élysées, or the Arc de Triomphe, all of which were options on their path. After passing a few beautiful streets on their way and looking up and down the sunlit facades of so many charming old buildings, Lala found herself forgetting to wonder or worry about where they were going.

"Yikes, I think I may be doing that 'living in the moment' thing," she confessed to Clive. "That is *so* not me."

It's such a lovely day and I am having such a lovely time, Lala thought. *I'm going to take a sabbatical from worrying or overthinking or maybe even from thinking at all. Just for a day. I'll be fine just for today. As long as I don't get tipsy at any point and start thinking again about David maybe not being immortal. And as long as they don't have some clichéd, crazy, terrifying idea for this double-date like going to the top of the Eiffel Tower.*

Ohhh, fuuuuuuuuuck, Lala thought.

"What a great idea!" she said. She held her hands together and clapped them in tight, rapid bursts, grinning as though she were a toddler unable to control her delight.

What the fuuuuuuuuuck? I haven't told any of them that I'm terrified of heights, have I? Of course I haven't. How would that come up in conversation unless we were about to go up into the sky somewhere? Into the sky somewhere not in an airplane. Fuuuuuuuuuuck!

"I think we should walk up!" Clive said.

"Absolutely!" Marie-Laure said.

"Absolutely!" Gérard echoed.

"*Absolument!*" Lala cheered with every ounce of her legendarily bad acting skills that she could muster.

Clive and Gérard and Marie-Laure flinched in unison. Lala wasn't sure if it was because of her transparently false gusto, or because of her universally vilified French accent. When she next spoke, she tried to mix a wounded tone with a proud one.

"Okay, once, when I was performing with this comedy group I was in in New York, I said this one line and it got a very big laugh, so I must have some talent . . . never mind . . . Anyway, my fiancé-to-be-my-fiancé thinks my French accent is very good. He said that. Once. When we first met. Just before we were about to . . . never mind."

Marie-Laure scrunched her shoulders in a paroxysm of delight that was utterly confusing to Lala.

What is that all about? Lala thought.

"Ohhh," Marie-Laure said, "he must love you *soooooo* much!"

Hmm, Lala thought. *I'm not sure if that's a backhanded compliment or a forehanded insult.*

"I remember when we met briefly when I moved to New York," Marie-Laure continued.

Oh, merde, *you're not going to mention my public nervous breakdown, are you?* Lala thought.

"I remember being so impressed by your command of French grammar and vocabulary and syntax."

Aaaand not my accent. Still kind of a backhanded-compliment-slash-forehanded-insult . . .

They were standing a small distance from the base of the Eiffel Tower. There was a long line for the elevator leading to the top. There was no line for the stairs.

"Come on," Lala said. "Let's get this done. Let's do this. Now."

No one will know. I will be confidence personified.

Lala sprinted over to the entrance to the stairs and wondered what she would be dealing with.

Please, god, let it be entirely enclosed. Fuuuuuuuuuck!

The seemingly infinite steps leading up the tower loomed before her. For an unnerving moment, Lala thought they might be undulating. Surrounding the steps were wire mesh walls. Through which one could easily see. Because they were not in any way an enclosure around the stairs.

"Oh, fun!" Lala said.

Oops, I think a note of sarcasm may have slipped through . . .

"Fresh air! Fun! Let's go!"

Okay, just don't look down . . .

Lala sprinted up the first flight of steps and turned toward the interim landing to tackle the second set of steps.

I'm just going to count to myself and just focus on the numbers and I'll do it in French because that will certainly keep my mind occupied, and if I'm doing it to myself no one can disparage my accent, merci mille fois.

On the second set of stairs, Lala paused for a moment to wave and smile at Clive and Gérard and Marie-Laure, who were just starting their ascent.

"Let's go, people! Last one to the top is a rotten egg! Do you have that idiom in French? Isn't that the one of the oddest idioms ever?"

And she was off again, keeping her eyes straight ahead and not looking at the rapidly retreating ground.

Dix-sept, dix-huit, dix-neuf, vingt . . .

Lala kept going, and she kept reminding herself, in between counting and giggling because "eighty" in French is "four twenties," that this "fucking nightmare" had a limited shelf life and that one day, perhaps even one day soon, it would all be a distant, terrible memory, and she was very surprised when an upbeat, inspiring song came into her mind out of nowhere and forced itself out of her mouth with confidence and vigor.

"It's the EYE of the TIGER, it's the THRILL of the FIGHT!"

"Lala!" Clive yelled from somewhere below. "Don't sing!"

"Okay, okay," Lala grumbled.

Seven hundred and four steps later, Lala emerge onto the second floor, where the steps ended.

"WHOA! WHOA! WHOA!"

Clive came sprinting up behind her and wrapped his arms around her in a protective hug.

"What's wrong? Are you okay?"

"There's a champagne bar!"

Lala dragged him over to the *Bar A Champagne* with his arms still around her in a kind of exercise in slapstick physical comedy. They stood in line, and Clive still had his arms around her when Gérard and Marie-Laure joined them.

"He's doing this because he's heroic because he's a movie star and he plays heroes a lot and apparently it rubs off. This is not us flirting. I think we need a bottle of champagne, *oui*? *Une bouteille, n'est ce-pas?* I am gonna need some serious fortification before I approach that ledge and that indescribable view."

They walked back down the stairs. Lala was uncharacteristically quiet and was moving at a much slower pace than she had on the way up. Indeed, she was lagging behind the other three, and Clive had to keep turning around to check on her.

"Are you okay?" Clive finally asked.

"We were up there on our honeymoon. It was raining then, but the view was still spectacular. In a kind of wonderfully gloomy and intense way. I don't think I ever told Terrence I'm terrified of heights. Oops, cat's out of the bag. That's kind of a funny idiom, too, huh?"

When they were back on *terra firma* and Lala's feet hit solid ground, she stumbled just a little. Clive caught her.

"Seriously, are you okay?"

"I am feeling a little lightheaded," Lala said.

Clive steered her toward an empty bench nearby. Gérard and Marie-Laure followed. Lala eased down onto the seat and put her head back with her eyes shut.

"Big improvement. Immediate. I love when that happens."

"Do you need to go home?" Marie-Laure asked.

"Nah," Lala said. "I think I was having the widow vapors. All better now! Why are you two looking so conspiratorial?"

Marie-Laure and Gérard smiled at Lala and Clive.

"Did you bring a gown with you?" Marie-Laure asked.

"A . . .? I don't . . . I'm pretty sure I don't own a gown . . ."

Marie-Laure insisted that Lala and Clive come to their apartment so that Lala could borrow one of Marie-Laure's dresses. As they walked to the nearby building on a charming side street, Lala pestered.

"Why would I need a gown? WHAT are you up to?"

"Patience," Marie-Laure said.

She pronounced it "pah-see-ohns."

Damn it, that damn sexy language is so damn sexy when she uses it, Lala thought.

Their apartment was every bit as sunny and airy and perfect as Lala expected.

"Please tell me you paid a professional to decorate this place," Lala said in the welcoming entryway.

"No, no," Marie-Laure said. "I love interior design. It's so relaxing to make a house a home."

Oh, for fuck's sake, Lala thought. *How delightful is that?*

Clive and Gérard decided to sit on the terrace and polish off a few bottles of Alsatian beer while Lala and Marie-Laure went shopping in Marie-Laure's massive closet.

"Seriously, Marie-Laure," Lala said. "How many time zones does this thing cross?"

Lala and Clive left the apartment an hour later with Lala carrying a dress bag under her arm. They had promised to meet Gérard and Marie-Laure back at their place at seven o'clock. Gérard would arrange for a car to pick up Clive and then Lala. Clive had assured Gérard and Marie-Laure that his white tuxedo jacket would work well for whatever elegant surprise they had planned for that evening.

"You travel to your film locations with a white tuxedo jacket?" Lala asked. They were back walking along the Seine toward Lala's apartment.

"Well, I am a movie star," Clive said.

"Yes, I've noticed that."

"And I do rather fancy myself a bit of a James Bond. Specifically a Sean Connery James Bond. A Sean Connery James Bond in *Dr. No.*"

"I can see that," Lala said.

After Clive dropped her off and she showed Minou the

beautiful deep purple gown that was temporarily hers, Lala decided she needed to catch a nap on the couch along with her foster cat, who had not been so impressed by Lala's new duds that she was going to actually open her eyes.

Lala slept through the alarm she had set on her phone at a too-low volume, and only woke up when Kenny knocked on her door because he was feeling like having Minou come over to his place early so he could watch television with her purring on his lap.

"*Merde!* What time is it?" Lala stood at the front door. She had been sleeping on the couch on her stomach with her face mashed into the cushions. Her face had fabric creases in it and there was a not unsubstantial deposit of drool in her hair.

"It's almost six o'clock."

"*Merde!*"

"Actually, I wish you'd just say 'shit' instead of 'mairrrrd'," Kenny admitted.

"Really? My accent's even bad with monosyllables?"

"Yeah."

"Shut up. Listen, you have to sit with Minou on the couch while I take a quick shower and get dressed and do a catwalk for you both, okay, I didn't even think about Minou when I said catwalk, and then you both have to tell me I look fabulous, okay?"

Kenny dutifully took his place on the couch and was there, watching an episode of *Les Feux de l'Amour* with Minou sleeping on his lap, when Lala emerged from the bedroom in her finery. She stood in the doorway to the living room and did a twirl. Lala thought, if her full-length mirror was reflecting accurate reality, that she might be looking better than she expected. And then she saw that Kenny had either not heard the bedroom door open, or her appearance had not been enough to distract him from the show on the screen.

"I do not understand why Jack doesn't just deck Victor," Kenny muttered to himself. "And what is up with Ashley and her sucky taste in men?"

"KENNY!" Lala yelled. Kenny whipped his head around. "I am going to need your FULL attention!"

"Wow! You look great!"

"Really? I can pull off strapless? I don't think I've worn strapless since I graduated from college."

"Well, it's about time you did. You look great!"

"IIIIIIIIIIII don't know what I'm doing with my liiiiiiiiiiiiife."

"Who does?" Kenny said. "I'm thinking don't worry about it tonight. Just go have fun."

There was a knocking on her front door, and Clive called out.

"Scribe! We gotta move it!"

"He's got a bit of a James Bond thing goin' on, don'tcha think?" Lala said. She winked at Kenny. "I like that in a man."

She opened the door. Clive held a single red rose. Lala took it and smiled.

"Even I would feel silly saying this is not a date. I would, however, like to point out that it's a semi-platonic date. I'm not sure what I mean by that."

"Whatevs, m'lady. You look beautiful. Let's book it. Hey, Kenny, how are ya?"

The car Gérard had hired definitely fell into the grand limousine category. The wet bar included a bottle of champagne. Clive popped it open and poured two glasses. He asked the chauffeur to take them to their destination by way of the Champs-Élysées, and to please "spin us on that grand traffic circle around the superb Arc de Triomphe twice, my good man, if you would, please, sir."

"WHOOOAAAAAAAAA!" Lala yelled as their car plunged at highway speed and with no hesitation into the inchoate mass of traffic that resulted when a dozen boulevards converged around one of the most famous monuments in the world.

Lala had her arms up above her head in the way that she

had seen on footage of people riding monster rollercoasters, an experience she would never personally have because she had once ridden on a "choo choo train for babies," as her older and way cooler cousin Louise had described the Big Thunder Mountain Railroad, when their families were visiting Disneyland when Lala was ten, and the memory of that event still gave her the shivers. She had determined on that long-ago terrifying day at the Happiest Place on Earth that she would never again go anywhere near anything that in any way resembled a rollercoaster.

"This is flippin' FABULOUS! I might barf, but it will be SO worth it!"

Gérard and Marie-Laure were waiting for them at the entrance to their building as the car pulled up. When Marie-Laure came into Lala's line of vision, Lala's shoulders crumbled.

Lala remembered that Monty's daughter Helene, a friend whose success had always intimidated Lala just a bit under the surface of their affectionate relationship, had once told her about going to an awards ceremony and making the mistake of wearing black.

"When you wear black, you're wallpaper, Lala," Helene had told her. "No one notices you if you're wearing black. It's been done, what, five million times already?"

Marie-Laure, Lala reflected as she tried to reignite her rapidly extinguishing confidence, would never be considered wallpaper in any context in the black gown she was wearing.

Marie-Laure's short, bright silver hair was slicked back in a severe style that looked sexy in a threatening way that Lala suspected every man and a substantial selection of women would find a challenge impossible to resist. The dress was off the shoulder, and Marie-Laure's arms were covered in sheer black lace. There was a slit going up the front of her dress that ended just below the top of her thighs. Lala watched Marie-Laure turn toward Gérard to adjust his bow tie, at which point she was able to see that the back of Marie-Laure's gown was essentially non-existent. The fabric plunged down to the top of her tush, and her shoulder blades were bisected by a long line of pearls.

Awwwwwww, man, she looks so effortlessly gorgeous. Awwwww, MAN, fuuuuuuuuck, Lala thought.

The chauffeur opened the back door and Gérard and Marie-Laure entered the car. Clive handed them each a full flute of champagne. Gérard raised his glass.

"In French, *à la vôtre.* In English, bottom's up."

Lala downed her newly full glass in one gulp.

"Marie-Laurie," she said, "you look *trop belle.*"

"My dear, if I could write a story as charming as your *Dressed Like a Lady, Drinks Like a Pig,* I would never even give a passing thought to how I looked."

"Thanks!" Lala said.

I think? she thought. *Hmmm, was that a backhanded compliment? Or a forehanded insult? Like I don't care how I look? Fine. Who cares. I wrote a book. And I've got champagne. Life is beautiful.*

Lala smiled and raised her empty glass and twirled it in the air to get Clive's attention. She had just enough time to finish the glass he poured for her before their car arrived at the Quai de Grenelle. The chauffeur drove them to the end of the street, which was in fact the Seine. And where a small yacht was docked.

"Ohhh, boy," Lala said. "If that's our destination, I am thinking it is time to do some serious partying! There's more champagne on board, I assume?"

Gérard escorted them to the ship. Lala saw a man waiting for them on the deck. A man in a chef's uniform, complete with the traditional tall, puffy hat that Lala always felt made the wearer look like a character in a Disney cartoon. A man who looked exactly like Gérard.

"*Chers amis, je vous présente mon frère, Lucas.*" Gérard said.

Lucas took Lala's hand and kissed it. Then he kissed Marie-Laure on both cheeks. Lala's jaw had not yet reconnected with her upper lip.

"You have an identical twin brother?" Lala said. "I mean, obviously you do. I guess I'm trying to convey that I'm amazed I didn't know that."

Why am I amazed? Lala thought. *We worked together. I was in love with Gérard. He liked me okay. And had a girlfriend. And still has the same one. And he never shared any personal information with me, because why would he? Hey, Lucas, want to hear something funny? You and your bro look exactly like my dead husband!*

"Okay, enough inner monologue," Lala said. "Let's shift this shindig into high gear, shall we?"

Lucas escorted them to a small dining room where a table was set for four. He led them to the bar area of the room and popped open a bottle of champagne. He filled five glasses.

"Is this your yacht, Lucas?" Lala asked. "And you're a chef? How cool! When did you decide you wanted to be a chef? What's your favorite part about being a chef? I bet you have some really fun chef stories, huh? I'd love to hear them sometime!"

Lucas smiled nervously.

"My English. Not so good as my brother's," he said.

"Oh, that's okay," Lala said. "I'll speak French!"

"No, no, no," Gérard said. "I'll be happy to translate."

Lala was already too tipsy to be offended.

"Fine, fine, *je ne vais pas parler français*, ya big sensitive baby. Wouldn't want to hurt anyone's big sensitive baby ears. This champagne is lovely!"

The yacht began its voyage on the Seine. The room had floor-to-ceiling windows, so the bar and their table had unobstructed views of all the monuments that were beautifully lit along the river.

Gérard and Marie-Laure had informed Lucas that Lala was a vegetarian, and the evening's repast was a tribute to the culinary delights of the legume and the noodle and the herb-based-broth sauce.

Chocolate soufflé, thankfully, was and always had been vegetarian.

Over dessert, Lala found herself noticing that Clive was giving her glances that could best be described as quite adorably furtive.

"Why haven't I mentioned earlier that you look lovely?" he said.

"You did, actually," Lala said. "When you picked me up."

"Well, it bears repeating."

Lala saw Gérard and Marie-Laure smile at each other.

Have I told them that I'm engaged-to-be-engaged? Lala silently asked herself. *God, that sounds so stupid.*

"My dears, what are you doing to celebrate *le Quatorze Juillet?*" Marie-Laure asked.

"Also known as Bastille Day," Lala elucidated for Clive in a stage whisper.

"Yes, love, thank you, quite aware of that," Clive said. He smiled, wrapped Lala's hand in his, and kissed it. Lala noted that this affectionate gesture was met with approving nods from Gérard and Marie-Laure.

Maybe I forgot to tell them about my fiancé-to-be-my-fiancé, and I sound demented even saying that in my mind, don't I?

"Gérard and I are having a party *chez sa grand-mère* in Reims."

"Reims as in the Champagne Region Reims?" Lala gasped. "Clive, we have to go!"

The yacht brought them back to their point of embarkation. There were hugs and thanks by the shore, and Lala kissed Lucas on both cheeks more than twice. She just kept going back and forth between either side of his mouth with loud smacking noises that divided the words in her rapid and hushed sentences.

"That . . . was . . . the . . . best . . . dinner . . . I . . . have . . . ever . . . had . . . *mon* . . . *trop* . . . *cher* Lucas!"

The limousine brought Gérard and Marie-Laure to their building on the way back to Lala's apartment, and the evening's penultimate leave-taking abounded with copious, sincere, and gushing thanks, and with promises to get together again very soon, for fun and, as Marie-Laure initiated, to discuss having Lala's novel translated into French.

On the way to Lala's street, Lala asked Clive if he would mind if the chauffeur dropped them off by the river so they could take in her favorite view of Notre Dame before the evening ended.

Standing by the Seine, Lala nearly wept, as she was always fearing she might do, from the timeless beauty of Paris. A strong wind came off the water, and she shivered. Clive took his jacket off and wrapped it around her and hugged her to keep her warm and the next thing she knew, they were kissing and trying to do the equivalent of a body snatching science fiction classic wherein they were the only two people in the world in danger of having their souls physically invaded by an outside force, that outside force being embodied in the person right there next to them.

They were neither of them in any rush to break away from each other. When they finally did, Lala spoke first.

"That," she said, "was nice."

"Very nice," Clive agreed.

"Very, very nice."

"Very, very, very nice."

"You can't walk me home."

"Lala, I am not going to let you walk home alone at this hour."

"You can walk ten feet behind me. And you can stand in the entrance to the courtyard and watch me walk into my building. That's my best offer, pal."

Lala and Clive would remain affectionate friends for the rest of their long lives. They would always stay in touch and would be closer in their relationship on numerous occasions, depending mostly on proximity through work and changing mutual social circles. It would be at the Academy Awards ceremony during which Lala made history as the oldest person to ever win an Oscar for Best Adapted Screenplay that the first and only time they would reference the stolen kisses they had shared in Paris so many years earlier would occur.

Clive would be nominated for the second time for Best Supporting Actor for his role as the crotchety grandfather with a heart of gold in the screen adaptation of Lala's bestselling novel, *A Woman of a Certain Age*, which had taken longer to get the green-light for production than anyone had expected. By the time the director yelled his first "Action!" on the set, Clive would be too old to play the character his glib comment about Lala's age had inspired when he first said it in Paris. And he would whine mightily about that fact.

"It's not fair! Ageism in Hollywood isn't fair!"

"Are you fucking kidding me," Lala would respond. "You're just now realizing this? Welcome to every female actor in history's world, my pouty friend. Now memorize your role and hush up."

Standing in line next to each other at the bar during a break in the awards ceremony, Lala would introduce a major non sequitur into their discussion of the insane property values in Malibu that they were both benefiting from.

"You kissed me. In Paris. Repeatedly."

"Oh, my dear Lala, you were the one who kissed me. Repeatedly. In Paris."

"You leaned in first."

"I beg to differ. I distinctly remember you leaning in first."

"Nuh uh."

"Uh huh."

"Shut up. Hi, may I have another champagne, please? Aren't you adorable? What's your name, sweetheart? Want to be one of my adopted nephews? I should warn you, it is not the easiest gig on the planet . . ."

AND ANOTHER

The sun had only recently appeared on the horizon. It was, in Lala's words to one of the production assistants on the set, "colder than fuck out here." And yet Lala was feeling cozy and thrilled. She was on location at a horse farm, where they would be filming the scene she wrote as payment for the real estate blackmail her building's former owner had demanded in order to be willing to sell her the haven for feral cats that was now hers.

The set that day was a mini-family reunion, when "family" is defined as people you have around you because you want to, not because you have to. Clive, of course, was there. He looked as tired as Lala felt because it had been late when they had gotten back to their respective homes after their yacht adventure the night before.

Lala was terrified when she first saw him, and then indescribably relieved when he appeared to have agreed—without any communication regarding the subject actually occurring between them—to pretend nothing unusual had happened.

"Hey, how are ya?" Clive had called out when he first saw Lala.

"Great! You?"

"Great!"

"Cool! Well, I won't keep you! I imagine you're wanted in the make-up tent, huh?"

Matthew was there. Lala had, in the course of visiting the various film sets, grown quite fond of him. His brother, Atticus Finch (that never got old for Lala, and she generally insisted on calling him by his full name whenever they spoke, which made Atticus giggle with embarrassed delight), was also on the set, having come along for the fun of it and to help out if any rewrites were needed. His boyfriend (his definitely committed boyfriend and there would probably be a wedding in the near future), Lala's much-adored neighbor and highly-valued employee and wonderfully-dedicated rescue colleague Kenny, was there to help with craft services. Kenny had brought three large trays of his superb croissants and strawberry jam for breakfast. Lala ate five of them before shooting started.

Clément Barrault, the former owner of Lala's building, had gotten there before anyone else. He had arrived at the location while it was still very dark out and almost walked smack into the side of a barn because it was so hard to see anything.

Though this would be Clément's first turn as an actor at the age of sixty-seven, he would prove to be a consummate professional that day. He had all his lines down letter-perfect. He would help the other actors run their lines during the breaks between shots. He was warm and cheerful, and he actively sought ways to make the day's experience pleasant and successful for everyone. They all fell in love with him.

Clément would be nominated for an Oscar for Best Supporting Actor for his performance in that one scene in the film version of Lala's novel, despite the fact that his screen time in the final edit would be far shorter, clocking in at just under two minutes, than that of any actor who had been nominated to date.

He would not win. In an unprecedented slate of nominees, there would be two non-Americans who were also non-Brits nominated for Best Supporting Actor, and Clément would lose to an astonishingly brilliant performance by "that kid from that weird Finnish sitcom," as Lala had christened young Kalevi

Korhonen. But the acting bug would have taken hold for the rest of Clément's life, and he would transfer his passion to the stage, becoming, in very short order, one of the resident character actors at the acclaimed *Comédie Française*.

His daughter, who would remain grudgingly devoted to her duties as the caretaker of an aging parent, would post a major hissy fit whenever her father's theatrical fame in the French capital would garner more attention than her own brittle beauty could muster from the public. Which was all the time. Because Clément was adorable and everyone in his audience treasured him. And because Celestine would remain exceptionally off-putting for the rest of her life.

Lala had left for the set too early that morning to Skype with David. Which was a blessing in her unstable world because it gave her more time to convince herself that her make-out session with a handsome British movie star had not in actual fact occurred and had only been an entirely innocent, drunken hallucination. She was determined to prove to herself that the more you told yourself a lie, the more it would set you free.

The early morning segment of the shoot went very smoothly. Clément's and Clive's characters stood at the entrance to the barn while they were grooming their horses and had an intense conversation wherein the older man shared his insights about life and all the risks that committing to love involved. And also tennis. The characters talked about tennis a lot.

That part about tennis ended up on the cutting room floor. Matthew explained that it was "just a wee bit off topic, but clever, very clever, kiddos" when Lala and Atticus whined about their best punchlines being cut.

The sun was strong that day, and the lunch break was like a wonderful picnic. Matthew had a very continental view of the atmosphere he wanted on his set, and since there was no stunt work to be done that day, some lovely French white wine was served along with the multi-table spread of salads and pastas and fruits and breads.

With the agreement of the cast and crew, the production had become cruelty-free as a result of Lala's impassioned promotion of animal welfare. Which had only made Lala love them all that much more.

Lala had a delightful conversation with the owners of the farm, an older couple who had lived in Chicago for many years before they returned to their native land to take over the farm they had inherited from the wife's family. Lala and the location scout had chosen the property to film because the family raised only crops there . . . all the animals at the farm—horses, goats, bunnies—were family pets. For Lala, being there was like being in kindness heaven.

Henri and Edith, the farm's owners, spoke impeccable English. The subject of Lala speaking French never came up during their chat.

The afternoon shoot was to begin with Clément and Clive sharing tea and intense conversation. The dialogue in the scene about competitive ping pong would be cut in the editing room. Lala and Atticus would complain that Matthew was deleting some of their best stuff. Matthew would tell them to shut their mewling pie-holes already, a comment he would make with tremendous affection. Years later, Lala, would give a speech at an American Film Institute tribute to Matthew's work and would thank him for their many superb collaborations and for "editing the shit out of my work, which always made it leaner and meaner and funnier and better."

Just before the scene was about to begin shooting, Lala caught sight of something, and what she saw got her to twitching. With delight.

"Wabbits," she whispered.

Switching her seat to the periphery of the next scene had brought Lala within view of a small outdoor structure that looked like a cottage out of the Brothers Grimm. A little girl was sitting on the steps leading up to the cottage. She had a basket on her lap. Lala could see the impossibly adorable heads of little baby rabbits poking out over the top of the basket. She was instantly oblivious to the need to comport herself professionally on set. Thankfully, though, she sprinted in the direction of the cottage moments before Matthew yelled "Action!" Her exit didn't create a disruption.

Lala passed by a craft services table on her path and grabbed a gorgeous red apple. She took a big and delicious bite.

Am I remembering this correctly? Lala thought. *I think baby rabbits are called kittens. OMIGOD, they are adorable!*

Lala stopped in front of the little girl. She smiled at her, and the little girl smiled back. She held up one of the rabbits.

Okay, no need to frighten her with my mangling of her beautiful language. Let's get this out of the way right up front.

"*Tu parles anglais?*" Lala asked.

Lala saw the little girl's eyes widen with mirth and mischief. The next thing she was aware of was a hard substance butting her butt. She stumbled forward and had to brace herself not to fall flat on her face.

Lala twirled around and saw a large goat looking up at her with fierce determination. She had a brief moment during which she remembered, on a superficial level of understanding, that one of the worst things you could do when confronted by an aggressive animal who could outrun you without breaking a sweat was to flee.

"FUUUUUUUCK!" Lala screamed.

The cast and crew all turned in the direction of her dismay. Matthew yelled "Cut!" Lala was unaware of all of this because her heart was pounding so desperately as she turned and ran as fast as she could.

She had no plan in mind other than to keep running. She heard a ruckus behind her.

"Throw the apple away!"

"He's not chasing you!"

"He just wants the apple!"

"Okay, seriously," Lala said. Lala instantly realized that speaking aloud was not a good decision, as it only made her feel more winded.

Seriously, she thought. *I can't hear a word any of you are saying.*

"LALA!" she heard a chorus of voices yell.

It's possible that the excessively pumping oxygen had made her delirious, because her next decision was also a bad one. She turned on her heels and yelled back at the cast and crew.

"WHAT?"

Running backward for even the small amount of time that it took to launch that monosyllable slowed Lala down enough for the goat to catch up with her and butt her thighs. Down she went in a backward crumble.

"Oof," she said.

The goat calmly took the apple out of her hand and trotted away happily with it in his mouth. Lala lifted her head and stared at his retreat.

"That's what you wanted?" she gasped. "Why didn't you just say so?"

Lala let her head fall back down on the ground just as a herd of people came running over to her.

"Don't move!" Matthew yelled.

The crew paramedics had Lala on a stretcher in no time.

"I'm fine! Thanks for worrying, but I'm fine!"

"Just stay put and let them make sure you haven't damaged anything," Matthew ordered. He walked beside Lala as she was carried inside the farmers' house.

"Did I screw up the shoot?" Lala asked.

"Of course you screwed up the shoot. We could see you running around like a lunatic in the background. And then there was all that yelling. So, yeah, we're gonna need to start all over again."

"So you're okay?" her aunt barked into the computer screen.

Jeez, Lala thought. *Try to sound a little less disappointed.*

"Yup!" Lala said with all the forced cheerfulness she could muster, given how much her head still hurt. "The paramedics gave me a clean bill of health. I just have to rest for a day or two."

"DAVID!" Geraldine yelled. "You can talk to her if you want."

Geraldine, who had been sitting at her desk on the Skype call with Lala and had been hugging Petunia, leapt out of the chair and scowled at David as she brushed by him. Lala saw David stare with a troubled look after Geraldine's retreating figure. He sat in the chair and smiled at the screen.

"I'm so glad you're not hurt."

"Oh, David, honey, thank you. I miss you. I love you. That's not the French version of Extra Strength Tylenol with Codeine talking."

And then, without warning, there was an awkward pause. Lala and David smiled nervously at each other.

"How are the dogs? How long are you home?"

"I'm just here until tomorrow. The dogs are great," David said. "They miss their mama. We all miss you."

Ever since she received the Skype call from Manhattan Beach, Lala had a vague but consistent feeling of wooziness, which she assumed was from her nervous heart pumping blood just a little too quickly. As a result, she was a tiny beat behind fully hearing what Geraldine and David were saying to her, as though there were a delay in the transmission. She smiled at David as she processed what he just said before she responded, and he jumped in again before she could say anything.

"Are we okay?" David asked

"Mmm—"

"Because I'm not sure where we're—"

". . . hmm. Mmm hmm, I'm okay. Am I okay? Is that what you asked me?"

"No. I mean, of course I want to make sure you're okay. No one told you to just throw the apple to the goat? What I asked just now was if we're okay?

Ohhh, merde, Lala thought.

"Mmm hmm! Yup!" Lala said.

"David! Dinner's ready!" Auntie Geraldine brayed from

some dark and forbidding space beyond the computer.

"Be right there!" he called over his shoulder.

He looked back at the screen. There was another awkward pause. Lala had to struggle to keep her voice steady as she stumbled into the silence.

"You better not keep the general waiting," she said.

"Yup. Love you."

"Love you."

She didn't give herself a chance to hesitate breaking their virtual connection. Her index finger slammed down on the mouse so that the call would disconnect as quickly as possible.

Lala shut her laptop and put it on the coffee table next to the couch. She turned the television back on and snuggled beneath the two cozy quilts Kenny and Atticus had covered her with when they brought her home from the set while the rest of the cast and crew stayed behind to reshoot the scene and try to make up for the time she had cost them.

Minou was on her lap sleeping the peaceful repose of a treasured pet. Lala held the cat closer and was comforted by snuggling with an animal.

"Minou," she whispered. "I'm all off balance. Did I tell you that my star sign is Libra? It's the scales. Stop me if I'm repeating myself."

Lala picked up the remote control and flipped through the channels. She settled on a documentary about—as far as she could tell from what she could catch of the narration and from the photograph and video montages—the fashion choices of the 1970s that were, in hindsight, especially unfortunate.

She watched for a few minutes, and then she started to feel really tired again. She put her head back on the pillow and pulled Minou up right under her chin. The cat started purring loudly, and the sound of her and of the low volume on the television was just what Lala needed to help her relax. She closed her eyes and sighed.

"Minou, did I ever tell you about this time Terrence and I

were going to the Hollywood Bowl? Stop me if you've heard this before. No? Okay. So we were visiting my parents for a few weeks and Steely Dan was playing at the Bowl, so of course we had to go. But you know parking at the Bowl is just hellish. So my friend Theodora told us about this swell street nearby where parking is actually not restricted and not many people know about it. So we park there and she's given us instructions on how to find the staircase that leads right down to Highland Avenue right by the Bowl, and we can just walk across the street and we're right there. And of course I didn't write down the directions because they sounded so easy when she was telling them to me. And of course I thought I was following them. And of course I couldn't find the stairway."

Lala heard quiet yelling in English coming from the television. She opened her eyes, lifted her head, and turned up the volume. The archival video showed a group of young people standing outside a disco in midtown Manhattan. Lala gasped when she saw the outfits they were wearing.

"Sweet Baby Jesus," she said.

She couldn't take her eyes off the screen. It wasn't until her head started hurting again that she was forced to shut her eyes and lean back down on the pillow.

"Where was I, Minou? Oh, yeah. So it's getting later and later. We're in danger of not getting to the Bowl in time for the show. I'm getting frantic. I keep looking and looking and we're running around and then there it is. It just appears. With no effort. I'm looking in front of me, and I look maybe a few inches to my right, and there's the staircase. As though it had been there all along. I must have looked at that spot where it was a dozen times while we were searching. Somehow I didn't see the staircase until that moment. Until the last second. And then everything was okay."

Lala's voice was trailing off during the last two sentences, and she fell asleep again. When she woke up, she wasn't sure how long she had slept. She peered at the television. The documentary had ended, and the channel was now showing a talent competition. Lala immediately closed her eyes again. She didn't feel the need to try to find anything more compelling to watch, because she had the distinct impression that she wouldn't be awake for long. Minou did not wake up, and had not stopped purring.

"You're such a love, Minou," Lala whispered. "Want to hear a story? It's germane to what I was talking about before our most recent nap. It was when my parents and I were visiting my grandparents in England. I was a teenager. I had such a blast with all my cousins. They're so cool. Anyway, I was taking a bath at the hotel and there weren't any screens on the window because, you know, Europe 'n' stuff, and this huge fly comes buzzing in. The poor thing starts frantically bumping into the walls, and of course I immediately feel sorry for it, so I'm thinking I'll get up if it doesn't find its way back to the window soon and I'll just herd the big beast outside. So it gets back to the general area of the window, so I'm thinking it's going to be fine, and the stupid insect is hitting the wall all around the window and it's going everywhere right next to the window, and I start yelling, 'It's right there, you idiot! Just move over one inch! It's right there!"

Lala titled her head without lifting it and looked down at the cat.

"I can see that you're hanging on my every word," she giggled. "In case you're wondering, I did have to get up out of the bathtub and I used my towel to guide the fly toward the window, and it finally got out." Lala shut her eyes.

I'm hungry, Lala thought. *And I'm much too lazy to get up. Oh, well.*

And then she sighed. "The window is just an inch away. The staircase is within my field of vision. I feel like the answer is right there. The solution is right there. I just can't find it."

Lala slept on and off for the next day and night. She was reasonably conscious when Kenny and Atticus came up to check on her and to bring her comforting soups and breads. They sat with her while she ate, and they left her with lots of hugs and with promises to check on her and to not wake her if she was asleep.

Clive and Matthew also came over. Lala was asleep when they got there, so they left her a box of gorgeous red apples and a note that said, "Throw them! Just throw them!" Lala chortled when she woke and saw the gift and the note, and muttered "Those cheeky bastards think they're funny" to Minou. She thought about eating one of the apples, decided she would save that for later, and then promptly fell asleep again.

The next time she woke up, Lala was surprised to find that she had something going on in her body and her mind that almost felt a little bit like energy. She stayed curled up on her left side with Minou snuggled against her chest while she debated if the sensation was real or a phantom memory from the days when she was actually peppy. She opened her eyes and looked at the television. Matthew's film, *Tooters*, was showing again.

Did that cheeky bastard put a DVD of his abomination on repeat? Or is that being broadcast again? Why do the French love that stupid movie so much?

Lala turned over on her back, clutching Minou and taking her with her as she rolled. She lifted herself up a bit on the pillow and blinked at the light in the room. The curtains were drawn, but bright sunlight was streaming in around the edges.

"Wow, Minou," Lala said. "I may be done sleeping. For now."

Lala sat up. She swung her legs around and put her feet on the floor.

"Okay! So far, so good."

Lala sat quietly and just looked around the room for a bit. When she was confident that sitting up felt good, she decided it might indeed be time to reconnect with the world. Opening her laptop seemed like a good first step.

The first thing Lala saw when she checked her inbox was an e-mail from her aunt.

"READ THIS RIGHT AWAY" the subject line blared.

Yikes, Lala thought.

She steeled herself as she clicked to open the aggressive missive. Lines and lines of text ran in front of her as she scrolled down. Even as she was avoiding actually taking in any of the words and as she was trying to ignore all the exclamation points, Lala was marveling that the internet in fact had the capacity to transport a tome of such intense volume. She took a deep breath and headed back up to the top of the e-mail. She glanced down at Minou, who had turned around in a circle a few times right after Lala sat up, and was now curled up and fast asleep on the couch next to her with the top of her little head resting up against the edge of Lala's laptop.

"This communication from Auntie Geraldine is the reason the phrase 'magnum opus' was coined. Do you want to hear what she has to say, Minou? You do? Okay. I'll read to you. Wait. I better get something liquid. Go back to sleep."

Lala brewed a lovely, extra-large mug of English Breakfast tea and carried it back to the couch.

"Shove over," she said to Minou. She snuggled next to the cat and started at the top of the screen. There was no salutation for her to read. Auntie Geraldine got right to it.

"'Of course I'm glad that you're okay,'" Lala read. "'But I'm done pretending your behavior is acceptable any longer, young lady! You could be losing him right now! What if some graduate student or sexy colleague has turned David's head because you've been ignoring him?'"

Lala paused and took a big gulp of tea.

"Okay, I haven't exactly been *ignoring* him," she said. She shrugged and continued reading.

"'What would you expect David to do if you died first?'"

Damn you . . .

"'Con—'"

Damn you and your making sense 'n' stuff, Auntie Geraldine, Lala thought.

"—tinue his life,'" Lala continued as her answer to Geraldine's question. "'I'd expect him to find happiness again. And take really good care of my dogs. But he hasn't had to go through it yet. I'm weakened by it.'"

"'I know you think you've been weakened by losing Terrence,'" Lala read.

Lala's eyes widened and she shook her head in disbelief.

"Wow. She is good, Minou. I think I mentioned that once or twice a long time ago. I'm hungry. Stay here. I'll be right back."

Lala ran to the kitchen and returned with a warm croissant and a pot of Kenny's jam to dip it in. Lala was so mesmerized by her aunt's ability to predict her response while Geraldine was writing the e-mail that she had almost entirely forgotten to be dreading the lecture she was receiving. She plopped back down on the couch, took a big bite of croissant, and started reading again with her mouth full.

"'Or you're strengthened by your terrible loss. Because you know that it gets better. It gets easier. It never gets easy. But it does get easier.'"

Damn her, Lala thought. *She's right.*

"'And we go on. Because we must. You know what Terrence said to everyone when he was sick.' *God*, Auntie Geraldine plays dirty, Minou."

Lala had to stop reading while she remembered, very clearly, as though she were again hearing and seeing Terrence ask their friends and family to please promise him that they would always make sure that Lala was okay.

She remembered all these scenes, but she was remembering them in her imagination, because Terrence had never had any of those conversations when she was there with him. It was only after he died that so many—that all of their friends and family had told her that nothing mattered to him but her welfare.

"Ahhh," she sighed. She brushed away many tears with the palms of her hands and went back to the screen.

"'All he asked us to do was take care of you. All he wanted was for you to find love again. And you have. If you throw it away, I swear to god, I will slap you so hard.'"

I'm scared, Lala thought. And then she clarified, as though Minou had heard her thoughts.

"I'm not scared of her slapping me, Minou," Lala said. "She's tall and she's feisty as fuck, but I think I could take her. I'm scared of ever again feeling the way I did when Terrence was gone. Goodness, I need more tea. Wait just a sec."

She ran to the kitchen and came back with a full pot and another croissant.

"'I don't give a royal rat's patootie how scared you are of losing David the way you lost Terrence.' Yikes, Minou, that is a bit strident, don't you think? 'I could lose Monty tomorrow. TOMORROW, do you hear me? And it would all be worth it. ALL of it. Don't you dare let David go because you're scared of losing him. I will NOT put up with anything as ironic as that in your life or in my life, do you understand me?'"

Lala realized she just had to take a break. She closed her laptop and walked toward the bathroom, shedding her clothes as she stepped. She took a very long, very hot bath, and then got dressed in her exercise clothes, with the idea of taking a long and brisk walk along the Seine. But she decided she did want to finish her aunt's e-mail before she left the apartment.

Minou was asleep between the layers of the multiple blankets on the couch. Lala patted the flannel mounds to ascertain where the cat was. A warm, large lump and a meow followed quickly by a soft little growl established the space next to which Lala should sit.

"Those first two years were a non-stop nightmare," Lala said. "I couldn't survive that again. I couldn't."

She opened her laptop and read aloud:

"'I know the years after Terrence was gone were a nightmare.'"

Lala slammed the laptop shut as though it had suddenly come completely alive and was spying on her with a not-clearly-benevolent goal in mind.

"Okay, this is just getting weird now, Minou. Is Geraldine here? Is she typing her responses remotely while she's listening to me? *And* reading my thoughts?"

Lala slowly opened the laptop again and peered beneath the screen as it lifted.

"'I hope you don't have to experience that tragedy ever again, but if you do, we'll all be there to help you. And you'll get through it.'"

An angry and unkind thought occurred to Lala. She felt guilty, but she had to give it voice. And it probably wouldn't bother the cat, who was continuing to be deeply unconscious.

"I'm sorry, Auntie Geraldine, but would you be saying all this to me if—poo, poo, poo god forbid, Monty's tumor hadn't been benign?"

"'I realize I may sound glib,'" Lala read, "'And you may be wondering if I would be feeling the same way if Monty's tumor had been malignant.'"

Okay, either Geraldine just knows me really, really, really, really, really well, or Minou is somehow communicating telepathically with her, Lala thought.

"Minou," she said, "if I find out you two are in cahoots, I will be very annoyed." And then she went back to the screen. "'I would be sad and I would be crying and I would still be saying exactly the same things to you that I am saying now. Because all the sadness and the tears would be worth it for the time I've already had with Monty, and please don't even try to tell me that you don't feel the same way about the time you had with Terrence.'"

Fuuuuuuuuuuck, Lala thought.

And, as much as she wanted argue with her aunt, to scream that she couldn't stand to be widowed a second time, because maybe that would somehow vaccinate her against it ever happening again, she knew her aunt was right. If it ever did happen again, she would get through it. Somehow.

"Okay, enough for now. Air. And movement. I need both. *Aussi vite que possible*. Sorry about my mangled accent, Minou."

Lala calmly shut her laptop and put it back on the coffee table. She tied her shoelaces and stood. She patted the small feline lump beneath the blankets.

"Don't get up. I'll be back in an hour or two. When you communicate with Auntie Geraldine, which I assume you'll be doing as soon as I leave, please tell her I promise to reflect on everything she's yelled at me."

IN SEARCH OF LOST *BOULEVARD PÉRIPHÉRIQUE*

Someone in the car behind Lala was honking at her in an unpredictable rhythm of long and short blasts that made Lala think he might be trying to communicate via Morse code. She lowered the driver's side window and leaned out with her head turned over her shoulder.

"Listen, buddy, at this point I don't know if you're pissed at me or if you're flirting with me, but in case you hadn't noticed, NONE of the cars are moving!"

Damn, Lala thought. *He probably doesn't understand me. How do you say all that in French?*

Lala put Kenny's car into park and leaned her head back on the headrest. She closed her eyes and remembered how enthusiastic she had been feeling on the evening before that fourteenth of July.

The plan had been for Clive and Lala to drive to Gérard's family estate for the celebration of Bastille Day and to spend the night there.

"In separate bedrooms," Lala had declared, over and over and over again, during the coordinating of details. "Do not get any ideas, pal."

"No ideas gotten," Clive had assured her, over and over and over again.

They had planned to leave early so they could have the option of stopping anywhere along the way if an especially charming location appeared. But when Lala's phone rang and woke her up an hour before the time she had set on the alarm, she jolted awake with the immediate and very unpleasant feeling that something must be wrong.

"WHAT?" she bleated at her phone.

"I'm so sorry. The good news is, your virtue will be especially safe. The bad news is, I can't go to the party. We have to reshoot all the scenes at the farm. You know, the ones we did on the day the goat molested you."

"I remember, Clive," Lala growled. "I remember the goat, and I can hear you trying to suppress a long series of giggles. Why do they have to reshoot? Did you see the dailies? Did Clément suck? Oh, god, I forced him on the production to serve my own selfish, albeit very caring and humane, needs, and he sucked? I knew I shouldn't have imposed an amateur on the film. I get so tunnel vision with animals, and now I've put the entire—"

"Lala, take a breath. Yes, I saw the dailies. Clément was amazing. I mean, he was brilliant. It's me. I sucked beyond belief. I think Matthew wanted to fire me on the spot. I've got to redeem myself pronto or else I am fucked."

"Oh. Okay," Lala said.

"Listen, since I can't drive you, I think you should take the train."

"Why?" Lala huffed. "I'm perfectly capable of driving myself."

"You're a terrible driver."

"What makes you think I'm a terrible driver?" Lala demanded.

"You told me. Those were your exact words."

"Oh. Okay. Well, I was kidding."

As she remembered her conversation with Clive, Lala opened her eyes and looked up at the ceiling of the car.

I wasn't kidding, she thought. *Driving myself today has already earned a top spot on my long list of dumbest ideas I've ever had, and I'm not even half of the way to my destination.*

After she hung up with Clive, Lala was feeling defiant and irritated and like she had something to prove to patronizing men everywhere, so before she got the car from Kenny and headed out, she deliberately programmed the GPS on her phone to give her directions in French.

"Do you really think that's a good idea?" Kenny had asked when she told him about her bold and confident decision. "It's just an added layer of difficulty that maybe you don't need when you're—"

"Kenny," Lala said through tight lips, "I know you mean well, but the patriarchy is really busting my ass this morning, so I'm in no mood."

Lala shut her eyes again. Just as she did, the driver behind her leaned on his horn with a steady pressure. She thrust her head up and looked in the rearview mirror. The man was standing up as much as he could in a car and appeared to be pressing the full weight of his body on the center of the steering wheel. Lala leaned back out the window.

"Are you KIDDING? *Aucune voiture n'avance*, you big jerk! So why don't you just calm the fu . . . Oh . . ."

Something had caught Lala's attention out of the corner of her right eye and had taken her focus away from the car behind her. That something was a boulevard newly devoid of the traffic jam that she had assumed would be her destiny, if not until the end of time, then certainly for at least the next hour.

"Okay, okay," she muttered. "I'm shifting into drive, *Monsieur*. My mistake. Sheesh."

Lala hit the gas pedal and pulled over to the first free space at the curb that she saw. She turned the car off and covered her face with her hands. She shook her head and sighed.

We will be doing this, Lala told herself. *We will take a deep breath and we will not be bested by le Boulevard Périphérique. We are strong. We are invincible. We are woman. We have no idea why we are using the royal "we" in our internal pep talk.*

Kenny had changed tactics that morning when he felt the vibrating wrath of Lala's irritation, and had decided to be overly encouraging because it might save him from any additional glaring. He had explained to Lala that she would be heading out of Paris toward the countryside via *le Périph'*, the multiple-lane road that circled the historic center of Paris and loosely defined its classic borders.

"It's just like a freeway in Los Angeles," Kenny assured her. "It'll take you right to the A-4 and you'll be in Reims in no time. Piece of cake. Nothing to worry about."

"I'm not taking the highway to get to Reims," Lala had explained.

"What are you talking about?" Kenny had asked, with an expression that immediately telegraphed grave concern for Lala's grasp on sanity.

"I'm programming my GPS to avoid highways. It's what I do in LA I take side streets. I don't like Southern California freeways. I don't like any freeways. I swear, I have no idea what the difference is between a freeway and a highway. In either case and in any event, I'm taking the scenic route to Reims."

"Well, then you'll get there on Tuesday. Late Tuesday or early Wednesday. Of the week after next."

"Very funny," Lala had sneered.

"I'm not trying to be funny," Kenny had said.

"Oh, this cannot *possibly* be the right address . . ."

Lala had passed many charming locales on her way to Gérard's grandmother's home. She had only had time to give each of them the briefest of longing glances as she motored through them at the quickest speeds that French travel regulations would allow.

Once Lala had finally driven outside Paris, guided by a new and stuffy British voice speaking clipped English on her GPS, it had become agonizingly clear that she would not be getting to Reims quickly on the country roads. As loping minute after minute after minute passed, she drove onward, silently debating different courses of action and unable to decide on any of them.

Turn around and call it a day and get hammered at the restaurant with Kenny and his grandfather and Atticus? Search for the nearest train station on the GPS, park the car there, and hope that a train to Reims is leaving sometime today? Park the car and speedwalk, because at least then I'll be getting some exercise and I probably might even get there more quickly than at this rate on these gorgeous cobblestone streets and all these winding paths through these impossibly adorable villages?

And now she was driving up what looked like either an endless, diminutive public road or an endless, huge private driveway. Majestic trees bordered the car on both sides and bent toward each other to create a canopy for Lala to drive beneath as she talked to herself and fretted.

"I think I distinctly remember that Gérard described his grandmother's place of residence as a *house* and not a freakin' *château* . . . I really don't think I packed anything fancy enough for this flippin' *castle* . . ."

Lala turned into the circular path in front of the immense wooden double door at the center of the structure's endless facade. The doors flew open and Marie-Laure came running out. She smiled and waved and rushed over to open the driver's side door.

"There you are! *Vite, vite!*"

Marie-Laure took Lala by the elbow and helped her out of the car. She kissed Lala on both cheeks and then opened the back door to grab Lala's weekend bag.

"I had no idea the house is this big," Lala said. "Is this a fancy party? I don't think I have anything fancy enough for a house like this."

"*Ma chère*, it's a picnic! Do not worry, you will look perfect! Now, you've got half an hour to rest in your room before the festivities start, so let's get you upstairs."

Marie-Laure escorted Lala inside. The entry hall had soaring ceilings and ended, after what Lala estimated was probably the full length of a football field, in a wide staircase.

"That *Boulevard Périphérique* thing?" Lala said as she peered at the portraits and tapestries that covered the walls. "*Le Périph*'? I got on and off that damn thing about a thousand times before I finally was headed in the right direction. I am serious, give me that swirling overpass on the 405 South just past the Getty Center, or that section downtown where you're going from the 110 to the 10 and you have to get across five lanes of traffic from left to right in like two minutes? I mean, I've only ever done it as a passenger, but I would cheerfully do it as a driver any day of the week, including rush hour heading home on a Friday, rather than get anywhere near that damn *périphérique* again. I assume there's champagne in my room?"

"*Bien sur*," Marie-Laure said.

"Then I'll be downstairs again in twenty-nine minutes, and I will be in fine fettle."

Lala's guest room for the holiday was considerably larger than the first apartment she had in New York City when she moved there after college. And it was rather a bit more opulent, given that her fifth-floor walk-up with a bathtub in the kitchen wasn't quite up to the standards of an *Architectural Digest* spread.

A bottle of champagne sat in an ice bucket next to her bed. Lala popped it open and poured a full glass.

Lala lay down on the lush canopy bed for just a moment and woke up forty-five minutes later when Marie-Laure knocked on her door. The first thing she noticed when she opened her eyes was that she hadn't had any of the champagne before she fell asleep.

"Are you ready, *chère* Lala?"

Lala grabbed the glass and chugged the contents.

"I'll be down in five minutes, Marie-Laure! I fell asleep! That drive must have been way more stressful than I realized."

Lala put on her sundress. It was a lovely soft cotton in light blue and it had a wide belt in the same fabric. She had specifically bought it for the Bastille Day celebration at a cozy boutique near her apartment that was owned by a friend of Kenny's. Kenny had dragged her there under protest.

"I hate shopping! I look stupid in just about every outfit I ever try on! I have no visual taste and I don't know what I'm doing! I'm not going to the party! I don't want to go shopping!"

Once in the dressing room, having been given a selection of items by Kenny's very warm and welcoming friend Simone, protest turned to praise as soon as Lala tried on the first dress.

"Omigod! This dress makes me look like I have a waist! I can't wait to show it off at the party!"

Lala walked down the staircase with the bottle of champagne in one hand and her glass in the other. She was barefoot and had gotten a manicure and pedicure the day before, because Marie-Laure told her there would be lots of "adventures without shoes and much bathing" that weekend.

Lala didn't normally get pedicures because it was hard for her to sit still that long and because she didn't much like her toes. A friend in college had seen her toes for the first time a year or two after they met and was shocked and worried.

"Were you in some kind of horrible farm accident?" the friend had asked.

"I . . . No, I didn't grow up on a farm. I haven't spent much time on a . . . Why do you ask?"

"Why didn't you warn me that you have these strange little hobbit toes?"

Lala's friend had then taken to referring to any sandals that Lala wore as her "so-called open-toed shoes" and had ostentatiously made air quotation marks as she said that, and had cackled at her cleverness every time as though it were the first time she had ever come up with that memorable quip.

Lala had lost touch with her friend after they graduated. A bit by design. And had been a bit self-conscious about her toes ever since.

The second glass of champagne she was drinking as she walked through the doors that led to the endless lawn and gardens behind the house, and the image of herself in her new dress that she had enjoyed in the mirror before she left her room, had helped to put that thought about her feet on the back burner of a stove in a different time zone.

That and the fact that Gérard leapt up from the vast picnic blanket he was sitting on with a group of people to greet Lala with a radiant smile.

Oh, merde, Lala thought. *How do you still make my heart race? And why do you look so much like my Terrence? That is just the weirdest thing on record.*

"Lala! Come meet our friends!"

Lala did her best to focus on all the names she was hearing for the first time. It was a little hit-or-miss throughout the day and the evening, both of which involved lots of delicious food and more champagne than Lala thought she had ever seen in one place at one time, including at her wedding to Terrence.

"Pierre? Is it Pierre? Am I remembering that correctly?" she said to the debonair older man who had joined her on the terrace to open a new bottle. She had discovered when they were standing next to each other in line at one of the many buffet tables that they were both vegetarians, and she had grabbed every opportunity since then to flirt with him.

"It is Pierre," the gentleman said, smiling. "I like the way you pop. Did Gérard tell you that all of this is from his family's vineyard?

"Get outta town!" Lala said. "That is wicked cool! Oh, and just to confirm, that's an American idiom. I don't literally want you to leave Reims."

Lala had, early on, given up the idea of trying to speak French to anyone at the party because they all spoke English so perfectly and because she didn't want to hurt their ears.

"Pierre," Lala continued. She filled their glasses and winked at him. "Apropos idioms, I heard the most adorable French one recently. The grumpy fruit vendor near my apartment said it to me the other day, and I don't think she meant it as a compliment. It seems that I *parle français comme une vache espagnole!*"

Lala saw Pierre recoil and just as quickly try to hide that he was doing that.

"Aren't you gallant!" she said. "And is that an adorable way of describing not speaking French well, or what! Like a Spanish cow! Which I've never heard speak French, but I can't imagine it sounds very good! I should, in my own defense, point out that it's my accent, as you just noticed and don't pretend you didn't, you sweet man, that causes the problems. My syntax and vocabulary and grammar are, I think, quite *pas mal*, if I do say so myself. Oh, look, they're choosing teams for *pétanque!*"

Though Lala's physical skills were almost exclusively to be found at the gym or on a hike, she had heard about this popular French version of bocce before, and on that Bastille Day she ended up being quite good at it on her maiden foray into the sport. Possibly, as she theorized somewhat stridently, because the champagne was loosening her pitching arm.

She sent her steel ball rolling toward the small wooden ball that the players were trying to get their aim closest to. Lala's ball landed, rolled, and came to rest just a few centimeters from the goal. Lala pumped her fist in the air and turned to one of her teammates.

"*Oui!* The bubbly is kickin' in, *mes amis*! *Pas mal* for a beginner, huh, Clothilde? Did I get that right? It is Clothilde, isn't it? We are winning this thing, huh!"

Gérard was on the losing team and was very noble in defeat when Lala ran up to him waving her steel ball in his face at the end of the match.

"*Nous avons gagné*, SUCKA!"

"*Toutes mes felicitations, chère Lala*," he said.

"And we're having your family's champagne? What? You weren't perfect enough already?"

Oh, jeez, Lala thought. *Way to act like you're still in love with him. Change the subject. STAT.*

"You know, something just occurred to me, Gérard, and I'm feeling very ungracious that I haven't asked about this before now. Where's your *grand-mère*?

"She'll be here a bit later. She's at a demonstration in town. Her women's political group organized a protest against the mayor. He called a female reporter a little tart, loosely translated. That didn't sit well with my grandmother. If he knows what's good for him, he'll issue a public apology. My grandmother doesn't give up easily."

"She sounds great! I can't wait to meet her!"

Lala paused and smiled at Gérard and suspected that she looked like a crazy person. Like a crazy person in love. That was something she had done more than once when she worked with Gérard in New York and had a painfully overwhelming crush on him. Something she had done more than once a day. Often repeatedly in one hour. Before she knew that Gérard had a gorgeous girlfriend named Marie-Laure.

Lala could only keep smiling and bobbing her head at Gérard while she searched for an exit line. At last, one popped into her mind.

It's not melodic, but it'll have to do, she thought.

"Okey doke. See ya around!"

Just before the fireworks in town were to begin, the buffet tables were once again loaded with an infinite spread of savory and sweet treats. The champagne bottles, Lala suspected, were spontaneously regenerating themselves in a legendary wonder of

228 • Heidi Mastrogiovanni

nature that had no actual basis in scientific fact.

The view from the estate was gorgeous, and Lala was sent into paroxysms of delight with each explosion of lights and colors. She was sitting on one of many picnic blankets, and had chosen her spot to be as far away from Gérard as possible so that she wouldn't be tempted to embarrass herself again by wearing her heart on her sleeveless arms. That concern being momentarily abated, Lala gave herself free reign to wax loony about the patriotic fireworks display.

"Wow! Look at that one! That is incredible! Omigosh, look at that one! It's even bigger 'n' better 'n' brighter than the last one! Wow! That one might be the best so far! Wow! Wow Wow Wow Wow WOW!"

Lala turned to the man sitting next to her on the blanket and raised her champagne glass.

"Those are some fabulous *feux d'artifice*, huh!"

The man smiled and nodded and clinked his glass against Lala's.

"*Vive la France!*" Lala cheered. "Listen, Pascal, can you get someone to hit 'Pause'? I really need to run inside for a brief bathroom break, and I don't want to miss any of this! It is Pascal, isn't it?"

Lala scrambled up off the blanket and ran into the house. As soon as she got inside, she felt just a little dizzy, possibly from having stood up too quickly and having jogged the short distance to the house too exuberantly after having so much delicious champagne. Lala noticed that there was a door ajar just down the hallway to her left and glimpsed a wall of books through the opening. She immediately thought that the trip to the bathroom could wait, and that her equilibrium would no doubt benefit from being in a library. She slipped inside the dimly-lit room and peered at the titles on the shelf nearest to the door at her eye-level. The books all looked old, and all of the titles were in French. She continued on along the wall and saw several titles in English and Italian in the next sections of the shelves. She returned to the first shelves she had seen and stood on her toes to search the titles higher above her head. One of the first books she saw on that upper level made her gasp. Lala carefully extracted a thick volume with ornate letters on the spine reading *Le Comte de Monte Cristo*.

As Lala turned to the center of the room with the idea of picking out a comfortable chair to sit in so she could wallow in the original French of her favorite classic novel, she was startled when a door at the far end of the room opened and a petite woman in a sleek black pantsuit entered the room. The woman had a tight grey bun and she wore a large pair of glasses that somehow managed to look elegant even as they took up much of her small face.

"*Oh, je suis désolée, Madame. Excusez-moi,*" Lala said.

The woman smiled and strode across the room with her hand extended.

"Ah, Gérard and Marie-Laure's American! Welcome. *Je suis* Arlette, Gérard's grandmother." She spoke with a voice that sounded somewhat strained and raspy.

Arlette shook Lala's hand, then kissed her on both cheeks and took a look at the book Lala was holding.

"You have excellent taste, my dear! That's my favorite."

"Mine, too!" Lala said. "*Je m'appelle* Lala, and I am so happy to meet you. How was the protest?"

"Effective," Arlette said.

"Brava! I'm so sorry I snuck into your library. It is heavenly."

"Not a bit. Come sit with me for a moment. I've been standing all day shouting and waving signs."

Arlette led Lala to a small sofa. They sat down next to each other, and Arlette put her clenched hand to her lips and tried to clear her throat.

"Wait," Lala said. "Perhaps some of your family's incredible champagne would help soothe your voice?"

Arlette smiled and said, "I feel sure it would."

"I'll be right back."

Lala ran out to the lawn, grabbed a bottle off the buffet table, secured two clean glasses, and rushed back inside, calling back to Gérard, who was on the patio as she zipped past him.

"Your grandmother is, I suspect, utterly *fabuleuse!*"

Lala scooted back onto the couch, where she popped the bottle, poured, and handed a glass to Arlette. Arlette took a deep sip and patted her collarbone with her fingertips.

"Much better. *Merci mille fois.* My dear, am I remembering correctly? Did you and Gérard work together in New York?"

Ohhh, merde, Lala thought. *She knows. He told her.*

"Mmm," Lala said.

Lala paused. Arlette covered Lala's free hand with hers and gave it a quick squeeze. They both took several sips of champagne before Lala spoke again.

"I had such a crush on your grandson. Of course I didn't know about Marie-Laure until . . . and then . . . I kind of had a bit of a complete and utter meltdown at work."

"Mmm," Arlette said.

"Gérard looks just like my late husband."

"Oh, my dear. You were widowed? I'm so sorry."

The door Lala had entered the library through opened wide and a gangly older man stopped in the doorway when he saw the two women inside the room.

"Ah, Étienne, *mon cher,*" Arlette said. "Come meet my new friend, Lala. She's the American."

Lala stood and Étienne took her hand and kissed it.

"*Enchanté,*" he said. He bent to kiss Arlette on both cheeks and clasped his hands together in supplication as he straightened again.

"Will you two lovely ladies forgive me if I leave you so soon? I must retire." Étienne tilted his head toward Arlette and smiled at Lala. "Protesting with my wife is exhausting for an old fellow like me. I shall see you tomorrow, yes?"

"Absolutely," Lala said.

The women watched Étienne leave the room and close the door behind him.

"How nice that Gérard's grandfather supports your causes," Lala said.

"It is nice, indeed," Arlette said. "Étienne is not, however, Gérard's grandfather. My first husband died many years ago."

"I'm so sorry."

Lala paused and took another sip of champagne.

"And you found love again."

"Twice," Arlette said. "Étienne is my third husband."

"Wow," Lala said. "You are brave. And you are my hero. I've found love again. Once. What happened to your second husband?"

"He died."

"Oh, I'm so sorry. You were widowed twice. I imagine the second time was just as awful as the first time. Or worse?"

"Worse in some ways, yes. It was a long time ago. Are you and your second love getting married?"

Lala shook her head and shrugged her shoulders.

"I don't know. Maybe I'm too scared. I don't think I can do it again. I can't be brave like you. I can't be widowed again."

Arlette picked up the bottle and filled their glasses.

"This is why the Good Lord made champagne," she said. "And why he made us strong."

"I don't know. It's just that . . . I keep thinking about how I have no hope of ever seeing or speaking to Terrence again. Not in this lifetime. Afterlife? I hope so. But I miss him now."

Arlette nodded.

"He had this way of saying 'sure' that was a little different from the way I say it, and I always thought it was so adorable. And he said it a lot, because he was so agreeable. I'd say something and he'd concur, and he'd express that by saying 'Shore, shore.' Not 'shur,' the way I pronounce it. It was 'shore.' I have video of Terrence. I haven't been able to watch any of it yet. But I know I don't have video of him saying 'Shore, shore'."

Lala paused and tried to catch her breath so she could then whisper a thought that she often returned to.

"If I could just have dinner with him once a year. Once every ten years. That would be enough. I could look forward to that and it would be enough now."

"You know I understand," Arlette said. "Most of us who have experienced what you have understand."

"David is wonderful. Kind and lovely and wonderful, just like Terrence. And he's alive. Now. Even if he breaks up with me because I'm basically a high-functioning lunatic, at least I could still see him every five or ten years. Unless he takes out a restraining order. And even then I could at least force a hug on him and hear his voice before the police show up to enforce it."

Arlette let out a hearty, dirty laugh that sounded like a bark. It made Lala love her even more than she already did. Lala beamed at her.

"You're so *fabuleuse*. You remind me of my favorite aunt. You two have to meet sometime. This may be the best champagne I have ever had. Kudos to you and your family. If David dies, I'll never be able to see him or speak to him again. No matter where I go, no matter what I do. I don't think I could stand that again."

Arlette took Lala's hand. Neither of them put their champagne glasses down.

"My dear, may I tell you a little story?"

"Of course," Lala said. "I would love that."

"I was devastated when Gérard's grandfather died. I felt as though my life was over, as though I wanted it to be over because I couldn't bear to be in so much pain. And then I met Antonio. He was Italian and he was wonderful and he was fifteen years younger than I was."

"Wow," Lala said. "That is very cool."

And a much better bet, statistically speaking, Lala thought.

"And very safe, wouldn't you expect?" Arlette asked.

"That's actually exactly what I was thinking," Lala admitted.

"By rights, he should have been the one to lose me. But it didn't work out that way. Because there are no guarantees."

"Mmm. It would be nice if there were," Lala said.

"Mmm," Arlette agreed. "Étienne is several years older than I am. Who knows what will happen? Perhaps we'll both die on the same day, within minutes of each other. That happens sometimes. Sometimes you just get lucky. And how lucky we are to find more than one person to love us."

"But . . ." Lala began. "If we're widowed again . . ." She realized that she had to wipe away a few tears.

"Oh, I'm not going to be widowed again," Arlette announced. "Everything I just told you is entirely theoretical. I have made it very clear to Étienne that I will be going first. I have told him this many times."

"Oh?" Lala said. "And what does he say when you tell him that?"

"He doesn't say much. He usually just wags his finger at me in a very affectionate way, which I take as an indication that he knows that I know how poignantly ridiculous my demand is. And then we have lovely sex."

"Oh," Lala said. "Nice."

I think I've found a new mentor, Lala thought. *Not to replace Geraldine. In addition to . . .*

Arlette tapped the cover of the book Lala was holding.

"Our favorite," Arlette said. Lala nodded her head vigorously.

"It's my Bible. My Talmud. My Qur'an. My Baghavad Gita. My Atheist's Guide to the Universe. I just made that last one up. I don't know if it actually exists."

"The last words of our favorite book?" Arlette asked.

Lala nodded again.

"Wait and hope," Lala said at the same moment that Arlette said, "*Attendre et espérer.*"

"And the subtext?" Arlette said.

"The . . . the subtext of what?"

"Of those words?"

Uh oh, Lala thought.

"Umm . . . gimme a sec . . . That we should wait and hope?"

"That we should live. Without fear. As I have learned, my dear, if you give up on love you give up on your life."

Lala smiled at Arlette and nodded.

"I'm very literal, so subtext is not my forte. That's why I need a writing partner when I work on a screenplay. You know, where subtext counts for a lot 'n' stuff.'"

There was a knocking at one of the tall, wide windows and they both jumped up a little at the sudden sound. Thankfully, no champagne was spilled. They looked over to the window and saw Gérard standing outside on the patio, peering into the library. He waved at them. Arlette went to the window and opened it. Gérard leaned in and enveloped his grandmother in a very loving hug.

"When did you get back?"

"Just now, *mon cher*," Arlette said. "I have been having a lovely visit with our dear Lala, and I think now you want to have her back, *oui*?"

"*Si je peux*," Gérard said. "The pool beckons."

"It's excellent timing. I shall join my husband and you young people shall go swimming."

"Wonderful. *Vite, vite*, Lala."

Gérard shut the windows and waved at them again before he hurried out of their range of sight. Arlette walked back to the couch and took Lala's chin in her hand. She looked Lala in the eyes with a warm and earnest gaze.

"Please tell your dear aunt and your dear David that I will hope to meet them one day soon. Perhaps on a very celebratory occasion. And I suspect you may have some idea of what my subtext is when I say that. If not, ask your writing partner."

Lala had hugged Arlette and had promised her that she would reflect on Arlette's example. Then she had rushed upstairs and had put on her favorite bathing suit of all time, and in fact the only swimming ensemble she currently owned. She bought it many years ago when she still lived in New York for a bachelorette weekend at a resort in Montauk for one of her college friends. Like a classic little black dress, it was one piece and slimming. She loved the way she looked in it.

Yes, she had thought as she did an enjoyable once-over in

the mirror, *no one will notice my hobbit toes in this.*

And then she had paused for a moment to remember how her critical friend had once asked Lala if she was concerned that her lack of foot digits might one day result in her not being able to stand upright, and basically just tumbling forward whenever she stood because her feet had nothing with which to balance and grip? To which Lala had responded, "It's worked for me so far, you snippy bitch." And then Lala had laughed insouciantly to indicate that her friend's cutting observations were of no consequence to her. Which they kind of were. And kind of always would be to an extent as tiny as her toes.

When Lala got downstairs and approached the pool, the first thing she immediately noticed was that no one else was wearing a bathing suit. Or a tee shirt. Or a pair of shorts. Or anything at all.

Because, what with the naked shoulders bobbing out of the pool and the unclothed bodies lounging in the lounge chairs, it was a detail that was hard to miss.

Oh, Lala thought. *Well.*

Gérard saw Lala and swam over to the edge of the pool. He walked up the stairs and approached her. Naked.

Yikes, I've never seen his wiener before, she thought. *I've never actually even seen his bare chest before. Don't stare. No need to stare. Everything probably looks exactly like Terrence's. God, how am I not going to swoon? How am I not going to do something crazy tonight?*

"Hey! Hi! Yeah! Fun!" Lala said. "I'm overdressed!"

I sound demented, she thought.

"*Pas du tout*," Gérard said. "Nudity is not obligatory. I need more champagne."

He put his arm around her waist and led her to one of the buffet tables.

Don't stare, she thought. *Do not stare. I would absolutely love to get a good look at it, though. Omigosh, there's Marie-Laure. God, her boobs are fabulous.*

"There you are!" Marie-Laure said. She jogged over and

kissed Lala. On the mouth.

Whoa, Lala thought. *Hello. That was very pleasant. And more than a little surprising.*

Marie-Laure grabbed a champagne bottle, grabbed Lala's hand, and ran back to the pool with her. Lala planted her feet halfway there and stopped. Marie-Laure gave her a questioning look. Lala quickly slid the straps of her bathing suit off her shoulders, wriggled it down her hips, stepped out of it, and kicked it off to the side. Then she grabbed Marie-Laure's hand and continued to the pool.

"I was feeling conspicuous," Lala explained. "Don't look at my toes."

The two women stood at the top of the double-steps that led into the center of the pool. They grasped the middle rail as they walked down together. Lala tried not to make it obvious that she was checking out the other guests checking her out.

I feel good, she thought. *This is fun. I wish David were here. So we could have fun like this. Together. Naked.*

"You have such lovely breasts," Marie-Laure said.

"Ditto," Lala said. "And I think I'm blushing." *And how's your boyfriend's wiener?* she silently asked. *I'm guessing great, n'est-ce pas? I've kind of always wanted to know. Not kind of. Actually.*

"This water is amazing," Lala said. She stepped off the stairs and the water, which was as warm as a Jacuzzi, enveloped her up to her shoulders. She noticed that there was no chlorine smell to bother her nose. She dipped her index finger in the water and touched the tip of it to her tongue.

"Are you serious? This is saltwater? This is a saltwater pool?" Marie-Laure nodded happily and Lala shook her head admiringly. "Damn it, y'all are so cool!"

Marie-Laure drank directly from the champagne bottle she was holding and passed it to Lala. As Lala took a big swig, Gérard landed next to them in the water in the form of a smooth cannonball. Lala and Marie-Laure laughed and spluttered and wiped saltwater off their faces. Gérard emerged from the water like a male Venus. Lala fully expected him to be standing on a gigantic half clamshell.

The champagne bottle made a full round through the trio and then was passed around one more time in the opposite direction. Lala could feel her fingertips starting to prune. She was staring at her right hand and rubbing her fingertips together when Gérard calmly handed the champagne bottle back to Marie-Laure and grabbed Lala and kissed her. Their bodies were suddenly right up against each other in the pool. And she was kissing him back. And then while she was reeling from having a years-long fantasy become a tipsy reality, she was suddenly kissing Marie-Laure, and it was a great kiss, and it was even better than the kiss she had shared with Gérard. The two women released each other, and Lala saw that Gérard had been watching them kiss and that he was really enjoying it.

"Is it just me, or is their unbridled delight at girl-on-girl both adorable and irritating?" she asked Marie-Laure.

"Not just you," Marie-Laure said. "Both. *Pas de question.*"

"God, this is so much fun," Lala said. "But you know what's missing?"

"Clive?"

Lala noticed Gérard responding to Marie-Laure's uncensored enthusiasm for the British movie star with a quick flash of irritation. And she gave him credit for just as quickly changing his expression into a classic Casanova's "I'm up for any permutation" stance.

"Well, sure, Clive's adorable, but I was thinking of my fiancé . . ."

. . . *to-be-my-fiancé?*, Lala thought.

"David," Lala said. "My fiancé. Full stop. If he'll still have me. Please forgive me. I've got to be somewhere."

"You are somewhere," Gérard said. He winked at Lala and looked very pleased with himself.

Oh, and how bilingually clever do we imagine we are? Lala thought. *Stay cocky, mon ami. And, no, I just can't entirely stop thinking about your penis.*

Lala smiled at Gérard and patted his wet shoulder with her dripping hand. She realized that she wasn't being very successful in keeping her smile or her pat from seeping over into the realm of the patronizing. And so she reconciled herself to the near certainty that her next words would also be rather condescending.

"Somewhere else," she said. "*Vite, vite.*"

It was agreed, reluctantly by Lala and only after extensive lecturing by everyone except Pierre, who had given up trying to "persuade this woman of anything because she is an American and they are notoriously stubborn," that it was far too late and Lala was far too drunk to drive back to Paris that night, and she would just have to wait until the morning.

"And, no, there won't be any trains running at this hour, Lala," Pierre had huffed on his way to his bedroom. "This is France. We aren't as obsessive as you Americans are. We're not a twenty-four-hour society, *merci beaucoup.*"

Clearly Lala had whined the question, "But can't I catch a traaaaiiiiiin?" once too often for Pierre's liking.

Lala marched up the stairs in a snit of drunken petulance. If Lala's beloved mother was watching her daughter from Heaven, she would at least have been comforted to note that her sometimes bossy child was making a point of putting her feet down very gently as she stomped on the steps, and was whispering her outrage rather than shouting it so as to "not wake your lovely *grand-mère*, Gérard, though if she were awake, I feel *sure* that wonderful and inspiring lady would agree with me that love is patient, love is kind and it does not envy, it does not boast, it is not proud, and that those words *especially* apply to driving to Charles de Gaulle in the middle of the night."

Lala took a hot shower when she got back to her room, and for a minute she felt entirely confident that she had sobered up enough to drive. She was going to march right back downstairs, declare her conviction to everyone, and demand that they get her car out of the multi-car garage that was somewhere on the property, right after she took a tiny little five-minute cat nap.

When she next opened her eyes, the glass in the windows was covered with torrential rain. She had been sleeping naked on her stomach the whole night and well into and beyond the morning. Lala hadn't managed to dry her wet hair or even free it from the towel turban she had created.

She lifted her throbbing head and her bloodshot eyes saw that a large breakfast tray had been set up next to her bed. She smelled the tantalizing aroma of especially fragrant coffee.

I think I need to barf, she thought.

She put her head back down on the bed and waited for the moment to pass, which it thankfully eventually did. While she was trying not to have to vomit, Lala silently prayed that it had not been Gérard who had delivered the food to her room, not because she was, in principle, opposed to him seeing her naked, as her willing participation in the skinny dipping had clearly substantiated, but because she felt confident that splayed on a bed with her limbs twisted in unnatural directions was probably not a staging that would be showing her at her best.

As soon as she was sure she wasn't going to be sick, Lala, without stopping to think that it might be a bad idea given the possibly tentative calming of her hangover, ate the scrambled eggs and the flaky, buttery croissant (to which she paused to add apricot confiture) and the sautéed new potatoes, and chugged all the coffee straight from the pot because pouring it into a cup seemed as unnecessary a step as transferring Häagen-Dazs Vanilla Swiss Almond from the container to a bowl before she ate it all while watching yet another episode of an irresistibly addictive television show.

Lala sat straight up after swallowing the last mouthful and scrunched her lips upward in an expression of nervous anticipation. After three very loud burps, she felt that maybe her future held respite rather than disaster, and she decided she was willing to risk standing. She tottered upward and stood swaying for several moments.

Okay, I think I'm good.

She tottered to the bathroom and peered in the mirror.

Oh. Well. Okay. Maybe those creases will eventually come out of my face.

Lala unwrapped the terrycloth from her head. Her still-damp hair, which had essentially been tightly trapped in an impromptu steam room for hours, was crimped and crinkled in some sections and dreadfully flat and lifeless in others. It also smelled vaguely of mold.

The shower she took that rainy day in that exquisite estate in that lovely, world-famous town outside the French capital lasted forty-five minutes. When Lala would speak of it in the future, she would describe it as "the closest I have ever come to communing with the divine."

She held the blow dryer to her strands until they were bone dry. Then Lala quickly dressed, quickly packed up her belongings, and ran down the stairs carrying the tray with her. She found Gérard and Marie-Laure and Arlette and Étienne in the kitchen, where they had just finished having lunch. All the other guests had already headed home.

"I had a wonderful time!" Lala said. "Thank you so much for everything. You must promise me that you will come stay with us in Manhattan Beach so I can reciprocate. I don't mean to be abrupt, but I'm in a terrible hurry, as I suspect I may have explained, repeatedly and in a slurring voice, last night. Breakfast was delicious! Thank you so much! Gérard, you weren't the one who brought it up to my room, were you?"

Lala's car, as it happened, was already waiting for her in the circular driveway, having been brought out of the garage by her new life coach, Arlette. The four of them walked Lala outside, each one brandishing a large umbrella against the still pouring rain. Gérard put Lala's bag in the backseat. Lala got in the driver's seat and buckled her seatbelt.

"Godspeed, my lovely girl," Arlette whispered to Lala. She

kissed her on both cheeks. "No matter what the outcome, please remember that I am proud of you for doing this." Lala grasped her hand and squeezed it.

"I think there's a good chance that I wouldn't have the courage to do this if I hadn't met you," she said.

"Then I'm especially glad we met," Arlette said.

Lala closed the door and rolled down the window. Gérard leaned in and caressed her cheek with his palm for a moment. As suddenly as Lala had felt the pressure of his hand on her face, it was gone. She blinked and shook her head imperceptibly and focused on not blushing.

"You will be okay driving back?" Gérard asked.

"Of course!" Lala said. "I'm very good on freeways. Highways. Motorways. Whatever the fuck y'all call them."

Lala's hands had been clenched in white-knuckled terror for so long, she was starting to suspect that arthritis might be the permanent result of her misguided bravado.

She had just pulled into a rest stop at the side of the . . . she still didn't know what it was actually called, so she kept thinking of it as a freeway, but in a futile attempt at distraction from the hell she had inflicted on herself, she was thinking of the route in the literal French translation of free and way, *manières libres*, which had been good for exactly one silent grunt of a chuckle as she tried to stay calm while maneuvering along the road with semi-trucks and high-class automobiles that were giving no adjustment to their driving because of the torrents of rain all around them.

Lala sat in the parking lot of the rest stop. The lights of the small snack shop behind the gas pumps read as blurry and melting through the water cascading down the car. Lala stretched her stiff fingers over and over again.

I'm not a good driver in sunshine, she thought. She shook her head and was surprised to find herself beginning to hum The

Wedding March. *God, I really have to pee.*

Lala threw the door open and ran into the store. It wasn't much of a distance, but she was soaked by the time she got inside. She blinked to adjust to the bright lights. A woman was standing behind the counter with her back to the door. She was reading a magazine. Lala walked up to the counter. She assumed the woman must have heard the door open and close. She assumed the woman must have felt the increasingly irritated energy of Lala's unacknowledged presence. The woman did not, however, turn around or take her eyes off the magazine.

Oh for fuck's sake, Lala thought.

"*Excusez-moi?*" she said.

The woman took a full beat to even lift her head, let alone turn around, which took another full count of ten.

Omigod! Lala thought when she finally saw the woman's face! *It's the dreaded daughter! What the fuck is her name again?*

"Madame Pettt-eeeettttt-BOWWWNNN," the woman sneered with a pronounced look of aggressive disappointment.

Omigod, no, Lala thought. *No, no, I do not have the energy to deal with this . . .*

"Oh, gosh, please, call me Lala," Lala said.

"Nice to see you again, LaLAAAAA," the woman said, with no hint of pleasure in her voice or face.

Oh god, Lala thought. *No. That's almost worse.*

"Bathroom?" she begged.

The woman made a quick jerking motion with her head toward a short hallway in the middle of the far wall. Lala ran in that direction, yanked the door open, scooted inside the bathroom, and bolted the door behind her like one being pursued by a mythical beast.

What is her damn name? she thought.

Lala came out of the bathroom a few minutes later, after soaking her hands in hot water, which made them feel much better. She smiled at the woman and tried to sound gracious.

"How's your dear papa?"

"My pa-PAAAA?" the woman said. "Oh, he is very fine, thank

you. He was very much enjoying working on the movie for which you hired him, and he is now an actor and he is very happy."

"That's nice," Lala said uncertainly. The woman's clear disdain was making her increasingly nervous.

"He is fine, my pa-PAAAA," the woman repeated. "I, however, am not."

"Oh," Lala said. "I'm sorry to hear that."

I realize that dashing out right now without another word would be very rude, even in the face of her appreciable lack of courtesy, Lala thought. *That's not the issue. The issue is, do I care?*

"Yes, well, my FATHERRRR has insisted that I work here, you see, since I no longer have a building to manage for him because now that building is YOURRRR building."

"Uh, yeah," Lala said.

"And now he says I must learn some proper VAAAAAL-UES, and I must work here because it is owned by a friend of his, and my father got me this job so I can LEARRRRRN."

I may be having a mild stroke, Lala thought. She realized that she had subconsciously decided to start moving herself, millimeter by millimeter, toward the urgent but distant promise of the exit.

"My father is now only paying for my rent and my credit card bills. Everything else, I must pay for with what I earn here, La-LAAAAA."

Lala winced at the sound of her name, then twitched, and then jerked her head back involuntarily as though to get her ears as far away as possible. She almost hit the base of her skull against a rack with magnifying eyeglasses on it that she had somehow moved herself dangerously close to.

"And what I earn here," the woman said, "is a pittance."

She does speak English very well, Lala thought. *"Pittance." You don't hear that every day in Manhattan Beach. What is her name? This is going to drive me nuts . . . Why isn't she wearing a name tag? Isn't that the law, or something? Maybe not in France . . .*

"Right, well, okay," Lala said. "Good luck, then."

And with that, Lala bolted for the door. And skidded to a

stop just before she opened it.

"Umm . . . what is this called?" she asked, and gestured outside.

"This?" the woman repeated with unfettered disdain. "Rain?"

"The road? What is a big road, a highway, freeway . . . What is it called in French?"

"Ohhh," the woman groaned as if she had been inconvenienced and insulted beyond the outermost boundaries of civilization. "*L'autoroute?*"

"Omigosh, of *course*," Lala said, and actually slapped her forehead, just in case her words weren't enough to indicate her exasperation with how dense she had been.

And, Lala thought, *I think I may be starting to get subtext, because the clear unspoken message that last word she spat at me is that I am, in her estimation, a complete idiot.*

Lala smiled at the woman, waved good-bye, and ran out into the rain. She lunged for the door to her car and slid inside, even more soaked than she had been when she had entered the store.

Actually, I'm a bit pipped at my Gallic Heartthrob, Lala thought. *I don't know why Gérard didn't just tell me it's an autoroute before I drove away. It might have brought me some measure of, well, if not peace, then at least closure, during this shit show of a journey.*

And then Lala suddenly remembered something because she hadn't been trying to remember it for the past few minutes since her focus had been distracted by the French word for "freeway," and she once again slapped her forehead in a universal gesture of regret and recrimination.

"Celestine! Of course! Her name is Celestine!"

That was going to drive me nuts all the way to Paris, Lala thought as she started the car up again and shifted it into gear. *Okay, let's get this shit show of a journey back on the road, shall we?*

There's No Place Like Home(s)

Lala was still not so delirious that she was unable to realize that she was nearly delirious with exhaustion. Unfortunately, there was no time to waste and thus no time to rest.

She had gotten back to her apartment after hours of tense driving, swearing to herself as she parked the car that she would not only never again drive on an *autoroute* of any kind, domestic or foreign, she would, in fact, never again get behind the wheel of a car as a driver. Not on side streets in Los Angeles. Not on country lanes. Not while playing video games with the many adopted grandnieces and grandnephews she looked forward to having.

I swear, she said to herself as she trudged up the stairs to her apartment, *I will never ever ever ever ever again turn the ignition key to a motorized vehicle. Never. Fuck that noise. I fucking hate driving.*

The first thing she did when she got inside her apartment was call Kenny and ask him to please come to her apartment and please bring Minou so she could say "Good-bye for now."

Kenny rushed upstairs. He had Minou cradled in his arms. The cat was sound asleep. Lala could see how much they loved each other. She felt happily teary.

"Look at you two," she sighed.

"How was your weekend? Did you actually make it there?" Kenny asked.

"I actually did. And it was a very enlightening time. Listen, would you do me a huge favor and promise you'll come to LA for my wedding, if I have one?"

Lala hugged Kenny and squished Minou between them as she did. Kenny started to say something.

"*Non, non, mon cher, pas maintenant,*" Lala said. "I'll explain all via a joyous e-mail from California, if I'm lucky. Now, scoot! I love you both, and I'm in a big hurry!"

Lala's next call was to Clive.

"How are you?" he asked. "How was the party?"

"Enlightening. Listen, I know how irritating unsolicited advice can be, but if I were you, the moment that Matthew yells 'That's a wrap!' I would get on a plane to Stratford, and I would find Tara, and I would tell her that she's the love of my life, and I would do whatever I needed to do to get her back. And then I would marry her, if she would still have me. And then you must bring her to my wedding. If I'm lucky enough to have one."

"What are you—"

"Clive, my dear boyfriend in an alternate universe, I'm sorry to dictate and run, but I'm in a mad hurry. I'll e-mail you as soon as I have some news, good or otherwise, oh please, universe, let it be good."

As Lala was throwing a few essential things into a carry-on bag, there was an urgent knocking on her door. She heard a familiar voice, always much loved and currently rather feared, despite Lala's immediate and obedient plans to change her life completely.

"Lala!" Geraldine yelled through the door as she continued to pound on it, "are you in there? You better be in there and you better open up, right now!"

Lala ran to the door and threw it open.

"What are you doing here?"

She took a step forward to hug her beloved aunt. Geraldine swatted her niece's arms away as though they were a swarm of especially annoying mosquitoes.

"I am not going to hug you, because I am here because I am *very* irritated with you."

Geraldine stormed past Lala and threw herself and her small suitcase down on the couch. Lala stared at her.

"You're here because you're irritated with me? You couldn't be irritated with me long distance?"

"Well, I tried that," Geraldine huffed, "but I frankly got quite fed up with you not responding to my e-mail. It was a work of love to put all that into words, and I got tired of not getting an answer from you."

"But I did answer you," Lala began, and then stopped.

I guess maybe Minou wasn't communicating telepathically with my aunt? Oops . . .

"I'm sincerely sorry," Lala said. "But, listen, I didn't realize it at the time, but I do now . . . You are now preaching to the choir. Don't even take off your coat. Let's get back to the airport."

"What?" Geraldine said. Her eyes narrowed. "What are you up to, young missy?"

"I'm going to do everything I can to take the 'to-be-my-fiancé' part out of the equation. I don't know why it took me so long to realize how ridiculous that sounds."

Geraldine jumped up off the couch and nearly knocked Lala over in her rush to hug her.

"You are? Oh, my dear! I'm so relieved! I'm so happy!"

"Me, too! And we'll be officially engaged as soon as I can make David promise not to die first!"

Every cell in Geraldine's body froze. The cells in her arms unfroze long enough for Geraldine to thrust her niece away from her, and her facial cells unfroze long enough for her to stare at Lala with an expression of pure and utter exasperation.

"I'm sorry, but it doesn't work that way, Lala!" she yelled. "Did you not comprehend anything that I wrote?"

"Kidding! I'm kidding!" Lala said. "Lighten up! Now, let's get going, because I need to be on the next flight to San Francisco."

Much to Lala's surprise and rapidly escalating dismay, Geraldine smiled at her, gave her a hug, and sashayed in the direction of her kitchen.

"What are you doing?" Lala called after her aunt. She heard the refrigerator door open and close, and she heard a cabinet open and close. Her aunt came out carrying a bottle of white wine and one glass.

"What are you *doing*?" Lala repeated.

Her aunt spoke to her as though Lala had suddenly had a precipitous drop in her IQ standing.

"Getting a drink?" Geraldine said. "I'd offer you one, but I don't think you have time."

"Aren't you coming to the airport with me?"

"Goodness, no. I'm calling Monty and telling him to join me. Your apartment is adorable. And I need a vacation. Where should we get *pain au chocolat* in the morning? I assume you have a favorite place by now. And, by the way, what made you change your mind about getting married?"

"You did. You and the French you. If you were ten years older and were on your third husband. You two will love each other. She can't wait to meet you. I'll explain another time."

Lala had every intention of getting a little sleep at the airport while she waited for her flight. And by any reasonable metric that shouldn't have been a problem, since the earliest she could get on a plane to San Francisco was nine hours after she got to Charles de Gaulle and bought a ticket at the Air France counter.

Lala made the bold and unorthodox decision to check

her carry-on bag, thus negating the very nature of its carry-on aspect, so that she could, as she explained to the clearly uninterested young woman behind the check-in counter, "travel lighter than I've ever traveled before in my life, because I have got a life-altering *job* to do."

"That's nice," the young woman said, apparently quite confident that she had a secure handle on the exact minimum amount of politeness she was required to display before she would be fired.

Having taken her passport, her wallet, her phone, and the book she was currently reading out of her carry-on and stuffed them in next to her laptop in her computer bag, Lala scanned the signs and found the arrow pointing in the direction of the Air France lounge. She walked with determination toward the sanctuary.

I'll have a soothing cup of chamomile tea, she thought, *and then I'll find a comfy chair in the corner and I'll doze until they call my flight. If I turn the chair to face the wall, I should be able to banish any concern about being seen with my head tilted sideways, drooling onto my shoulder.*

The first thing Lala saw when she entered the lounge was a long counter with lots of food on it.

Oh, she thought. *I bet having something to eat would make me drowsy, and I bet that would help me sleep. I'll just grab a quick little snack.*

After piling cubed cheese, olives, crackers, and dried apricots on one plate and finding that only one plate was not going to do the job, Lala filled another plate and carefully carried both to the next expanse she set her eyes on.

Lala swung herself onto a stool and smiled at the robust older gentleman who was tending the bar.

"*Bonjour, Madame*," he said.

"*Bonjour, Monsieur*. I'm thinking a lovely glass of red wine will help me nap a bit before my flight, don't you think?"

"Absolutely," the gentleman said. "I have a favorite I would like you to try."

He picked up a bottle and gave Lala a heavy pour in a large glass. She sniffed the wine, sipped it, and grinned.

"Ohh, so nice," she said. "Thank you. I'm just going to take this all over to that cushiony chair over there so I can already be in my nest when I collapse from exhaustion."

The gentleman gave her a caring smile and a soothing nod, and Lala toddled off to a chair that was far away from the center of the large lounge. She got herself comfortable, and she gazed out the window at the landing and taxiing and taking off airplanes. She ate all the food she had brought with her and debated getting up to get some more because it was delicious. She finished the excellent wine and mustered enough energy to go back to the bar and ask her sweet new friend for a refill, which she finished with even more urgent enthusiasm than the first glass.

She sat quietly and looked around her. The lounge was fairly empty. Lala debated finding someone to engage in a little light-hearted conversation, but thought better of it when she realized that she would probably fall face forward in the middle of a sentence and start snoring, which she reasoned would be very rude, especially given that she had been the one to initiate contact.

Lala considered taking out her laptop and doing some work on the manuscript for *A Woman of a Certain Age*, but she decided she was probably too tired to write anything of passable quality even for a shitty first draft.

She took out the book she was reading, a collection of short stories by one of her favorite *New Yorker* writers, and read the first paragraph of the new story that began on the page separated by her Strand Bookstore bookmark. She read the six sentences of the paragraph once. And then again. And then a third time. She began to read them a fourth time, but gave up halfway through when she was forced to concede that the book had somehow been magically transformed between then and the last time she had picked it up from English to some unclassifiable language she didn't recognize. That, Lala paused to reflect, was happening to her more often than she liked.

Lala put the book back in the computer bag. Her fingers brushed against her phone. She had to stop herself from calling or texting David.

You must not blurt, she silently commanded herself. *This must be a grand and dramatic and supremely romantic surprise! You need every advantage on your side if you're going to pull this off.*

She slammed the computer bag shut and ran back to the bar to ask for and receive a set of earphones from the "lovely bartender, really, you are such a dear and sweet man and I appreciate you very, very, very much." Lala leaned back in the chair, stretched out, and watched the fare that the large television on the wall opposite her was providing for the assembled travelers.

This will be great, Lala thought. *I have no idea what's going on in this show. I don't even know if it's a show or a documentary or a movie or a reality mishmash. They are speaking way too quickly for me to catch any words that I could have any hope of understanding. I'm not even sure if that's actually French that they're speaking. I'll be asleep before I can bring this inner monologue to a close . . .*

Six hours later the loudspeaker announced boarding for Air France Flight 84, non-stop service to San Francisco. Lala mustered every fragile remaining milligram of strength and consciousness she had left and hoisted herself up out of the chair. Her eyes were bloodshot and her back ached. Two hours earlier, after watching the entirety of what her best guess assessment decided was a Spanish-language mini series set in Barcelona that had been dubbed into French and concerned the bodice-ripping exploits of a docent-by-day at the Picasso Museum who spent her evenings as a concierge at her family's boutique hotel, Lala had managed to fall asleep, only to be woken after five minutes by a thundering crash of trays and cutlery and glassware from the lounge kitchen. After that, she hadn't fallen asleep for another moment. She was, however, relieved to see that Sofia, the heroine of the mini series, found true and hopefully lasting love in the final installment.

Oh, well, Lala thought as she shuffled her way to the gate and considered for a moment flagging down an airport cart and begging the driver to let her hitch a ride, *I'll just sleep through the whole flight, and then when I get to San Francisco, I'll be rested and renewed and ready to conquer this monumental, life-altering challenge.*

Lala smiled at all the lovely people waiting to greet her and the other passengers at the entrance to the plane. She stumbled over to her Business Class seat. The configuration of the plane had a single seat at either window and two seats together in the middle, with ample room in each location for the passengers to be comfortable. Lala had gotten the last seat available on the plane, in the middle. She collapsed onto the large and cozy seat, adjusting it so that it would lean backward. Even with a passenger right next to her, she would have sufficient privacy, and Lala hoped that she would finally be able to relax and fall asleep for at least a few hours.

Lala shut her eyes and tried to empty her mind of worry and anticipation. She couldn't stop herself from imagining what she would say to David when she saw him again.

I'm so sorry.

I was scared.

I'm still scared.

I would love to get married. I would love to take that ridiculous "to-be-my-fiancé" out of the equation. As long as you promise not to die before I do.

Kidding! I'm kidding!

Not really.

I need a glass of champagne or something. And an eye mask.

Lala put her seat back in the upright position. She saw a woman and what was presumably her teenage daughter coming right toward her. They were both tall and thin and brunette and attractive, and they were both wearing stylish, elegant clothes that looked very expensive. And they were both scowling to such an extent that their features were distorted with irritation.

Uh oh, Lala thought, *I'd better get myself into the "I'm asleep and I can't chat" position . . .*

Just as the thought materialized, the daughter scurried into the seat next to Lala's, while the mother sat down in the window seat across the aisle. The next thing the daughter did was to completely change her expression by giving Lala what Lala read as a sweet and sincere smile.

Well, damn it, I can't very well be rude to this nice young lady and ignore her . . .

"Hello!" Lala said.

"Hi," the nice young lady said.

Lala leaned forward and waved to the nice young lady's mother, who was still looking quite annoyed.

"Would you two like to sit together?" Lala asked. "I'm happy to switch seats, if you—"

"No!" the two women yelled.

"That's very nice of you," the mother added with exaggerated good cheer. "But we're fine. Thank you."

"Thank you," the daughter said.

Ohh boy, Lala thought. *Well, I may not know what it's like to be the mother of a teenager, but I certainly vaguely remember being a teenager . . .*

Lala smiled and nodded at both the women. She debated trying to fall asleep right away, but then she thought she might wait for that glass of champagne after all and maybe see how long after takeoff dinner would be served.

The nice young woman opened her carry-on bag and took out a thick book. Lala saw the title on the cover. It was one of the volumes in a trilogy she didn't know much about, other than that it concerned a young woman in a dystopian future, it was globally and outrageously popular, and the movie versions were just as successful as the books. The young woman noticed Lala noticing the cover.

"It's really good," she said.

"Mmm," Lala said. "I've never read it." Lala saw the young woman's face register disappointment and what looked like pity. "I've read all the *Harry Potter* books," Lala offered.

The young woman reached into her bag and pulled out another hefty volume. She handed it to Lala.

"It's the first book in the series," she said. "It's really good.

I've read it seven times."

When dinner was served two hours later, Lala and Bethany discovered that they were both vegetarians. While Bethany's mother, Jennifer, enjoyed her dinner in her private island seat and watched a movie on her personal screen, Lala and Bethany enjoyed their first chance to talk, because eating necessitated both of them releasing for the first time the books they were reading since the plane had taken off.

"It's just so . . . this book . . . I just . . . the courage and the injustice and the romance . . . yikes . . ."

"I know, right?" Bethany said. She chewed on a big twirl of pasta and nodded.

They chatted through dinner and dessert. Bethany told Lala that she wanted to go to college at UCLA and study creative writing and film production. Lala gave Bethany her business card and told her that she would have an internship waiting for her at Lala's production company any summer that she wanted one, starting right now. Bethany got teary when Lala said that, and then Lala got teary, and Bethany's mother was asleep by then and missed the whole episode, which was probably fine with her.

As soon as their dessert plates had been taken away, Lala and Bethany went back to their books. Lala finished the first volume of the trilogy half an hour before the pilot informed the passengers that they were beginning their descent into San Francisco International Airport. Lala shut her eyes and fell into a deep and not at all restorative sleep. After fifteen minutes, she woke up feeling even more exhausted than ever.

Lala and Bethany gathered their things and stood to exit the plane. Bethany stepped into the aisle first, and Lala motioned to Bethany's mother to go ahead of her. Jennifer smiled at Lala.

"Your daughter is a very smart and gracious young person," Lala told her.

"Thank you," Jennifer said. "Sometimes I forget that."

Jennifer gave Lala's hand a grateful squeeze and rushed ahead to catch up with her daughter. Lala watched Jennifer put her arm around Bethany's shoulder and Bethany put her arm around her mom. Lala watched them lean their heads together as they walked out.

Lala headed for the exits leading to ground transportation, and then she remembered that she had checked her carry-on bag. She sighed, rued her earlier foolishness, and dragged herself to the baggage claim area.

Her carry-on bag was among the very last to be ejected from the plane.

I can't believe I didn't think this through, Lala told herself as she watched the baggage carousel slowly and relentlessly trudge past her. *This may break me. This may be the last straw. I think I'm going to barf.*

When Lala finally saw her bag, she lunged for it, grabbed it, and ran outside to find a taxi stand. She was convinced that she was about to pass out, and she wanted to at least be in a car on the way to David's apartment before that happened.

After she gasped David's address to the driver, she put her head back and essentially fainted, coming to only when, just over an hour later, the car stopped in front of a cute old one-story building of garden apartments surrounding a small courtyard.

She found Apartment #4 and stood in front of the door for a minute, taking deep breaths. She knocked very tentatively. There was no answer, so she knocked again, a bit harder this time. No response.

Merde, Lala thought. *What do I do now?*

Lala considered taking a cab to the UC Davis campus to find David's office at the veterinary school, but decided it would be better to keep their reunion more private than that. She took out her phone and looked up the main number for the veterinary school. She asked the person who answered if he could tell her if Dr. McLellan was in class at the moment? The man asked her to hold, and when he came back on the line, he informed Lala that Dr. McLellan was on vacation for the week.

"He's . . . on . . . vacation for the week," Lala repeated. "Right. Okay. Thank you so much."

Lala disconnected the call and sat down on the step in front of David's door. She mashed her carry-on bag like it was a pillow, and put her head on it while she stretched her legs out. She looked up at the sky and wrinkled her nose.

Fuck it, she thought.

Lala sat up, grabbed her phone again, and hit David's number in her contacts list. The call went straight to voicemail.

Fuck this, Lala thought.

She typed a text, "Where are you?" and hit the arrow that sent it to David's phone.

She waited. And waited. And then her phone rang and she answered and yelled.

"David! I'm outside your apartment!" Lala yelled.

"I know," David said.

"You know?" Lala said. "How . . . Who told you . . . Where are you?"

"I'm in Paris. I'm at your apartment with Geraldine."

"It's crazy, huh?" Lala heard Geraldine yell in the background. "If I had known, he could have brought Monty with him."

"David," Lala said, "what the continental fuck are you doing in Paris?"

David explained over dinner at his favorite restaurant in New York City, an upscale vegan establishment on 79th between Lexington and Third that former president Bill Clinton often frequented, that he had suspected that something had to be done, that something was "up" with Lala, and that his concerns had been confirmed when he witnessed Geraldine acting so weird and annoyed when they had Skyped with Lala while David was taking a short break from his teaching duties and was back home in Manhattan Beach for a quick visit.

"She acted as though she hated you. She would never do that unless something freakish and weird were going on. I knew drastic measures were required. I gave the one lecture I was committed to and I got a colleague to take over my seminar for a week. And I got on a plane."

"I'm still really irritated with my aunt for ruining my grand and dramatic and supremely romantic surprise by being such a snippy pill to me on that phone call, but I totally get where she was coming from," Lala said. She speared the last piece of seitan scaloppini on her plate and brought it to her sated-but-not-slowing-down taste buds.

"I'm debating ordering another serving of this," Lala added. "It is just way too delicious."

"Yup. But maybe think about saving room for one or two or five of their incredible desserts?"

Lala and David had met at John F. Kennedy Airport the day before. Lala's flight from San Francisco arrived five hours before David's flight from Paris landed. Lala spent the time she was waiting for David sitting in a Starbucks in the International Arrivals Building getting refill after refill of iced tea, operating at a more or less consistent level of low-grade nervousness, and reading *Jane Eyre*, the book she had picked up at a newsstand when she landed, not because she was specifically looking for it, but because the book had caught her eye while she was scanning the floor to ceiling shelves of paperbacks and hardcover bestsellers.

"This is one of the many big gaps in my reading list and I'm ashamed to admit that," Lala explained to the very nice young barista who kept filling her plastic trenta cup. "Spoiler alert, I'm definitely identifying with Rochester more than with Jane. He's widowed. Kind of. If you haven't read it yet, I've said too much already. You know what? I think I might have another scone. P.S. I've also never read anything by James Joyce, which is just a *schande*."

Lala made her way over to the doors leading from the customs section to the baggage carousels about an hour before David's plane was listed on the Arrivals board as being anticipated to land. She stopped at every bathroom she saw on the walk over, having basically consumed her body weight and then some in iced tea. Then she stood at the edge of the crowd of people who were waiting for traveling loved ones to appear, holding a sign she had created at the airport in San Francisco when she was waiting for her flight to New York to take off. She had the idea in a sudden wave of inspiration on the way to the airport, and she asked the cab driver to stop at a stationary store. She ran in and bought a large piece of posterboard and a handful of markers in different colors. She did her best to be artistic and creative as she wrote out the sign, and then she kept it with her carry-on luggage when she got on the plane, stowing it flat under the seat in front of her. The grandmotherly woman sitting next to her caught a glimpse of the sign and smiled at Lala.

"I'm not very visual," Lala admitted with no small degree of embarrassment.

"It's lovely," the woman said. "I hope he'll say yes."

And then the woman fell asleep almost immediately after takeoff and snored loudly across the United States, which Lala chose to interpret as an optimistic sign for the vital romantic mission she was undertaking.

Lala saw David walking down the hallway leading to the exit doors. Her heart started racing. She held up the sign. She saw David see her in the crowd, she saw him read her sign, and she saw him smile.

DAVID: WILL YOU BE MY FIANCÉ, FULL STOP? (I'M NOT VERY ARTISTIC . . .)

They had caught a cab from the airport to the Library Hotel on Madison and 41st Street. Lala wasn't familiar with that boutique hotel, though she imagined she must have walked by it dozens of times during her many treasured hikes around midtown.

"It looks gorgeous on the website," Lala explained to David in the backseat of the cab as they drove out of Queens and the much-loved skyline of Manhattan appeared in front of them. "I booked us one of their Love Rooms."

Damn it, Lala thought. *I didn't mean to bring up the issue of us being in love and me finally being ready to take the next, very, very, very terrifying step in my life, assuming he still wants to get married, in the cab. With the driver here. And stuff. Sheesh. Way too much to talk about and not the right time to start talking about it. Damn it.*

"Because of . . . you know . . . the name of the room having *love* in it . . ." Lala sputtered. "Look, the Empire State Building!"

They checked in and got up to the room and it was indeed lovely. The bed was strategically strewn with rose petals. They had sex on the thick carpet, and then they had sex in the bed, pulling off of the blankets of which had sent rose petals flying around the room. They ordered room service and ate delicious pasta and drank delicious red wine in bed. They watched political commentary shows and yelled at the television and had sex again before they fell asleep.

The next day, they stayed in bed and ordered breakfast and lunch from room service. Lala thought she might be getting a urinary tract infection, so she ordered several glasses of cranberry juice and called her gynecologist, who phoned in a prescription for antibiotics, which Lala had delivered to the hotel because she didn't want to get out of bed with David.

They finally showered and got dressed and walked the mile and a half to the vegan restaurant without having yet had an actual conversation about their relationship, unless moaning and panting with porn film enthusiasm in their hotel room counted as having a discussion.

Three vegan desserts arrived at their table. Lala grabbed her spoon and stabbed the crusty top of a raspberry crème brûlée and fretted and then forced herself to speak.

"I haven't actually apologized to you, and you haven't had the opportunity to reject or accept my—"

"There's nothing to apologize for," David said. He ate half

a chocolate chip cookie and then fed the other half to Lala. "I can't imagine what a leap of faith it takes to get married after you've been widowed. I admire you. I can't wait to be your husband."

And then Lala burst into loud tears, fueled by great relief and even greater adoration. And she saw that the other diners and the wait staff were staring at her with the questioning concern of not knowing if those were happy or sad tears, and that's when David announced that they had just gotten engaged "for real." The dining room erupted in applause. Lala didn't remember much of the details of their walk back to the hotel, other than having a vague and joyous sense that every building and person and subway station they passed on Lexington Avenue was exceptionally special and delightful that night.

They flew back to Los Angeles on the red-eye the next day, after having an early breakfast in the room and then walking to the main branch of the New York City Public Library on 42nd and Fifth so Lala could kiss the lions, Patience and Fortitude, who guarded the entrance, and tell them that she missed them desperately and she promised to visit again as soon as possible with her new husband. Catching a late plane also gave them enough time to walk to Lala's favorite antique jewelry shop in Greenwich Village, where they picked out a small, elegant Art Deco engagement ring.

Geraldine and Monty and the dogs were waiting for them in the courtyard when they got back home. Lala went nuts.

"My babies! My babies my babies my babies my BABIES!"

Petunia and Chester and Eunice acted like puppies. They whined and wriggled and kissed their mama. Lala wrapped herself around them and kissed one, and then passed that one to David so he could kiss that one. The dogs went around in a circle like that until Geraldine notice the ring on Lala's finger.

"OMIGOD! We have to go out and celebrate!"

"Absolutely!" Lala crowed. "As long as we go somewhere that has outdoor seating so we can bring the babies, because I never want to be separated from my babies for so long EVER again!"

When they got home, Lala and David hugged Geraldine and Monty at the door to their apartment, and then skipped up the steps with the dogs cheerfully trotting behind them.

"They know their mama and papa are happy," Lala whispered to David as she giggled and tried to figure out how her keys worked.

Once they got inside, they got into their robes and sat on the couch. The dogs were snuggled there with them, and Lala felt safer than she could remember feeling since Terrence died. David took her hand and kissed it.

"What do you think? Is October too soon to plan a wedding?"

"October? Mmm . . ."

"Or Christmas is such a festive time to celebrate a marriage."

"I have a date in mind," Lala said and winked at him. David didn't get it right away. And then he remembered how many times he had heard the telling and retelling of the several iterations of that blighted day.

"Seriously?" he asked. "You don't think that might be tempting fate?"

"Let's do it! I'm not scared! I will walk up to that date with my eyes wide open and say, 'I fucking DOUBLE dare you!'"

Petunia gave a big beagle yelp in the middle of an urgent dream, and Chester the greyhound turned over and covered his borzoi/Shar Pei sister Eunice with his front leg. Eunice grunted contentedly when the added weight landed on her. Lala grabbed David's face and kissed him.

"Plus," Lala said, "there's a TV show I need to be on . . ."

"I feel the same sense of breathless awe and wonder I imagine Henry Hudson must have experienced when he sailed up the majestic river that would one day bear his name, and saw the Palisades on one side and the pristine island of Manhattan on the other. Except indoors 'n' stuff."

Lala's head was turning around in every direction. She had just entered the epicenter of all things bridal, the Kleinfeld Manhattan showroom on West 20th Street. Also known as the setting for *Say Yes to the Dress*, Lala's episode of which would be taping that day.

Lala and Auntie Geraldine and Monty's daughter Helene had flown to New York the day before. Brenda, Lala's best friend from high school in Santa Monica, had picked them up at the airport. Brenda lived in a palatial apartment on the Upper West Side and her husband, Frank, was in Europe on business, so the four women had a slumber party at Brenda's home.

The four of them consumed two bottles of champagne and a large tray of vegetarian lasagna that Brenda had ordered online from her favorite Italian restaurant, one that the website defined as being intended for "8-12 guests."

"Okay, maybe, but those would be very, very, very, ridiculously small portions," Lala had declared while she was devouring her fifth serving at two o'clock in the morning.

Sleep had not been a priority for any of them.

Before Lala had a chance to steer her entourage to the reception desk of the store, a young woman wearing a headset ran over to them.

"Lala Pettibone?" she said, and then added, not waiting for an answer, "I recognize you from your book cover! I loved your book!"

"Thank you so much!" Lala said.

Will receiving praise for my work ever lose its heady luster? Lala thought. *No. Definitely not. Never ever.*

"I'm Olivia," the young woman said. "Wow, we had a late night last night, huh, ladies? Let's get you all to make-up right away."

Olivia took their coffee and tea orders, and lead them to the make-up room. She quickly returned to find them all sitting in their chairs and staring into the mirror, just after Lala had announced to her make-up artist that it sure looked like those dark circles under her eyes would require some industrial strength spackle.

"Okay," Olivia said. "Just a few things, and then we'll go right into filming. I hear the bride has seen our show!"

"The bride," Geraldine said, "is obsessed with your show."

"That's great! So, Lala, you're familiar with the elements that make an episode especially compelling."

Here we go, Lala thought.

"Conflict," Lala said.

"Yes!" Olivia cheered.

"Lala doesn't like conflict," Brenda said.

"I can rise to the occasion," Lala said with absolutely no conviction whatsoever.

Why did I promise that? Lala thought. *I'm a terrible actress. Everyone will know I'm creating inauthentic drama for drama's sake. Oy vey.*

"It's okay," Olivia assured Lala. She patted Lala's shoulder. "We don't need a big fight. We just need a few different opinions."

"That shouldn't be a problem with this group," Helene snorted.

"Also," Olivia said, "you're a widow, so that already adds a great element to your appointment, because who doesn't love a widow getting married again?"

What? Lala thought. *My late husband, maybe? Wait, that's not actually true. Terrence very much wanted me to build a new life. Olivia's right. I have loved seeing widows on this show, and I have cheered for them getting married again. I think Terrence loves that I'm getting married again. I think he and David would love each other. Omigod, I cannot start crying yet.*

When the women had their make-up finished, Olivia led them to the main showroom. Geraldine and Brenda and Helene sat on a long, white sofa, and Olivia placed Lala in an ornate white chair next to them. There were several camera operators who were being wonderfully unobtrusive, but Lala still started to feel a little nervous when she saw them.

"Okay," Olivia said. "We're going to start, and we're going to just keep going, unless I yell 'Cut,' of course. Even if I shout out directions, just keep going because we can easily edit in post. Let's have fun!"

I think I may need to barf, Lala thought.

The camera operators began filming, and Lala tried to make the frozen smile on her face look at least a little natural. Her consultant, Julie, a statuesque blond woman who was probably around Lala's age, and was someone Lala had seen on the show many times, came over to start the segment.

"Hi, who's my bride?" Julie said with a big and lovely smile.

"I am," Lala croaked.

"Take that again, please, Lala," Olivia said with no hint of irritation. "It's okay, we're doing great."

"I am," Lala repeated, this time around in a slightly less amphibious voice. "I'm Lala." Olivia gave her a cheerful thumbs-up.

"Welcome!" Julie said. "Who do you have with you today?"

"My adopted aunt, Geraldine, and my best friend from high school, Brenda, and also my friend Helene, who is my aunt's stepdaughter."

Julie shook everyone's hand. Lala definitely had the sense that the other women were as beguiled by Julie's warmth and her welcoming nature as she was.

"So what kind of wedding dress did everyone have in mind for Lala?"

"I like cotton," Lala said with enthusiasm. Out of the corner of her eyes, she registered her aunt looking at her with disdain.

"You're not going to a picnic," Geraldine said.

"Cotton," Brenda said, shaking her head.

"What? You're going to the gym?" Helene asked.

Off-camera, Olivia gave them all a very enthusiastic thumb's up.

Before arriving for the appointment, the four women had

agreed not to reveal what style they each thought Lala should be wearing in advance of the actual taping of the episode, with the hope that Lala would then have the best chance of presenting a genuine reaction of surprise or delight or irritation or disgust, reasoning that if she had to recreate the moment, they would probably be asked to leave the building because of the dreadfully bad acting that would involve.

Lala suddenly felt very ganged up on and very hurt. She debated challenging the patronizing assessments of her entourage, but realized that doing so would immediately up the conflict quotient to a level that might torpedo her ability to finish taping the show. So she opted for pivoting.

"I also like pockets," Lala said, nervously.

Merde, Lala thought, *that is absolutely not what I should have said next.* Merde!

"Pockets?" Geraldine and Brenda and Helene sneered.

"Umm," Lala jumped in. "Umm . . . I definitely want sleeves—"

"Well, you can certainly try on at least one strapless dress," Geraldine ordered.

"Aaaaand, I am incredibly short-waisted, so I don't think a ballgown—"

"There's no reason to not at least *try* on a ballgown," Brenda said. "If you don't at least *try* it on, you'll never know if it looks good on you."

"I'm not wearing white. I want an ivory or a very pale blush. No pure white."

"Well, just try on *one* white dress," Helene said.

"And I definitely want an off-the-shoulder look," Lala announced, a little more loudly and with a little more vehemence that she intended because she was rapidly getting enormously sick of being told what to do. "You know, something Oprah or Dame Helen Mirren would wear."

"Ohh, yes," the three other women cooed, nodding their heads in loving solidarity.

"Is there a price point we should be respectful of?"

"Well, here's the thing," Lala said. "Whatever I spend, the four of us are going to double that amount and use it to start a foundation that brings senior shelter animals to assisted living facilities and to group homes for kids, so the cats and dogs can spend their golden years staying with elderly people and young people. It's a natural match, and we're going to provide the coordination and support needed to make it a viable program around the country. We've got a commitment for matching funds from several companies and public figures, including absolutely adorable Clive Ellis, who is starring in the movie version of my novel, *Dressed Like a Lady, Drinks Like a Pig,* and also I think I didn't time my inhalations correctly and I'm running out of breath . . ."

Lala gasped for air and looked over nervously at Olivia, who was smiling. She made a circular waving motion with her right hand.

"It's okay, keep going," she said. "We'll edit the blips."

"Umm, right," Lala said. "So, I guess the answer is, the higher the price, the better. And I've probably watched all the episodes of the show at least once, so I do know that there are some ridiculously high-priced dresses here. I mean, seriously, who needs to spend thousands and thousands and thousands and thousands of dollars on a dress?"

Lala noticed that Olivia was frowning at her.

"That's not going to make it into the final cut, is it?" Lala asked.

"No," Olivia said. "Not a chance. Let's get you into the dressing room."

Olivia and the camera operators followed Lala as Julie led her through the showroom and down a hallway to a fairly small dressing room. Only one of the camera operators, a woman, joined them inside the room, with the other camera operators waiting in the large anteroom with several dressing rooms off it outside Lala's room.

Julie motioned for Lala to sit, and sat down next to her.

"Tell me about your fiancé, Lala," Julie said.

"Oh, David is absolutely wonderful," Lala began.

Uh oh, Lala thought. *I . . . I think I'm going to . . .*

Lala looked straight into the camera, as though she wanted to speak to Terrence.

"My first husband died. He was absolutely wonderful, too. I miss him all the time. He really wanted me to find love again."

"I'm sorry," Olivia whispered. "That was lovely, Lala, and very touching, but do you think we can do it again without you looking into the camera?"

Again? Lala thought. *Oh, no. I can't recreate—*

Julie took Lala's hand in hers and drew Lala's focus back to her.

"Lala, I understand this is going to be your second marriage?"

"Yes," Lala said, thinking about David and Terrence and how lucky she was much more than trying to act like she was thinking about David and Terrence and how lucky she was.

Lala told Julie about how Terrence had been diagnosed with stage 4 stomach cancer and how he had died less than six months after. She told Julie about how much love and care their family and friends gave them when Terrence was sick and after Terrence died. She told Julie how painful and awful it had been to miss Terrence as much as she did, and how time had helped ease the anguish. She told Julie about meeting David and being engaged-to-be-engaged to him at first and about how terrified she was that David would die before she did and she would be widowed again, and she didn't think she could survive that much pain twice, but she had decided that being married to David was worth any risk.

And then she showed Julie a picture of her with Terrence, one that had been taken when she first met him and that she had scanned onto her phone and put in her laptop so that it would always be near her. It was a shot of them standing by the stage of the Shakespeare in the Park theatre in Central Park on a gorgeous fall day in New York. And then she showed Julie a picture of her with David. They were walking along the boardwalk in Santa Monica. And then she told Julie about how she met Terrence and how she met David, leaving out the part where she slept with both of the men on the first night she met them, because she figured that might be a bit much for a basic cable channel.

"Okay, I'm sorry," Olivia said, "we have to stop for a second. I think the mic on the camera picked up the operator crying. And if it didn't catch her crying, it probably caught me crying. That was great, Lala. Let's take a break."

"That was kind of a long speech, huh?" Lala said. Olivia come over and hugged her.

"Oh, goodness, yes, it was much too long. We'll keep maybe one-fifteenth of it. But it was lovely. It really was."

"I am NOT coming out!" Lala yelled.

That was the fifth time that afternoon that she had spoken those exact words.

"Can I just announce my subtext to my entourage?" she asked Olivia. "You can edit it out, right?"

"Go to town," Olivia said.

"I am NOT coming out because I am getting very sick of all of you and your bossy bullshit!"

"Whoa, yeah!" Olivia said, grinning. "We might keep that in. Bleeped of course."

"Cool!" Lala said.

Lala was still in the dressing room. Geraldine and Brenda and Helene had moved from their chairs in the main showroom and were now sitting in the smaller anteroom outside the dressing room.

Lala's entourage had committed one of the cardinal sins of

the show by wandering around the salon to pick out their own selections of dresses for Lala to try on. They had even found their way into the hallowed stockroom that housed the hidden treasures of Kleinfeld, a place of legend into which no civilian was meant to tread and from which no lay person could emerge unaffected. This trespass was met with extreme irritation on the part of Lala's bridal consultant and extreme satisfaction on the part of the producer of Lala's segment.

Julie had reluctantly agreed to bring the armfuls of dresses that Geraldine and Brenda and Helene had picked out for Lala to her dressing room.

Lala had hated all of them on their hangers. She agreed to try them on only because Julie told her it would "make for good TV." From outside the door, Geraldine and Brenda and Helene had gotten into the annoying habit of chanting, with growing determination, "Show us the dress! Show us the dress! Show us the dress!"

And each time the chanting began and crescendoed, Lala announced that she would not be coming out of the dressing room.

"No! You can see it when the episode airs! Unless I can bribe someone to delete all this misguided fashion mishegoss."

Lala was in a sweeping ballgown. She looked in danger of being suffocated, and ultimately absorbed into and disappearing beneath the folds of fabric.

"I look like I'm in a third-rate bus-and-truck tour of *Gone With the Wind*," she said.

Lala heard giggling from outside the dressing room, and she was instantly suspicious and on guard.

"We don't care if you come out or not!" she heard her aunt crow.

"We're drinking champagne out here!" she heard her best friend say.

Lala grabbed the bountiful skirt of the dress she had on and lifted it up so that she wouldn't trip and fall on her face. She threw open the door of the dressing room and stomped out, and immediately registered that there were no champagne glasses and no champagne bottles and no one was imbibing.

"SUCKA!" Brenda yelled.

"But some champagne would be lovely," Geraldine jumped in to say. "Hair of the dog and all that."

"Oh my god, Lala, that dress looks terrible on you," Helene groaned. "And I'm the one who picked it out. You are submerged in that much fabric. And it looks like your waist has *literally* been surgically removed. I'm intentionally using 'literally' incorrectly to highlight my point about your waist having disappeared."

"Okay, that's it," Julie said. "Lala, get back in the dressing room. You three . . ."

She pointed an accusing and furious finger at Lala's entourage.

"You three stay right there. I am going shopping now. *Alone.*"

Julie strode away with her head held especially high and her shoulders especially squared, much as a 1940s movie star might stride into battle in a classic film. Lala saw her aunt raise her eyebrows in amusement and, as she walked back to the dressing room and shut the door behind her, heard the three women giggling like schoolgirls herded outside the principal's office for an amusing infraction that they knew would not result in any permanent blot on their records.

Julie knocked on the dressing room door after not quite a quarter of an hour and carried in three dresses. She hung them up, and Lala studied them.

She liked them all, and her first impression was that she liked them all very much, actually. One of them, she realized with increasing confidence, she loved.

"That one," she said, pointing at the dress hanging in the middle.

Julie nodded and smiled.

"I had a feeling it would be that one."

Julie helped Lala into the dress. She clipped the back of it so that the sample size would fit Lala. Lala looked in the mirror. The dress was off-the-shoulder, with sleeves that ended just below her elbows. The material was a very soft and comfortable lace. The dress was tightly-fitted on top and them flowed outward at Lala's hips. The sample size was much too long for her, a fact which caused Lala no concern at all because she had watched endless examples of the magic created by the alterations department at Kleinfeld. She was instantly enchanted.

"We weren't kidding about the champagne," Geraldine yelled from outside the door. Lala and Julie rolled their eyes in unified bemusement. Lala spun around to take a look at the back view of the dress.

"It looks like I have a waist," Lala whispered.

"That color is called 'champagne'," Julie told Lala.

"That," Lala said, "is a clear sign from the universe."

Lala and Julie walked out of the dressing room. Geraldine and Brenda and Helene gasped.

"Turn around," Geraldine ordered. Lala did. The women all uttered an extended "Ohhhh" that covered varying octaves.

"You better love it. Do you love it?" Brenda asked. Lala nodded and shrugged her shoulders in joyous disbelief.

"That's the one," Helene agreed.

"Yup," Geraldine said. "You don't need to try on any others."

"Yup," Brenda said.

"Done. Ring it up and wrap it up. Let's start drinking," Geraldine said.

"Yup," Brenda and Helene said.

"Uh oh," Lala said. She turned to Olivia, who was standing next to one of the camera operators and was beaming. "Should we reshoot that? It's my first dress that I showed them. It shouldn't go this smoothly, should it? I mean, for purposes of storytelling 'n' conflict 'n' stuff?"

Olivia shook her head and grinned. "That's okay, we have a very good amount of conflict already. Julie, go ahead and ask the question."

"Lala," Julie said, "are you saying yes to the dress?"

Lala lifted her arms up over her head and yelled, "I am saying FUCK yes to the dress!"

She thrust her hands downward and covered her filthy mouth and mumbled, "Oh *shit*, should we do that over again?" and everyone started laughing.

"Nah," Olivia chortled. "We'll bleep it. It'll be a hoot. Okay, people that is a wrap! Who's popping the champagne?"

"Yes!" Geraldine said. "We are parched over here, and we are saying YES to the bubbly!"

SHE DOES AND HE DOES AND THEY DO

The courtyard of the fourplex where Lala and David and Geraldine and Monty lived had a bit of the air of a meeting at the United Nations, without the polyglot quality, since the *lingua franca* of the festive day was unabashedly English. Despite that monolingualism, many air miles/kilometers crossing the Atlantic and the Great American Continent had in fact been logged by guests at the wedding.

Kenny and Atticus and Kenny's grandfather had arrived from France a few days earlier. Matthew had flown in for the day from the location of the next movie he was directing. Clive and his girlfriend Tara—the love of his life who agreed to forgive him when he surprised her at the Shakespeare Theatre in England and said she would be willing to "take things very slowly and you better not fuck it up again, Buster"—were there. The wonderful French veterinarians who were part of the feral cat coalition that Lala had helped to establish with Kenny and that now had six maintained feral colonies in several neighborhoods in Paris had come to celebrate. Gérard and Marie-Laure and Gérard's grandmother and step-grandfather were there, having arrived in the U.S. two weeks before to tour up and down the splendid California coast and check out the rival vineyards of the Golden State.

Local guests included their neighbors Craig and Stephanie and their baby, along with Thomas the Salman Rushdie twin and his girlfriend, and Lala's producing partners, Zoe and Eliza. David's grown sons had come from San Diego and Long Island, respectively and, at the rehearsal dinner the night before, Lala had initiated her not-very-discreet project to get them matched up with her young partners.

"YOU! You four MUST sit next to each other!" she had loudly commanded. "Talk! Get to know each other! Flirt! I'm the bride! Do what I say!"

And now the wedding day had arrived, and everyone was enjoying a bountiful Happy Hour with a full bar and a wide array of vegan appetizers before the ceremony. Had Lala been looking out over the railing of the balcony outside her apartment, she would have seen Zoe and Eliza and Ben and Warren chatting animatedly together, and she would have been very pleased and proud of her yenta skills.

David and his best man Monty, along with Brenda's husband Frank and Helene's boyfriend Clark, were standing up front at the pergola, where the judge, who had gone to Wesleyan with Lala and who had been a delightful rediscovery via the wonders of social media after he and Lala had lost touch post-college, would be uniting the bride and groom in matrimony. David kept checking his watch nervously, as did Monty, both men wanting to get to their places with several minutes to spare.

They needn't have worried about the hour. It was Ides of March, and Lala Pettibone was not going to be on time . . .

Upstairs in Lala's bedroom, her trio of attendants, Geraldine, Brenda, and Helene, were with the bride. Joining them for the preparations were Lala and David's four-legged children, who now numbered five.

As soon as Lala got back from picking out her wedding dress in New York City, she told David she was ready to adopt again. They went to Dogs of Love and adopted a brother-and-sister Chihuahua pair who had been abandoned by the family of an old woman who died. The dogs were estimated to be around 15 or 16 years old, and they each weighed no more than three pounds. Lala lost her mind when she met them.

"I . . . I . . . I love them so much already, I can barely breathe." She turned to David and grabbed both his hands in a desperate plea. "David, I'm going to want to pick them up and hold them and kiss them all the time. Please keep an eye on me so I don't go overboard. This will, as I know you are already imagining, require your constant vigilance."

They had come with the names Squeaky Boy and Squeaky Girl, which Lala deemed "so wrong, they're right," and it was decided by their new mama and papa that the monikers the precious seniors had known all their lives would of course be retained. Lala did come up with the idea of adding their own special flair to the new family members' names by referring to the dogs, at all times, as *the* Squeaky Boy and *the* Squeaky Girl.

"At all times?" David had asked when she made the pronouncement at the shelter.

"It's like with *the* Bronx," Lala told him. "No one says, 'I'm going to Bronx.' No one. Ever. It's always got a definite article, right? Trust me, this will be exactly the same thing."

The five dogs were dressed in formal wear for the ceremony and were all asleep in their beds. They would all be escorted down the aisle by Brenda and Helene, who would enter for the ceremony first, and then Geraldine would escort her beloved adopted niece to the pergola.

There would be no music accompanying Lala and Geraldine down the aisle. Instead, the wedding invitations had specified that the guests were requested to please offer a version of the Wedding March by either snapping their fingers to the timeless tune or clapping out the rhythm, which Lala thought would be a "freakin' hoot and would set the tone for the day very nicely," and which Geraldine had deemed, while giggling, "the silliest fucking idea I have heard since that crap you pulled about being 'engaged-to-be-engaged' when you were out of your fucking mind."

Lala's hair, as coiffed by Geraldine, looked beautiful. Geraldine had made it softly wavy and had gathered it in a gentle updo. Brenda was responsible for Lala's make-up, and had done a gorgeous job of riding that fine line between simple and fussy.

The three attendants' dresses had also been selected on their trip to New York, with the cost also being doubled as donations to the new animal welfare foundation. They were matching short, navy cocktail dresses. Geraldine had spied them the moment the four women had entered the designer dresses department at Macy's flagship store in Herald Square.

"We're wearing those," she announced. And then she slowly turned her head to peer at Lala. "Anyone want to argue with me?"

"Not I," said Lala. And she didn't regret abdicating any decision-making responsibility then, and certainly not on the day of the wedding, because the dresses looked breathtaking on her attendants.

"You all look so beautiful," Lala sighed with infinite contentment.

"And as beautiful as our dresses may be," Helene said, "they will pale in comparison to yours."

Indeed, the only thing left to do before they made their elegant way to the ceremony, was to get Lala into her wedding gown.

"Wait a sec," Lala said. She ran out of the room, shoeless, in her bra and control-top stockings.

"Where are you going?" Geraldine demanded.

The three women heard Lala's words coming from the direction of the kitchen.

"It's going be a deliciously long day," Lala yelled to them, "and so I got some of those energy boost pepper turboshot things you love at Whole Foods."

"Oh, that's a good idea," Geraldine said. "Just make sure you don't—"

"AAAAAAGGGH!"

Geraldine and Brenda and Helene bolted out of the bedroom into the kitchen. They saw Lala standing next to the open refrigerator, clutching at her throat.

"My GOD, that is *hot!*" she rasped.

Geraldine grabbed the small bottle Lala was clutching in her hand.

"That's not a turboshot, that's a tincture! It's just cayenne pepper! The turboshot has lemon and maple syrup . . . You're supposed to dilute this tincture stuff big time! Like one drop in a gallon of water! We need bread!"

Geraldine started digging through the full shelves of the refrigerator. "We need lots of bread and lots of milk... Lala, how do you not have any bread or milk in here? Brenda, go downstairs to my fridge and get all the bread and milk in there! STAT! NOW!"

Brenda threw the front door of the apartment open and scrambled down the stairs. As soon as the sound of the door opening and the footsteps pounding were heard, the guests and the groom and his best man turned toward the second-level apartment. Brenda saw them all rush to their chairs and she saw David and Monty rushing to join the judge.

"No!" she yelled. "No, don't scramble to the pergola! Everything is fine! We've just got a teeny tiny delay, nothing to worry about! Everyone have another drink!"

By the time Brenda rushed back past everyone, clutching a bag of sourdough rolls and a half-gallon of Lactaid Fat-Free milk and completely ignoring their confused and concerned looks, she found the bride and her attendants back in the bedroom. Lala was drenched in more sweat than she had probably produced in any of her many workouts or hikes over the years, including the ones she used to do during the most humid summer months when she lived in New York City. Geraldine and Helene were desperately fanning her with magazines.

Brenda thrust a roll at Lala.

"Chew!" she ordered. Lala obeyed. When she was done with the roll, Brenda took the cap off the milk carton and handed that to Lala.

"Drink!" Brenda said. Lala did. She finished the carton and slammed it down on the bureau.

"I think I'm going to barf," she managed to rasp. "Christ, that stuff is HOT."

"Ohhh, Sweetie," Geraldine cooed. She grabbed a tissue and mopped Lala's drenched brow. "You are covered in schvitz. I think we're going to have to redo your hair. And your makeup. I just don't know why the Ides of March are always so cruel to you."

"Are you kidding?" Lala giggled, just before she segued into a major coughing fit. "This is my favorite day of the year from now on and for the rest of my life! Tell you what, I'll just jump in the shower and we'll start all over again, yeah? It's all good! We'll be partying before I know it!"

The actual delay of the ceremony was just under an hour, which all the guests and her new husband assured Lala at the reception was really to be expected at just about any wedding, and it was in fact the rare and possibly bizarre marriage that actually took place precisely on time.

Lala didn't believe a word any of them were saying, but she loved them all that much more for lying to her about it. Especially her new husband.

Just short of sixty minutes overdue, the door to Lala and David's apartment opened. Helene exited first, carrying one sleeping Chihuahua under each arm. Brenda came next following her down the stairs, leading Eunice and Petunia and Chester on their leashes.

Geraldine held Lala's arm as they walked through the door in tandem. Lala and Geraldine paused at the top of the stairs as they waited for the procession to reach the pergola.

Lala peeked over the railing of the balcony. She saw David look up and see her. She saw him look at her in a way that Terrence had once looked at her on an equally lovely day. When Brenda and Helene and the dogs were standing by David and Monty and the judge, Geraldine gave Lala's hand a loving squeeze and kissed her forehead.

"Ready?" Geraldine asked her niece. Lala bobbed her head and smiled.

"Snap those fingers and clap those hands, people," Lala whispered. "The Act Two curtain is coming down to thunderous applause. A wonderful Act Three will follow after a festive intermission."

ABOUT THE AUTHOR

Heidi Mastrogiovanni is a graduate of Wesleyan University and was chosen as one of ScreenwritingU's 15 Most Recommended Screenwriters of 2013. The comedy web series she writes and produces, *Verdene and Gleneda*, was awarded the Hotspot on the Writers Guild of America's Hotlist. Heidi is fluent in German and French, though she doesn't understand why both these languages feel they need more than one definite article.

A dedicated animal welfare advocate, Heidi lives in Los Angeles with her musician husband and their rescued senior dogs. She loves to read, hike, travel, and do a classic spit-take whenever something is really funny.

Along with fellow Amberjack Publishing author Teri Emory (*Second Acts*), Heidi is delighted to be bringing their Writing While Female Tour to bookstores and libraries around the country. *Lala Pettibone: Standing Room Only*, the sequel to *Lala Pettibone's Act Two*, continues to explore the themes present in all of Heidi's work . . . It's never too late to begin again, and it must be cocktail hour somewhere.

http://heidimastrogiovanni.com/